DOOMSDAY RECON

RYAN WILLIAMSON   **JASON ANSPACH**

WARGATE

An imprint of Galaxy's Edge Press

CHAPTER 1

Panama City, Christmas Day, 1989

"Guns N' Roses or Aerosmith?" Sergeant Wilson asked as he tore open his MRE pouch. The three of us were sitting in our Humvee, waiting for something to happen. We'd been waiting for a long time.

"Beastie Boys," Arizona chimed in.

"No one asked you, Arizona. Chicken a la King *again*?" Wilson grumbled. "Wanna trade, Bennett?"

"Trade 'em for your stripes," I said.

"You can't handle these stripes, Specialist. Whatcha got, Arizona?"

"Frankfurters. And no trade, Sarge."

"Bogus. I love franks. So anyway, Roses or Aerosmith?"

"Welcome to the Jungle," I said.

"Most definitely. Crawford or Ireland?"

"Macpherson," Arizona said.

"Shut *up*, Arizona."

"No, he has a point," I said.

But Wilson wasn't having it. "Come on, man. Kathy Ireland is choice."

"She is," I conceded, "but we require more research. I think Arizona needs to recon Sanchez's *Sports Illustrated*."

"Affirmative," said Wilson.

Arizona shook his head. "Why do I gotta do it?"

"Because you got mosquito wings and we don't," I said.

The kid remained unconvinced. "Are you mental? Platoon Sarge would dust me."

"So don't get caught," I said. "Are you a badass scout or what?"

"You're a lean, mean fighting machine, Arizona," Wilson added, pumping his fist. "Scouts Out!"

"Fine, I'll trade," Arizona said. "Gimme your Chicken a la Grody." He passed over his MRE—properly known as *Meals, Ready to Eat*, or, as we referred to them, *Meals, Rarely Edible.*

Sergeant Wilson chuckled as they exchanged packets.

I rested my head on the back of the truck's rooftop hatch, sitting on the sling, and hummed the bass line from "Higher Ground." It was mid-afternoon and hot, but not too hot, and there was a breeze carrying with it a hint of salt from the Pacific. Fortunately, it was the beginning of the dry season in Panama, so the humidity and the mosquitos were tolerable. It felt good.

Sergeant David Wilson was the same age as me, twenty-three, but had been in the uniform two years longer. He was a bodybuilder from California, tall and seriously pumped. A surfer. Arizona's real name was Paul Balmochnykh, but nobody could pronounce his last name. He was a decent kid from Phoenix, fresh out of One Station Unit Training, or OSUT. He'd only been with us a few months. Skinny and cursed with bad acne, his pride and joy was the fuzz growing on his top lip he insisted on calling a mustache. It wasn't. Not like our section leader, Staff Sergeant St. James, who had as close as you could get to a perfect *Magnum P.I.* 'stache without breaking grooming regulations. He was constantly on Arizona's case to shave the caterpillar off his lip. The kid wouldn't hear of it.

I closed my eyes and listened to the monkeys and parrots fighting to be heard over one another. It was only five days since America had invaded Panama. Things were buttoned down already, more or less, aside from bands of "Dingbats"—Noriega's Dignity Battalions —who hadn't gotten the memo that the war was over.

Special Forces, Rangers, and the 82nd had effectively shut down the Panama Defense Forces in short order. Cavalry Scouts like us were just there to provide protection for convoys, do some route reconnaissance, and secure landing zones for the birds we supported in the Air Cav. Aside from providing the Dingbats with sporadic target practice, nothing exciting had happened to us since we landed with the 7th Infantry Division as part of Task Force Atlantic a few days before. We'd missed the main event.

"You served your mission around here, didn't you?" Wilson asked me.

"No, up north. Mexico Veracruz Mission."

"Lotta betties up there?"

"I tried not to notice."

"Man, I couldn't do it. Two years wearing a white shirt and tie and no *señoritas*. Forget it, bro."

I shrugged. "It wasn't so bad."

Wilson had a devilish gleam in his eye. "Yeah, but you're still a virgin."

"Mmhmm."

Arizona's acne-filled face erupted into a grin. "Bennett's a virgin?"

"Shut up, Arizona," Wilson and I said together.

Before the conversation could go any further, I caught our section leader walking over to our mount. "Here comes trouble."

Staff Sergeant St. James leaned into Arizona's window and smiled. *Tom Selleck, eat your heart out.* It was always trouble when he flashed that trademark grin.

"How're you boys doing?"

"Righteous," Wilson said. "Lemme ask you a question. Crawford or Ireland?"

"Macpherson," he replied.

"Told you," Arizona mumbled from behind the steering wheel.

"Shut up, Private," St. James said. "And shave that caterpillar off your lip. Listen up, we're moving out in fifteen mikes. Tankers are coming through and Brigade wants to make sure the road's clear up ahead. The Dingbats have been felling trees to make roadblocks. Wilson, squad leader meeting at my mount, now."

"Yes, Sergeant." Wilson donned his Kevlar helmet and unlatched his M16 as he exited the vehicle.

Arizona started drumming his fingers on the steering wheel and bobbing his head. I nudged him with my boot.

"What?" he asked, annoyed.

"Better do your maintenance checks, Private."

"Did 'em earlier."

"Do 'em again," I said.

"Bogus, man," Arizona grumbled. He kicked open his door and grabbed the laminated checklist.

"Don't forget your Kevlar and weapon," I reminded him.

"Yeah, yeah." Arizona tossed his helmet on and slung his rifle over his shoulder.

"Yeah, yeah, what?"

"Yeah, yeah, *Specialist*."

"And do up your chinstrap, John Wayne."

Arizona flipped me the bird as he started around the Humvee, checking off boxes.

Meanwhile I busied myself with double-checking the love of my life. I was the assigned gunner on our mount, and my responsibility was the sleek black MK-19 automatic grenade launcher mounted on the turret. She was finicky and required just the right touch to pull back the charging handles, but when she let loose, it was a beautiful thing to behold as she belched out belt-fed 40mm grenades once per second, *thump-thump-thump*. I could drop an egg down a tank hatch at one thousand meters. Hole in one. Put that in your pipe and smoke it, Jack Nicklaus.

Fifteen minutes later the platoon fired up the Humvees and we pulled out of the assembly area, our mount taking point down the dusty hard-packed dirt road.

***

"Red Two, this is Red Seven," I heard Sergeant Wilson shout into the prick's handset—that's what we called the heavy PRC-77 radio, "the prick"—trying to be heard over the driving rain that beat on the roof of our Humvee.

"Go for Red Two," replied our section leader, Staff Sergeant St. James.

"Be advised, road is washed out. Sending dismount to see if we can ford it. How copy?"

Dismount. I was up in the turret manning the Nineteen when I heard that. Water pooled around my boots, and I had no desire to invite it *into* my boots.

"Roger that," the staff sergeant said. "Charlie Mike, out."

Charlie Mike. Continue mission. Awesome.

Sergeant Wilson glanced back at me and flashed a grin. "Showtime, bro."

"Moving, Sergeant."

I ducked down and unlatched the rear door as Wilson took my position up in the turret, only for a gust of wind to rip it free from my hand. Outside the rain fell in driving sheets so thick I couldn't see beyond a few meters. Fat droplets drummed on my Kevlar helmet and poncho. Lightning forked overhead, lighting up the dense jungle on either side of the road and washing out my NODs for a moment. A tremendous thunderclap shook the heavens.

The Humvee's blackout lights shone in my NVGs on a torrent of water that had taken out a good section of what *had* been a hard-packed dirt road. Now it was a quagmire that sucked at my boots as I trudged forward, leaning into the howling wind.

The washout didn't look any better from out here than it had from inside the Humvee. Water was still moving in a white-capped brown froth that greedily ate away at the road, carving a deep channel. If we were riding in the old M113 armored personnel carriers, we could make it across no problem. But these new trucks? Not so sure. Either way, I wasn't about to step into the washout and cross it on foot. I moved back to the truck and told Wilson as much.

"Hop in, Bennett, and let's see what these trucks can do," he replied.

I nodded and remounted, absolutely drenched and dripping water all over the Humvee's interior. The vehicle revved as if Arizona was trying to build up the courage to move by making the engine roar.

"Take it easy, Arizona," said Sergeant Wilson, trying to calm the kid, who held on to the steering wheel white-knuckled like it was a lifeline. "Give her a little gas, not too much. Just ease into the water."

I felt the front wheels drop as the road disintegrated beneath them. Arizona hit the gas too hard, and we were suddenly in the middle of the current, listing sideways as the wheels lost purchase.

"Slow is steady, steady is fast," Wilson said, trying to keep his voice calm, his volume just south of a shout. "You can make it, man."

Water foamed up over the hood, and Arizona revved the big diesel engine slowly. A moment later the wheels caught on something, the truck straightened out, and we were up and over the far bank and back on the road.

"Righteous!" Wilson yelled, performing a trademark surfer boy fist pump.

The grin on Arizona's face went for miles.

Wilson got on the radio. "Red Two, this is Red Seven."

"Go for Red Two."

"We're across. Washout is fordable."

Fordable if you're insane, I thought. And I was right, because Wilson was, in fact, insane. He was an adrenaline junkie. Surfing, snowboarding, whatever. He'd been to the Air Assault and Pathfinder schools. Just because.

"Roger. Sending Red Three."

One by one the mounts of Red Platoon, Apache Troop, Second Squadron, Ninth Cavalry Regiment forded the washout. To my amazement no one got stuck, sucked in too much water, and cracked an engine block, or worse, washed downstream. Maybe these new trucks weren't so bad.

Captain Brown's voice came over the radio. "All Red elements, this is Red One. Charlie Mike."

"You heard the man," Wilson shouted to Arizona. "Move out. Nice and slow."

"I can't see shit, Sergeant."

Wilson pointed a knife hand at the heavy fat rain-obscured windshield. "Just follow the road."

The kid shrugged his shoulders while maintaining his death grip on the steering wheel. "What road?"

"Guide him, Bennett," Wilson yelled up to me.

Rain assaulted me as I tried to peer through the storm. I could barely make out the road, a dark patch of black cutting through thick jungle, everything a mottled fuzz of green on green. There was another flash of lightning, far too close, and my NVGs washed out, blinding me. A thunderclap followed immediately, making my ears ring. I ducked back down.

"Sergeant, I'm gonna get fried if I stay up there!"

"Someone has to man the Nineteen," he answered. "Find Arizona that road."

"Yes, Sergeant. Arizona, just keep moving forward."

"Nice and slow, bro," Wilson added. "Feel out the road. You'll know if you leave it."

St. James's voice came over the radio. "Red Seven, this is Red Two."

"Go for Red Seven."

"Red One says there's a clearing up ahead, half a klick. We'll coil up there. How copy?"

"Roger, Red Two. Coil up at the clearing."

It took far too long to make those five hundred meters. Arizona left the road and crashed through brush more than once, but eventually we made the clearing and took up a position at the twelve o'clock while the rest of the platoon filed in, parking our ten Humvees in a tight circle, all facing outward, keeping about twenty meters' separation between vehicles.

I guessed the clearing was about the size of a Major League Baseball field, but with the driving rain it was impossible to tell for sure, and my NVGs kept fogging up.

"How long I gotta stay up here, Sergeant?" I called down to Wilson. "I can't see anything and nobody's going to be out in this weather."

"Captain wants all eyes on the perimeter," my fearless squad leader replied.

It took an hour for the rain to let up, although the thunderstorm continued. By then Captain Brown had ordered us to fifty percent security. It looked like we would be staying in the clearing overnight. Wilson sent Arizona up to man the Nineteen and I wedged myself into the back seat. Water drenched me through to the bone, and even though the nights in Panama seldom dropped below seventy degrees, I felt cold and clammy.

A word about Captain Brown. He was an interesting officer, to say the least. A towering, burly man, he was a former heavyweight boxer and a scrolled Ranger—which meant he'd served in the 75th Regiment, not just went through the school for the tab like a lot of officers. He was a dead ringer for Larry Holmes, except he was bald as a cue ball. And he was a captain, which might sound unusual for a platoon CO, but wasn't uncommon for Cavalry Scouts. He was also obsessed with the X-Men. Somehow every briefing contained snippets of wisdom from the comic book series. For Captain Brown there was only one Uncanny God, and Chris Claremont was his prophet.

All that aside, he was a good officer, the best I'd served under. He listened to his NCOs and had an open-door policy. If you had a problem, he'd talk you through it, provided you were willing to listen to the wisdom of Mr. Claremont.

As to why a former Ranger captain was commanding our platoon, we could only speculate. Specialist Bond had a pool going with a list of outlandish options to bet on, ranging from the ridiculous to the outright scandalous. My money was on one of the longshots—that he was on some secret squirrel Ranger mission and needed us and our trucks for some upcoming direct action. A man can dream.

I changed my socks and tried to get comfortable in the Humvee's confines. As I drifted in and out of sleep, I heard snippets over the prick about a loss of comms with higher up. It seemed we couldn't raise Apache Troop, or anyone in the 7th Division. I figured it was just the weather.

As it turned out, I figured very, very wrong.

The drums that started that night were my first clue.

CHAPTER 2

It was a couple hours before dawn, and I was on watch again, stationed behind my MK-19. I couldn't see anything, but I could hear the rhythmic pounding of drums growing slowly closer. Every few minutes a low-pitched whistling sound would rise between the beats and make the hair on the back of my neck stand up. It made me think of what a banshee wail might sound like because it wasn't human. It also didn't sound like any animal I'd ever heard before.

The tree line was about fifty meters away and lit up in a fuzzy green-on-green haze in my NVGs. By the book, fifty meters is too close to safely engage with a MK-19, although the grenades arm themselves within about fifteen to thirty meters. Still, anything closer than seventy-five meters isn't safe, doctrinally speaking. So if anyone burst out of the jungle, I'd be just about useless. Theoretically.

By now the thunderstorm had stopped, but we still didn't have comms with higher up. The captain was debating heading back to base, but the roads had been barely passable in getting this far, and after several more hours of the stuff, the road would be a major hazard to navigate in the dark, even with night vision.

And then of course there were the drums. Nobody had any idea what that was about—other than that it was creepy as hell.

The radio squawked. "All Red elements, this is Red One. I need eyes in that tree line."

Sergeant Wilson thumbed out toward the jungle. "You're up, Bennett. Arizona, go with him. Quick sneak and peek. Don't get lost."

"Affirmative," I said, ducking down from the hatch and grabbing my rifle.

"How come you get to stay in the mount, Sergeant?" Arizona asked.

"Someone has to man the Nineteen and monitor the radio, bro." Wilson flicked at the chevrons pinned to his lapel. "Merry Christmas."

Still grumbling, Arizona joined me outside the truck. "This sucks," he said, fumbling to attach his NVGs to his Kevlar.

"Affirmative," I agreed, pulling the charging handle on my M16 to load a round. Arizona followed my lead, and we bounded forward across the open ground in a crouch. The drums were hella unnerving.

Once we were a few meters into the trees, I signaled Arizona to stop, and we took a knee. Water dripped loudly from leaves in the canopy high overhead.

"What are we waiting for?" Arizona whispered.

"Patrol voice," I subvocalized. "Whispers carry, man. Better to talk real low. Better yet, Arizona, don't talk at all. We're stopping to get our bearings. Just scan your sector and listen. Don't fixate on anything. Keep your eyes moving."

We waited for about ten minutes, keeping as motionless as possible before I waved Arizona to follow me. The jungle floor was thick with deadfall, making movement difficult. I cringed as the kid stumbled behind me. If there was a twig to step on, somehow he found it. Every time.

"Stop walking like an ox," I hissed at him.

"Sorry."

We moved another dozen meters before I called a halt again to watch and listen. After a few minutes Arizona plucked excitedly at my sleeve.

"What?" I grumbled.

"I think I saw something!"

"Keep your voice down. Give it to me as a SALUTE report." I was testing him, asking for a standardized Size, Activity, Location, Unit identification, Time, and Equipment report.

"Uh, three—no, five men approaching from, uh, fifty meters to the south. Dingbats I bet. 0423 local. They're carrying uh, spears, maybe?"

I had my NVGs on and was about to call Arizona out on several shortcomings in that report as I peered in the direction he'd indicated. But his equipment report gave me immediate pause. "*Spears?*"

"I… I think so, Bennett."

"How desperate are the—oh, hold up."

It was hard to make anything out, just green on green, but for a moment I thought I'd seen a really short man, or maybe a child, duck behind a tree. And yeah, it really did look like he had a spear in his hand. Moments later another one popped up from behind a screen of vegetation and rushed to cover. That one I got a good look at. He appeared to be a man, not a child, but very short. Half-naked and carrying a bundle of three or four short spears. Javelins really. Were there unreached tribes here in the Panamanian jungles? I didn't know, but it sure looked like it.

Whoever they were, they were closing on us, using a kind of bounding overwatch. The single tube on the NVGs gave me zero depth perception, so it was hard to accurately estimate distances.

"What do we do?" Arizona whispered, his nerves evident in his voice.

"Just get ready," I said.

"Ready for *what*?"

"If they get too close, I'll fire a warning shot to alert the platoon. You know the ROE."

The Rules of Engagement we'd been given were very specific: we were not to fire until fired upon. I wasn't a fan, but orders were orders.

Another little man jumped up and silently ran a few meters before vanishing in the undergrowth. I was on one knee now, scanning through my M16's iron sights.

"They're getting closer!" Arizona hissed.

"Just watch your sector." I thumbed off my safety and glanced at Arizona. "Finger off the dang trigger, man."

"Right," he said. "Sorry."

For several long moments nothing happened.

Then, as if by some unseen and unheard command, five little men materialized all at once, not twenty meters away, and unleashed a volley of javelins. Not just normal throws either, like those guys in the Olympics. They used some kind of hooked sticks, about as long as your arm, to launch the javelins with tremendous velocity. I had a sudden memory of making one of those stick-things one summer in Boy Scouts. A word came to mind: *atlatls*. That's what the Aztecs had called them.

All such thoughts vanished as I felt a javelin rip through the hood of my poncho and deflect off my Kevlar. Another hit me square in the stomach. Fortunately, I was still wearing my flak vest. Still hurt though, like a punch in the gut.

I didn't hesitate to pull the trigger.

One of the men caught my round in the chest and went down. I was already pivoting to the next and firing. Another volley of javelins flew at us, and I felt a searing heat as one grazed my right bicep. Another slammed into my flak vest, hitting my solar plexus dead center. I gasped for air as I returned fire, putting two rounds center mass into another one. I hadn't heard Arizona fire once. Kid must have frozen in fear.

I tried to shout for him to start engaging, but only a sort of cough came out of my mouth. That spear to the chest had taken my breath away. Swinging my muzzle, I tracked a third target and fired. Rounds zipped into his head, and he dropped while I tried to steady myself. I had aimed for center mass.

That left two, and they pounced with the grace and speed of jungle predators as they rushed me.

Twenty meters isn't very far once people start sprinting at you. I managed to drop one, and then the other was already right on top of me, swinging a tomahawk at my throat.

Time does funny things in moments like that. For me, it got really slow. I could hear the sharp crack of M16s firing, everyone in the trucks shouting, but it sounded distant. And my attacker, he was so close he blurred in my NVGs, but I got the impression of a snarling old man's face, oddly feline, with big bat ears sticking out of the sides of his head. *Two* pairs of ears, I registered later, one smaller set, long and pointed, the other much larger and higher up. But at the time, I didn't even process the fact that something from *Weekly World News* was jumping at me out of the Panamanian jungle. It was all instinct and survival.

I didn't know it then, but these little creeps would soon become a *serious* pain in my rear.

I raised my rifle to block him, and he crashed into me, the two of us falling into the wet, muddy ground. Somewhere in the process he knocked my NVGs off and I dropped my rifle.

The guy's breath was foul, like rotten eggs, and he hissed, baring sharp fangs that gleamed in the darkness. He might have been small, but he was solidly built and heavily muscled. I had one hand gripped around a wrist to keep the tomahawk from hacking me to pieces and another around his throat, holding him back as he tried to bite my face off. I needed a third hand to stop the guy from repeatedly stabbing my flak vest with a knife.

I tightened my hand around his neck, trying to strangle him, but he just hissed and spat all the louder. So I did the only thing I could think of in the moment: I head-butted him. Hard.

Pygmy cat-boy, meet Kevlar helmet.

The blow stunned him long enough for me to draw my knife and jam it up under his jaw and into his brain. He twitched for a few moments and then went still.

I fumbled, found my rifle, and brought it up to my shoulder, looking for more little men in the darkness. I could hardly see anything. My mind went to Arizona, who still hadn't fired his weapon once that I could recall.

"Arizona," I shouted. "You okay, man?"

The shooting was happening elsewhere now, with my platoon firing into the tree line far away from my position. I pulled the flashlight off my load-bearing vest and shone the red light around me, feeling a sense of dread that the little savages had taken the kid off into the jungle. What I found was just as bad. Arizona was lying in a heap off to the side, twitching and kicking his legs.

Meanwhile the weapons fire wasn't dying down. If anything, it was intensifying.

I turned the kid over, still trying to keep a lookout on my surroundings. Arizona's panicked eyes stared up at me. A javelin was stuck through his throat—it looked to have snapped in half when he fell—and he was choking on his own blood, making sick gurgling sounds.

"Hang on, Paul," I said. "I'm getting us out of here."

There was no point calling for Doc. We were too far away. But I didn't know what to do so I shouted for him anyway. Maybe it would comfort the kid to think a medic was coming. But he needed help now. Only... I wasn't qualified to give it. I knew if I pulled out the shaft, he'd die for sure. The best I could think of was to rip out a field dressing, wrap it around his throat, and haul him up in a fireman's carry. So I did. Then I ran as fast as I could, stumbling and tripping over deadfall. I heard a javelin *thunk* into meat—whether it was Arizona or me I couldn't even tell, that's how hard the adrenaline was pumping—and another flew by my face, embedding itself into a tree only inches away.

I picked up the pace.

As I broke through the tree line, shouting out the running password at the top of my lungs so no one would shoot me, I could see Wilson up in our Humvee's hatch waving at me to hurry. My legs were burning, and I could barely breathe.

As we closed the distance, Wilson lit up the MK-19, *thump-thump-thump*, and I heard explosions resonating deep in the forest behind me. PFC McKee from Sergeant Clark's mount came running up to me and together we hauled Arizona behind my mount. Doc was already there as we laid the kid on the muddy ground. Arizona's eyes were glazed over, and he wasn't making any sounds. He wasn't breathing.

"Bennett, McKee, get on your rifles!" Wilson barked, but I didn't want to leave Arizona. Doc met my eyes and nodded for me to go.

I'd lost my NVGs, and I couldn't see anything except for muzzle flashes and tracers from the Fifties flying into the jungle. McKee pulled me after him and we hit the ground beside my mount. I could hear our platoon sergeant's voice over the radio in the truck calling a cease-fire. There were a couple last bursts of machine-gun fire and the *thump* of a grenade exploding a moment later in the trees… and then all was silent. Even the drums had stopped.

"McCoppin's missing, man," PFC McKee said under his breath.

"What?"

"We were on patrol, like you and Arizona. Then these *things* come out of nowhere—you know what I'm talking about, right? Those strange-looking little men? You saw 'em too, right? Throwin' spears and hissin' and spittin'. We got separated. McCoppin and me. I think they captured him."

"How'd you get away?"

"I ran, man. I just ran. Call me yellow. Go ahead. I don't care. Those things ain't *human*."

Doc crouched down beside me. "You okay, Bennett?"

"I—I think so."

"Let me check you out, just to make sure." He started patting me down, feeling for blood. He found the graze on my arm and bandaged it.

"Is Arizona gonna make it, Doc?" I asked, despite already knowing the answer.

"He's gone, Bennett." Doc's tone was cold. Just stating the facts. No emotion. Sergeant Johnny "Doc" Yazzie was a twenty-six-year-old former Ranger medic, a 91B attached to our platoon; he'd served in the batts before getting busted down to E-5 and transferred out of the regiment for some unknown indiscretion. He'd been there. He'd seen things. He was a legit professional.

Sergeant First Class Sanchez, our platoon sergeant, was making the rounds, ensuring everyone had ammo. He paused by Doc and me and took a knee.

"What happened, Bennett?" he asked.

I tried to compose myself and gave my report as clearly and accurately as I could, but my voice wavered.

Sanchez pursed his lips. "Run that description of the enemy by me again, Specialist."

"They were short, Sergeant. Under five feet. Half-naked. Faces like old men…"

"And?" he prompted when I hesitated.

"It sounds crazy, I know, but they… they had big ears, like bats, and seemed… I dunno… cat-like. Like their noses were—"

"He's been through a lot," Doc said. "The mind plays funny tricks under stress."

"I saw 'em too, Sergeant," McKee put in. "It was just like Bennett said."

Sanchez nodded. "I've heard similar reports from others." His voice was flat. The man was short and wiry but seemed seven feet tall when he was in your face about something, even though he rarely raised his voice. He was former Marine Recon and had been through the Army's Pathfinder and Recondo schools. He was about as hardcore as hardcore could get without putting on a green beret or pinning a trident to your chest. Nothing fazed him. Apparently not even little freakish Stone Age cat-men with bat ears.

That others had seen them too was exactly what I *didn't* want to hear. It would be much better if McKee and I had simply been hallucinating. I started to shiver uncontrollably.

"Get him some coffee," Sanchez said to Doc. "And dry clothes. You're off duty for now, Bennett. Doc will get you squared away."

"Come on," Doc said, helping me to my feet. "Little bit of Doc's famous brew and dry gear will do wonders for you."

"I—I don't drink coffee, Doc."

"Damn good time to start, Bennett."

CHAPTER 3

I sat wrapped in a field blanket on the tailgate of Sanchez's Humvee, nursing a canteen cup of hot chocolate. The sky was beginning to lighten in the east, just a touch of gray lacing the heavy clouds. The drums had started up again at first light.

Doc was conferring with Sanchez quietly when Captain Brown came marching over. He stopped in front of Sanchez and threw a knife hand in the opposite direction.

"Where the hell is my road?" he snapped.

"Beg pardon, sir?" Sanchez said.

"My road, Diego. We came through here on a damn road, and now it's gone!"

It occurred to me that I didn't know Sanchez's first name. Somehow, I kind of figured he didn't have one. Our platoon daddy seemed to me like he'd been born an NCO. Birth certificate listed first name Sergeant and all. I wondered if Diego was a family name. All that was more interesting to me at the moment than the lack of a road, but Sanchez was tuned in to Captain Brown's needs.

"We'll find your road," Sanchez said.

"And get my comms up."

"Will do, sir. Anything else?"

"I need coffee."

"Figured you would," Doc said, handing the captain a steaming canteen cup. "You can have Bennett's cup. He wouldn't take the plunge."

"Thanks, Johnny," Brown said. Then to Sanchez: "This is all screwed six ways to Sunday."

"Affirmative."

Brown sipped at the cup and frowned. "What do you think?"

"We need more intel on the enemy," Sanchez replied. "We've got nothing to go on. The clearing should be littered with their bodies, but they're just... gone."

Captain Brown turned to me. "You saw those little freaks up close and alive, Nephi. What's your assessment?"

I don't know what startled me more, hearing my first name or the captain asking my opinion—on anything.

"I, uh, sir—I don't have that information at this time, sir," I stammered.

"I asked for your opinion, not solid intel. Take a guess, Bennett."

"To be honest, I'm not even sure anymore what I saw. It was dark, and my NVGs kept fogging over... and..."

"You missed your calling in Military Intelligence, son," Brown said. "Somebody needs to get me some answers, yesterday. Good coffee by the way, Johnny."

"Thank you, sir," Doc said.

"Actually, sir," I said, surprised by my own boldness. "I was thinking something."

Brown waited.

"Those... men... that attacked us, they remind me of stories I used to hear when I was serving in the Mexico Veracruz Mission."

Brown took another sip and raised one eyebrow. "Go on."

"Well, sir, they're just folktales, but the locals believed in these little beings they called *Chaneques*. That's the Aztec word for them. In Spanish they're called *duende*—"

"My *abuela* told us stories about the duende," Sanchez interrupted. "They're like dwarves or gnomes. Leprechauns. Yeah... yeah, I can see it."

"Something like that, Sergeant, yeah," I said. "'Master of the House,' in Spanish. The Aztec translation would be similar, but the Yucatec Maya believed them to be spirits of the forest and guardians of nature."

"Interesting as all that is," Sanchez said, dismissing the idea with a wave, "knowing the bedtime stories that scare little Mexican children ain't exactly gonna help us. McCoppin's still out there. So what do they want?"

Brown stared down into his cup, lost in his thoughts. "Reminds me of the Awakilius from the Savage Land. They first appeared in *Ka-Zar the Savage* issue sixteen…"

He wandered off, drinking his coffee and muttering to himself. Like I said, he was an amazing officer, but he had some strange… quirks.

***

When the first wave of the little men—the Chaneques, as I'd come to start thinking of them—flooded out of the jungle I was back in the turret. Flooded? Yeah, that's the right word. It was like a dam bursting. Dawn was breaking and the sun was just peeking above the horizon when they came in that great wave. Hundreds of them, from all directions.

M2 machine guns and MK-19 grenade launchers came online almost simultaneously, ripping the advancing line of Chaneques to shreds. They charged fearlessly, clambering over the remains of their own dead, waving stone axes and spears or hurling more javelins. The first volley of javelins hissed through the air like a death rattle. I dropped into the body of my truck, listening to the *thunks* hitting the side of our vehicle. A few even penetrated the thin unarmored walls.

Taking a deep breath, I stood back up and swung the barrel of my MK-19 down, but they were already too close to safely engage. I readjusted my aim to target the rear lines still spilling out of the jungle and let loose with a burst—*thump-thump-thump*—watching as tree trunks exploded, showering the little men with deadly splinters. Wilson was out of the Humvee and leaning over the hood. He fired at the advancing line as fast as he could empty one magazine and reload another. Specialist Pierzchala from Sergeant Wright's squad had taken up a position beside him with our section's M60 and was laying down the hate like a professional. PFC Dee fed the Pig belts of ammunition.

The Chaneques picked up pretty quickly that a full frontal assault was suicide and retreated back into the jungle. But not before sending another volley of javelins our way as a parting gift. I ducked again as stone-tipped projectiles pelted my truck.

"Don't let up, Bennett!" Wilson shouted. "Level that jungle!"

Didn't have to tell me twice. I got back on the Nineteen and fired blindly into the thick trees, walking bursts of high-explosive, dual-purpose death across my sector of fire.

Sanchez was calling a cease-fire over the radio when another furious volley of javelins flew out of the jungle, followed by a roar of primal rage and fury that somehow deafened even the ear-splitting noise of the Fifties.

And then...

I know that this is the point where things go from weird to absolutely crazy, but it happened. In hindsight, it seems like a natural progression. But at the time... how do you deal with the fact that you're engaging not only little stone-aged cat-men but also... monsters?

That's what they were, though. Huge, scarlet beasts that burst from the trees and charged us from all sides. They were vaguely apelike creatures, but massive, easily fifteen feet tall, with powerful muscles that rippled under their sleek red fur. Each one must have weighed over a thousand pounds. And they were *fast*.

They charged on all fours, bellowing guttural challenges as they churned up the muddy ground beneath them. Like... like a bunch of Bigfoots who'd gotten into the hair dye. Bursts from the M2s hardly seemed to slow them, even as the fifty-caliber rounds tore off huge chunks of bloody meat.

One reached Sergeant Clark's mount to my left, grabbed the smoking barrel of the M2, and just ripped it right off the pintle mount. With its free hand it just as easily flipped the truck over and beat at the undercarriage, using the machine gun as a club.

So... *that* was terrifying.

But what came next was far, far worse.

Pierzchala got to his feet and shifted fire with the M60, going cyclic. 7.62×51mm NATO rounds can put down most anything that walks on two or four legs on this planet, especially when firing around six hundred rounds a minute. But it only seemed to annoy the monster. I know that sounds crazy, but the thing was full of holes and bleeding and *should* have been dead, but it stayed upright as if it were some impervious zombie waiting for just the right shot that would take it down.

It spun and backhanded Pierzchala with the M2. I saw the receiver of the Browning contact my platoon-mate's body. Time compressed into an instant and yet stretched out for eternity as I listened to the terrible cracking of bone and ripping of flesh…

… and then Pierzchala was simply—gone. Vanished in a cloud of red mist.

I learned later that parts of him flew as far as two hundred meters off into the jungle. It's a moment frozen in my memory, a prelude to the many horrors yet to come that would be branded on my consciousness. I can still see the moment—hear it, smell it. Taste his blood spatter on my lips.

The beast locked eyes with me as I stood frozen in the turret. It had cruel horns twisting out of the sides of its head. The monster roared, exposing terrifyingly huge tusk-like canines. The only defense I could think of against getting crushed was to swing my MK-19 over and fire the grenades, hoping the blunt force of the impact might scare the thing off. But that was… unlikely. And, for me at least, impossible. I was too afraid. God forgive me, but I could only watch helplessly as it raised the M2 in an overhand strike, preparing to bring the full weight of the eighty-pound weapon down on my head.

Sergeant Clark must've gotten on his mount's Fifty, because a burst raked over the monster, sending huge gouts of blood and chunks of flesh spraying everywhere. This time, whether due to greater proximity or mere accumulation of damage, the assault got the job done. The monster's roar turned into a weak cough, and it toppled and fell.

Later I would learn why those things were so tough. I'm not telling you now because you wouldn't believe it. *I* wouldn't have believed it, back then.

By then the other Fifties had turned aside the rest of the savage crimson beasts too, assisted—I learned later—by Sanchez and a couple of disposable AT4 84mm recoilless guns.

My legs buckled and I fell inside the Humvee.

I hadn't signed up for this crap.

***

PFC Lawrence was our third major casualty. He was badly wounded in the assault, hit in the back by a javelin that pierced his lung. The kid wasn't doing well. I could see that plainly when I returned to the improvised med station set up in the back of Sanchez's truck, nursing what was probably a concussion I'd sustained when I fainted. Doc and two other guys were trying to keep him from thrashing around, the pain was so bad.

"Dammit," Doc snapped. "Bennett, come over here and help us keep Lawrence still."

Lawrence was moaning in pain, frothy pink blood foaming from his lips, and I ran over and grabbed his legs. I tried not to watch as Doc injected the PFC with morphine, then taped three sides of a portion of an MRE wrapper over the wound, leaving one side open.

"What's that for?" I asked.

Doc ignored me and pointed to one of the other men. "I need you to periodically lift the edge of that wrapper and 'burp' it, now that he's calmed down a bit, so that air doesn't collect in his chest cavity. We want to avoid him developing pneumothorax."

I watched the goings-on at Lawrence's side. The morphine had kicked in and he was calm as could be. Doc didn't say how often the "burping" thing should be done, but he kept his focus on me and my problems, so his helper's timing must have been okay.

"All right," Doc said. "Now let's check out that head of yours, Bennett."

He shone a light in my eyes and felt around the back of my skull.

"How do you feel?" he asked.

"Little dizzy," I said. "Little nauseous. Head hurts. Not too bad. Also maybe it's affecting my eyes? Everything feels way too dim outside for daylight, you know? Even with the clouds."

"Your eyes are fine. It *is* dim outside. As far as your head goes, though… probably just a mild concussion. I'll tell Sergeant Sanchez you're on light duty. Try to get as must rest as you can. This isn't something you want to tough out. I'll give you some Motrin for the headache."

"Thanks, Doc. Don't know how much rest I'll be able to get with… everything that's going on."

"Yeah, this is surreal," Doc agreed. "Feels like a bad dream."

Lawrence started up with a dry, hacking cough and looked like he was having trouble breathing. I looked over and saw his skin was turning an alarming shade of blue.

"Dammit," Doc said. "His lung just collapsed. I'm going to have to perform a thoracostomy." He sent one of the other guys to grab a scalpel, then bent down and looked into Lawrence's eyes. "This is going to hurt me more than it hurts you."

"Already… hurts… like hell, Doc," Lawrence said almost sleepily.

Doc motioned for me to stand over the PFC's head. "Bennett, hold his arm over his head. Keep him good and steady."

Doc probed his fingers down Lawrence's side, counting ribs before he found the planned incision point, which he wiped with iodine. He took a scalpel and made a small, deep cut. Lawrence stiffened and cried out. Air and fluids bubbled out of the cut with a burbling, hissing noise. Then Doc inserted a rubber tube, sutured it in place, and applied a dressing.

"What now, Doc?" I asked.

"Pray. And get some air. You're looking pale. All of you. I can handle it from here."

I grabbed my rifle and climbed from the cramped back of the Humvee, standing unsteadily. Specialist Bond, the guy who ran the pool, came over and put a hand on my shoulder.

"You look like crap, Preacher."

I hated that nickname. "Been a long day already."

Bond nodded. "If you need to, you know, talk about—"

I cut him off. "I don't want to talk, Chris. I've had two of our buddies get dusted not ten feet from me in the last twenty-four hours, McCoppin is missing, and Lawrence probably isn't going to make it. I mean, I'm still picking pieces of Pierzchala out of my hair and BDUs. I'm tired, and I'm scared, and I just want *out* of this frigging *nightmare!*"

I didn't realize it, but my voice had been rising to a shout and most of the platoon was looking at me.

Sanchez called me over. "Bennett," he said. And then, in a lower voice, "Walk with me."

I followed him out of the circle of Humvees and we proceeded around the battlefield. The heat and humidity were rising as the sun rose behind thick clouds. The smell was already horrible. Crows were flocking and feeding on the mounds of Chaneque dead. Those creatures were even more alien out here in the oddly subdued, almost reddish daylight than they were in the dark of night. This nightmare was very real.

At least our platoon sergeant now had solid intel on what they looked like. I guess we killed too many this time for them to pull all the bodies out. Maybe we even killed them all. I hoped that was true.

"I'm going to tell you a story, Bennett," Sanchez said eventually. "It's a story that never happened, and one you'll never repeat. Not to anyone. This goes to your grave. You read me, Specialist?"

"Lima Charlie, Sergeant."

"Good. So it goes like this. It was 1976. I was about your age. Vietnam was over, officially, but some of us were still in-country hunting down POWs. I was part of an eight-man team leading a platoon of indigenous rebels. We had a couple of Green Berets and SEALs, a Spec Ops guy from the Air Force, and three of us Recon Marines. I was the youngest. Just a buck sergeant. Most of the guys had served in the Studies and Observations Group before Nixon shut it down in '72. Anyway, a few years later someone in the Pentagon spins us up. Some general. No one knew who. We didn't have an official name. I don't know if President Ford even knew about the operation.

"We set out in April with twenty Hmong soldiers. By June we were down to five Americans and a bad case of dysentery. Then we lost the colonel to a punji trap. He didn't go quickly, either. We didn't have comms or resupply and were so far off the grid no one would know where to look for us. If anyone would be looking. Which they wouldn't. Remember, this never happened.

"But we kept pushing. We knew our guys were out there, rotting in some tiger cage, we knew we were close, and we weren't about to give up on them. By July it was just me, a captain from Special Forces, and the two SEALs. We were all walking wounded."

He stopped as a break in the clouds finally exposed the sun. Only, it didn't get any brighter. Not really. At first, I was riveted with the story and so it took me a moment to realize that Sanchez hadn't stopped for dramatic effect. He was looking up. I did the same and, to my surprise, saw that the sun was totally eclipsed, but this eclipse was… not right. The corona was a bright red halo of flame, almost the color of blood.

That explained the strange, hellish light we'd been walking through. I didn't know whether to feel relieved that I hadn't been imagining it… or terrified to know it was real.

A muscle in Sanchez's cheek twitched. We stood there for a while, listening to everyone else chatter about the solar oddity. But eventually, I couldn't contain my curiosity any longer.

"What happened then?" I asked.

Sanchez looked down and seemed to consider whether he wanted to finish the story, or go off and maybe talk to the captain about the eclipse. Then he gave me a hard look. "We found them. The POWs. In a Chinese camp deep in Laos. Two pilots and a SOG operator. They were in real bad shape. We spent weeks observing the camp, eating snakes and scorpions, looking for an opportunity. One of the

SEALs cracked. He became a security risk. We had to… neutralize him."

I could feel my eyes widening in surprise. "You killed an American? A teammate?"

"Had to be done. We drew straws. I got the short one."

"I don't think I could ever do that." I paused… and then it hit me. "Wait. Why are you telling me this?"

"You need to get your head squared away, Bennett. We're at *war*, and war is hell, and horrible things happen. Horrible things happen *to* you, and *you* must do horrible things to others. You've lost some buddies. I get it. But you'll lose more before this is over. Trust me on that. So you need to box up that pain and terror and bury it deep. Maybe some pretty shrink can help you unbox it when we get back to the world. But here, now? Here and now you man up and push on. You read me?"

Not going to lie. I was feeling real small right about then. Not to mention even more terrified of Sanchez than I already had been at the start of the walk. My troubles seemed like a bad day at the beach.

"Read you loud and clear, Sergeant. It's in the box."

"Good. Because I can't have you going Section Eight on me after just the first day."

I chewed on that as we made our way back to the assembly area. The eclipse still hadn't ended, which struck me as odd, but I had other things on my mind at the moment. Like not being murdered by my platoon sergeant.

"Sergeant Sanchez?"

"Mmhmm?"

"What happened… next?"

He stopped again to check on the eclipse with a glaze over his eyes, like he was looking a thousand years into the past. I could hear him gritting his teeth, and when he spoke his voice cracked.

"The Chinese captured Captain Sullivan and Master Chief Davis. I got away. Somehow, I made my way to Thailand and managed to hook up with these CIA spooks that got me out of the country real quiet. The government knows where the camp is. I volunteered to go back. Nothing came of it. Far as I know our guys are still out there, rotting in those tiger cages. It's a hard thing to live with."

"And you just… box it up?"

He seemed to realize his image as a hardcore platoon sergeant had slipped and he cleared his throat.

"Nothing to box up. Remember, kid. It never happened. Just a nightmare I get sometimes."

CHAPTER 4

Turns out everyone else was as freaked out by the odd eclipse as I was—they had just been made aware of it earlier. Apparently it had made its first appearance from behind the clouds, just above the horizon, while I was still temporarily out of commission. The sight had caused some consternation, to put it mildly. But by now everyone—everyone other than me anyway—had grown somewhat accustomed to, if not comfortable with, its ongoing presence.

And that was the weirdest thing about it. The odd eclipse didn't end, even as the sun continued to rise. Such a thing wasn't possible... but neither were the Chaneques or the great crimson beasts that we would later learn were called *sisimitos*. Nor was the complete disappearance of a wide road through the jungle, for that matter.

We still didn't have comms with higher-up—or anyone else. The radios worked fine within the platoon, but it was as if the rest of the world didn't exist. It felt as if we were marooned in this small clearing that was a strange world all unto itself.

It felt that way. What we didn't yet know, and wouldn't have believed, was that it *was* that way.

In hindsight, the eclipse should have been the first indication that things had gone not just pear-shaped but... entirely beyond our understanding. The ape-beasts and the cat-men—they were unnatural but *possible*. You could, perhaps, justify to yourself that, like Bigfoot or the yeti, these creatures had been living in the wilds for centuries, and just had never before been encountered by humans. But the eclipse... that was *supernatural*. There simply was no possible explanation for it. Eclipses don't stick around. They can't. It's physically, astronomically, impossible.

But at the time, the eclipse wasn't top of anyone's mind. Because unlike the Chaneques and the giant beasts, it wasn't trying to kill us.

Our Humvees had been peppered by javelins, which managed to puncture several tires. The sisimitos had completely totaled Sergeant Clark's mount. Luckily he had been alone in the truck manning the M2 when the giant ape monster flipped it, and even more luckily—miraculously, really—he'd escaped unharmed. See, our MIA, McCoppin, had been his gunner, and PFC McKee had dismounted before the engagement. Had both been there during the flip, there was no way we would've gotten off so easy.

Tensions in the platoon were rising, and several arguments and even a fistfight broke out. We were all scared and confused. Security was at a hundred percent as we waited anxiously for the next attack. There were no drumbeats in the distance any longer, but that hardly comforted us.

"Yo, Bennett," Sergeant Wilson called. "Ruck up. We're going on a walk."

Ruck up? That sounded like a *long* walk. We rarely took our rucks on dismounted patrol. But, unlike on my last walk with a sergeant, this time I at least had some confidence that Wilson wouldn't hint at killing me during the hike.

"Who's 'we,' Sergeant?" I asked.

"Alpha Section. Get your gear—all of it. We might be gone for a while. Oh, and here." He handed my NVGs up to me. "You dropped these. Make sure you got fresh batteries in them. No Kevlars. Wear your boonie. Section meeting at St. James's mount in five."

That meant I had two minutes to repack my ruck and shove some extra MREs in it. I moved with a purpose and then hurried over to my section leader's Humvee. Guys were already milling about, putting on camo paint and checking weapons. There were just nine of us left in Alpha.

SFC Sanchez and Staff Sergeant St. James came over and ordered us to take a knee.

"I'll keep this short," Sanchez said. "We have a man missing and we need intel. You're to conduct a dismounted reconnaissance of the surrounding area. Priority One is finding Specialist McCoppin. Second to that is finding the captain his road and gathering whatever information you can about the hostile indigenous forces we've encountered. Strength, areas of operation, anything you can discover. You are to avoid engaging the enemy unless it's a matter of life or death. Remember, we're scouts. Our job is to gather intel, not fight battles. That said, the rules of engagement have changed. Your squad leaders will make the call whether to engage or not. Anyone carrying a weapon is to be considered a hostile element with deadly intent. Is that clear?"

We *hooahed* the affirmative.

Staff Sergeant St. James snapped his fingers then clapped his hands in front of him. "We've lost men, so I'm reorganizing the section into three squads. I'll assign squad leaders by seniority. My squad will retain Specialist Bond and PFC Evans. Sergeant Clark will take Sergeant Wright and retain PFC McKee. Sergeant Wilson, you will retain Specialist Bennett, and PFC Dee will join you. We will be on patrol for as long as it takes, so pack extra food and iodine tablets. PFC Lawrence is still in critical condition, so Doc will not be joining us. Who here has taken the Combat Lifesaver course?"

Sergeant Clark and I put up our hands.

"You're our medic now, Bennett. Get what you need from Doc. Evans, you're my radio man. Get the prick from our mount and extra batteries. Sergeant Wright will field the Pig. McKee is your AG. I want everyone in the section to grab a hundred-round belt of seven-six-two. You may not have noticed, but our compasses aren't working, so we'll be marking our trail. Squads will take turns on point. Any questions?"

McKee asked the question that all of us were thinking. "What the hell is going on, Sergeant?"

"It's best to avoid speculation at this point," Sanchez answered. "Improvise, adapt, and overcome."

Right, Platoon Daddy. Tremendous help there, bro.

We all had our theories. Bond was convinced we were experiencing a mass hallucination. Part of some sick CIA experiment. Other thoughts ranged from an alien invasion to experimental mutants created by the Soviets. A few of the guys, PFC Evans being the most adamant among them, were convinced we'd all died and gone to Hell. And then there was the popular *Land of the Lost* theory that Sergeant Wilson had started.

You remember *The Land of the Lost*, right? I guess if you're reading this you might be too young. It was a Saturday morning TV show back in the seventies where this family gets trapped in a time warp or alternate universe or something, and they end up in a world that's really primitive and inhabited by dinosaurs and lizard-people and ape-men. Odd things like that. Every Saturday morning was another fun adventure of them trying to overcome some environmental obstacle or outwit the evil lizard-men or avoid the mean T-Rex they called Dopey... or was it Grumpy? I can't remember. Anyway, it was fun in all the ways whatever what was happening to us right now wasn't. But if you think about it, a real-life *Land of the Lost* would totally suck, right? And whatever was going on right now most definitely sucked.

Bond, as always, had a pool going.

I was personally leaning toward Wilson's theory, but I wasn't about to discount Soviet mutants. Although that didn't explain the strange perpetual eclipse. So maybe Bond was right, and we were all hallucinating. But I knew I hadn't imagined Arizona or Pierzchala's deaths. Those were both as real as real got.

Guys started hustling as squad leaders barked orders, and I double-timed it over to Sanchez's mount to see if Doc could scrounge me up an aid bag.

"How's Lawrence?" I asked.

"Touch and go, man," Doc said. "I drew some of his blood and fed it through the air tube. If we're lucky, it'll form an autologous patch on his lung and seal the air leak. Best we can do without surgery."

"They teach you that in the Bats?"

"Nah, this crusty old SF medic showed me how once. Totally unorthodox. Lawrence consented to try it and Captain gave the green light. We figured it was worth a shot. Right now, he's on an IV drip with enough antibiotics to treat a Navy boat crew on shore leave."

"I didn't know we carried antibiotics in the field."

"We don't. But I never like being without some, so I liberated a stash from the clinic. You never know."

"Dang, Doc. We're lucky to have you."

"Just doing my thing. You heading out on that recon?"

"Yeah, I'm the only one not leading a squad who has Combat Lifesavers, so I'm the default medic. Think you can scrounge me up an aid bag?"

"No problem. I always pack extras. I'll get you squared away." Doc began rummaging through the back of the truck and shoving stuff in a bag. "And listen, I know it goes without saying, but make sure the guys don't drink untreated water. I'd even be careful with iodine tabs. God only knows what's swimming in these streams."

"Like what?"

He started ticking a list off on his fingers. "Cryptosporidiosis, Escherichia coli, giardiasis, schistosomiasis, dracunculiasis, oh, and don't forget primary amoebic meningoencephalitis. Little bugger that travels up into your brain and causes meningitis. Almost always fatal."

"Sorry I asked."

"You'll be sorrier if you don't treat the water properly. I'll throw in some chlorine tablets too, just to be safe. Just tell the guys there's a bacterium in the water here that'll make their most prized appendage fall off. That usually does the trick."

***

By noon Alpha Section was geared up and ready to go. Squad leaders double-checked everyone's kit, made sure we were weapons hot, safeties on, and doubled us up on canteens. I'd given the speech about the local water, including the part about the precious appendage-eating bacteria. The guys seemed to take me seriously.

The temperature and humidity were rising when we marched out of the clearing and into the trees. It was unseasonably hot for Panama in December. Assuming we were still in Panama.

"You still think this is a CIA psyop?" I asked Bond. "Because I'm leaning hard toward Sergeant Wilson's theory."

"Mos' def," Bond replied. "It's Occam's razor, man. The simplest theory is the correct one. What's more likely, an airborne hallucinogenic or getting sucked into an alternate reality?"

"I didn't hallucinate our friends getting killed."

"Of course not, man. You just hallucinated *what* killed them."

He made a compelling point, but I still wasn't quite buying it. The stench in the clearing from the rapidly decomposing bodies was real enough to me. Bond said that was because there *were* rotting bodies, only they were Dingbats, not ugly little cat-like pigmies with the faces of old men.

"Lucky bastards," said my new squad mate, PFC Evans, looking back at Bravo Section pulling security in the assembly area with the vehicles. "They get to chill in the AA while we go sweating and humping through the bush."

"They won't be chillin', bro," Sergeant Wilson said. "Bravo Section has body detail. All those dead kitties are gonna spread disease. They gotta bury or burn 'em."

"Kitties?" I asked.

"Yeah. You know. 'Cause the little freaks look like little cat-people. Close enough."

"I was calling them Chaneques, Sergeant," I said.

"Kitties," he replied.

Once in the trees, we spread out into a wedge formation. Sergeant Clark's squad took point, with us on the left flank. The plan was to strike out in the direction the road *should* be and make a clockwise spiral outward. We would avoid the abundant game trails and paths, which could be booby-trapped or lead into ambushes.

The forest was ancient, with little undergrowth and a ton of deadfall. The canopy rose like the ceiling of a cathedral high overhead, the sickly light of the never-ending eclipse filtering down through the broad leaves. The air was thick and heavy, muting the hoots of monkeys and screeches of birds. There were other sounds too, the incessant chirping of insects and a strange call sounding like a bullroarer that would occasionally break out.

Given the number of Chaneques—I refused to call them "kitties"—who'd attacked us, there was very little sign of their tracks. It seemed they had stuck mainly to the maze of trails that we kept crossing in our search. Every now and again we'd halt, secure a trail, and bound across it.

By mid-afternoon we were all soaked with sweat and caked with salt, and the mosquitos were out in force. They were huge suckers too, bigger than any I'd seen before in Panama. Our insect repellent didn't seem to have much effect. Eventually I just got used to being a walking buffet and didn't even bother to swat them away.

Our squad was leading the wedge now and I was on point. Through the trees I made out a towering hill covered with vines and other vegetation. I called a halt and Sergeant Wilson moved up beside me.

"What do you think, Sergeant?" I asked. "Top of that hill is above the canopy. Could be a good chance to get the lay of the land."

"Righteous call," he replied. "Lemme check with St. James."

He scuttled off silently and returned a few minutes later. "It's a go. St. James will take his squad to the summit while Clark and us pull security at the base. Lead the way, Specialist."

I waved the section forward and crept toward the hill. As we drew closer, I noticed clumps of vines covering ancient stelae—tall, sculpted stone shafts like the Mayans used to erect. These monuments were carved out of a dark stone, almost black, and the reliefs sculpted on the weather-pitted surfaces were terrible scenes of torture and sacrifice. Mass suffering. Genocide. Many of the hieroglyphs seemed to waver with a life of their own. They literally hurt to look at for too long. So that was weird.

It was only then I realized the hill itself was in fact a great pyramid of black stone rising over the jungle. Something about the whole temple complex—I had no doubt it was some kind of temple —gave me the chills, despite the oppressive heat. This was an ancient place of unspeakable evil. You could just feel it.

Or at least I could. Staff Sergeant St. James seemed unaffected and led his squad up the face of the steep temple, clambering among the snaking vines and twisted trees that covered the crumbling surface. When he reached the top, I could see him up there crouching with his maps, trying to orient himself. PFC Evans was beside him, fiddling with his radio antenna while St. James talked into the handset. Bond was crawling around the summit, careful not to expose himself against the skyline and pausing every so often to peer through his binoculars and report back to St. James.

"This place gives me the creeps, man," Sergeant Wilson commented at my side, his eyes scanning the jungle. "There's some seriously bad mojo here."

"Roger that, Sergeant," I said.

PFC Dee had been studying one of the stelae. He should've been watching his sector. I saw him running his hand along the carved relief. Then he gave a choked scream and stumbled back, eyes wide with fear as he clutched his hand. Without warning he doubled over and vomited.

I rushed to his side and helped him sit down. He held his head between his knees and dry-heaved.

"What's going on?" I said.

"My hand," he managed to groan between retches.

He continued to clutch his hand close to his chest.

"Let me see your hand, Jay," I said.

His arm trembled as he held it out. It was a mess. His fingers were charred, the skin split, and dark lines ran up the veins of his hand into his forearm.

Wilson appeared at my side. "What the hell happened to Dee's hand, man?"

"I dunno, Sarge," I said as I dug into my aid kit. "He touched one of the stelae. The carved columns," I added quickly before he could ask.

Dee was moaning and threw his head back, his eyes showing only the whites.

"What the f—his veins, man!" Wilson shouted.

"I know, I know, it's spreading."

The dark veins leading from his hand began to rise above the surface. It was like watching a time-lapse video of ice crystals forming, but instead we were getting a vascular road map of all the bad stuff that was working its way up Dee's arm.

Sergeant Wilson swore. "What should we do? Tourniquet?"

"I don't think that'll help. Just let me think."

"It's going up his arm!"

"I know! Let me think!"

"You gotta amputate, bro!" Wilson insisted.

"With what, Sergeant? My knife?"

"Hold on." Wilson shucked his ruck and dug into it, retrieving a wicked-looking machete. "Here, use this—"

"I'm not chopping off his arm! You know how many hacks it would take with that thing?"

"Well you gotta do *somethin'*, man! I'll do it!"

Wilson readied the weapon.

I held up a hand to stop him. "No! Neither of us knows how to do a field amputation. He'll bleed out!"

Then… Dee spoke. And it wasn't English.

"What the hell is he saying?" Wilson cried.

The sergeant's question was rhetorical, but I knew the answer. "Something about death," I said. "Ravenous, living death. I don't know—it doesn't make sense. Just let me think, Sergeant!"

"You *understand* him?"

"It's Nahuatl. He's not making any sense. Dear God. The poison is going to reach his heart soon. I don't know what to do."

Wilson forced the machete into my hand and then shoved Dee down and clamped his hand on the kid's arm, holding it away from his body. With his other hand flat on Dee's chest, he held him as still as he could. Dee was convulsing.

"Do it," Wilson growled, locking eyes with me.

"I—I can't, Sergeant."

"*Do it!*"

The machete felt like it weighed a hundred pounds. As I raised it, my vision tunneled.

"Goddammit, Bennett! Grow a pair! He's going to die!"

The whites of Dee's eyes flooded with inky blackness and his free hand shot up, clamping around Wilson's neck like a vise.

Wilson let go of the infected arm and clawed at the hand that was now wrapped around his neck. The veins in his forehead bulged as he tried to break Dee's grip, but he couldn't do it. Dee was just locked on. It didn't make sense. Wilson was jacked and Dee was half his size.

The scrawny kid's lips pulled back in a leering rictus, and he snapped his teeth as he pulled Wilson's horrified face closer.

"*I hunger!*" Dee hissed, speaking in a corrupt-sounding Nahuatl dialect with a voice I had never heard him use before.

Pure, primal fear gripped me, and my eyes snapped back into focus.

"*I am the living death,*" Dee moaned, chanting in sing-song. "*The undeath of eternal hunger. I am the Father of Death. Ah, sweet eternal suffering! I hunger!*"

I brought the machete down as hard as I could—on Dee's skull instead of his arm.

CHAPTER 5

"He tried to eat my *face!*" Sergeant Wilson rasped, trying to raise his voice above the general shouting. "He tried to eat my effing face!"

His actual words were a lot more... colorful, but my mom might read this and, well, I'm just a Mormon boy from Utah so I'll be taking certain liberties when quoting people directly, which is some work because troopers swear, like, a lot. Like, all the time. More f-bombs than nouns, verbs, or adjectives, really. It's rather... impressive.

Anyway...

Several rifles were pointed at me, but I just sat on the ground staring off into the jungle.

"I told you," Bond said. "We're all hallucinating and now Bennett's *murdered* Dee!"

"Shut up, Bond," St. James snapped. "Everyone, just shut up. Bennett, what the hell happened?"

I raised a shaking arm and pointed at Dee's corpse. He was already rapidly decomposing, his belly swollen, his skin blackened and seeping a dark viscous fluid. We had all moved a safe distance away, upwind of the putrefying body. Wilson's machete was still embedded in Dee's skull.

Where I had put it.

"Jay was... possessed," I mumbled.

"What part of 'He tried to eat my face' aren't you all registering?" Wilson yelled in support of me. "And does this look like a frigging hallucination, Bond?" Wilson pulled down his collar, exposing the dark bruising on his throat.

"There's got to be a rational explanation," Sergeant Wright began.

"*Rational* up and effed off about twenty-four hours ago," Wilson said. "There's nothing *rational* about any of this, bro."

McKee wandered over to one of the stelae, and I jumped to my feet. Bond, Wright, and Evans brought their rifles up to their shoulders and aimed them at me.

"Don't touch it, McKee!" I cried. "Don't touch anything!"

St. James backed me up. "Get away from that, McKee!" Then he turned to me and said calmly, "Run it all by me, Bennett."

"Dee touched one of those—those monuments—and… and something… infected him," I stammered. "It *changed* him. His hand, his… arm. He was chanting in Nahuatl about… about the hunger of the living dead. About a whole lot of stuff that doesn't make sense. How he was the father of death and pain and suffering. How hungry he was. It wasn't even his voice, Sergeant. Then he attacked Sergeant Wilson."

"He tried to *eat my face*," Wilson repeated.

"You think there's a contact poison on the monuments?" St. James asked.

"It wasn't just poison, Sergeant," I said, my voice rising. "He was *possessed*. It was something *evil*. This whole place is evil!"

"All right, calm down, Bennett. And everyone, stop pointing your rifles at him."

I saw St. James and Bond exchange a look.

"You guys…" I began, "you guys didn't touch it, right?"

"No," St. James said flatly.

"You're sure?"

"We didn't effing touch the totem pole, Bennett!" Bond shouted at me.

"It's a stela," I corrected. "And good."

Wilson moved to retrieve his machete.

"Don't touch that either!" I shrieked.

"What?" Wilson asked. "Bro, that cost me forty bucks."

"Stay away from the corpse, Wilson," St. James said. "It's obviously infected with something."

Wilson backed up, rubbing his palms on his pant legs. "He touched me, bro. You think I'm already infected? Shit, guys, I haven't been baptized, you know? Bennett?"

I closed my eyes and rubbed my temples. "I don't know, Sergeant. I don't think so. He turned so fast."

"Ho-lee shit," Bond said. "We just walked into the Panamanian version of *The Thing*."

"I need to call this in," St. James said, motioning Evans to follow him with the radio. "Everyone, cool down and stay away from the body *and* the monuments. As a matter of fact, don't touch *anything*."

As the staff sergeant stepped away, Wilson moved over to me and put a hand on my shoulder. "Don't beat yourself up, bro. You did the right thing. Maybe if we'd taken the arm off, we could've saved him, maybe not. But you did the right thing. I owe you, bro."

I just shook my head. Jay Dee was a good kid. He'd been with us less than a year, but he was motivated and squared away. Had a wife back in Fort Lewis, near Seattle.

I think she was pregnant.

What the hell had I done? What if Bond was right, and I'd just murdered a guy because of some hallucinogenic jungle spores?

But the words Dee had chanted kept running through my head. About the living death, the death that is not death, the hungry death... He'd said he was the father of death; that he was pain, he was suffering. Sweet eternal suffering. *I hunger.*

When I spoke, my voice felt far away. "Chopping that arm off, even if we could have done it, wouldn't have stopped him," I said. "He was possessed."

"Roger that," Wilson said. "Dee could hardly pass a PT test, but he got so strong at the end. I couldn't break free. This is some seriously bad mojo."

Bond was standing nearby. Listening. "Possessed?" he scoffed. "Like by the devil? Get real. This ain't one of your Mormon tent revivals, Preacher. This is the real world. Occam's razor, man."

"I'm with Bond," Sergeant Wright said.

"Dude, trust me when I say I've had some *seriously* gnarly trips," Wilson said. "But nothing close to this. I'm telling you, we ain't on *Earth* anymore. This is some kind of sick alternate reality."

And just like that, the argument about who was right about what was going on restarted.

I was relieved when St. James came back and put his hands on his hips, looking at each of us in turn. "Talked with the captain. He says Charlie Mike."

"Charlie Mike?" Wilson said. "Seriously? Did you fail to mention that Dee tried to eat my face, Sergeant?"

"Charlie Mike," St. James repeated flatly.

"What about Dee?" McKee asked.

We all looked at the corpse. It was beginning to liquefy, and maggots were crawling out of the mouth and eye sockets.

"Leave him," St. James said. "Listen up. Nothing out there matches anything on our maps. We're not remotely close to Panama City. I don't even think we're in the isthmus anymore. Geography is all wrong. Assuming we can rely on that for compass directions"—he threw a knife hand in the direction of the still-eclipsed sun as it fell toward the horizon—"there's a mountain range far out to the east that sweeps around the south. To the north there are highlands and a huge lake. West of us the jungle turns into savanna. About a klick southeast of here there's what looks like a large village. Captain wants us to check it out. See who the indigenous are. Try to gather intel on our location. We have a few hours of daylight left; let's make use of it. I'm reorganizing us into two squads. Wilson, you're with me. Bennett, go with Clark. My squad will take point for now."

Sergeant Clark had been silent up to this point. But before we moved out, he pulled me aside.

"You squared away, Specialist?" he asked quietly.

"Doing my best, Sergeant."

"Listen, don't let the other guys rattle you. From what I've heard, and I've heard enough, you made the right call. Whatever you killed, it wasn't Dee. Not any longer. Read me?"

"Lima Charlie, Sergeant."

"Whatever doubts you might have, box 'em up and send 'em packing. I need you sharp."

That was the second time someone had told me I needed to put any hindrances to our survival in a box. It was advice that would turn out to be crucial the longer we stayed in this nightmare of a land.

"Affirmative, Sergeant."

Sergeant Clark slapped my shoulder and moved off to confer with the rest of the squad.

***

The perpetual eclipse was sinking low as we approached the village, casting thick, dark shadows across the jungle floor. The impossible celestial event resembled a void in space itself, a hole punched through the sky, haloed in flame. A *black sun*, if you can imagine such a thing.

Tree frogs began to chorus as the light faded, and monkeys chittered at us from the canopy high above. We moved cautiously and silently through ferns and sedge in the wide spaces between massive trees with gnarled trunks draped in vines and orchids. The forest felt ancient. It was palpable, like walking through a realm untouched by time.

Bond was on point and signaled a halt. St. James went to consult with him for a minute and then returned, gathering us into a huddle.

"The village is just ahead. We'll hold here and observe, see what we're dealing with. Watch your sectors closely but *do not* engage unless directly threatened. Hooah?"

We all nodded and spread out, getting low and hidden. From where I was positioned, I had a view of the village through the trees. It wasn't particularly large, maybe twenty wattle-and-daub huts surrounded a few stone and adobe buildings and a small stepped pyramid. I didn't spend long checking the village out, however, because my attention was immediately drawn to what was perched atop the pyramid. Two large timbers had been erected in the shape of an X, and what appeared to be a man had been bound to the cross. St.

James was observing with his binoculars and swore softly. He called Evans over and got on the prick.

From the snippets of what I overheard, he'd identified McCoppin as the crucified man. It appeared he had been flayed, the skin cut and peeled from most of his body.

I felt nauseated.

"Listen up," St. James called out softly. "Those frigging savages have McCoppin. They tortured him to death. Captain's given the green light to go in and get him down. We'll hold tight until dusk to assess the opposition, and then we're going in fast and hot. And I mean *hot*. I couldn't give a damn about collateral damage. Nobody else is gonna get it like he got it. I don't give a shit what the rules of engagement say. Hooah? We're getting him out, and whoever did this is going to pay."

Raiding villages and rescuing captives wasn't exactly part of our job description, but that hardly mattered now. I nodded along with the rest of my section mates.

"Looks like the villagers are kitties, Sarge," Bond said.

"Dead kitties," St. James replied, peering through his binos. "They just don't know it yet."

I was sure he didn't mean *all* of them. A village like that would have elderly, juveniles, females. We'd round up the warriors and priests or whatever, and some of them would get themselves killed fighting us, but even with what had happened to McCoppin, we weren't going in there to burn the village to the ground and salt the earth.

And besides, as best we could all tell, there were no warriors in the village. Maybe they were hiding in the huts, but why? They didn't know we were there. What we saw through the binos was mostly females: smaller than the males, more graceful, and lacking the faces of old men. They reminded me of those hairless cats. Sphynx, I think they're called, except they had messy blue-gray hair on the tops of their heads.

After dusk fell, St. James motioned Clark to join him and they conferred briefly in low tones. Clark nodded one last time and then crept over to Wright and McKee, tapping them both on the shoulder.

He gave my shoulder a tap too as he passed by, and I got up and followed. By now it was getting dark enough we'd broken out our NODs.

The village was surrounded by a few acres of cleared ground planted with corn, and we skirted the field for a few hundred meters before Sergeant Clark called a halt.

"Okay," he said as we huddled close. "There hasn't been any sign of armed combatants like what we encountered before. Either they're holed away in the huts or they're out doing whatever kitty warriors do. We're going in fast and things might get real chaotic real quick, so watch your sectors of fire. Remember, St. James's squad is coming in from the twelve o'clock. Don't shoot them.

"Bennett and I will hit the huts and drive the kitties out. Wright, you'll cover us with the Pig. Evans, you're on crowd control with Sergeant Wright. We'll herd them to the square in front of the temple and sort out who's responsible for what happened here. Captain wants intel. If you see someone with a weapon, you drop them. No hesitation. Hooah?"

"Wouldn't it be easier to just kill 'em all and let whatever god these freaks pray to sort it out?" Wright asked.

"We're not gunning down females and juveniles in the street, understand?" Clark said. "I know we're all hungry for payback, but that's not how we do things. Are we clear?"

"That's not what St. James said," Wright growled. "They ain't even human, Clark."

Clark scowled. "Stop trying to read between the lines of what St. James said because he sure as hell isn't the type to commit mass murder. I'm your squad leader, and I'm telling you we're *not* going there."

"'Don't give a shit about rules of engagement,' that's what he said," Wright insisted.

"Get your damn head squared away, Wright. Captain would never authorize us wasting an entire village. That's not what St. James meant. You know that."

Wright shrugged, but that wasn't good enough for Clark.

"Are we clear, Sergeant Wright?"

"Crystal," Wright grunted.

"Good. Okay, guys, we're going to wait for dark, then we'll move in. Stay alert. Heads on a swivel."

As we waited and watched, the words Dee had been chanting ran through my head like a tape set on repeat. I'd picked up a decent amount of Nahuatl in my two years of proselytizing in Veracruz, where I'd often spent months in the lush hill country. Everyone there spoke Spanish, but I had been fascinated by the ancient Aztec tongue and found plenty of people out there who still knew it. Most of what Dee had chanted was in a dialect I was unfamiliar with. It sounded ancient, but I could somehow understand the gist of it. The essence. Enough to make a shiver run down my spine.

Wright tapped my shoulder twice, and I jumped. Oh, man. Not how I need to be operating in a situation like this. He put a finger to his lips and pointed to Clark, who waved me over.

I joined my squad leader and went in the direction he knife-handed. Even with my NODs it was hard to make out much in the moonless dark. Three shadowy figures coming from the north crept through a field of squash. That would be St. James, Bond, and Evans. Wilson was hidden somewhere out there, watching our backs.

"Bounding overwatch," Clark subvocalized. "Be as silent as possible. We hit that hut first. You see it?"

"Roger, Sergeant."

Forty meters of open ground lay between the cornfield and the first hut. Along the way was a pen that contained turkeys. There was no cover.

Clark slapped my shoulder, and I moved as swiftly and silently as I could, covering ten meters before I dropped prone. Clark bounded past me another ten meters before going prone himself. I got up and moved again. Some of the turkeys began to make noise and I dropped once more, trying to make myself as flat as possible against the damp ground. The turkeys' single, staccato notes of alarm intensified for a moment and then slowly fell off until only the sounds of the nocturnal jungle remained.

Why not have edible guard dogs, I guess.

Clark low-crawled beside me and raised his head to see what St. James was up to.

"They're about to hit their first target," he subvocalized. "Let's move. Don't worry about the turkeys. Things are going to get real loud, real fast anyway."

We scurried the remaining distance and took positions on either side of our targeted doorway. When we entered, he would clear left, and I would clear right. He held up a fist and waited, motionless.

We heard the loud *whoomph* of a grenade detonating, and Clark dropped his fist into a knife hand. Apparently St. James had chosen to clear his first hut with explosive force. Literally. I swept aside the door-covering and entered, swinging my muzzle to the right.

The wattle-and-daub hut was a small, single room lit by a sputtering pine resin torch. I cleared my corner, which contained only a loom, then swung my rifle to the center of the room where three Chaneques crouched on reed mats. All looked female. One I took to be a juvenile, the other perhaps her mother, plus a much older female. All three laid back their big ears and hissed, revealing sharp, needle-like teeth as they backed up against the far wall.

"How do you want to do this, Sergeant?" I asked. The plan was to flex-cuff the inhabitants of the houses and march them out to the temple square, but now that I was staring down at three hissing and spitting creatures with nasty-looking claws, I wasn't so game to go in and restrain them.

Sergeant Clark glared at the Chaneques and pointed to the floor with his off hand. "Get down on your bellies. Now. Understand?"

They might not have ever seen an M16 before, but they seemed to comprehend that the weapons held by the two relative giants were a threat. Whether they could also understand English, I doubted.

"*Face down,*" I commanded in Nahuatl, also pointing to the straw mats. The one I assumed to be the mother spat at me, and I jerked my muzzle, repeating the command. "*Do you understand?*"

She understood. She hissed quietly to the older female and then pushed the juvenile face down before lying down beside her in the same position.

Outside I could hear more grenades and heavy rifle fire. Something was going down.

"Sounds like we found the warriors," Clark said. "Get that old one down, Bennett."

I tried, but the older female hissed in defiance and drew a stone knife out from under one of the mattresses. Sergeant Clark shot her before I even registered what was happening.

"Cuff 'em, Bennett," he ordered over the yowls of the others. "We gotta get out there."

The mother pushed her face into the mattress and made a strange mewling sound as I moved behind her, slung my rifle, and got out the zip ties. Things sounded kinetic outside. The rest of the team needed us in whatever fight was going down.

"Screw it. We're not going to have time to cuff everyone," Clark said. "Just get them out."

"Roger, Sergeant."

I unslung my rifle and prodded the mother's back. *"Outside! Move!"*

As we emerged from the hut with the two females, we immediately encountered panicked Chaneques in the street. No young men, no one who looked like a warrior, just females, juveniles, and *very* old males. You could just tell, even with their old man faces. Wright and McKee were moving up the street toward us, herding them. We pushed our females in with the rest, then rushed to clear other huts as more rifle fire erupted from across the village. The warriors must have been concentrated near St. James's squad.

Clark and I were just exiting another hut, this one unoccupied, when we encountered more resistance: a female with a stone axe, coming right at us. Clark reacted first, dropping her with a quick double-tap. A second female caterwauled and raised a war club, and was abruptly cut down by a burst from Wright on the M60.

The threat had been neutralized, but Wright didn't stop there. He laid into the terrified crowd, mowing down the Chaneques indiscriminately.

"Cease fire!" Clark shouted, trying to be heard over the thunderous grunting of the Pig. "Dammit, Wright! Cease fire!"

I was immobilized by the sight of tiny bodies literally flying apart as the heavy rounds tore into them. The Chaneques were small to begin, and the females looked almost as childlike as the juveniles. The devastation was horrifying, but maybe Wright saw something I didn't.

That's what I told myself, anyway.

Wright stopped firing when his belt ran out, then started loading a new one, almost frenzied. Clark was still screaming at him, but I don't remember what he was saying. I was too absorbed by the surreal carnage that littered the street. I desperately wanted to look away, but I couldn't. It was gruesome and alien all at the same time.

"Bennett!" Clark shouted in my ear.

"Yes, Sergeant?" I asked, tugged free from whatever spell I'd been under. Juveniles clung to the shredded remains of their mothers and mewled. Just across from me an old male was sprawled against the wall of a hut, staring at his intestines. The street reeked of blood and excrement.

"Bennett!" Clark repeated. "Look at me!"

I snapped fully out of my daze and faced him. I couldn't read his eyes.

"Get these things rounded up and to the square," he ordered.

I motioned to the dead and dying. "Lot of them can't move, Sergeant."

"Then move the ones that can."

"What about the wounded?" I asked, suddenly remembering that I was the designated medic. Should I try and save these creatures? Could I even figure out their anatomy?

"Just get them moving, Specialist."

Speaking in Nahuatl, I ordered them to move, to hurry, to go to the village square. Wright and McKee were shouting the same thing in English. And McKee... he had a look of amusement on his face. As if all of this were somehow... funny. But they were following Clark's lead now. Gone was the weird frenzy that Wright had shown in his shooting and hurried, frantic reloading.

We moved the survivors forward as best we could, and soon linked up with Bond, who was pushing forward his own group of females.

I ran over to him. "Everyone okay?" I asked. "That sounded intense. You must have run into every warrior in the place."

Bond laughed. "Not a one, Preacher. Not a single one."

I looked back the way he had come. The ground was strewn with bodies, many of them blasted completely apart. And some of the huts had begun to burn.

"No warriors?" I asked dumbly.

"Nope," he said. "But that just made our job easier. How many kitties you dust? I lost count, man. That was some epic shit."

I was thoroughly confused at that point. And Bond... this wasn't like Bond. Not at all. He wasn't that guy. *None* of the guys, as far as I knew, were that guy.

"Bennett!" Clark screamed. "Get your ass over here."

I rushed numbly to rejoin my squad in the village square. St. James was already there, standing on the lowest step of the temple, with another group of Chaneques huddled in the courtyard below him. Evans stood off to one side, covering them. Juveniles were mewling and females were hissing.

Altogether, there were perhaps two dozen females assembled and maybe a handful of old males.

That was it. That was all that was left of the village.

It had been a massacre.

CHAPTER 6

The hellish light of the burning huts was bright enough that I could stow my NVGs. "Who's the head honcho here?" a livid St. James barked, staring down at what few Chaneques were still alive. "I want the big man. Who's in charge?"

I moved to translate, since it seemed these creatures could understand my poorly spoken Aztec, but an ancient Chaneque male limped forward without my needing to. The elder was assisted by a young female.

"I am Tlamatkitlajtoli. I am the village headsman," the ancient one said in Nahuatl, proudly squaring his shoulders.

"Good," St. James replied in English. "Then explain that to me." He threw a knife hand up to the top of the temple.

I was taken aback. I'd had no idea that St. James could understand their language. How was that even possible? I could barely speak and understand it myself, and that was only because for two years I had made it my weird missionary hobby.

The headsman looked from McCoppin and back to St. James. He blinked once, slowly, but didn't seem bothered by the implications of it all. "The warriors captured the Outworlder and gave him to the priests as a sacrifice to Tezcatlipoca. You should be proud. He sustained his ordeal with honor, as is expected of a warrior."

I edged over to Clark and whispered: "The old guy said we should be proud because McCoppin died like a warrior, with honor."

"I ain't deaf, Bennett," he whispered back.

I shook my head. That was too weird. "You can understand Nahuatl?"

"What the hell are you talking about? Everyone's speaking English, Bennett."

Color me confused. To my ears we spoke English and the Chaneque spoke Nahuatl, and yet no one had any difficulty understanding each other. It made so little sense that I couldn't help but give a little more credence to Bond's hallucinogen theory.

"Bond, Evans, get McCoppin down," St. James ordered.

"No! You must not!" the headsman shouted. Crazy how *this* was the thing that finally got him riled up, and not what had just been done to his people. "It would give grave offense to Tezcatlipoca!"

"Tezcatlipoca can kiss my ass," St. James said flatly. "Bond, Evans, do it."

"I must protest!" Tlamatkitlajtoli said, taking a step forward. "This is desecration! You shame your warrior!"

St. James snapped his rifle to his shoulder and shot the headsman in the belly. The old Chaneque yowled in pain and fell forward.

"Grandfather!" cried the female beside him. She flattened her ears and hissed at St. James, coiling her body like a spring to pounce.

He calmly pointed his rifle at her. "Down, kitty."

She crouched and spat but didn't move.

"That's a good pussycat," said St. James.

Bond and Evans, ignoring the old Chaneque's protests, had gone up to McCoppin, and now Bond started shouting. "Oh, god! Oh, god!"

"Report, Specialist!" St. James called back.

"Sergeant, he's still alive! Bennett, get your ass up here! McCoppin ain't dead!"

I took a step, unsure what I could do for a man who'd been skinned alive. But St. James stopped me. There was a hardness in his face. In his eyes. A sort of, I don't know... venom. I'd seen the staff sergeant get angry plenty of times, but never like this. This was a whole other level.

"Bennett can't help him," St. James said. He jerked his head at Clark. "He's your man, Kenneth. Your responsibility."

"Affirmative," Clark replied gravely.

"I've got morphine in my bag," I told Clark.

Clark gave a quick shake of his head. "Just mind the prisoners, Specialist."

Sergeant Clark climbed the temple steps stiffly and told Bond and Evans to go back down, leaving him alone with McCoppin. They practically stumbled down to us. Evans paused just long enough to vomit, and a frightening memory of Dee just before he was... taken over, came unbidden to my mind. But Bond's face was livid, every bit as hard and cruel as St. James's.

A single gunshot echoed through the night, and I immediately understood. A mercy killing. And it had been Clark's job to perform it.

"Bennett, secure the female," St. James ordered, motioning to the young Chaneque who still knelt beside her dying grandfather. "Bond, cover him."

"We should just shoot her too, Sergeant," Bond urged. "Shoot 'em all. Finish the job."

"Negative," St. James said, but not until it looked as though he'd strongly considered it.

Bond didn't bring it up again. At least not directly. Instead, he sort of chanted to himself in a whisper. "We gotta... We gotta..."

It was weird.

"Shut up and cover Bennett," St. James snapped. The staff sergeant paced back and forth, a feral look on his face.

I slung my rifle and cautiously approached the female. She bared her teeth at me, her sharp claws sheathing and unsheathing as she flexed her fingers. But she was also making a soft mewling noise that sounded like crying. Pathetic as that was, the Chaneque females were every bit as ugly as the males, and I couldn't help but be a little repulsed by her.

Bond moved up close and shoved his rifle's muzzle in her face. "Don't even think about it, kitty."

Her hand moved deftly behind her back, and I leapt forward, grabbing her wrist and twisting her arm in one of the jujitsu locks Sergeant Takahashi had taught me, all while forcing her to the ground. It wasn't difficult; she wasn't any bigger than your average six-year-old.

Jamming my knee between her thin shoulder blades I pulled the stone knife out of her grip, tossed it aside, and cuffed her arms behind her.

"You shame me," she mewled. "Let me die with honor by my own hand."

It hadn't occurred to me that the knife was for her, not us.

"Sorry," I said, not really meaning it.

I pulled her off the ground and hauled her to her feet, taking care to keep my hands well out of reach of those wicked teeth.

"She's your responsibility, Bennett," St. James said. "Captain wants a prisoner. If anything happens to her, it's your ass, clear?"

"Lima Charlie, Sergeant."

"What about the rest of 'em, Sergeant?" Bond asked. "We gotta…"

We all knew what he meant.

St. James had that darkness in his eyes. "Dust 'em."

I shivered, and then felt sick.

***

Sergeant Wright's M60 made short work of the surviving prisoners. Bond whooped and hollered as the Pig spat out death at close range. Mothers shielded their children with their bodies as the M60 grunted and tore them to bloody shreds. Old men stood in defiance as they were gunned down.

It was slaughter and there was no honor in it.

Bond called it justice.

But it was murder.

And honestly, I was afraid that if I said anything or did anything to stop it, they'd kill me too. It wasn't that these guys had just snapped from two days out in the crazy and seeing terrible things happen to McCoppin. It was more like they were completely different people. Bond was a friend. I knew him. Knew what it was like when he was at his wit's end. What had gotten ahold of him? Of all of them?

When Wright finished his bloody task, Bond and McKee eagerly sifted through the carnage, ensuring every last man, woman, and child was good and dead. Then they drew their knives and started taking trophies. Morbid, ghastly trophies.

"C'mon, guys," I said.

They ignored me like they hadn't even heard.

My prisoner mewled pitifully throughout it all. She cried again as the others set fire to the crops. Sergeant St. James ordered a pyre built for McCoppin out of timbers from the houses. He demanded it be made in the shape of a pyramid with McCoppin on top, and then set the whole thing ablaze. The jungle seemed awash with hellfire.

"What's your name?" I asked the prisoner.

"I am dead," she replied. Her eyes were vacant. Her ears hung limp. "I have no name."

"But you had a name. What was it?"

"Epasotl," she eventually whispered without emotion.

"That's a pretty name," I lied. It meant "skunkweed."

"Your warlord is without honor and your warriors are dumb beasts," she hissed, staring daggers at me with her big green-and-gold eyes, her pupils narrowed into tiny slits. "They behave as servants of the dark one."

"I'm sorry," I said. And I was. Completely.

But I don't want it to sound as if I wasn't angry about what had happened to McCoppin. I was. I wanted vengeance too—as much as anyone. He had been my friend. A good friend. He was a good man.

But I knew him well enough to know that he wouldn't have approved of what had happened tonight. Brian McCoppin was a man of honor.

"Your words are the hollow bones of rotting birds," Epasotl said.

I ignored the remark. "My captain will want to know where your warriors are."

"And if I refuse to speak?"

"I don't know." That was the truth. I had no idea if St. James would even allow this prisoner to reach the captain. What else was the man capable of? Torture? Before tonight, I would have told you not in a million years. Now… I didn't know. The sooner we got her back to the captain and the rest of the platoon, the better.

"If I answer your questions, will you sacrifice me to your gods?" Epasotl asked after a prolonged silence. I assumed she was worried we would until she added, "I pray it is so. I cannot live with my shame."

"What's there to be ashamed of?" I asked. "There's nothing you could've done to prevent what happened."

"I am no peasant girl. I am the daughter of a warlord, and you have taken me captive. There is no greater shame. I am dead to my people. Is it not the same with you?"

"No," I said. "If we're captured, we're expected to escape, if we can, and are welcomed home as heroes."

"Heroes die in battle. Only cowards are captured. They live in shame. Only through facing death by torture without fear can they regain their honor."

"And my friend…" I said. "He regained his… honor." It wasn't a question, and I felt almost nauseated saying it.

"His bravery moved me deeply," Epasotl whispered. "You should be proud to call him a friend."

I was.

Right then, Staff Sergeant St. James power-walked up to us. A man on a mission.

"Where are your warriors?" he shouted to Epasotl. "Right now. Tell me."

She laid her ears back and bared her teeth.

"Listen, pussycat, I'm not going to ask twice. Talk, or I'll start carving pieces off you." St. James waved his knife in front of her face for emphasis.

She didn't even flinch. The pint-sized creature was brave, I gave her that much. St. James towered over her like a giant. Sergeant Wright stood behind him and laughed, the M60 resting across his shoulders. Wright wore a necklace of Chaneque ears fashioned out of

550 paracord. Bond and McKee had similar macabre trophies. Evans still looked sick; he was shaking. Clark was watching McCoppin's funeral pyre.

Wilson had rejoined us by then. He caught my eye and gave me a look that made it clear he wanted to know how this had all happened. I could only shrug.

"It's no use, Sergeant St. James," I said. "She *wants* to be tortured."

"Say again?"

"In their culture, withstanding torture proves one's bravery," I explained. "She belongs to the warrior caste. It's a matter of honor. Besides, Captain Brown wanted a prisoner. He won't be happy if you carve her up before he can question her. All due respect, Sergeant."

"The little freak's got four ears, for eff's sake," Bond erupted. "Take half and there's still enough of her for the captain."

"Yeah, she can spare a couple ears," Wright chuckled. He flicked one of the same on his necklace.

Clark finally spoke up. "Can it, Billy." Then he addressed the staff sergeant. "We're not torturing anyone right now. The questions can wait. We need to finish our exfil before anyone gets too interested in this colossal signal flare we've created."

"Roger that, man," Wilson said. "Staying here is hella tactically unsound, bros."

St. James thought for a moment before sheathing his knife. "All right. We're moving out. My squad'll take point. Bennett and Miss Kitty keep to the center of the formation. Single file. I don't want anyone getting lost."

***

We rucked for about a dozen klicks before St. James called a halt to wait for dawn, which was only a few hours away. He set us on fifty percent security, and Wilson came over to sit beside me and Epasotl.

"Catch some winks, bro," he said to me quietly. "I'll watch the kitty-cat."

"If anything happens to her it's my ass," I replied.

"Nothing's gonna happen." He lowered his voice even more and took a quick look around. "Bro, what happened back there was screwed up. How the hell did St. James lose it like that, man? Most of the dudes went feral. That's bad mojo."

"It was murder, Sarge," I said, still not quite believing what had happened.

"Facts," Wilson agreed.

"I kept thinking Sergeant Clark would stop it."

"What did you expect him to do? He did what he could, man. Listen, what happened, happened. Nothing you or I can do about it."

"Maybe not," I said, thinking. "It's just... I dunno. It doesn't feel right."

"Yeah, no shit."

"No, not that. It's like, even before it all went down, Wright was acting weird. Like his mind wasn't working right and all he could think about was mowing everyone down."

"Probably thinkin' about what happened to McCoppin."

"Sure. So was I. So were you and Clark." I let out a long breath. "Wilson... did you... did you see any of the guys touch anything back at that temple?"

Wilson shook his head. "No. I was watching my sector. Dee'd still be here if he'd done the same. Ruck out, bro. I got this."

I stretched out, using my ruck for a pillow. The change over Alpha was just so abrupt. I couldn't help but wonder. And worry.

I felt a tap on my shoulder. It was Wilson again.

"Hey Bennett, what do I call the prisoner in case she gets feisty?"

Epasotl sat next to me, motionless.

"Her name's Epasotl," I said with a yawn.

"That's pretty," Wilson said.

"Means 'skunkweed.'"

"Sweet. I've smoked that. Good dope."

"No, like the noxious plant."

"Never been desperate enough to try and smoke any of that."

I closed my eyes. I felt wired, but I must have been more exhausted than I thought because the next thing I knew Wilson was nudging me awake and the sky was the wolf-gray of predawn.

"Get some chow," Wilson said. "We're moving out soon."

I stretched and dug a couple MREs out of my ruck. I offered one to Epasotl.

"Chili mac or Chicken a la King?" I asked.

She tilted her head questioningly.

"It's food," I said. "Well, the Army claims it is anyway. I recommend the chili mac."

I shoved the Chicken a la King back in my ruck and tore open the chili mac. Her nose twitched and her pupils narrowed.

"It stinks," she said.

"You get used to it," I said. "But it's delicious."

I spooned some into my mouth, and she watched with apparent disgust.

"Want some?" I asked.

"I am not hungry."

"Your loss. Oh, I know. You'll love this." I pulled a small chocolate out of the package and unwrapped it. "Here, try some."

She sniffed at it suspiciously before taking it in her mouth. Her pupils dilated, and I swear I heard her purr.

"Good, isn't it?" I said.

"Look, Bennett's got himself a pet," Wright sneered. "Careful the pussycat don't bite your hand off."

"Stop fraternizing with the prisoner, Specialist," St. James growled.

"Yes, Sergeant."

I wolfed down the rest of my breakfast and stowed the packaging, shoving a packet of crackers and jalapeño cheese spread in my cargo pocket for later.

Epasotl's ears perked up and her nose twitched. "They have found us," she hissed.

"Who?" I asked.

"The vanguard of my father's war band."

"Where?"

"They have surrounded us. We will all die soon."

Mist shrouded the trees and all I could hear was the hoots of monkeys and chitter of birds greeting the pending dawn. I grabbed Epasotl's arm and hurried over to Sergeant Clark.

"Sergeant, I think we're about to be ambushed," I said in a low voice. "Epasotl says her father's war band is nearby."

Clark scanned the trees and brought his rifle up to his shoulder, sweeping it from right to left.

"She says they have us surrounded," I added in a whisper.

"I can see one," he murmured, pausing his sweep of the forest. His rifle barked and he yelled, "Contact! Contact! Contact! Hostiles on the perimeter! They're everywhere! All around us!"

I dragged Epasotl to the center of our camp and shoved her down before unslinging my rifle as more calls of "Contact!" echoed through the section and rifle fire shattered the early morning. The M60 grunted a long burst, and I heard Wright calling out for the ambushers to "Get some!"

Javelins whistled through our ranks, and I ducked instinctively. Then, like apparitions, Chaneque warriors materialized out of the mists waving stone axes and long spears tipped with obsidian blades. They caterwauled war cries as they broke through our perimeter. Two rushed me and I fired, dropping one at five meters. The second reached me and swung his axe at my stomach. I parried with my rifle and then shoved the muzzle hard into his chest, firing as quickly as I could reset the trigger.

Another warrior with a long spear flicked the tip at my face. I leapt back, stumbling, and fell on my ass. Epasotl was up in a flash. Somehow she'd freed herself of her flex cuffs, and she snatched an axe off the ground. I thought for about a second that a chop was coming my way, but instead she leapt inside the reach of the spear-toting Chaneque and swung her weapon with both hands at the warrior. The axe head hacked deep between neck and shoulder. Epasotl spun and pulled the weapon free before hurling it into the back of another warrior who was sparring with Wilson. The Chaneque fell in a heap and twitched at Wilson's feet. His eyes were just as wide and surprised as mine were.

It seems we had been wrong to assume the village had contained no warriors. Epasotl could fight.

She backed protectively toward me, her body tightly wound in a crouch, ready to spring, ears back, claws out.

Wilson hauled me up to my feet, spinning me around in the process. I snapped my rifle to my shoulder as more warriors broke through the trees. Wilson and I worked together, dropping them as they charged.

"Mag out!" I shouted as my bolt locked back. I fumbled to swap magazines as Wilson covered me. I hit the bolt release and dropped to a knee to fire again.

"Mag out!" Wilson echoed a moment later.

By now everyone in Alpha Section had backed into a rough circle, shoulder to shoulder. Wilson was on my left and Clark was on my right. More warriors charged and more warriors fell. I'd lost sight of Epasotl.

"Get some, motherf—" I heard Wright roar above the grunting chatter of the M60 from behind me before it suddenly fell silent.

"Medic!" McKee called out.

It took me a moment to register that he was calling for me.

CHAPTER 7

McKee was dragging a bloodied Wright into the center of the circle. I hurried to the spot.

"Get on that Pig, McKee," St. James barked.

McKee's eyes met mine for a moment before he hefted the M60 out of Wright's hands and returned to our rapidly shrinking circle.

Wright's face was a mask of blood, and he was shaking and moaning. I felt down his body for more injuries, turning him on his side to check his back. Just a wound to the face, it appeared. Those always bled like crazy and could look worse than they really were, but this one was legitimately bad. He'd been slashed with something razor-sharp, the cut running up the left side of his face into his scalp. It was deep, and when he shook his head, a hefty flap of skin flopped open, exposing bone. The guy was practically scalped.

I dug into my aid bag.

Wright moaned. He balled his hands into fists and gritted his teeth, his eyes rolling back into his head.

"Easy there, Sergeant," I said. I was trying to speak calmly but had to raise my voice above the cacophony of the battle. I turned my focus to the wound. There was so much blood I couldn't see exactly where it began and ended, so I took one of his canteens and poured its water over his face while dabbing at the blood with a field dressing.

"Sergeant, you need to keep your head still." I realized Epasotl was kneeling beside me. "Hold his head still," I told her.

Epasotl looked at me questioningly, but moved to cradle his head in her lap, holding his head with both hands.

"Get that bitch away from me," Wright said between gritted teeth.

"Just try to stay still, Sergeant," I repeated, folding the flap of skin back against his face. Doc had somehow obtained skin staplers and had added one to my bag. I held it above Wright so he could see it.

"I have to close the wound, Sergeant. This is probably going to hurt like hell."

Wright didn't even flinch as I worked from the top of his scalp, stapling his skin together with the stainless-steel sutures. He was bleeding so much I had to keep flushing the cut with water to see what I was doing. His legs kicked and he bucked, but Epasotl held his head firm as he swore up a storm. Wright was angrier about her holding on to him than he was about the injury or my rough ministrations. It was pure hate. He clearly believed she was going to kill him.

And why not? After what he'd done to her people, whose ears still hung in a vile necklace around his neck, whose blood mixed with his own to stain the front of his BDU... why wouldn't she kill him? I was the only thing keeping either one from killing the other, or so I thought at the time.

It took two dozen staples to reattach the skin to his face. Then I wrapped his head in gauze and covered it with a field dressing.

By then the forest was silent, save for the heavy breathing of the men around me. St. James noticed Epasotl and kicked her away from Wright as if she were a stray.

"She was helping me with Wright, Sergeant," I explained.

He grunted an expletive while Clark crouched down beside Wright and me.

"He going to be all right?" Clark asked.

"I think so, Sergeant. He'll have a nasty scar, but he should be okay if we keep the wound clean and get him back to Doc."

"Good," Clark said. "How you feeling, Billy?"

"Fine," Wright replied tersely. "Could use some morphine or something, Sergeant."

"You didn't give him anything for the pain?" Clark asked me in shock.

"Sorry, Sergeant," I said, digging in my bag for an autoinjector. "There was a lot going on. I forgot."

"You're an asshole, Bennett," Wright said. "And a moron."

"Roger that, Sergeant." I stuck him in the thigh. "I'll check on you in thirty mikes and give you more if this doesn't do the trick."

I stood and surveyed the carnage. Little blue-gray bodies littered the jungle floor. At least twenty of them. The battle had been a close thing.

"Anyone else hurt?" I asked.

Miraculously, the answer was no.

"For a minute there I thought we were gonna have to revert to harsh language," Wilson said.

"How the hell did she get out of her restraints?" St. James asked. He threw a knife hand at Epasotl, who was standing close beside me.

"I don't know, Sergeant," I replied. "But she saved my life. Probably Sergeant Wilson's too."

"For sure," Wilson said.

"Get some flex cuffs back on the prisoner, Specialist," St. James barked. "I'm holding you accountable for her getting loose. You'll be a private before the day's out. You read me?"

"Affirmative, Sergeant." I pulled Epasotl after me to get some distance between her and the men. Bond was staring daggers at her, and I didn't trust St. James one bit. I didn't trust anyone who'd decided to participate in that murderfest back at the village.

"I got to call this in," St. James said. "Ken, take Bond and search the kitties for intel. If there are any survivors, kill 'em."

"Roger," Clark replied.

"Wilson, you, McKee, and Evans are on security," St. James added. "We move in ten mikes."

"Hooah," Wilson said.

With some distance between us and the other men I crouched beside Epasotl and flex-cuffed her hands together—this time in front of her body.

"Why'd you do that?" I asked her quietly. "Why'd you save me?"

"Our fates are bound," she replied. "My duty is to you as my captor. I am your slave until you either restore my honor or send me to the underworld in eternal shame."

"But those were your father's men. You could have escaped."

"And heap shame upon shame? Where would I go? I serve you now. If I serve well, perhaps you will grant me an honorable death. That is my only solace. I am dead to my people. I am a ghost upon the land."

I shook my head. "Your own father wouldn't take you back? Even if you killed us when you had the chance?"

"My shame would be too great for him to bear. He would kill me without honor, and I would go to dwell in Mictlāntēcuhtli's kingdom forever."

She shuddered at the thought.

***

It was late afternoon when we reached the clearing and were reunited with the rest of the platoon. Bravo Section had been busy burning bodies and cross-loading the vehicles. We had no way to patch the tires punctured by Chaneque javelins, let alone inflate them, so we swapped out wheels. That left us with two inoperable trucks counting Clark's, which had been totaled by the enraged sisimito.

Bravo's section leader, Staff Sergeant Douglas, had led a patrol that discovered a game trail leading westward that was wide enough to accommodate the Humvees. What kind of game would make a trail that wide, we didn't know. Hopefully we wouldn't run across it.

But we had a way out.

Which was a good thing, because by dusk the drums had started up again.

I was beginning to think everyone had forgotten about me and my diminutive prisoner when Wilson came to our mount to inform me the captain finally wanted to see her.

"You get to meet the big kahuna," Wilson told Epasotl.

"Big kahuna?" she asked.

"The old man, the boss, the chief," Wilson said. "Captain Brown."

"The one you call Holy James is not your warlord?" she said.

Wilson and I shared a look. He'd heard it too. Whatever cosmic universal translator was active here had approximated "saint" with "holy."

"Nah, he's like a sub-chief," Wilson said with a laugh. "And he ain't holy. But he is my boss, just like I'm Bennett's boss."

She looked at me in surprise. "I did not know you were such a low-ranking warrior."

"Sorry." I shrugged, feeling oddly embarrassed. "Come on."

I felt the eyes of the platoon on me and Epasotl as we crossed the assembly area to the captain's mount. He was talking to Sanchez. I stopped a respectful distance away and stood at ease. Eventually he noticed me.

"Thanks for bringing the prisoner, Nephi. That'll be all."

"Yes, sir," I said. I didn't snap to attention or salute. We didn't observe those formalities in the field. Officers preferred it that way. They generally didn't enjoy being the focus of sniper target practice.

"I'd prefer he stay, with your permission," Sanchez said. "I have some questions for him too."

"As you were," Captain Brown said to me. He strolled over to us and crouched down in front of Epasotl. Sanchez stood behind him.

"Ugly little thing," Sanchez commented.

"Can you communicate with her?" Brown asked me.

"Yes, sir. I can understand her, because I speak a little bit of Nahuatl, but apparently so can everyone else. And she can understand them. It seems everybody but me hears her speaking English, but I hear her speaking Nahuatl."

"What's Nahuatl?" Brown asked.

"Aztec, sir."

"Fascinating," Brown commented, still studying the young Chaneque woman before him. She was small, as I've mentioned. Less than four feet tall. Next to the captain she appeared miniature.

"Her name's Epasotl," I volunteered.

"Hello, Epasotl," Brown said. "Have you been treated well?"

"I have, Big Kahuna," she replied.

Sanchez looked like he'd eaten something unpleasant. "She's been around Wilson too much already."

"Call me Captain or Sir," Brown told her. He jerked his head toward me. "Bennett over there claims we aren't speaking the same language."

"We are not," she said.

"That's interesting. Because it sure sounds to me like we're both speaking English. Can you explain that?"

"I speak Nahuatl. You speak your tongue. We understand each other. It is a gift granted to Outworlders by Tezcatlipoca," she answered with confidence.

"Tezca… Who is that?" Brown asked.

"He is the creator of this world and our chief god. He is omnipotent and omniscient. It is to him that your warrior was sacrificed, so that he might lend us his strength in our raid against you Outworlders."

"Seems to me those big… monsters you ran out there have all the strength you need. They stood up to almost everything we had. What were they?"

"Sisimitos," Epasotl said. "They withstood the power of your weapons?"

Brown nodded. "For a time."

"Then Tezcatlipoca did not abandon us. Your Outworlder magic must be very powerful for you to be alive."

"You refer to us as Outworlders," Sanchez said.

"Yes," said Epasotl. "For Tezcatlipoca reaches his hand across worlds and snatches beings to bring into his realm."

"And why would he want to do that?" Brown asked.

"Who can know the mind of a god? Perhaps it amuses him."

"Why did your warriors attack us?" Brown asked, changing subjects. I got the sense that he wasn't buying her theology.

Having grown up in the church I did, I wasn't either.

"We are the people of the forest. We make war on all who trespass into our domain. It has always been so."

"Where are your warriors now?"

"They retreated after the battle to the sacred places to regain their strength. They will make sacrifices to Huitzilopochtli. I believe they will return to seek retribution for the destruction of our village and the murder of their wives and children."

"Women and children?" Brown asked. He directed the question at me this time.

"Uh… yes, sir," I said, not knowing what to say or not to say.

"What happened at your village?" Brown asked Epasotl.

"A great slaughter," Epasotl said without emotion. "Your men attacked while our warriors were away. They attacked without honor, killing our old men, mothers, and cubs, even the young women. They burned our homes and fields. We did not provoke them. Not all of us. Why would your warriors do such a thing?"

Epasotl looked proud and regal in asking the question. She pressed it further.

"To raid a village for plunder or vengeance I can understand. It is the way of things. But to kill mothers and cubs? Maidens? Where is the honor in that? They should be taken as a prize for the warriors, to become their wives."

Brown locked eyes with Sanchez. "Her story has a slightly different color to it than St. James's, eh, Diego?"

"Yes, sir."

"That what you saw, Nephi?" Brown asked me.

"Yes, sir," I said, feeling like I'd crossed a line I couldn't go back over the moment I spoke the words. But there was no other way. I couldn't be party to any of this. "At first I thought St. James and the others must have encountered Chaneque warriors, but there were none. We knew that going in, and we saw nothing to change that assessment. We killed everyone anyway. It was a massacre. Ask Sergeant Wilson. He'll confirm it too."

"He's already spoken to us," Sanchez said. "Said he wasn't in a position to explain why the shooting started, but that non-combat casualties were a result. The other members of Alpha have acknowledged the civilian loss, but claim that it was unavoidable given the circumstances." He fixed me with a hard look. "These are serious charges, Specialist. I want you to think very carefully about what you say next. Are you claiming that Staff Sergeant St. James had no justification to use lethal force? You saw what *he* saw? It's your word against the rest of Alpha Section."

I felt flustered. Of course, I hadn't *seen* what kicked it all off. I only saw the aftermath.

"No, Sergeant. I didn't see how it started. I did, however, witness Staff Sergeant St. James give an order for the few prisoners we had —excluding Epasotl—to be executed prior to our leaving camp."

Sanchez looked to Captain Brown, and a short, non-verbal conversation quickly resolved itself before Sanchez's eyes went from Epasotl to me. "You been getting along pretty well with the prisoner, I hear."

I don't know how Sanchez would have gotten that impression unless St. James or one of the others had told him. This felt to me like I was being set up. My stomach twisted itself into knots.

"No, Sergeant. Just a prisoner."

Brown waited out the brief silence that followed. Then he and Sanchez asked Epasotl a few more questions and grilled me about PFC Dee and my part in his death. By the end I was convinced I'd not only be demoted but court-martialed and summarily shot on the spot. But Sanchez simply said I was being reassigned to Bravo Section, and Captain Brown dismissed me.

Epasotl was still my charge.

I assembled my gear and reported to Staff Sergeant Douglas's mount for reassignment. Douglas was a stout, slow-talking Cajun who'd seen action in Grenada. I'd heard he was a great section leader, and I was more than happy to be out from under St. James's command. Even before the Chaneque village, he'd been something of a butthole.

But leaving Wilson... that gave me mixed feelings. I couldn't understand why he would cover for St. James when I knew he disagreed with what had happened as much as I did.

To my surprise, Sergeant Wilson was also with Staff Sergeant Douglas, and his ruck was with him. He gave me a lazy mock salute.

"Sergeant Sanchez's shaking up the whole outfit, bro," he said. "Getting re-org'd into three sections."

I wanted to ask Wilson right there why he hadn't told Sanchez what I'd told Sanchez, but figured it wasn't the time or place. And I already knew the answer. As Sanchez had said, these were serious charges.

"Who's leading the new section?" I asked instead.

"Shrimp's got Charlie," he answered. "Takahashi's squad is joining him."

Sergeant Shrimpton was soft-spoken and always *very* squared away. With Takahashi as his assistant section leader, Charlie was going to be an incredibly high-speed, low-drag unit.

"Who're you joining?" I asked.

"I ain't no joiner, bro." Wilson laughed. "I get García's squad. Seniority and all. He's joining Douglas."

"So I'm still with you?"

"You think I'd let them break up the band?"

I smiled, but my heart wasn't in it. A feeling of extreme vulnerability still weighed on me. I couldn't help but think that everyone on that mission had me in mind to take any fall that might come from it.

If Wilson had García's squad, that meant I'd be serving with Specialist Pierce and Private James. I didn't know either of them very well, but García had run a tight squad, so I was confident they were squared away.

"Long as I'm still on the Nineteen I'm happy, Sarge," I said.

"She's all yours, bro. Pierce hates being a gunner. I'm making him the driver. Tired of being tossed around by privates."

Sergeant García came over and tossed his ruck into the back of Douglas's truck. He gave a long look back at his mount and then pointed at Wilson.

"You take good care of her," he said.

"What's her name?" Wilson asked.

"Beauty." García slapped Douglas's truck. "This one's Beast."

Our mount was named Apollo, but she was being reassigned to Shrimpton. He'd probably rechristen her something stupid like *Carnivore*.

"Word of advice, man," García said. "Don't let Pierce drive her."

"James any good?" Wilson asked.

"Better than good. Kid was born off-roading. Smooth as silk."

Staff Sergeant Douglas rambled over to us. "You boys squared away?"

"Cheah, Sarge," Wilson said, flashing a shaka sign.

"Dear Lord," muttered Douglas. "Another surfer. You an' Pierce goin' get along famous."

"Really. I didn't know Pierce was cool," Wilson said.

"He's a regular waxhead," García put in. "He thought Panama was going to be all waves and chiquitas. Welcome to the Army, eh?"

"Yeah, I was really hoping to hit Playa Morrillo," Wilson replied.

"Sorry to disappoint," said Douglas. "Mount up. We movin' out in fifteen while there's still some light, afore 'em kitties get here." He looked over at me. "She ain't goin' be a problem, is she?"

I'd honestly forgotten about Epasotl for a minute. She was quiet and caused no trouble at all. It was actually alarming how relaxed I'd gotten with a prisoner so close by. She just stood right beside me, like my shadow.

"No, Staff Sergeant," I said.

Wilson and I hurried to our new mount and stowed our gear in the back. Pierce was pulling security on the MK19 and nodded at us. James had been checking under the Humvee's hood and gave us a wave.

"Welcome to Bravo Six, or whatever we are now," James said. He was a big, cornfed kid who looked like he'd been tossing hay bales since he was a toddler. He slammed the hood down and latched it shut before wiping his hands with a rag. "Beauty's ready to roll, Sergeant."

"We're Havok Squad now," Wilson said as he got into the Humvee.

"That's better than Nightcrawler," James remarked, joining him in the driver's seat. "Why captain named us after an earthworm I'll never know."

"I keep telling you, dude, it's not a worm," Pierce called down from the hatch. "Nightcrawler is badass."

"Whatever, nerd," James shot back.

"Hey, Pierce," Wilson said. "Bennett's gunner now. Swap out."

"Thank God," Pierce said, shucking the flak vest. He was a solidly built guy. Not pumped like Wilson, but he looked like he could hold his own in a fight. He was a year or two younger than me and a couple inches taller, with a complexion like dark toffee. Reminded me of a young Lando Calrissian, complete with lady-killer mustache. "You can have it, man." He caught sight of Epasotl as she moved to follow me into the truck. "Whoa, man. What the hell is that? It's not riding with us, is it?"

"Don't sweat it, bro," Wilson said. "She's housebroken. Her name's Skunkweed. She's our new mascot. She's cool."

Pierce eyed her suspiciously as he got into the seat. "It doesn't bite, does it?"

Epasotl tried to mimic a human smile, with somewhat unsettling results. Too many sharp teeth.

"Hang loose, bro-ski," she said to Pierce, attempting to hold out her thumb and pinky like she'd seen Wilson do.

"See? She knows some tricks already," Wilson said. "And if you think about it, she's so ugly, it's almost cute."

"Almost," Pierce said, edging away from her. "Gonna have to be another few years in country before *that* starts looking good."

I held back a grimace. They were talking about her like she couldn't understand them. But she could. And she was right there. That was not how I was raised.

After slipping into the flak vest and making sure my NVGs were secured to my Kevlar, I stood up on the gunner's platform and inspected the MK19. I didn't like being assigned someone else's weapon and I missed my girl. Right now, Specialist Grant was probably running his grubby hands all over her.

"Damn, Pierce," I called down. "You ever clean this thing?"

"The grime makes her run better," he replied. "Trust me. She's finicky. Doesn't like being too clean. You know, like a stripper."

"Nah," Wilson said with a laugh. "He definitely *don't* know, bro."

The radio squawked. "All Red elements, this is Red Four. Fire in the hole."

I glanced over to where the Humvee with the flat tires had been towed beside Clark's overturned and clobbered truck. Two bright white flashes were followed by a massive plume of white smoke as incendiary grenades went off inside each mount. They'd burn for almost a minute at over four thousand degrees and cause enough damage to render the trucks permanently inoperable.

Sanchez got back on the radio and counted down the mark to start up our vehicles. We pulled out of the assembly area with Charlie Section taking point, and entered the narrow path through the jungle that Douglas had discovered. Bravo Section was at the back, so I had rear security.

As our Humvee pulled into the trees, I heard the prick squawk almost at the same time as some of the guns went live.

"Oh, shit!" Wilson said. "They're back!"

To say I was surprised to see a wave of Chaneque warriors and sisimitos entering the clearing was an understatement. We had picked up no signs that they'd regrouped, and even Epasotl seemed to think that they were off licking their wounds and bribing their gods for better luck next time.

We'd gotten rolling, but too late to avoid this fight.

"All Red elements," Captain Brown said over the radio, "be advised, hostiles to the rear. Let's pick up the pace."

I didn't wait for any particular order. The enemy was less than a hundred meters away and closing fast. Firing in long, sustained bursts, I walked grenades from the rear to the front and to the left and right, painting the battlefield with death.

Thump-thump-thump.

The destruction was devastating. A high-velocity M430 high-explosive dual-purpose grenade will obliterate anything in a five-meter radius and seriously ruin the day of anyone within fifteen meters. I was blasting huge holes in the massing groups of warriors and sending bloody chunks of sisimito flying in all directions.

Even after we had followed a bend in the trail and I'd lost sight of the clearing, I continued to pour fire, arcing the grenades through the canopy.

"Pierce!" I called down. "Get me another can."

He dug into the back of the truck and hoisted up a sixty-pound can of grenades. Maneuvering it onto the tray, I fed the forty-eight-grenade belt into my weapon, slapped the top cover down, and charged the handles.

We were careening through the dense jungle now and I'd lost sight of targets. I wasn't worried about the Chaneques following on foot, but the sisimitos were fast.

As if my thought had manifested it, a sisimito burst through the trees, racing alongside us, roaring and tossing its horns. Red fur rippled across huge muscles as it veered toward us. The thing was bashing its shoulder into our vehicle and attempting to force us off the trail. My weapon was useless at that range. The best I could do was hurl insults.

The jungle lit up with tracers as Specialist Woodward in Douglas's mount ahead of us laid down with the Fifty. I swore and dropped down from the hatch. The burst had come so close, I could hear the rounds cracking through the air. Wilson glanced into the side mirror and got on the radio.

"Red Five Golf, this is Red Seven Actual. Target neutralized. Thanks for the assist. Little warning next time, bro. You almost cooked my gunner."

"Red Seven, this is Red Five," Douglas replied in his slow drawl. "Don' fret, son. We're professionals."

A little shaken, but none the worse for wear, I stood back up in the hatch and secured the Nineteen as we bounced along the uneven trail.

CHAPTER 8

We were twenty-seven men lost in unfamiliar territory and facing unimaginable circumstances. We drove through the night and into the next day, fording a river and several streams as the jungle gave way to savanna. As day broke across the plains, we saw small roaming groups of giant, turtle-like armadillos that Epasotl said were called *ueyayotochtli*. Each was nearly the size of a Humvee. They didn't appear aggressive and were content to simply watch us roll by as they grazed on the tall grass.

So, at least we knew what had made the trail we followed.

Epasotl said her people wouldn't leave the forest to pursue us, but there were other dangers in the great expanse of rolling grassland. She spoke of giant warriors with the heads of beasts and monsters, and fleet-footed, ferocious predators that were part vulture, part wolf.

At this point, all of it sounded plausible. The earlier arguments about what was going on around us had given way to a general acceptance that, inexplicable as it was, one way or another... this was no hallucination. All of us, our equipment, everything... we weren't in Panama anymore.

For Tezcatlipoca reaches his hand across worlds and snatches beings to bring into his realm.

That's what Epasotl had told the captain.

It was as good an explanation as any.

And then there were the skull-faced bird-women.

"Run that by me again," I said, unable to get a mental picture of exactly what such a creature would look like.

"They are fierce warriors with the upper bodies of women and the lower body and legs of giant birds," Epasotl explained. "Their faces are skulls, crowned by a great plume of feathers. They were created by the moon goddess Coyolxāuhqui, as we were created by her brother and sworn enemy, Huītzilōpōchtli."

"Have you ever seen one?"

"Of course not, for we do not leave the forest, but we have always been at war, and there were many great battles in the days of my grandfather's grandfather. They are renowned warriors, and it is said they feast on the remains of their enemies like vultures. Their only virtue is that they hunt the Children of Mictlāntēcuhtli."

That rang a bell.

"*In iahmikis apismikini*," I muttered, remembering the litany Dee chanted before he tried to eat Wilson's face.

"Yes," Epasotl said. "Those who suffer the living death of eternal hunger. We have hunted and destroyed them in our forests, but Mictlāntēcuhtli's temples remain. They are forbidden places possessed by great evil."

"We encountered one of the temples," I said. "A man I knew became infected. He… changed."

"Then you are lucky to be alive," Epasotl said somberly, "and not one of the ravenous undead. To even touch such a desecrated place is to give your soul over to Mictlāntēcuhtli."

I thought about St. James and the others from Alpha Squad. They weren't infected like Dee. But they'd changed.

Or maybe I was just naïve about what men are capable of in the right—or wrong—circumstances.

Around noon the captain ordered us to coil up. Charlie Section had spotted something, and Captain Brown wanted to investigate. There was also the matter of fuel. A plan needed to be put together because we couldn't just drive around the savanna forever. We needed to get some sense of where we were. Where we were going. How to get out of this godforsaken place. It was the first real opportunity we'd had to regroup, and I knew that Captain Brown would want to make the most of it. That would include conducting a more thorough interrogation of Epasotl, who was our number one source of intel when it came to wherever we were.

Carrion birds circled overhead in the thermals and a hot wind blew across the plains, causing the tall grass to ripple and gleam like a golden ocean. Staff Sergeant Douglas ordered Pierce and me to join Specialist Woodward and Sergeant García on recon.

I slipped out of the heavy flak vest, glad to be rid of it in the heat, and swapped my Kevlar for a boonie. After ordering Epasotl to stay behind with Wilson, Pierce and I linked up with García. We waded through the waist-high grass and I could see the dismounts from Charlie, led by Sergeant Takahashi, patrolling from the north about two hundred meters away.

"What exactly are we looking for, Sergeant?" I asked García.

"Shrimp saw what he thought was the remains of a battle. Cap'n wants a closer look."

We proceeded in a wedge with Pierce on point. Soon he held up a hand for us to halt and waved García over. Woodward was carrying the prick and joined us.

"Red Four, this is Red Six," García called into the handset.

"Go for Red Four," Sanchez replied.

"Definitely was a battle," García said. "We've got the remains of a horse and a man here. Not much left of him. Blue uniform like from an old John Wayne movie. Real old-looking single shot carbine and a sword."

All of that hardly registered beyond invoking a sense of curiosity. This place was weird, and it was our life. I felt my mind starting to not even object to things that it wouldn't have dreamed of believing back home. Maybe this was how people went crazy. The crazy starts to make sense one day and you just roll with it.

"Roger. See what else you can find. Red Four out."

As we moved further into the battleground, we found more evidence of horses and men. Bones mostly, all of them picked clean, accompanied by bloodstained tatters of blue uniforms, black-powder rifles, and swords—sabers, to be specific. There were a lot of expended rifle cartridges too, piles of the brass here and there where someone had made a last stand. Mixed in with the men and horses were the carcasses of bird-like creatures with strange reptilian heads and mouths full of needle-sharp teeth. They were about the size of a large dog, and had strange, stubby wings ending in sharp talons. Their feet sported a middle toe ending in a wicked sickle-shaped claw at least four inches long.

One kick from a beast like that could easily disembowel a man—or a horse for that matter.

Specialist Woodward was getting excited. "These are US Cavalrymen," he said. He picked up a battered hat and showed off the crossed sabers. "See? Look, they were from the Ninth. These were Buffalo Soldiers."

"Or Civil War reenactors," García said. "Weapons look real enough, though."

Charlie's dismounts were on the radio, calling in the same thing we'd found. García got on the net to confirm.

"Tell 'em about the Buffalo Soldiers, Sarge," Woodward whispered excitedly.

García waved him away.

While he was on comms, we speculated over the little lizard-creatures that the soldiers had apparently died fighting. I'd never seen a lizard with feathers. Epasotl said they were the predators she'd told me about earlier, the wolf-vultures. They occasionally ventured into the forests and she considered them to be extremely dangerous.

Captain Brown joined us. He seemed quite interested in the possibility that we'd discovered the remains of a unit of Buffalo Soldiers. "You know what this is?" he said, turning a wide-brimmed hat over in his hands reverently. "This is history. These men were with Bravo Troop, Ninth Cavalry Regiment. Buffalo Soldiers. Just like my great-grandpa."

Like I said, it was eerie how easily everyone had started to accept the impossible.

The captain stowed his boonie and put the hat on, adjusting it slightly to straighten the brim. Then he picked up a saber.

"Collect whatever weapons and ammunition you can find," he said. "We might need to augment our own the longer all this goes on.

Then bury these men. We'll give them a proper send-off to Fiddler's Green. They were Cav, like us."

***

"Gotta dig it deeper," Bond said, flicking a cigarette off to the side.

It was the first time I'd been on duty with my former squad mates, and I couldn't shake the animosity I felt toward them over what had happened in the village. I rushed over and stubbed out the smoldering butt. "Idiot," I said. "You'll start a grass fire."

Bond shrugged and shook another cigarette out of the pack.

We'd have preferred to bury the troopers in separate graves, but scavengers had made such a mess of the bodies we didn't know which bones belonged together. So, a mass grave it was.

"Why don't you grab an e-tool and help?" Greene said to Bond.

"Because *my* job is to supervise," he replied, lighting the cigarette with a flourish of his Zippo.

"I hate digging," said James. "If I wanted to dig, I'd have joined the infantry."

"Burning daylight," Bond said. "Keep digging."

"Hey, James," said McKee. "How many spec-fours does it take to change a lightbulb?"

"Two," James shot back. "One to hold the ladder and one to find a PFC."

"Hey, Preacher," Bond said to me. "What do you do when a private throws a grenade at you?"

"Pull the pin and throw it back," I replied halfheartedly.

Bond had changed since the Chaneque village. He was more arrogant now, more callous. Everyone who'd participated in that slaughter was behaving that way. They didn't wear their Chaneque trophies openly—Sanchez would've smoked them to death if he knew the truth, especially after they'd lied about it—but I knew they still had them. Together with St. James they had formed an exclusive club. They had all been *in the shit*, as Bond said. But not me. I wasn't sure how Evans and Sergeant Clark fit into the clique, or if they did, exactly. And then there was Wilson, who at least was separated from the other guys. Maybe he felt it would be better for all of us to let it go. I hadn't worked up the courage to talk to him about why he hadn't told Sanchez, and the more time that passed, the harder it felt to bring it up. But it was clear to me that Alpha Section was drifting apart from the rest of the platoon. I didn't know if Sergeant Sanchez or Captain Brown saw it.

"How's your pet, Preacher?" Bond asked me.

"She's not a pet. And don't call me Preacher because I ain't one." I hated being called Preacher, and Bond knew it.

"You still feeding her chocolates?" Bond asked. "You find the special spot to make her purr when you stroke her?"

"Don't be gross, man."

He stepped up close and blew a cloud of smoke in my face. "You got the hots for that little freak, dontcha?" He poked my chest and before I could answer, laid in on me. "You're real sick, Preacher, you know that? Can't get laid, so you're hooking up with the local wildlife. That's the kind of sick shit your religion pushes, brother."

I snapped and gave in to my anger. I was calm, but furious. "*I'm* sick? Not you, the guy who was practically dancing in innocent blood."

I imagined making him eat his cigarette.

"They're *animals*, Preacher. No different than shootin' rats with a .22."

"No. *Animal* is wearing women's and children's ears around your neck."

"Oh, you mean this?" He pulled the paracord loop from his cargo pocket and dangled it in front of my face. "Ain't no different than having a lucky rabbit's foot. They ain't human. Pull the stick out of your ass."

"Damn, man," Greene said. He and James had taken a break from digging after initially trying to ignore what was clearly some bad blood going on between the two of us.

Bond continued to shake the trophy in my face until I turned away.

"This bother you, man? You don't *approve*? Whatcha gonna do about it? 'Cause whatever it is, we both know it won't involve having your squad mates' backs. Surrounded by those things and you didn't pull your trigger one frigging time. You're a joke."

"Specialist Bond," Sergeant Sanchez said calmly. We both jumped and snapped to parade rest. He was standing not ten feet away from us. "What is *that*?"

Bond swallowed hard. "Memento, Sergeant."

"Memento?" Sanchez held out his hand. "Let's see it."

"Yes, Sergeant," Bond said.

Sanchez glared, his eyes slitted like paper cuts. He was still holding out his hand, but Bond hadn't moved.

"Hand it over, Bond," Sanchez said.

Bond glared at me with the same hate I'd seen in the village, then slowly lifted his arm.

Sanchez snatched the necklace away and looked at it in disgust.

"Are these what I think they are?" he asked. His voice was quiet. Dangerously so.

"I… don't know what you mean, Sergeant," Bond said.

Wrong answer.

"Walk with me," Sanchez growled.

***

"What was that about?" James asked after Bond and Sanchez had left.

"Nothing," I said.

"I thought you two were about to rumble," Greene added.

"Nah," I said.

"I thought you two were buddies," James pitched in.

"Don't worry about it. Keep digging."

McKee looked scared and kept glancing back toward the assembly area. "Bennett, I, uh, need to go get something from my mount."

"Keep digging." I knew exactly what he wanted to go get and stash now that Sanchez was homing in on the truth of what had happened. "If it's no big deal to kill a few 'animals,' it won't matter what he finds. Will it?"

"You think they're gonna do a health and safety inspection?" he asked nervously.

"Probably."

"Come on, man," McKee begged. "If they find it, it'll be my ass."

"Find what? Your *memento*?"

"Shit," Greene said. "You got one too, McKee? What the hell happened on that mission? Platoon Sarge was *pissed*."

"Yeah, I never seen him so mad," James added.

McKee moved to bolt, but I grabbed the back of his collar and swept his legs out from under him. He crashed hard, and I put a knee on his chest. All the anger I was feeling about what had happened was coming out now.

"You did what you did, McKee. At least have the decency to own it."

McKee started to swipe at my face. I held my chin back, and my hand wavered close to the knife on my LBE.

"It needed to happen, man. Had to do it. You saw what they did to McCoppin." McKee struggled against me and looked for help from the other men. "Get him off me, guys! He's gone mental!"

"Come on, Specialist," James said. "Let him go. This is bullshit."

I hauled McKee up, tossed him into the hole, and threw an e-tool after him. "Keep. Digging."

James watched me closely. Loomed over me, more like it. He was a big kid. "You okay, Bennett? Man, what happened out there?"

"Yeah, what's this all about?" Greene echoed excitedly.

"Nothing," I said. "I'm fine. Keep digging."

"Bullshit," Greene said. "You're making it *somethin'* right in front of us."

"Sar'nt St. James is gonna have your ass, Preacher," McKee called from the grave. "Nobody touches Alpha."

"Oh, shut up already, McKee," James said. The big man picked up his e-tool and hopped down into the pit. "As pissed as Sanchez was, I don't want him to find this pit unfinished when he gets back. Keep digging."

CHAPTER 9

When Sanchez came back, Bond wasn't with him. He approved of the work we'd completed and told us to get back to the trucks once the burial was finished. To McKee's relief, he didn't order an inspection.

I hiked with James and Greene back to Beauty from the gravesite.

"You don't have nothin' you wanna tell us about what the hell happened to Alpha out there?" James asked. "You and Bond used to be tight."

Used to be. Bond had been a good friend, one of my best, and now he was an enemy. He had a vengeful streak a mile wide, and he'd be gunning for me now. It was an uncomfortable thought.

"Things change," I said.

"You've got a problem, man," he said, but that was that.

I'm not sure why I didn't just come out and tell them. Maybe I was thinking that our captain and platoon sergeant were the ones who needed to spill it, not me. I don't know. Mostly I just didn't want to talk about it. But it was obvious that they knew what was going on. They had seen the necklace. They'd heard Bond and me spitting back and forth. I'd said out loud what his *memento* was, and I think I even said something about him dancing in blood.

I'd said enough.

We reached the mount and I slouched into the back seat. Epasotl crouched on the other seat in the back, spooning something into her mouth out of an MRE pouch.

"Whatcha got there?" I asked her.

"Chicken of Kings," she said around a mouthful. "It is… rad."

I locked eyes with Wilson, who had clearly taught Epasotl some new vocabulary.

"Get some chow," he told me. "Then swap out with Pierce on security."

As I nodded, I saw James open his mouth to speak. I knew what was coming. And truth be told, I was more than a little interested to see how Wilson was going to handle the inevitable question. He hadn't participated in the slaughter, but he'd seen it.

"Hey, Sergeant, you were on that mission to the village. What happened?" James asked. "Because you won't believe what just went down out there. I think Sanchez is going to get Captain to bust Bond down to private."

"What? How?" Wilson asked.

James was so eager to tell the story he ignored his own question. What I wasn't telling him was eating at him. "Him and Bennett got into it. I thought they were gonna start fighting, like knives out, you know."

"Oh yeah?" Wilson shot me a knowing look.

"Well, it started out with, Bond was ribbing Bennett about Miss Kitty here, crazy stuff," James continued. "Got real mental. Was going off about how he thought Bennett had the hots for her."

Wilson snorted at the thought, then began laughing. His laughter gradually increased until he was laughing so hard that tears ran down his cheeks. Maybe he was relieved that it was something so small. He had no idea how much James and Greene knew, though.

James started laughing, too. It was contagious. Pierce bent down to ask what was so funny, and Wilson told him. Then he was laughing. I probably would've joined them, because it *was* a mental thing for Bond to say, but I was still seeing red. And honestly I was still pissed at Wilson for making me the only guy to tell Sanchez and Brown the truth.

"I do not understand," Epasotl said. "Why do you laugh and cry? What does Ben-Ette have for me? What is 'hots'?"

"It means…" James was having trouble talking as he laughed. "You know. That Bennett wants to—you know—with you."

"Bennett and Skunkweed," Wilson howled. "Oh my God. Bond's lost his mind."

"It means," I said to Epasotl, "that he thinks I'm attracted to you. Sexually."

"Oh," she said, her ears hanging limply. "I am your slave. It is your right."

The Humvee got real quiet, real fast. Then broke out into howling laughter again.

"But I'm not—" I stammered. "I don't want to—no offense, but you're not my type."

She watched me closely for a long moment, then her face brightened, and she started making a staccato hissing sound I supposed was a laugh. "Gag me with spoons. I would rather mate with a *cipactli*. That is grody to maximum."

Wilson and James laughed even harder.

"Big time, sister. Barf me out," Wilson said, holding out his fist.

Epasotl bumped it with hers. "Cheah, bro-ski."

The laughter died down, and suddenly James sobered up real quick. "But then," he said, "Bond started waving something in Bennett's face. I saw what it was, Sergeant. Kitty ears. Bennett said it was women and children."

Wilson stopped laughing too. "Bond… he just took it out and showed you all? Right there?"

"He did," James confirmed. "Well he showed Bennett, but we were all right there. And then all of a sudden Sanchez is standing behind him with murder in his eyes."

I looked down.

"What the hell happened out there, Sergeant?" James asked again.

Wilson let out a long sigh. "Bad mojo, bro. Real bad mojo."

I waited, but he didn't say anything more. Maybe I shouldn't have been so disappointed in him, but I was. Sanchez wasn't even here to stare him down, and still he wasn't talking.

"They gunned them down at the village," I eventually said. "Old men, women, children. Just started shooting."

"Shit," James said. "That's messed up. Did… did you guys?"

"No," I said quickly. "Or Wilson or Clark."

"Guys in 'Nam used to do that," Pierce called down from the gunner's hatch. "Shit happens in war, man."

"Enemy soldiers, maybe," I said. "But women and children too?"

"Well, okay, yeah," Pierce agreed. "That's messed up. But it happened that way more than once in 'Nam, too."

"So how did it go down?" James asked. "You guys just gunned down the kitties and torched the place?"

"*We* didn't," Wilson said sourly. "*They* did. I don't know why and if you're smart, you won't ask them. This sucks, man."

I glanced at Epasotl. Her ears were laid back and her eyes had narrowed.

"Guys," I said. "Let's stop talking about this like Epasotl isn't sitting *right here*. Those were people. Her family. Friends. And stop calling them 'kitties.' They're people."

To his credit, James's eyes widened and he looked ashamed. "Damn. You're right, man. I wasn't thinking. Of course, maybe Bond is right about you, too." He chuckled at his own joke, but otherwise stayed sober. He nodded back at Epasotl. "Sorry, ma'am."

"It is in the past," she said in an even tone, but I could hear a soft growl beneath it.

"So…" James said after a long moment of uncomfortable silence. "What's going to happen?"

"About what?" I asked.

"Would you stop acting so damn dense, Bennett? About what happened at the village."

I looked at Wilson as I spoke. "Now that Sanchez busted down Bond and saw the necklace… I dunno what's gonna happen. But it's still *my* word alone against the rest of Alpha."

"Okay. Here's the problem with that, bro," Wilson said, and I knew the tension that I felt was getting ready to come to an end. "St. James said they had to start shooting and then shit was screwed six sways to Sunday by the time it was all over. Neither you nor me saw what kicked things off. So let's say there's an inquiry. Can you prove it, Bennett? Of course not, because you didn't see shit."

"I saw the aftermath."

Wilson sighed, exasperated. "Shit happens. It sucks, bro, but given the circumstances with McCoppin, you can count on a shit ton of leeway. And you do realize this ain't Panama."

"What about having the last of the survivors executed before we left?"

"That's gonna be for Captain Brown to decide," Wilson said.

"You didn't tell him about it."

"No. Because it was a bullshit call he had to make. You think those villagers would zip their lips and tell anyone pursuing us that they couldn't divulge the direction we'd left in? Of course they would. He had to decide whether to let them do that and endanger us or… or take the option off the table."

"Take the option off the table," I parroted.

"Yeah, dude. It's not all shits and giggles having to make these decisions, but it's sure as hell easy to second-guess, isn't it? Anyway, cat's out of the bag now, bro, so if Brown and Sanchez think something needs to happen, it'll happen. Clark and I were willing to give St. James the benefit of the doubt—I ain't crazy about those little psychos Bond and McKee wearing *ears*—but St. James was always solid, despite being a dick. You don't like it… sue me."

I frowned. I could see where Wilson was coming from, even if it still didn't sit right with me. I should have brought it up earlier with Wilson and I should have done it in private.

"Pierce," I said. "I'm coming up."

"About time," he said. "I'm going to try to get some sleep."

We swapped the flak vest, and I took over on the Nineteen, scanning the savanna while Wilson wandered over to Douglas's mount.

There wasn't much to see, just a shimmering ocean of grass dotted with lonely stands of broad-boughed trees with dark, wide leaves. Here and there groups of those giant armadillos roamed about, usually two or three adults with a juvenile. Sometimes a whole lot of smaller somethings would move in the grass, causing trails to streak through the waves of golden stalks. Maybe it was those things that killed the Buffalo Soldiers. I didn't like that they were out there, and I didn't like that I couldn't see them. But they were giving our assembly area a wide berth, for now.

The afternoon was hot, and the wind was dry. I felt like I was standing in front of a furnace, and I was sweating under the heavy flak vest. I wondered how bad it would be if the sun *weren't* under a continual eclipse. It was difficult to stay alert and not let the heat and undulating grasses hypnotize you. Pierce and James were snoring inside the Humvee.

Then I heard the unmistakable sound of St. James barking out my name from behind me. He was standing a few feet away with his hands on his hips, his eyes hidden by wraparound shades.

"Yes, Sergeant?" I replied.

"Get down here, Bennett," he ordered.

The last thing I wanted to do was dismount and take whatever he had coming for me.

"Negative, Sergeant," I said. "I'm on watch."

"I don't give a damn. Get down here."

"All due respect, Sergeant, but that would violate my First General Order. As you know, I cannot quit my post until properly relieved."

Yeah, that was cheeky. But you learn a thing or two about dealing with NCOs as a Specialist.

"Don't get cute with me, Bennett," he said, raising his voice. "You put a hand on one of my men. Get your ass down here."

"The specialist regrets to inform the sergeant, again, that he is on watch and cannot quit his post until property relieved."

"Then I'm relieving you," he barked. I could almost see the smoke coming out of his ears. "Down here. Now."

"The specialist regrets to inform the sergeant that the sergeant is not in the specialist's chain of command any longer."

Thin ice, Bennett. Really thin ice. All the same, I'd be lying if I said I wasn't enjoying myself.

"Dammit, Bennett," St. James roared. "Get. Your. Ass. Down. Here."

Staff Sergeant Douglas ambled over with Wilson in tow. Thank God. The cavalry had arrived.

"Somethin' amiss?" Douglas drawled to St. James.

"Bennett laid hands on one of my men and needs to be disciplined," St. James answered hotly.

"Bennett's my man, not yours. If'n there's somethin' to mete out, I'm the one to do it," Douglas said in his slow, soft-spoken Cajun way. He squinted up at me. "You lay hands on one-a his men, son?"

I'd run out of E-4 tricks. His question demanded a yes or no answer.

"Yes, Sergeant."

Well, that that was that. I was cooked. But then Douglas surprised me.

"Why?" he asked.

That's not a question you're asked often in the Army. I had to think carefully about my answer.

"PFC McKee was attempting to leave his post without being properly relieved, Sergeant. As the ranking person on the scene, I felt it was my obligation to see that he followed his orders and remain at his post."

"This is bullshit," St. James said. "Don't tell me you're being taken in by this, Douglas."

Douglas ignored him.

"That ain't no reason to lay hands on the PFC," Douglas said to me. "Why you ain't report it to th' NCO commandin' your detail?"

"Sergeant Wilson was not in the vicinity, Sergeant," I said. "I could not report the incident without leaving my post."

Douglas turned to Wilson. "That true, Sergeant?"

"Yes, Sergeant," Wilson replied. He was putting on a good show of formality. He even stood rigidly at parade rest. "I had posted Specialists Bennett and Bond in charge of the grave detail and was attending to other matters, Sergeant."

"'Bout settles it," Douglas said. "Sergeant St. James, I'm 'onna see to it Specialist Bennett is corrected right to handle such a situation if it comes about again. Specialist Bennett, you're denied leave for thirty days, hear? There'll be a written, uh, counseling statement your squad leader will prepare for you to sign. Y'all understand?"

"Yes, Sergeant," I replied.

"What the hell?" St. James was livid. "What kind of bullshit are you pulling, John? *He laid hands on my man.* I want his ass, and I want it now! You hear me? I. Want. Ass."

"Don' think so, St. James," Douglas replied calmly.

St. James got in his face. "You little son of a bitch, I'll—"

"Y'all what?" Douglas squared his shoulders and pulled the words out like taffy. "Jus' throw down? Right here? Right now? 'Cause I'll whup you good and proper, like your mama should've, and you know it, Couyon."

"Is there a problem, gentlemen?"

Captain Brown had come strolling over easy as a Sunday morning.

"No problem, sir," Douglas said brightly. "Sar'nt St. James an' I was just discussin' a matter with one o' my men."

St. James clenched his jaw and flexed his fingers, staring daggers at Douglas.

"That right, Angel?" Brown asked St. James.

"Yes, sir." St. James straightened and forced a smile. "Just a disagreement about the correct form of discipline."

Captain Brown rocked back on his heels and tipped his hat up. "Well, if it's about discipline and it's about one of John's men, seems to me there's nothing to disagree about, now is there, Angel?"

"No, sir," St. James answered.

"Excellent," said Brown. "Perhaps you'd best be off to see to *your* men's discipline then, Sergeant."

I had to bite my tongue hard to stop from laughing. Really hard. I tasted blood.

After St. James had left, the captain exchanged a few pleasantries with Douglas and Wilson before wandering off himself. Douglas waved me down. I hurried to drop out of the hatch and dismount, standing at parade rest before my section leader.

"At ease, son," Douglas said. "Listen and listen close: I don' want hear no nothing 'bout you touchin' another soldier 'gain. Y'all clear?"

"Crystal, Sergeant," I replied.

"As you were."

I climbed back into the gunner's hatch and resumed my watch on the endless savanna.

Wright lost his stripes and was demoted to Specialist, and Bond and McKee were dropped straight down to E-1. Their punishment for the interim was digging the latrine pit outside of our assembly area. I didn't know if we'd be in the vicinity long enough to require a latrine, but they were digging one anyway.

Since I was still on security, I missed the service that Captain Brown led for the fallen Buffalo Soldiers. Wilson said it was very moving and that the captain might have missed his calling as a chaplain.

As the black sun set for the third night, I felt a peace come over me. This strange, savage land was oddly beautiful. I rucked out with the newfound confidence that we would learn its secrets and survive.

It would be anything but easy.

CHAPTER 10

"The current situation we find ourselves in reminds me of *X-Men* issue one-oh-five," Captain Brown said. He was sitting on a jerry can with all of us taking a knee in a half-circle around him. All of us E-4 and over, that is. The privates were off pulling security. Epasotl was with us, too. Captain Brown rightly recognized her as our best source of intelligence and had taken to spending an hour minimum each day interviewing her. For a while at least, he had me sit with them too. But lately she'd gotten so familiar to us that the captain would speak to her in private.

Captain Brown swept his gaze over all of us, deadly serious. When he started citing *X-Men*, it was time to listen up; he was about to lay the Gospel of Claremont on you. "That was the issue when Xavier sent the X-Men through a space portal to rescue Lilandra."

I know, that sounds stupid when you read it. But if you knew Captain Brown and were in his presence when he said something like that… you didn't laugh. You wouldn't dare.

Brown paused a beat. "I strongly believe we've been transported to an alternate dimension."

"Just like *Land of the Lost*!" Sergeant Wilson said, snapping his fingers. "I *knew* it."

"Something like that, yes, Sergeant, very much," the captain replied.

"So we're screwed," said Sergeant García.

"We're scouts, man," Wilson quipped. "Getting screwed is our job."

Everyone started murmuring until Sanchez, who was standing behind the captain, cleared his throat, and then everyone shut up with a purpose.

"Before I get into the details of where we are and what I plan to do about it," Captain Brown began, "Sergeants Sanchez and Yazzie have some business we need to attend to. Sergeant Sanchez?"

"Thank you, sir," Sanchez said. "First order of business is logistics. My job as platoon sergeant is to keep you men supplied with beans and bullets, and we don't have an infinite supply of either. Food in particular is getting low. We'll need to start foraging."

Brown interjected. "Our indigenous ally here"—he motioned to Epasotl, who sat beside him—"has been a useful source of information and has proven to be most cooperative. She can help identify which plants are safe for consumption."

Epasotl gave her impression of a human smile, which I had told her stop doing. It looked predatory and a little bit crazy. Not a good mix. Her hands were no longer bound because, as the captain had said, she was an ally, a prisoner no longer. He had talked with her alone for a long time the night before and came away even more impressed with her than he already was.

St. James was unhappy about her change in status. Livid might be a better word.

Too bad, so sad, St. James. Suck eggs, man.

"Foraging includes hunting," Sanchez continued. "Our M16s aren't fit for taking down game of any reasonable size; the five-five-six cartridge is simply too underpowered. Fortunately, we have secured several forty-five-seventy caliber Springfield carbines. Sergeant Douglas has experience with black powder weapons and will begin drilling those with hunting experience.

"As for ammunition for our *modern* weapons, we are not in a critical state yet, but any further prolonged engagements will deplete our stores. To that end, you will all begin drilling in hand-to-hand combat. We did not recover enough sabers to outfit the entire platoon, so what we have will be distributed in order of seniority. Those without sabers will be drilled on knives and improvised hand weapons. Sergeant Takahashi will see to your training.

"Fuel is a critical concern. We have perhaps enough to travel another hundred klicks. Our range could be extended by abandoning vehicles and transferring fuel, but that is an exercise in rapidly diminishing returns. We must face the fact that soon our mounts will be inoperable, and the weapon systems are too heavy to realistically transport on foot. In a matter of days, not weeks, we will be operating in unknown terrain against unknown hostiles as a dismounted element with no heavy weapon systems. We will adapt, and we will overcome. Hooah?"

"Hooah," we chorused, some with less enthusiasm than others.

"Doc?" Sanchez said.

Doc stepped forward and crossed his arms. "The most critical elements to survival are water and shelter. In an environment such as this, shelter is less critical than water. Ideally you should each drink at least four liters a day. We topped off our water cans when we forded the river, and I treated the water, but it won't last. Do not—and I cannot stress this enough—do *not* drink untreated water.

"We are in an unknown environment with unknown pathogens. It is essential that you do not drink untreated water and do not eat undercooked meat. Water- and food-borne illness will kill you quicker than a hostile enemy. Historically, most armies suffer far more casualties due to disease than to combat, by an order of magnitude. So watch what you ingest. See to your personal hygiene. Use the latrines. Use insect repellent while supplies last. And report any injury. I don't care if it's a minor scrape or abrasion, you come see me. If you develop *any* symptoms of illness, come see me. That is all."

"Thank you, Doc, Sergeant Sanchez," Captain Brown said. "We'll hold questions for after. Now I will answer the most important question: *where* we are. Epasotl informs me that we are in the realm of Ocelotonatiuh." The captain sounded like he'd been practicing how to say the word. "Also known as the Land of the

Black Sun, a world she says was created by Tezcatlipoca, an entity known as the 'dreaded and all-powerful' Smoking Mirror God."

That news elicited frowns from everyone.

"Now, according to the legends of Epasotl's people, this Smoking Mirror fellow is bad news. He banished another entity, Quetzalcoatl, who Epasotl's people look upon as a god of light and goodness. Tezcatlipoca destroyed Quetzalcoatl's world and civilization and set up shop here, demanding blood sacrifice, among other unpleasant things. That's the CliffsNotes version. It gets complicated. Point is, she believes Smoking Mirror brought us here and is now toying with us."

Captain Brown held out his hands. "I know how that sounds. But it's clear we're not in Panama. It's equally clear that much of what we took for granted at home—on Earth—doesn't apply here. Therefore, it is my decision that we will treat this, all of this, as reality. And that means there's only one thing to do. Find Tezcatlipoca and demand he send us home. And if he doesn't, destroy him."

Spoken like a Ranger.

"We're going to war against a god?" Sergeant Wilson asked.

"There's only one God," Douglas said. "We're talkin' about demons."

"Theological doctrines aside, I believe Douglas is correct," Captain Brown said. "This Smoking Mirror fellow is no god. He's merely an extradimensional entity, and he's going down."

Merely an extradimensional entity. Captain Brown was talking like this was just another encounter with the Dingbats we were gearing up for.

"Sir, what's an 'extradimensional entity'?" Specialist Grant asked.

"They're beings who exist outside of time and space as we know it. People may *worship* them as gods, but that doesn't make them so. They're merely very powerful entities."

"In… comic books, sir," García pointed out.

"Yes, in comic books, Sergeant; but also in reality, apparently. Take a look around you. This isn't our home. If you deny that, *you're* the one who's denying reality."

"Sir, how do you defeat a god?" Takahashi asked. "Sorry, I mean, a *god-like entity*."

"You find its weakness," Brown said.

"And what if it doesn't have one?"

"They always do."

"In comic books," García pointed out again.

"Comic books are just modern myths, son," Brown said. "All myths have a foundation in truth. Like the myths of our friend here. Epasotl, tell us about this Smoking Mirror entity's purported weaknesses."

Epasotl bit her lip, an expression that made her seem more human. "His brother Quetzalcoatl. They have always been at war. One tricks the other, defeating him for a time, and the cycle continues throughout eternity."

"See? We locate this Quetzalcoatl and enlist his help." Brown slapped his hands on his thighs. "Now, I fully admit this course of action is based on limited intel, but it's as good a start as any."

"You make it sound simple, sir," García said.

"Every good plan is," the captain replied. "There's more, however. And this part is more immediately actionable. We are *not* the only humans here. You already know that from the soldiers' remains we found. But Epasotl tells me there is a large settlement of *living* humans out beyond these plains to the northwest. It's essential that we learn more about these humans. Find out if they're from our world. Determine if they can be trusted, if we can be of help to one another. Because if not, we're alone out here.

"Epasotl could tell me very little about the human settlement—her people, especially the women, do not travel far—but she says there is a 'half-bird' species, living in the forests to the east of us, that roams widely and may have more information. She is extremely distrustful of them, but I intend to make contact and see if a mutually beneficial relationship can be developed. Allies are allies, even if they're half-birds.

"Finally: there is an abandoned fort of some kind approximately thirty kilometers east of our position. We will be making for it in order to evaluate its suitability as a temporary base of operations until contact with the bird people can be achieved."

"Executing all of that may be difficult," García added.

"That's what NCOs are for," Captain Brown replied with a grin.

After the meeting was over, Epasotl sought me out. We sat down over our MREs. She seemed agitated.

"What's bothering you?" I asked.

"I do not think the Big Kahuna's plan will work. Quetzalcoatl was turned into the sun. How will you reach him?"

I had no idea how *any* of it would work. I was starting to tell myself that it would only be so long before we ended up like those Buffalo Soldiers. But if Captain Brown had a plan, at least it gave us something to work toward.

"If anyone can find a way, Captain Brown can."

"Perhaps we will find Quetzalcoatl in the west, where the black sun goes to sleep in the distant sea," Epasotl said thoughtfully. "But to go to war against Tezcatlipoca is unthinkable. Big Kahuna is either the bravest of men or the most stupid. I am not sure which."

"Well, you've spent a lot of time talking to him," I said. "Does he seem stupid or brave?"

"Not stupid. He asked many clever questions."

"And he sees you as a friend. You're one of us now." I ruffled her hair playfully—and then pulled back. That was... spontaneous. And a little demeaning.

But Epasotl didn't seem to mind. She didn't even seem to notice.

We walked around the perimeter of the assembly area, careful not to wander too far from the vehicles. Those big feathered lizards might be out there, stalking in the tall grass. Epasotl was deep in thought, so we stayed quiet for a long while.

"You treat your slaves strangely," she said at last.

"We don't keep slaves," I said. "And we prefer our enemies to become friends."

"You are a peculiar people."

"Yeah, but you're stuck with us, so get used to it. You're part of the family, whether you like it or not. Which means Sanchez will find a job for you soon enough. You can't just sit around eating Chicken a la King all day."

She made that staccato hissing sound I took for a laugh, and then stopped, suddenly serious.

"What?" I asked.

"For a moment... I almost forgot I am living in shame."

I shrugged. "That's good. You *should* forget about it. Make a new life for yourself. We judge a man by how he lives, not how he dies. Live a life of honor."

"Big Kahuna said much the same thing last night, when I pleaded for an honorable death to end my shame."

"Captain Brown is a wise man."

She was about to reply when her ears perked up and her pupils contracted into the thinnest of slits. Her body was tense, almost quivering.

"What is it?"

"Death," she hissed. "We must flee. A dragon is approaching!"

Before I could stop her, Epasotl bolted into the tall grass, leaving me alone, puzzled, and more than a little worried. I scanned the sky but couldn't see anything. But she *did* say "dragon," and at this point, I had no reason not to believe her.

Then I heard it: the unmistakable chop of a helicopter in the distance. Shouts went up from gunners atop the mounts as a speck in the northern sky grew larger. The beat of the blades was an iconic sound, the bass line of the movie *Platoon*, and soon we could make out a Huey, trailing a thin plume of black smoke.

Epasotl returned a moment later, tugging at my arm in a panic.

"Why didn't you follow me?" she mewled. "You could have died. Come, quickly, we must hide."

"It's not a dragon, it's an old Huey!" I said, nodding at the venerable bird as it continued its approach. "That's *us*—our army! I don't think it saw us. Shoot. Epasotl, you've seen those before? Are these the kinds of humans who you said live out beyond the savanna?"

The thought made my heart pound. If these other humans were *Americans*, people we could actually collaborate and work with to figure out what was happening, maybe even find a way back home... that changed everything.

Plus, they had helicopters.

"They are monstrous demons who breathe flame and summon whirlwinds!" She was yowling now, her eyes wide in terror.

"No, Epasotl, it's just a... just a machine, like our trucks." I crouched and forced her to look me in the eyes. "It's okay. If it's friendly, everything will be all right. If it's not, it won't come anywhere close to us. We have enough firepower to shoot it right out of the sky. Trust me."

The bird lumbered off into the west. Black smoked trailed after it. Not like it was hit or anything, more like it was running a little rough. Whether it saw us or not, I don't know. I didn't see a door gunner or anything like that. The pilot was flying pretty high and we were in tall grass. I'd like to think that we couldn't have been missed, but that's outside my area of expertise. I found myself wishing they would have set down, but then again, maybe it pays to be extra cautious in this world. In fact, I'd found that to be true already. Fact.

By now the camp was buzzing over the sighting. I pressed Epasotl for more information, not only because I knew it would be wanted but because *I* wanted to know. "Epasotl, where have you seen those before? In the forests?"

She nodded. "Yes. Long ago. They came in the night when I was a cub. They attacked our great city of Usulatán and laid waste to everything. Buildings crumbled. Our temple fell. The warriors could do nothing to stop them. They are a punishment sent from Tezcatlipoca because we failed to provide him enough sacrifices."

That... *definitely* wasn't true. It made me doubt whether, even in this crazy dimension or alternate reality or whatever, we ought not to put too much stock in Epasotl's intel. She was knowledgeable, yes, but at the end of the day she was also primitive. Her first instinct was to use myth and angry gods to explain anything she didn't understand.

I tried again to alleviate her fears.

"They're just machines, piloted by men," I said. "They're not monsters or demons. Epasotl, look at me. It's okay. It's all right. It can't hurt us. It's gone now. See?"

She scanned the sky, still trembling, her big ears erect and alert, twitching.

"Come on," I said. "The captain's going to have something to say about all this."

CHAPTER 11

The appearance of the Huey gave the platoon a feeling of hope. But Captain Brown was more cautious. Optimistic, but cautious. We didn't know who they were, after all, and now they, whoever *they* were, knew about us. Maybe. We at least had to be prepared for the possibility that they knew our size, our strength, and our position.

"I doubt it's a Chaneque flying that thing, which means Epasotl's reports of other humans are true," Brown told his NCOs while we waited to see if the bird came back for another visit. "It also means there's a fuel depot somewhere within that Huey's range."

"Either that," Sanchez agreed, "or that thing's runnin' on fumes, just like us."

"Or that," Brown conceded. "I was hoping they'd have come back around to make contact."

The captain decided to mobilize, and in short order the platoon was rolling over the savanna, spread out in a long wedge, still looking for the rumored stronghold. Epasotl hadn't steered us wrong yet, and I was sure we'd find it.

Epasotl and I had reported her stories of the "dragons" and the razing of Usulatán to Captain Brown. He listened sympathetically and asked her how long ago these attacks had occurred.

"I was only a young cub," she answered. "It was many seasons ago, over a dozen."

Assuming this place had four seasons, then we might be only talking three years or so. Yet Epasotl looked mature; she should have left childhood behind a lot longer than a few years back. At least, judging by human standards. She wasn't human.

I asked her how many seasons were in a year, and how long each season was.

"The rainy season and the dry season," she said. "Each is nine months of twenty days. There are also five nameless days. The ones belonging to Tezcatlipoca."

Her math came out to exactly the length of an Earth calendar year, and that interested Captain Brown the most. He had been convinced we weren't on Earth. The stars were different. The moon was missing. The sun… was black. And yet a year was exactly 365 days. I could see the wheels turning. Then he seemed to file that thought away for future consideration.

Meanwhile I was making sense of Epasotl's age. A dozen seasons would still be only six years ago. That seemed too recent for her to have been a mere cub. Maybe they had some sort of maturity ritual where you remained a "cub" until some specific ceremony that conferred adult status upon you. I was interested, so I asked.

"How old are you, Epasotl?"

"Nineteen seasons," she said.

Captain Brown raised his eyebrows. "Nine years old?"

She thought about that, then nodded.

I was shocked. "You look like a mature Chaneque woman."

She shrugged. "I am a very young woman. But not too young to be a widow already. My husband was twenty-six seasons and the leader of one hundred warriors."

Epasotl was a widow? This was the first I'd heard of a husband.

"How old are your warriors, generally?" Captain Brown asked. This was the sort of thing his Ranger mind would always gravitate toward. I was surprised he hadn't covered this with her earlier.

"Few live to see thirty seasons. My grandfather saw ninety-two. He was ancient! We feared he would die in his sleep, which would be exceedingly shameful. Those who die that way roam the underworld in sorrow for eternity. Fortunately, he died in honor, opposing Holy James."

"Humans are generally longer-lived," the captain said. "My grandfather would've been two hundred and six of your seasons when he died. But I admit that's rare."

"So old!" Epasotl exclaimed, marveling as she studied our faces, squinting like she couldn't quite believe it.

"You're surprised," I said. "Have you had so little interaction with the other humans in this world?"

"The Outworlders' children are all barbarians," Epasotl said with a look of disgust. "Practically animals. They are unworthy adversaries, cowardly and without honor. Few that we capture are even fit to be sacrificed. We do well to keep our contact with them limited."

"Guess we're not too popular with the locals," I mumbled. "Is there anything you *do* like about humans?"

Epasotl thought about that. "They do have a pleasant taste."

An awkward silence followed. Epasotl seemed to realize she had said too much.

"So sorry," she said quickly. "I forget sometimes that you are not like us, even though you are warriors. I do not know what to expect of the humans out beyond the plains, but those humans that have ventured into our forests were brutish and feral, little more than dumb beasts. You are not like them. Despite your strange ways, you are civilized and clearly intelligent. Have I offended you?"

"Not at all," Captain Brown said, dismissing it with a wave. "But I want to get back to the dragons. If a helicopter attack on your villages happened so recently, then the one we saw today could very well be from the same people who attacked you. Do you have any idea where it came from or who it belongs to? Or even why you were attacked?"

Not surprisingly, Epasotl had no answers for the captain. Until today, she hadn't known that the "dragons" *belonged* to anyone at all. But I continued to ponder the question as we rolled across the grasslands. I also tried to ignore the unsettling knowledge that my new friend had a taste for human flesh.

By mid-afternoon we spotted a tall hill in the distance. As we drew closer, we realized it wasn't a natural feature of the landscape. Someone, probably a few hundred or thousand someones, had erected a great mound by the banks of a river, surrounded by two rings of tall earthen ramparts. An ancient hill fort. The river served as an extra line of protection, surrounding the fort and its ramparts on three sides. On the fourth side, a winding path led up the slope. At the top of the mound, crumbling stone and adobe brick buildings stood open to the sky.

We found what we had been looking for and, better yet, the place looked to have been abandoned long before. We could not have asked for better luck.

Other than not being trapped in this hellscape nightmare to begin with.

The path leading up the mound was smooth and wide, and we drove our vehicles to the top. Once we got the trucks set up in defensive positions, we dismounted and cleared, then took in a commanding view of the surrounding area. To our south was a large thicket of trees, and to the west we could just see the beginnings of jungle we'd traveled from and a hint of blue mountains on the horizon. It was rolling grass as far as the eye could see in every other direction.

Captain Brown named the fort "Camp Arizona" in honor of the first of us to fall in this strange new world.

It was here that we caught sight of our first deer. Specifically, red brocket deer, according to Staff Sergeant Douglas. They didn't form herds, at least not that we saw, but individuals would come down to the river to cautiously drink from time to time. Douglas wasted no time in going out on a stalk, taking a couple men with him for security, and returned at dusk with two fine specimens already expertly field dressed.

I was just relieved that we wouldn't be eating giant armadillo.

As the black sun was setting, I found myself gazing down at a mother and a fawn on the bank of the river. I was wondering if the deer, like us, had been snatched from our old world into this one, when suddenly the water exploded and a creature leapt out. I expected a crocodile, but this thing resembled a hyena crossed with an opossum, with sleek fur like a beaver's. It was about the size of a small bear. Most astounding was its long prehensile tail, which had some kind of grasping tendrils at the end. It was these tendrils that grabbed the fawn as the mother bounded away in fright.

The creature slipped back into the river without leaving a ripple, carrying its prey along with it.

"What the heck was *that*?" I said to Epasotl, who sat alongside me.

"That was an *ahuizotl*," she said, thoroughly unimpressed with the *National Geographic* spectacle we'd just witnessed. "They are common in the streams and rivers and are very territorial. You must exercise much caution when drawing water. They take many of our cubs each year."

Always nice knowing the wildlife is just as eager to kill you as the native tribes are.

Over the next several days we dug fire breaks and burned the tall grass and shrubs that covered and surrounded the earthen fortress in order to create a killing zone. Guys would watch the sky for the Huey, but it never returned. Still, morale was up. There *were* other humans out there somewhere, and we had a fortress to call our own. It wasn't Panama, but it was a good sight better than being lost, alone, and on the run. We didn't know what Captain Brown's plan was for making contact with the bird-people, but the men trusted him; it would only be a matter of time. For now, we focused on improving our temporary dwelling. Brown reminded us that, remote as it all felt, this remained very much a combat operation.

According to Epasotl there were many legitimately hostile bad guys out here in addition to all the local man-eating wildlife. The captain kept up his daily ritual of interviewing her, and often she and I would talk later and I'd get a download of what they'd discussed. Among the more interesting threats she shared with me—and after the "dragons" I was never sure how much credence to give to her taller tales—was a race of some kind of giant manlike chimeras that lived far to the north. Too far for us to find in our routine patrols, but apparently it didn't work the other way around because these things could run for days and move as quickly as we did in our mounts. Only *they* weren't low on gas.

We kept a watch, thankful for the unhindered view our hilltop fort provided.

We ran out of MREs, but Douglas and the other hunters provided a decent supply of red brocket, and Epasotl helped us identify roots, berries, and mushrooms that were safe to eat. She also taught us how to make a kind of pemmican that was high in calories and would remain edible for several seasons.

Epasotl's knowledge proved invaluable in other ways as well. She taught us how to thatch the roofs of the buildings in the center of the fort—which soon became the NCO quarters and command center —and how to use the stomachs of the red brockets to make waterskins and the hides to provide bedding. The latter required curing, which involved smearing the skin with their brains and then smoking it. Tanning detail soon became everyone's least favorite assignment.

The days blended into a week, and then two, each one filled with work from dawn to dusk. If we weren't shoring up the earthen ramparts with our e-tools, we were building lean-tos, foraging, or being drilled by Sergeant Takahashi. Low as I was on the totem pole, I was issued one of the last M1862 light cavalry sabers. Although designed for use on horseback, it was an easy weapon to handle, with a brass guard and a thirty-five-inch blade, which Takahashi insisted we sharpen and hone until it had a razor's edge.

Epasotl was fascinated by the strength of our steel weapons. I think she admired them much more than she did our rifles.

By the third week we were getting ripe, but Doc wouldn't let us bathe in the river. Not that many of us were clamoring to do so; by now everyone had seen just how hungry and aggressive those ahuizotl things were. The grotesque monsters had charged more than one water detail. Doc was equally concerned about parasites and all the various and sundry ways they could make our "most prized appendages" fall off.

It was only nineteen days since we'd arrived in the Land of the Black Sun, but it felt like a lifetime. On the morning of the twentieth day, Captain Brown had decided that things were fortified well enough that it was time to expand our patrols in an attempt to find the bird-people. We were going to push out next morning and spend a few days searching.

But we never did. Because as it turned out, we didn't have to leave the fort at all to find them. That very evening I spotted the first of the mysterious bird-women who would change our lives forever—most especially mine.

***

Epasotl was sitting on the top of my Humvee, weaving reeds into a mat, as I pulled security behind the MK19. The black sun was burning low in the west, setting the vast sea of grass ablaze in shades of marigold. That was when I saw them. Three of them, in the distance.

I pulled out my binoculars to get a better look. To my surprise, they were human. Things had been so weird that I didn't think twice about Epasotl's description of them being bird-people. It sort of felt like, *sure, why not?* But these were definitely human females, each mounted atop a giant flightless bird. If you're thinking of something akin to an ostrich, you need to think in a more terrifying direction, because ostriches are sort of funny-looking, and there wasn't anything remotely comical about these beasts. They probably stood ten feet tall from head to foot, with long, thick muscular legs and necks, and their sleek heads were mostly all beak, hooked and serrated.

The riders wore elaborate plumed headdresses and thick, body-length cloth armor decorated with bright feathers. Most strikingly, their faces appeared to be skulls—either from a mask or the artful application of makeup. It was hard to tell at that distance, but it definitely activated the creepy senses. Each carried a long lance and had a round shield and wooden club at her side.

I remembered seeing clubs like that during my mission, on a visit to the museum in Veracruz. The Aztecs called them *macuahuitls*. The weapons resembled cricket bats with obsidian blades running along the edge. The little plaque in the museum said the warriors who used them could decapitate a horse.

I called to Epasotl. "Hey, I think I see some of those half-bird people you mentioned."

She hissed and flattened her ears back, then began to sniff the air. "Where are they?"

I pointed, though I wasn't sure how well she'd see them without binoculars. "Over there. See? They're not monsters, though. They're just people riding… giant birds. Humans."

The birds truly were giant, but they loped with surprising grace through the tall grass, moving in our general direction.

"There's just a few of them," I said. "Maybe they just want to check out their new neighbors." I was still looking through the seven-by-fifty optics. The magnification didn't give much detail, but there was enough for me to call in a SALUTE report once they stopped about a klick away.

Sergeant Sanchez asked me if they appeared hostile.

"Negative, they do not appear hostile," I replied.

"Roger, Red Seven Golf," he replied. "Keep an eye on them."

"Roger, out," I said. To Epasotl I asked, "Are you sure they don't have any male warriors that might be hiding somewhere nearby?"

"I have never heard of a male. But then, I did not know they were human." The way she said the last part made clear she still didn't believe it.

One of the skull-faced warriors spurred her bird, and the beast leapt into the air with a harsh cry before racing toward us at incredible speed. The warrior stopped about six hundred meters from us and raised her lance. Her high-pitched war cry carried across the savanna.

Then she wheeled her mount around and bolted back to the others, and all three sprinted off into the distance. I couldn't be sure, but if I had to guess I'd say those birds were clocking a solid fifty miles an hour or more.

Absolutely incredible.

Since they had come to us, Captain Brown called off the planned patrol and opted to wait and see if they returned. "They may have some sort of cultural greeting or expectation we're unaware of. Let's give it a few days, see what happens. If they don't return, that'll indicate the next move is ours to make."

Epasotl didn't have anything else to offer. She didn't know what to expect concerning the riders.

The captain was right though. We saw more of them the next evening. A dozen riders, including what I thought was the same woman who'd shouted, came racing across the savannah toward Camp Arizona. They got closer this time, maybe five hundred yards from our ramparts. The woman—apparently the leader—gave her war cry, and once more they all disappeared as quickly as they had come.

This turned into a daily event. Each evening the riders would return at around the same time—edging a little closer each day—the woman shouted her challenge, and then they all rode off. Some days there were upwards of thirty riders, other days only a handful. And each day they came from a different direction.

The captain had given us strict orders not to fire. The woman's actions were a ritual challenge, not an overt act of aggression. And it was definitely a woman. A fit one at that. Not quite Amazonian—they weren't any taller than the average woman—but they had some definite muscular definition. Wilson, our resident body builder, couldn't stop talking about it—or them. By now they had gotten close enough for us to see clearly that the elaborate skull designs on their faces was just paint, so he started calling them "the Sugar Skull Gals."

The name stuck.

At the end of the week, the leader came right up to the edge of the farthest ramparts. And this time, she didn't immediately retreat after issuing her challenge. Instead she paced her giant bird back and forth, shaking her lance at us.

Captain Brown responded by hopping atop a Humvee and drawing his saber. He held it aloft, the rays of the setting sun glinting blood-red off the polished steel.

This seemed to either satisfy or frighten her, and she sprinted away.

The following evening brought no challenge. Instead, six warriors, all of them female and carrying woven baskets, rode at a slow pace to within a few yards of the winding ramp leading up to the top of the fortress. They dismounted, placed the baskets on the burnt stubble of the killing ground we'd cleared, then remounted and loped away, graceful and silent.

St. James and the rest of Alpha were sent to retrieve the offering. They brought back baskets containing fresh fruits, flat bread like corn tortillas, dried spiced meat, small pots of honey, and a sweet corn mush wrapped in broad leaves. To everyone's surprise, Doc let us dig in after doing a cursory inspection. It was delicious, especially after weeks of eating nothing but bitter berries, boiled roots, mushrooms, and the occasional bit of smoked venison. There was hardly enough for all of us to have much more than a taste, but we were in heaven.

The next day, we all hoped for another care package, but it didn't come. Neither did the riders.

That special delivery was the last we saw of them until the battle.

CHAPTER 12

Excited radio chatter woke me up a few nights after our unexpected feast. Someone had eyes on intruders slipping over the first ring of defenses. A moment later I heard an M2 bark out three measured bursts, then another three, followed by one long, sustained burst.

We were all up after that, but nothing more followed. The only word I got was that something big had climbed the outer rampart, and that Specialist Grant had fired the shots that took the thing down. But it wasn't until morning light that I saw what the "something big" was. Lying at the bottom of our fort were the bodies of two giant humanoids. There were tracks belonging to a third, which must have gotten away.

The big monsters looked remarkably human apart from their size —each was twice as large as a normal man—and the huge tusks protruding from their lower jaws. They wore thick padded cloth armor stitched in a diamond pattern, and each was armed with a macuahuitl, like the Sugar Skull Gals, but on a massive scale that was frankly terrifying. It was easy to imagine being cut in half if you made the mistake of getting in the way of one of those things. On their backs were six-foot-wide hide-bound shields. Their helmets were wooden, one carved in the shape of a jaguar, the other some bat-like demon or devil.

"Are these the giants you told us about?" I asked Epasotl.

"*Quinametzin*," Epasotl confirmed. She examined the creatures, their helmets now removed, and I could see on her face the moment when she realized that they weren't chimeras of beasts and men at all, just giant humanoids. "These are small for what I know of their race."

"Small?" I said. If these were small, I'd hate to see the big ones.

"Oh yes," she answered. "The largest of all throws the sun into the sky each morning."

"Are they friends of the Sugar Skull Gals? I see they have the same weapons."

"No. They are not friends. They war."

"I wonder if they came from somewhere nearby," I said, looking out across the broad plain. "Let's go find Captain Brown. I'm sure he'll want to talk to you about them again now that we've bagged a couple."

We found Brown at the command center conferring with Sanchez, who left on some other business as soon as we arrived.

"My next order of business was finding you, Epasotl," Captain Brown said. He gave me only a nod. "I take it we've been attacked by the Quinna... Quinn..."

"*Quinametzin*," Epasotl said. "Yes. These are small for their race."

"Hmm," was all Brown said about that. "We've scouted extensively, but we haven't seen any settlements. Not for miles around. But you said these creatures could cover vast amounts of territory, so what I'd like to get at is just how far these two traveled, how long it would take them to reach us, and anything else you can think up relating to their tactics."

"They are fast runners, with great endurance," Epasotl said. "It is said they can run almost thirty *xiquipilli cuahuitl* in a single day."

"How far is a... xiqui...pilli... that thing you just said?"

I found it interesting that some words didn't translate. The others all heard Epasotl's words as if she were speaking English—even I did at times, I realized—but every now and then a word or phrase would pop out that no one understood. It seemed that Tezcatlipoca's "gift to Outworlders" had some glitches at the margins.

Epasotl stretched out her arms and wriggled her fingers. "A cuahuitl is the distance of a warrior's outstretched arms. Farther than I can reach. Perhaps the distance between the ground and here—" She reached up and jabbed a finger at the base of my throat.

"About five feet then," I said, wincing. "And xiquipilli means eight thousand, right? So, if a mile is fifty-two hundred and eighty feet, that would be…"

"Two hundred and twenty-seven miles," Captain Brown said without hesitation.

Ranger captain and a walking computer.

"Three hundred and sixty-five klicks," I said, trying to show off my own math skills. "In a single day? That's a long run!"

"But their scouts often post relief runners, so they could be very, very far away," Epasotl said. "Still, their army could be here in only a few days. Your presence will offend them."

"How large could this army be?" Brown asked.

"I only know the stories of generations ago," Epasotl replied. Given the quick maturity rate of her people, Brown and I both knew that might not be as long ago as she made it out to be. "Enough warriors to shake the ground with their approach from a great distance. When they hurl their mighty javelins, the sun hides his face in fear."

"How did your people defeat them?" the captain asked.

"With much cunning and our knowledge of the secrets of the forest. We struck at them like an ahuizotl, always swiftly and unseen. We made deep pits with poisoned spikes and dropped trees on them. We lured them to confined places where our sisimitos could tear them limb from limb. To fight them in the open is very brave, and brings great honor, but is also very stupid."

"Sounds like we need to get ourselves ready for another fight," Brown said, standing up as if he were about to go do just that.

Epasotl shrugged. "Perhaps they do not come at all. The way to us will likely take them before other foes."

Brown nodded. "We'll be ready, either way." And with that, he headed off.

"If they come," Epasotl called after the captain, "we will all die with honor!"

She meant it to be encouraging.

***

Sergeant Shrimpton had recovered the armor and shields from the dead giants and performed ballistics tests on them. The results were less than optimal. Their armor was constructed of densely packed, unspun cotton stitched between two layers of fabric at least two inches thick, and the shields were made of densely woven agave and cotton covered by animal hides that could stop a round from an M16. Incredibly, it would even slow down seven-six-two enough to prevent those rounds from penetrating, though it would still likely knock the wind out of you. No wonder it had taken so much firepower to drop them.

Given all this, Sanchez had ordered the M2 BMGs loaded with our small supply of Raufoss Mk 211 ammunition, a multi-purpose anti-materiel high-explosive incendiary and armor-piercing round used against aircraft and lightly armored vehicles. Shrimpton had tested it against the giants' shields and armor, with dramatic and fiery results. Unfortunately we didn't have much of the ammo in supply, so gunners were ordered to avoid pick their targets carefully and try for one-shot kills. We'd attempt to identify leaders and take them out first.

We would also make use of the Springfield carbines we'd recovered—but for headshots only. The forty-five-seventy black powder rounds could blast through the giants' wooden helmets and cave in their skulls—another thing Shrimpton had demonstrated by use of the corpses. But the carbines were single-shot weapons, utilizing a hinged breechblock for loading, which opened like a trapdoor. Douglas, once a sniper always a sniper, insisted on drilling us until we could sustain a rate of fire of at least twelve rounds a minute. Not exactly a blistering pace. But not easy to pull off, either.

That was what now brought me to the inner ramparts with the other sharpshooters. I had handled the Springfield well enough to earn the dubious honor of being a designated marksman. The Springfield had an effective range of a thousand meters—Douglas said it had been known to hit targets as far as thirty-two hundred meters away—but to take accurate headshots we'd have to engage within one hundred meters at most.

"All y'all are too slow!" Douglas barked. "Open that trapdoor, extract th' brass, draw from th' box, load a'gin. All got to be one smooth motion, boys. Why you fumbling th' cartridge, Grant? Y'all got buttafingers? On me, boys. No, not like that, Bennett. Y'all clumsy like an ox, sha."

He ordered us to stop, exasperated, and brought his rifle to his shoulder.

"James, y'all time me," Douglas said as we waited in position. "Call out after a minute. Bennett, y'all keep count. Say when, boy."

James looked at his watch and then shouted, "Go!"

Douglas flipped the breech-lock open, drew a dummy round he kept in the cartridge-box at his waist, loaded it, closed the lock, and dry-fired. He repeated the steps, repeatedly, smooth as silk, the rifle never leaving his shoulder, his aim never wavering.

"Time!" James shouted.

"How many was that, Bennett?" Douglas asked.

"Twenty-five, Sergeant."

"All y'all see? Slow is smooth. Smooth is fast. Don't think 'bout it. Just shoot, reload, shoot. Hooah?"

We did minimal live fire, drilling by dry-firing in order to conserve ammunition. The Buffalo Soldiers didn't have a ton of ready ammunition, but we'd also recovered lead bars, bullet molds, powder, and primers. Hand-loading the cartridges could be done with simple tools and was a relatively easy task that occupied our evenings. We had enough to drill with and fight with, but ammo was still a concern. Out here, wherever here was, no resupply was coming. Ever.

Even so, what little lead we did throw downrange left us all enshrouded in a blinding fog of white smoke reeking of sulfur. It was the main drawback of the black powder weapons—that and the black soot that covered our faces. We all had powder burns on our cheeks.

The next day, my arms were sore from the shooting, but I finally felt confident that I'd handle the weapon competently in the attack. I would soon find out for sure.

It was an early Saturday morning—the twenty-seventh of January, back in the world—when Specialist Grant got on the net to report a dust cloud far to the north. From the top of Camp Arizona, the horizon was about twenty klicks away. I grabbed a pair of binos and got on top of our mount beside Pierce in the gunner's turret. Soon a dark gray mass appeared on the horizon. I couldn't make out much detail at that distance, but it looked like a column of men marching.

Grant was already on the net. "All Red elements, this is Red Ten Golf. Massed column of figures approaching from the north. Size unknown."

Ideally he'd call out an azimuth, but our compasses didn't work.

"What I wouldn't give for arty support," Pierce muttered.

"Hell, man. Even mortars would be nice," I said.

The MK-19 has an effective firing range of fifteen hundred meters but can reach out and touch someone up to twenty-two hundred meters away. That still wasn't enough; they'd be on our doorstep before we could drop any indirect fire. The M2 BMG wasn't much better. We were loaded with precious Raufoss Mk 211, but we wouldn't be wasting that on long-range massed groups; we were saving it for sniping. And yes, in the right hands you can totally snipe with the Ma Deuce.

It took the column just thirty minutes to close the gap between us another six klicks, which meant they were marching at a blistering pace of eight miles an hour. Rangers march at four miles an hour, and that's a brutal pace to maintain. The river might slow them down, but then again, these were giants. Longer legs equal faster pace and easier wading.

At about three klicks away we could feel the ground shaking, even from the top of the mound, and their column spread out into a line four ranks deep and perhaps a third of a mile across. Through the binoculars I could now see that the front rank was composed of the largest of their warriors, each carrying an oversized macuahuitl and a shield decorated with bright feathers and ornaments of gold and silver that reflected the rising sun in a dazzling array.

They began beating their war clubs against their shields. Some spun bullroarers in the air. Even from that distance we could hear them clearly.

We were twenty-seven men against an army of a thousand giants.

I'll be perfectly honest with you.

I was terrified.

CHAPTER 13

The line of giants continued to advance, beating their war clubs on their shields and whipping their bullroarers in the air. Douglas, who commanded the detachment of marksmen, shouted for us to get a move on. We grabbed our Spencer carbines and cartridge-boxes to follow him down to the inner rampart on the northern side. We also took our M16s, just because, and we'd loaded up with as many fragmentation grenades as we could find.

Staff Sergeant Douglas and three other NCOs had grabbed the M203s from their squads and would provide close support for those of us tasked with preventing anyone from crossing first the river, then the moat to storm the inner wall. We'd snipe for as long as we could, use the grenades when they got close, and then it would be down to sabers, knives, and harsh language. Retreat wasn't really an option: we didn't have anywhere to run to. If the giants overran us, Camp Arizona was lost anyway.

There were only nine of us, not counting Douglas and the NCOs, and our line along the rampart stretched a hundred meters, leaving uncomfortable gaps between the men. I had Sergeant Wilson to my right, Private James to my left. Together we watched the giants approaching. They advanced to about a klick and a half, then stopped.

A handful of their largest warriors broke ranks and strutted up and down the line, shouting challenges at us. The resident demon-god's little language trick worked just fine. Were we warriors? Would we meet them on the field of battle and prove our honor?

Hell no. We'd stay behind our ramparts, thank you very much.

"They're staying put," James said. "Wonder why they're holding back?"

"Probably encountered Outworlders before, bro," Wilson replied. "They know we can reach out and touch 'em."

The giants kept it up for a long time. The black sun rose higher, and still they strutted and shouted insults from a mile away, their deep voices carrying across the plain as they tried to shame us into charging forth from our defensive position. It was getting hot, and boredom set in hard.

Flocks of buzzards and crows had begun collecting in the thermals overhead. They could sense a feast coming. Some landed on the ramparts and cawed at us. It felt ominous. I was sure Epasotl would've said it was a bad omen. Or maybe a good omen. She *did* want us all to die in battle, after all.

Around noon the giants started having mock fights with each other, one on one. Just to show us how badass they were, I guess. Not gonna lie, it *was* pretty badass. I wouldn't want to be stuck one-on-one in a fight against those things.

Captain Brown decided that the time had come for us to show these guys we weren't pushovers. His deep voice came on the net.

"Red Niner, this is Red One Actual."

"Go for Red Niner," Takahashi replied.

"Think you can take out the biggest one?"

"Roger, out."

Takahashi was like that. No bluster. No ego. Can he take out a target a mile away with a frigging Ma Deuce and iron sights? Roger. Out.

We heard the thunder of an M2 firing, and a couple seconds later the biggest giant, who was showing just how badass he was by mock-fighting three opponents at once, simply exploded, showering one of his opponents with incendiary fragments as his cloth armor caught fire. I was watching with my binos and wasn't disappointed in the least.

Badass warrior, meet the Red Waterfall.

That's what *Raufoss* means in Norwegian. They don't mess around when naming their ammunition. Red waterfall was right. Bloody glorious. Literally.

It was a one-in-a-million shot too. Just incredible. I think the legendary Carlos Hathcock made a shot like that back in Vietnam with an M2. Maybe Taks was channeling the dude. But if I hoped that display would make the giants think twice and just go home, I was in for a serious disappointment.

The strutting warriors dashed back into their ranks, and some kind of priests, or that's what I assumed they were, stepped out and walked up and down the line, splashing the warriors' shields with a dark liquid.

Probably blood.

Then the line broke into a march at double time, making the ground shudder. At the rate they were moving, they'd reach us in less than five minutes.

Douglas barked at Bond, Evans, McKee, and James to cross the swampy moat and douse the abatis with our nasty fuel-oil mixture. They moved with a purpose.

Sanchez got on the net and ordered the MK19 gunners to open fire. That would be Specialists Stanley and Pierce. They started bracketing fire in short bursts, and then laid on with sustained fire once they'd zeroed in on the swiftly approaching line of giants. The thumpers blasted ragged holes in the giants' formation, and mutilated corpses began bleeding out of the ranks as the line advanced. At a thousand meters Sergeant Takahashi and Specialist Woodward brought the M2s online, obliterating giants one by one.

Eventually the giants must have decided they'd taken enough punishment. They halted at four hundred meters out and turtled up in a shield wall that proved to be quite effective.

We sent thumpers at them, but they splashed off the interlocked shields like water balloons. A high-velocity M430 HEDP grenade can punch through two inches of rolled homogeneous armor, and here they were simply bouncing off hide-bound shields.

What the heck? I began to wonder if whatever their priests had done had actually improved their defenses. Epasotl had said that their sacrifice of McCoppin had been answered by the way the sisimitos withstood our direct fire. She wasn't around at the moment to ask, though.

The giants started moving again, while maintaining their shield wall. This had them advancing at a much slower pace, but they came on all the same. Takahashi and Woodward hit them with the fifty-caliber Raufoss rounds, but like the grenades, these were ineffective except for when they managed to find a gap in the shields.

At two hundred meters the shield wall opened briefly, and warriors with atlatls launched a volley of fourteen-foot-long spears, hundreds of them blackening the sky. We ducked behind the rampart as the huge projectiles rained down on our position, thudding powerfully into the turf. Miraculously they failed to impale anyone in the platoon.

Evans and the other privates crossed back over the moat, trailing our improvised 550 paracord fuses. They were all covered up to their armpits with the slurry, and Bond was swearing enough to make a sailor blush.

"Look sharp, boys," Douglas called out. "Find 'em gaps in the shields and make 'em pay."

Two hundred meters, one hundred and fifty, one hundred…

Close enough.

We opened fire with the Spencers, aiming at holes in the interlocked shields, hoping for headshots. We might have scored a few. And then they were at our abatis, larger than life, an entire line of giants hacking and shoving at our defensive fortification of branches. It looked impressive when we built it, but now, next to the giants, it seemed pitiful.

"Light 'em up!" Douglas shouted from somewhere within the hazy cloud of black powder smoke. "Hurry, boys!"

We lit the gunpowder fuses that led to the incendiary slurry, and smoking fire raced across the moat. Two went out only halfway across, but the third made it all the way and the abatis caught fire. I was expecting a *whoomph* and an explosive wall of flame, but there was nothing so dramatic. The fire kind of took its time, easy like a Sunday morning at first, before gathering speed and spreading. Diesel fires can be somewhat underwhelming.

It did the trick though, and giants started bellowing in pain and rage as black smoke roiled and the sticky fuel-oil mixture they'd been pushing through lit up.

The pause in the action gave us a target-rich environment, and we snapped off headshots as quickly as we could fire, grab a cartridge, reload, and fire again.

But the massed formation of giants continued pushing forward, shoving those in the front rank off the rampart and into the moat, along with large sections of flaming abatis. We kept firing as Douglas and the other NCOs sent grenades across the moat and into the massed ranks behind. With the screen of black smoke, we couldn't see if they had any effect. Smoke from our own weapons was becoming a problem as well, making it progressively more difficult to pick out targets. But I knew that giants were pouring into the moat, ignoring the burning branches that stuck to their armor.

Douglas ordered us to cease fire and ready grenades. We pulled the pins and waited for his order to toss them.

"Now!" Douglas cried. "Fire in the hole!"

We all chucked our grenades simultaneously and then ducked behind the inner rampart as they went off with a thunderous wave. The slurry in the moat must have contained pockets of methane, because now there *was* a tremendous series of *whoomphs*, and giant blue fireballs exploded above us. Bits of flaming scum and bloody chunks of giant rained down.

Then we were back on our Spencers as the next wave of giants stormed over the outer rampart. We took as many headshots as we could, and when the giants began massing in the moat, we threw another volley of grenades.

This time, some of the attackers got through to us.

One giant leapt over the inner rampart and landed not five feet from me. I was in the middle of reloading and froze as he whirled his eight-foot-long macuahuitl. I heard James shout, "Get some—" and the giant's face exploded.

James was still standing there, shrouded in white smoke and grinning from ear to ear, when another giant leapt down behind him and clove him in half diagonally from shoulder to hip.

I fumbled to reload as the giant sprinted toward me. Wilson was ready, and a bloody hole appeared between the giant's eyes. He crashed onto his back.

Thankfully there weren't a lot of them. Only a few had gotten through, otherwise we'd already be dead. Douglas shouted for us to keep after it and then someone was screaming for a medic. Where was Doc?

"Yo, Bennett!" Wilson shouted. "That's you, bro."

Shaking my head, I followed the cry to find PFC Harris lying on the turf staring up into the sky. Sergeant García was next to him, holding his hand and shouting at him to hang in there.

"I—I can't feel my legs, Sergeant," Harris moaned.

I was still in shock myself after witnessing James's brutal death, and it took me a second to realize the poor kid's legs were missing; they'd been cleanly severed above the knee. Working as fast as I could, I applied tourniquets to both legs.

"I can take it from here, García," I said.

The sergeant nodded and hurried off. As much as I could have used a hand, García needed to be in the fight a whole lot more.

"Am I gonna be okay?" Harris asked me. "I'm gonna be okay, right?"

"You're gonna be just fine, brother," I said, doing my best to hide my doubts as I injected him with morphine.

I propped Harris's rifle up against a rampart wall and then got out a bag of saline and hung it from the weapon. "I'm gonna start an IV," I said, fumbling to find a vein in Harris's hand. I drove the needle in and hooked up the tube.

"I'm tired, Sergeant," Harris said.

"Just stay with me," I warned.

"I'm gonna die, aren't I, Bennett?"

"You'll be fine, man," I lied. He'd lost a lot of blood. Too much blood.

Someone else was screaming for a medic. I locked eyes with Harris. "You're gonna be okay, but I gotta check this out. I'll be right back."

"I'm not going anywhere," he replied. "It's not so bad. Dyin's not so bad."

I took off, taking some small relief that the morphine was making things easier on him.

Before I could reach the next wounded man, a giant vaulted over the rampart and landed on the far side of Bond and Shrimpton. Bond charged him with a machete, but the giant lunged and shield-bashed him, sending him flying. Sergeant Shrimpton, saber drawn, slashed at the giant's thigh, but the padded armor was just too thick. The giant dropped his shield, grabbed Shrimpton by the head, lifted him off the ground, and roared a challenge, flashing his huge tusks.

I wasn't sure what to do beyond throw myself into the giant's knee and hope to cause a dislocation. I was taking the first steps to that end when Shrimpton twisted in the air and drove his saber into the giant's mouth and up into his brainpan.

The giant fell to his knees and convulsed, but as he did so, his powerful hand crushed the sergeant's head with explosive force, showering me with bone and brains.

The scream for a medic came again, and I forced myself toward the cry, stumbling blindly through the white smoke. Over the radio I thought I heard Sanchez ordering the gunners to cease fire. It didn't make sense. I could still hear the war cries of giants. Why would we stop engaging?

They were slaughtering us up here to the point that the men had given up firing down on them and were doing what they could to engage those who had broken through. But there were still enough of us in the fight that I felt like my job should be to take care of the casualties. Maybe that was a mistake. Maybe I should have gotten back into the fight too. But the only giants I saw around me were dead and I could see Staff Sergeant Douglas leaning against the wall of the inner rampart, holding the stump of his left arm. PFC Jensen was beside him and also wounded. The kid looked pale and was trembling, holding his hands tight against his stomach.

"Y'all see to th' boy first, now," Douglas said to me, gritting his teeth. I noticed he'd used his own belt as a tourniquet on his arm.

"Let me have a look, Jensen," I said. My voice and heart were racing. I expected the looming shadow of a giant to blot out the sun behind me at any moment.

Jensen shook his head, his eyes wide with fright. "My guts are gonna burst out, man," he said. "It's all I can do to hold 'em in."

I cut off his LBV and then helped him lie down, drawing his knees up. Specialist Cohen was nearby and apparently not busy fighting. In fact, the shooting had stopped altogether. Had we won? My mind raced over possibilities. Maybe it was bad here but the trucks made it worse for the giants down there and they'd called it quits.

Didn't matter. I called Cohen over.

"Abdominal wound, think it's perforated," I said. "I need you to apply pressure while I wrap it. Try to keep his insides where they belong. Jensen, listen, you gotta let Cohen take over holding you in place so I can work."

He fought us for a little while, but finally let go after we counted down from three. Cohen held his hands firm over the slash in Jensen's belly and met my eyes. He looked scared.

"Feels like a mess of eels is trying to burst out, man," Cohen said.

"Just try to keep the wound closed and keep applying pressure." I pulled out a roll of bandages. I needed to soak them first, or they'd stick to his exposed intestines, causing even more damage, but I was out of water.

"You got any water?" I asked Cohen.

"Nah, man. I'm bone-dry."

Douglas shoved a bloody canteen at me. "Here."

"Thanks, Sergeant."

After the bandages were good and soaked, we rolled Jensen onto his side and I swapped with Cohen, firmly pressing a wet dressing over the wound. Then, working together, Cohen and I carefully wrapped Jensen up.

"Now your turn, Sergeant," I said, turning to Douglas. "Sorry… I'm out of morphine."

"Well, shit," Douglas drawled.

"What happened?" I asked as I inspected his field-expedient tourniquet. It wasn't bad, but needed replacing.

"Damn sonofabitch got th' jump on us," he said, motioning to a headless giant a couple meters away. "But I got 'im good. Took th' bastard's head clean offa him shoulders, an' with just one arm, too!"

He laughed and then grimaced.

"I'm going to have to swap tourniquets, Sergeant," I said. "This will hurt."

"Roger that," he said. "How're th' men?"

"Doing fine, Sergeant. I think we won."

"Call me John. We brothers in blood now, son."

"You know I can't do that, Sergeant. Here, hang on."

I applied a proper tourniquet higher up and considered removing the belt but decided to leave it on as a stopgap. If Doc could get him a transfusion and clean up the stump, he might make it. Cohen was helping Jensen drink from the last of Douglas's canteen.

"You guys hang tight," I said. "I'll be back to check on you. Have to do the rounds."

Honestly I needed to clear my head, but there was still work to do. And I wanted to verify that this wasn't just a lull in the fighting. We'd lost too many men to have anyone fighting-capable away from the firing line.

Sergeant Wilson, standing atop the rampart with Wright and the radio, called me up. I could tell from his tone of voice that we were in the clear.

"How's it looking?" Wilson asked. "Sanchez wants a sitrep."

"James and Shrimpton are dead," I said. "Harris isn't going to make it. Jensen is critical. Sergeant Douglas lost an arm, but I think he'll pull through. I still gotta check on everyone else, but I wasn't sure what happened and didn't want to leave you another rifle short. It's over? We won?"

Wilson nodded and called in what I'd told him while I checked on every man in the detachment. We'd suffered our share of wounds, but everyone else was ambulatory and would recover. My curiosity over *how* we won was killing me, but I began to piece things together from talking to the guys. As bad as it was for us, it could have been worse. In short, we were bailed out by our new friends.

I peered through the thinning black smoke at the battlefield beyond the ramparts, wanting to see for myself the truth of what I'd heard. There I saw Sugar Skull Gals roaming over the plain, dispatching wounded giants while their huge birds feasted on the corpses.

I looked at Wilson, who was also admiring the aftermath—and admiring the bodies of those scantily clad, bronze-and-toned warriors —and he smiled.

"Yeah, bro," he said. "The craziest thing happened…"

CHAPTER 14

Everybody had their own variation on what happened. I quickly deduced that I was the only non-injured or dead person who hadn't seen it unfold firsthand. It seemed the Sugar Skull Gals had come out of nowhere and charged the giants from the left and right, rolling up their flanks. The giant birds they rode struck with their powerful necks like lightning, biting off heads and tearing at limbs with their sharp hooked beaks. The riders charged first with lances and then, once among the ranks of the giants, hacked and slashed with their macuahuitls. They were so effective that they not only broke the assault but absolutely decimated the giants' force, leaving few survivors to flee across the savanna.

"I don't understand it," Pierce said to me. "We could hardly touch them with thumpers and fifty-cal, yet those gals came in and slaughtered the bastards with Stone Age weapons."

"It was the shields," I said, thinking again of that ritual splashing of blood, or whatever it was, that the priests had performed before the battle. "There's something strange with them... some black magic or voodoo."

"Maybe," Pierce said. "Because they didn't have much chance to use them once the Sugar Skull Gals were in close contact."

Doc and others had come to us with stretchers to load Harris, Jensen, and Douglas, even though the staff sergeant insisted he could walk. In a sad bit of predictive medicine on my part, Harris didn't make it back to the med station alive. Jensen was alive but in critical condition. He needed a hospital, and the nearest one was an entire world and possibly another dimension away. Doc did his best, but he wasn't a field surgeon.

He did an amazing job stitching up Douglas's stump though, and kept him sedated on a heavy dose of morphine, if only to keep Bravo Section's leader from getting back into the action. Doc said the staff sergeant would recover. The amputation had been a clean cut right above the elbow, like from a giant scalpel.

Pierce gave me the most detailed description of the battle before the arrival of the Sugar Skull Gals. The loss of James, Harris, and myself, really, opened the way for a detachment of giants to storm the palisade guarding the ramp up to the mound. Captain Brown and his driver raced their truck to meet them and then used the weapons systems to keep them back. The captain had figured out the trick of the shields and targeted the Fifty to eat away at whatever was exposed, whether it was heads or legs. The detachment didn't stand a chance.

It should be said that St. James and the rest of Alpha also distinguished themselves in combat. By all accounts they fought with a furor that was unmatched, even by the giants. From what I hear, I may even be understating it. Pierce said they fought like they were possessed. Whatever swagger Alpha had lost after getting busted down, it seemed to be back. They had been strutting around camp like killers, and when the time came, they delivered. In spades.

All the movies say that war changes a man. Maybe there's something to that. The men I once knew had become something else. Something deadlier.

I still didn't like them.

Late into the afternoon the Sugar Skull Gals were still roaming the battlefield dispatching wounded giants while their mounts feasted. We were all wondering if Captain Brown would take the opportunity to make contact, but the SSG (the guys had already shortened the official nickname of the Sugar Skull Gals) hadn't paid any attention to us to that point. We would wait for them to say hello first.

Flocks of buzzards and crows blotted out the sky as they descended on the carnage, cawing and hissing angrily as they fought over corpses. It was a sweltering day, and even from the top of Camp Arizona the air hung heavy with the fetid stench of the dead. The smell would only get worse if we didn't deal with the remains of the giants. But I wasn't sure we could. How could twenty-four men, one of them too banged up to help, clean up a battlefield with what had to be hundreds of dead giants? Moving even one giant wasn't easy.

Shortly before dusk, when the black sun was low on the horizon casting a hellish red glow across the battlefield, a detachment of Sugar Skull Gals approached the ramp. One wore an immense feathered headdress and came flanked by six warriors. Captain Brown ordered Wilson to form a detail to go with him to meet them. Wilson selected me and five others, and we marched in formation down the ramp with Wilson calling cadence. We looked like crap, but we were troopers and had our pride; we marched like we were on a parade ground.

Wilson called a halt ten meters from where the female warriors waited, and the captain stepped forward one pace to greet them.

The woman with the impressive headdress also stepped forward one pace. She looked older than the others. Not elderly, per se, but at least two decades beyond many of the warriors around her. The champion who had ridden out to challenge us was there too, in the older woman's honor guard. They were all covered in blood and grime, like us, but their beauty struck me, especially the champion's. Somehow the intricate sugar skull makeup only enhanced it. She was young, perhaps not yet twenty, but it was hard to tell with the war paint. They were much shorter than I expected now that I saw them up close and dismounted; most were less than five feet tall, including the champion. But they were powerfully built.

Or as Wilson put it later: "Those babes are stacked and jacked, bro."

I tried not to stare and focused on keeping my eyes front as I stood at attention. But yeah, I noticed.

"It is a good day for slaughter, Outworlder," the older woman said after spending a silent moment sizing up the captain. She bowed slightly and touched her forehead.

"Yes, ma'am," Captain Brown agreed, copying the gesture. I noticed he bowed more deeply than the woman had. "A fine day."

We didn't know what the protocol was for this sort of meeting. Epasotl had had no idea. The captain was winging it.

"I congratulate you on the defense of your fortress," the woman said. "Your men have much fortitude."

"And we thank you for assisting us," Captain Brown said. "Without your support, the day would have been lost."

"We did not act in your defense," she replied bluntly. "There was an opportunity to strike at our enemy."

"We are grateful for your assistance all the same. We have a saying: the enemy of my enemy is my friend. Might we be friends?"

"That remains to be seen." The woman paused, allowing an uncomfortable silence that lasted for several long moments. When the captain said nothing more, she added: "It is customary to invite one's friends into one's home to feast after a battle."

"Yes, yes of course, excuse me," Brown said. "Welcome to Camp Arizona. May we escort you?"

"Lead, and we will follow."

Just before we turned, the young woman, the champion, caught me staring. I looked away quickly, but not before I saw the corner of her mouth turn up in what might have been a smile.

Wilson ordered us about face and marched us back up the ramp, with the Sugar Skull Gals in tow. They murmured quietly at the sight of our vehicles, but otherwise were silent as we walked to a fire pit we'd built near the command center. Our detachment took up position on one side of the pit, and the women stood on the other. Troopers in the platoon gawked from a respectful distance.

"You do not know our ways and so I will not take offense," the older woman said. "It is customary to invite the commander of the war host to sit."

"I apologize," the captain said. "Please, sit, ma'am. And please, do me the further honor of guiding and correcting me when my manners are lacking."

She nodded slightly and sat cross-legged on the ground. Captain Brown followed her example. Her warriors remained standing, and so did we.

"Sergeant Wilson," Brown said. "Some food and water, please."

"Yes, sir," Wilson replied. He ordered Woodward and me to fetch something.

I was disappointed to be sent away; I wanted to witness every moment of this strange meeting. But I was also relieved to escape the gaze of their champion. Now that she had caught me looking, she kept stealing glances at me, laughter in her incredible amber eyes. I was sure I was blushing furiously.

We didn't have much ready, but Woodward and I scrounged up some cold stew of roots, mushrooms, and venison, and a few canteen cups. I wasn't sure how to properly serve the leader of the sugar skull warriors, so I knelt in front of her and doled out a canteen cup of the stew and another of water. She took both without acknowledging my presence.

We also tried to serve her warriors, but they refused all but the water. The young champion met my eye boldly, and I felt my face grow hot.

As Woodward and I rejoined the formation, he elbowed me. "She's got a thing for you, man," he whispered. "Your days as a virgin are numbered."

By then I had to be glowing beet red.

Their leader sampled the stew and took a long drink of water, then set both aside, folded her arms, and introduced herself. I won't bother transcribing her long name, which was one compound word with about thirteen syllables, but it basically meant "revered skull-dancing warrior queen of the Kuauchanejkej." That name, the name of her people, meant "tree-dwellers."

"I am called Captain Brown," our platoon leader replied. "It is a great honor to meet you, Your Majesty."

He didn't try to pronounce her name and title, which was probably wise.

"I apologize for the food," he added. "We have little, and it doesn't compare to the gifts you brought us. We thank you for those."

"It is what neighbors do," Queen Skull-Dancer replied with a dismissive wave of her hand. "You did not attack my daughter, but saluted her as a warrior. We are not yet enemies."

So, the young woman who kept looking at me was not only a champion, but a princess.

I didn't stand a chance.

"Not yet enemies, not yet friends," Captain Brown said. "I would like to be friends, Your Majesty."

"Perhaps in time," the queen replied. "Outworlders are not to be trusted."

"Perhaps we can prove we are to be trusted."

"Perhaps. Tell me, how long have you been in our world?"

"Not long, Your Majesty."

"And there are only two dozen of you?" She was an astute observer.

Captain Brown hesitated. Giving away our size could put us in a position of weakness, but there was no point in lying: she could see the truth for herself. And besides, we *were* in a position of weakness. She must have had three hundred mounted warriors outside our fort.

"Yes, Your Majesty." Then he decided to gamble. "And though we have just arrived, we do not intend to stay. We seek to defeat Tezcatlipoca so that we may return home."

Queen Skull-Dancer laughed—a pure belly laugh. "Is that all, Outworlder? You seek to battle the very devil who rules our world?"

"If we must," the captain replied calmly. "We first seek his brother, in hopes that he will help. Perhaps you can guide us. Do you know where we can find Quetzalcoatl?"

The old woman shook her head with a look of disgust. "He cannot help you, Captain. The Wisest-of-Men is an outcast. Banished. *And* a drunkard. He drinks to dull his sorrow and shame beyond the Blue Mountains, where the great sea extinguishes the black sun each evening. You must forget your home, Captain. It is lost to you. This is your home now, for as long as you live, though I suspect your days will be short."

"That remains to be seen. We came out this way, in part, to find you."

The queen arched an eyebrow. "And what did you hope to do once you found us?"

"To seek your aid. We did not believe you to be human, but we were led to understand that you might lead us to more of our kind. More humans. Outworlders."

"There are many such as yourself beyond these lands," the old woman said. "But their fate is the same as your own. You are the playthings of Tezcatlipoca. Meant to entertain him until you perish."

I didn't like the sound of that, but Captain Brown took everything in stride. He was unflappable.

"And what of you and your people? Are you his playthings?"

"No. We are not." The queen sounded insulted by the idea.

"I meant no disrespect. Please, how are you different?"

"We are descendants of the men brought into this land. Their fates were sealed when they were chosen. But they live on through us."

I wanted Captain Brown to get into that, because I was interested. There didn't seem to be any males among these people. Was that because the males were all back home? Effeminate girly men unfit to fight? I doubted the Sugar Skull Gals self-reproduced. Not with the way the princess was teasing me with her looks.

Instead, the captain kept the discussion on Outworlders. "We saw a helicopter—a flying machine. Our native guide called it a dragon. It would likely be piloted by a human Outworlder, one likely to share our own history and culture. Do you know where it came from?"

The queen was clearly intrigued—not by the dragon, but by our association with a native. "I would speak to this guide."

Captain Brown turned to me. "Bennett, where's Epasotl?"

It was a good question. I realized I hadn't seen her since before the battle. I told him as much, and he dispatched me to find her and bring her back. It just goes to show how much Epasotl had become part of the fabric of our unit.

She wasn't in any of her usual haunts. I tried the command center and the building we'd converted to a kitchen. Eventually I found her deep in the back of a Humvee. Clearly hiding.

"What are you doing in here?" I asked her.

"You have invited the bird-women here!" she hissed accusingly. "They cannot be trusted."

"They saved our lives, Epasotl. Without them we would all be dead. Besides, you knew we were looking for them. They might know where we can find more of our kind."

"I did not think you would invite them to your camp!"

"Well, Captain Brown did, and now their queen wants to meet you."

Epasotl laid her ears back. "Never! They will skin me alive and eat my flesh!"

"But then you will die with honor," I pointed out. "Or is that not what you want anymore?"

She considered that for a moment, and her ears relaxed. "What will be will be. It is as the gods will."

She followed me back to the fire pit, trying to make a brave show of it.

When Queen Skull-Dancer saw Epasotl, her reaction was as virulent as Epasotl had predicted. She leapt to her feet and drew a long obsidian dagger. Her warriors raised their war clubs and formed a protective half-circle around her.

"What is this?" the queen cried. "You invite us into your camp as friends, yet you have a demon among you!"

Epasotl crouched and hissed, her ears flat back and her teeth bared.

Captain Brown hurried to his feet and got between them. "It's just a misunderstanding," he said. "Please, Your Majesty, we meant no offense. We captured her, she was a prisoner, but she has proved a helpful guide. We trust her."

"I would sooner trust an ahuizotl," the queen spat. "You are exceedingly foolish to keep one of her kind in your presence."

"Be that as it may, Your Majesty, she is no threat to you," Brown assured her. "I give you my word as a warrior and a leader of warriors. Please, sit down."

Queen Skull-Dancer narrowed her eyes to study Epasotl. "Is it true? Have you tamed this animal? She is a dangerous pet, Captain."

"She's not an animal," I blurted.

"Bennett!" Captain Brown barked, looking more angry than surprised at my outburst.

The queen's daughter whispered in her ear, and Skull-Dancer smiled.

"Are *you* her keeper?" the queen asked me.

I looked to Captain Brown, who nodded for me to answer. "I am her *friend*," I clarified.

"I see. And was it you who captured her?"

"Yes, Your Majesty."

"Then she is duty-bound to listen to you. Isn't that right, little savage?"

Epasotl hissed in reply.

Queen Skull-Dancer sat back down and sheathed her dagger, but her warriors remained on high alert.

The captain resumed his seat as well, though far more warily than before.

"Bring her to me," the queen ordered.

I crouched close to Epasotl and whispered, "I won't let anything happen to you. Let's just let this play out. And stop snarling."

She was able to hide her teeth, if not stop snarling completely. I was glad she was at least attempting to do what I asked of her. I led her gently by the shoulder to the fire pit and knelt.

"Make her kneel as well," the queen said.

I had expected Epasotl to follow my lead, and was a bit embarrassed at the defiant and haughty way she stood before the person responsible for saving all of our lives. I now gave her every visual cue I knew of to get her to show respect.

"I won't," she hissed at me.

"I don't want to order you, but I will," I said softly. "And you are duty-bound to obey, right?"

The look of betrayal in her eyes cut me to the bone, but she knelt and composed herself, although her ears remained flat back against her head.

"I have never spoken with a savage of the forest before," Queen Skull-Dancer said. "Can you understand me?"

I had learned from Epasotl that the gift of tongues granted to Outworlders didn't apply to the indigenous races of this world, but Epasotl's reactions thus far had made it clear that she could understand the queen nonetheless. The queen spoke something very close to Nahuatl; to my ear the difference was primarily one of dialect.

"Well?" the queen said.

"Yes, I understand your ugly speech," Epasotl growled. "You sound like a crow choking on its own entrails."

The captain coughed, but Epasotl's words seemed only to amuse the queen. "And your caterwauling I can barely understand at all," she replied. "Tell me, savage of the forest, isn't capture the greatest shame for your kind? How do you live with it?"

Epasotl looked at me and then said proudly, "I have learned to seek honor in life, not death."

A chagrined smile came to the queen's mouth. "Does it shame you to kneel before your enemy?"

Epasotl turned to me. "Are these barbarians your enemy?"

I glanced at the captain, who gave me a slight nod. "No," I said. "We would wish them to be friends."

"Then," Epasotl said, her ears perking forward slightly as she addressed the queen once more, "the friend of my master cannot be my enemy, and so there is no shame." She paused a moment before adding, "Your Majesty."

CHAPTER 15

Captain Brown sent Epasotl on her way, sensing not only her discomfort but also that her presence might unnecessarily complicate discussions he'd been wanting to have since we'd first heard about these "bird-women." There was now no doubt that other humans—Outworlders like us—were in this realm. Judging by the Huey, they might even be American. We just needed to learn how to find them.

"I appreciate your candor and your patience with me," Captain Brown told the old queen. "If it's not too much to ask, I'd like to hear what you know about the helicopter—the flying machine that crossed these plains not long ago."

The captain made an imitation of a whirling propeller with his finger, then pantomimed with his hand something flying over the earth.

"We saw this thing that you describe," Queen Skull-Dancer said. "And not just recently. It has traveled this way many times before. Sometimes the men riding in it kill animals on the savanna with their guns. They do not harvest the meat."

The actual word she used was not *guns*, but *arcabuces*, which is the plural Spanish form of *harquebus*. Not Nahuatl. I was intrigued.

"Captain, sir," I cut in. "If I may ask Her Majesty a brief question?"

He nodded.

I used the queen's full thirteen-syllable title when addressing her. "You used the word *arcabuz*. Where did Your Majesty learn that word?"

"From our spiritual leader, Friar Bastía," she replied, looking confused by the question.

Captain Brown raised an eyebrow. "*Friar* Bastía?"

She nodded.

"Forgive me, but in our language, Friar indicates a familiar religion and religious profession. Is this Friar… a Christian?"

"Of course. As am I. As are all my people."

Brown gave a curt nod and smiled. "Then that is something we have in common. I am also Christian."

"Do you follow the true faith or are you one of the heretics claiming to be Christian?" she asked.

"I believe the answer to that question would probably be best answered by Friar Bastía," Captain Brown said diplomatically. "Most people, even if they are heretics, wouldn't consider themselves so."

The queen seemed pleased by that answer. "You have a skillful tongue, Captain."

"Can you tell me about this Friar Bastía? Is he an Outworlder, like us? Did he bring Christianity to your people?"

"Perhaps he will discuss this with you directly. His answers are his own as mine are my own."

"You also have a skillful tongue, Your Majesty," said the captain.

She seemed pleased by this as well.

"Is there anything more you can tell me about the flying machine?" the captain asked. "Where it travels? Who the men are who ride in it?"

"It comes and goes in all directions," the queen replied. "I do not know these men, for they merely pass over our lands. But some say it is the property of the Silver Eagle."

"Silver Eagle?"

"Another Outworlder. There are more there than you may realize. You were wise to seek the truth from us. Silver Eagle is a great warlord. His people arrived twenty years ago and conquered the city of Amoloyan. Many of the local tribes worship him as a demigod, but they are a savage and superstitious people. He is of the Knife and Thunderbolt People.”

The shoulder sleeve insignia of the Special Forces is a dagger with three thunderbolts. I was certain that couldn't be a coincidence.

“I notice you all wear his war banner on your right shoulder,” the queen added.

The captain looked at his shoulder. “The American flag?”

“I do not know this word *ah-marican,* but I have been told of the Silver Eagle’s colors. Red and white stripes and a blue field containing many stars. This is the emblem you wear.”

The captain ignored the implied question. “What sort of man is this Silver Eagle?”

“It is said he is severe and ruthless, but just. I have not met him. I only hear the rumors from the savages we encounter.”

“Is Amoloyan far from here?”

“Perhaps two weeks on foot, perhaps three, but to get there you must travel through the forests of Tekuanloyan, and we do not go there. It is a dangerous land with many threats. There are fierce tribes of savages and terrible beasts... and much worse things. The ravenous Children of Mictlāntēcuhtli stalk the forest, as do wraiths.”

“Wraiths?” Captain Brown asked.

“The restless spirits of singularly evil men who drift through the darkness consuming souls and leaving a trail of tortured and mutilated corpses.”

The captain clearly had questions about this—about everything in this world for that matter. Epasotl had been invaluable to us as a guide, but her knowledge was often filtered through a lens of myth and superstition. Here, in the queen, the captain recognized a source of real, valuable intel.

But Queen Skull-Dancer had other ideas. With a glance at the setting sun, she stood. “It grows late, Captain. We must leave you.”

The rest of us stood as well.

“Your information has been most valuable, Your Majesty,” Captain Brown said. “I would very much enjoy speaking with you again.”

"Perhaps," the queen said. "Perhaps we will invite you to visit Kuauchanko. We thank you for your hospitality." She bowed, again touching her forehead, and Captain Brown followed her example.

Wilson led our detail as an honor guard to escort the queen and her retinue of warriors out of Camp Arizona. They mounted their terror birds and sprinted off to the south, but not before the princess caught my eye one last time and gave me a flicker of a smile.

***

Captain Brown sat us down for another family chat after they'd gone. I was expecting him to open with another X-Men reference, but he didn't. This time even the privates were invited, all except a few who were assigned to scan the darkened horizon for any nasties coming our way. We added wood to the fire pit, and sparks drifted into the night sky as we gathered around.

"We've obtained some new intel that's worth sharing with the platoon," the captain began. "I believe it's actionable, but I don't want to make a decision without hearing everyone's input on this, not just team leaders."

That was very un-Army of him, but not unappreciated. This little powwow was starting to feel downright cozy.

"First, though, I must give credit where credit's due. You men performed admirably today. We faced insurmountable odds, and we prevailed. Each man in the platoon did his duty above and beyond. And for that I commend you. We are cavalrymen, and today you demonstrated what that means. I'm proud of you.

"But there's no shortage of difficulties, either. We're down to two dozen combat-effective now, ammo for our heavy support weapons is critical, and today made clear that we simply cannot hold against such a vastly numerically superior force on our own. Additionally, we're barely keeping enough food coming in. We'll have to range progressively farther out to forage and hunt, and that comes with an increased risk."

Sanchez nodded along with all of that. Bullets and beans were his thing, after all. "That said, sir, this was never meant to be home. Just a waystation until we made contact with indigs who might have intel on other humans."

"And so they have," Captain Brown agreed. "The Kuauchanejkej warriors who came to our aid today informed us there's a city, two or three weeks' march away, that has been controlled by American forces for the last two decades. It also appears they have the support of the indigenous population. I believe their leader to be a Special Forces colonel, hence his nickname: 'Silver Eagle.'"

I hadn't made the connection, but in the Army the insignia for a full bird colonel is, you guessed it, a silver eagle.

The news of fellow Americans, and Special Forces no less, not only alive but potentially thriving in wherever this place was that we'd been transported to, got the group into an excited buzz. This was better than anything I'd hoped for. We had just been hoping to find any sort of civilized humans, and we'd done that with the Sugar Skull Gals. But American servicemen? I couldn't wait to set out to join them.

Wilson raised his hand.

"Yes, David?" the captain said.

"Uh, sir, just for the sake of argument, are we sure the dude is American?"

"Our guests said they wore uniforms with the American flag on them."

Wilson nodded. "Right, but anyone can put on a uniform. Especially if there's no Ron Jon's to buy something new. I mean, if they're Americans, why didn't they bring the Huey down to make contact?"

"What other reason would they have to wear an American military uniform?" Sanchez asked.

"To pick up chicks?" Wilson quipped.

As the others laughed, Sanchez furrowed his brow and got back to his point. "My concern isn't that they aren't American, it's that these guys have apparently been here for twenty years and haven't figured out a way home yet."

Captain Brown held up his index finger. "Maybe that's because they haven't considered the direct option like us."

"Maybe," said Clark. "Either way, I'm all for getting back to whatever passes for civilization around here. A city sounds pretty good right about now. It's either that or give up and go native."

Wilson smiled. "After seeing those Sugar Skull Gals up close, going native doesn't sound so bad either."

"Hell yeah, seconded," said Pierce. The two surfers high-fived.

"That's enough," Sanchez grumbled.

"I vote we link up with this colonel," St. James said from the shadows. "I believe I speak for everyone in Alpha Section."

Members of Alpha more than murmured their assent. They were behind St. James all the way.

"We're not voting," Sanchez said. "We're just having a discussion. It will be the captain's decision."

"Why *not* put it to a vote?" St. James said. He stepped forward into the light of the fire. "It's *our* lives we're talking about here. Our future. If Americans have gained a foothold in this shithole, we should join them."

"Hooah!" Wright shouted.

"That's *enough*," Sanchez said in his quiet murder voice. "You're out of line and need to stand down, Staff Sergeant."

St. James took a step back and held out his arms. "I'm just saying. We're a long way from the chain of command. Captain wanted our input, right? Well, that's my input. We vote."

Sanchez gave a look but didn't say anything. With that look, he didn't have to. St. James sat down.

"Your input is noted, Sergeant," Captain Brown said calmly. He didn't even look over at St. James as he spoke. Instead he was inspecting his nails, like there was something disgusting under them. "Traveling to this city will be dangerous. It will take up to three weeks, on foot, with hostile elements the likes of which we haven't encountered before. The SSG queen made that very clear."

By enemies, the captain meant the ravenous undead. And the soul-sucking wraiths, of course. I guess he was saving the fun details for later.

"But the day I give up on getting you men back to your families and loved ones is the day I'm buried," he continued. "That is my sole purpose and my solemn oath to you, as God is my witness."

And that right there was why we'd never mutiny, not even with St. James stirring the shit pot.

If only we'd known then how much he'd be willing to stir it.

****

Captain Brown called me to him as the meeting broke up. "Nephi. A moment."

I hopped up to him. "Sir?"

"I need you to find our little guide and smooth things over. That business with the queen wasn't pretty."

"I wouldn't be surprised if she's not speaking to me. We gravely embarrassed her. I hated doing it."

"It was necessary," Captain Brown said. "She'll get over it. Because you'll see to it that she does."

"I don't know. Chaneque honor is a touchy thing."

He just quirked an eyebrow at me.

"Yessir," I said. "I'll do my best."

"That's what it will take to survive this place and get home, son. Our best. We each of us must give one hundred percent and then some. Every day. Don't forget that. I expect no less."

"One hundred percent and then some. Understood."

"Carry on, trooper."

I nodded and wandered back to my mount, the exhaustion from the day finally catching up to me. I had only two hours before my watch, and all I wanted to do was sleep forever.

Epasotl was sitting on the berm in front of our Humvee, staring off into the night. I couldn't see anything out there without my NVGs, but I knew she could. I sat down beside her.

"Whatcha looking at?" I asked.

Her ears were laid back and she made a soft growling sound.

I ignored it. "I still haven't gotten used to the stars here. Nothing is familiar. I did a lot of stargazing as a kid, knew most all the major constellations. My dad got me a telescope when I was ten. I spent hours gazing through it."

She was still growling.

"What's that one there?" I asked, pointing at a cluster of stars. "It looks like a deer, or a stag maybe, like with huge antlers."

She said nothing. The growling continued, but at such low volume I could feel it more than hear it.

After a few minutes of silence I said, "I'm sorry, Epasotl."

"A master does not apologize to his slave," she hissed.

"I'm not your master, and you're not my slave. You're my friend. Can you forgive me?"

Another long period of silence passed before Epasotl spoke.

"It is not a stag," she said in disgust. "It looks nothing like a stag. It is the Two Snakes."

"What are they doing up there?" I asked.

"They are dancing. They are male and female, separate, but inseparable. Two halves of the same oneness. They are balance and harmony."

We watched the two snakes dancing for a long time.

"Can you forgive me?" I asked again.

"There is nothing to forgive. I forgot my place and shamed myself. Shame upon shame. I am your slave. It is correct for me to remember my place."

"No, Epasotl. Dammit. You're my friend."

She turned to me, her eyes glowing in the starlight. "If you were my true friend, you would grant me an honorable death and end my shame."

"Guess I'm not that good of a friend then. What about finding honor in life instead of death?"

"That is foolishness. The gods do not care how you live, only how you die."

I thought briefly of the friar the queen had mentioned, which led me to thoughts of my own religion. One I hadn't exactly been keeping all that closely. I hadn't even so much as thought to pray this entire time. Not once. But now, I was.

"Yeah, well, that's not how my god sees it," I said. "In fact, he let himself die a death of shame so that we could live."

Epasotl sounded like she was hacking up a hairball. Apparently the thought disgusted her. "How can you worship a dead god? A god who died in shame?"

"Because…" I began, knowing the answer I'd been taught and yet not being sure how much I believed it. Not knowing how much of me was just… going through the motions. But it felt like something Epasotl needed to hear if she was ever going to overcome this destructive need to end her life in order to find worth. "Because only through his shameful death did he save us from death and shame."

"I do not understand."

I laughed. "Neither do I, sometimes."

"You are very strange, Ben-Ette."

"Look who's talking."

I ruffled the hair on her head and we watched the stars together in silence.

CHAPTER 16

Captain Brown decided we were setting out asap to find this "Silver Eagle." Though I got the sense that he would have liked to have gotten more information from the queen before leaving our new friends behind entirely. Not to mention meet the friar.

The good news for us was that there was no need to spend days breaking our backs trying to clear out all the dead giants. Or waste our limited fuel trying to burn away the dead. We'd leave body detail to the abundant scavengers, many of whom had already gotten started. That, unfortunately, scared any game away. Which made the arrival of our skull-faced allies the next morning, loaded down with food, even more welcome.

Most every guy in the platoon continued to refer to the Kuauchanejkej as the Sugar Skull Gals, or SSG, like they were some kind of pop band, but the captain insisted that we use their proper name in their presence. The gift of tongues was no help here, so the guys had to practice, and more than one came to me for help or for confirmation that they were getting it right.

The translation thing was still weird to me. To my ear, the Kuauchanejkej were speaking a singsong dialect of Nahuatl that sounded very old—only, since I'm not fluent, the words that I didn't understand came out as English. To everyone else, they spoke plain old English all the time, with the occasional untranslatable word thrown in—mostly proper names, but a few other things too, like animals and plants specific to this world.

Sanchez had us hard at work, preparing to roll out, our faces covered with our shirts or whatever else we could fashion to keep the stink out of our noses, when a dozen Kuauchanejkej riders, led by the princess, came riding straight up the ramp like we were old friends. Unlike us, they pretended not to notice the atrocious stench rising from the battlefield.

Captain Brown welcomed them warmly and invited them to sit around the fire pit with him and Sanchez. The smoke from the fire made it so you could almost ignore the giant stink. Almost.

We wanted to gawk, naturally, but our NCOs kept us busy. I lucked out, however. Queen Skull-Dancer was not present, but she had instructed her daughter that "the one who speaks" should attend.

That, it turned out, was me.

"The Gift of Tongues is bestowed on Outworlders by Tezcatlipoca," the princess explained, "and he is an evil and capricious devil who is not to be trusted. It is good you have a man among you who speaks our tongue without magical aid. It will protect us from Tezcatlipoca's mischief."

Her name was *Siuapilxochicuauhtli*, which literally meant "Princess Flower-Eagle," a translation that pales in contrast to its meaning, which is a poetic expression of the majesty of an eagle and the simple beauty of a flower united. I thought the name suited her. She was fierce, mysterious, and, yes, beautiful.

I tried not to stare.

"We thank you for the gift of food," Captain Brown began. "And once again, for your assistance in the battle against the giants."

"The Quinametzin sent a large battle host, but not the largest we have seen," Flower-Eagle replied. "It may take them time to gather a new army, but they will return. This time they will not attack you so boldly as before, but will use stratagems to defeat your defenses."

"When that day comes, Your Highness, they won't find us here," the captain said. "I intend to lead my men to the city of Amoloyan. But I would very much like to know more about this Silver Eagle, the city, and how we might reach it."

"I am sorry, but we know little of the Knife and Thunderbolt tribe," Flower-Eagle replied. "While we sometimes make raids into Tekuanloyan to hunt the Children of Mictlāntēcuhtli, we have little contact with the tribes that live in those forests. They are savage peoples."

"Your mother mentioned wraiths," the captain said. "What do you know of them?"

"Only stories. They stalk the forest, invisible in the night, and steal the souls of the living. Their victims are often found terribly mutilated, for the wraiths hate all life and delight in torture and desecration. It is said they cannot be destroyed by any means known to man. Only Silver Eagle can defeat them, by binding them to the underworld with his magic."

And to think my family worried about me going to *Panama*.

Flower-Eagle hadn't come just to deliver food and chat around a fire. After a bit more small talk, she got to her real reason for coming. "My queen believed you would go to seek out Silver Eagle," she said. "It is the obvious choice. But the way is hard and very dangerous. My people can make it easier for you. We will provide you a guide and help you avoid pitfalls unknown to you."

Captain Brown nodded his thanks. "We would appreciate that. You have been a tremendous help already. I would like to know if there is some way we can repay you. As friends."

I noticed how the other warriors exchanged looks. Flower Eagle's reply came quickly.

"There is," she said. "We have need of your help in an urgent matter."

I'd had a feeling that all of this wasn't just out of the kindness of their candy-coated hearts. Not that I was opposed to helping them. They'd basically saved our collective butts. Now they'd likely seen us making our preparations to leave and figured this was their chance to get a favor back.

Captain Brown was gracious as ever. "What is it that we can help you with?"

The problem, as Flower-Eagle laid it out for us, turned out to be… *witches*.

"But the *tlahuelpuchi* are not *mere* witches," she went on. "They are extremely powerful creatures, they feed on the blood of infants and children, and they can assume animal form at will. They have plagued us for generations. So much so that suffering the theft of our daughters has become a way of life for us. Our only respite is that they are few in number. But we are powerless against them."

"If that's the case," Captain Brown said, "what is it that makes you believe we might fare any better?"

"Because you are men. Warriors." As she said this, Flower-Eagle turned and looked directly at me.

I laughed despite myself, feeling totally unworthy of the stock she was apparently putting in me. And in us. "I've seen you fight," I said. "You're just as much warriors as we are."

"No. You are *men*. The *tlahuelpuchi* cannot be killed by women, and our men have foresworn violence. The *tlahuelpuchi* are powerful, but they are few. They hunt only at night in the depths of darkness. To destroy them for us would be a great blessing to my sisters and I."

Sanchez, who had been watching Brown closely, now spoke quietly to the captain, his voice so low that I barely heard it. "Sir… is this necessary? We could make straight for the city. It may be better not to get entangled in native affairs." I was surprised to hear our platoon sergeant so openly question the plan. That wasn't like him. I learned the reason for his words, though, when he added: "I'm worried about Alpha Section. Something's gotten into them. They're on the edge."

The captain answered Sanchez and Flower-Eagle together. "It is still my desire that our two peoples be friends. We will go and make every attempt within our power to return the favor you bestowed on us in coming to our aid in battle. And then… we will gladly accept your guidance in safely reaching Silver Eagle."

I appreciated how Captain Brown made it clear that our plan was still getting to the colonel. No matter what else happened, the plan was to make it back home.

The warriors with Flower-Eagle had difficulty hiding their excitement and pleasure at this decision. But the princess herself remained calm and poised. "Your help in this matter is greatly appreciated."

With that settled, Flower-Eagle rose.

"Your Highness," Captain Brown said quickly. "If you could spare another moment, there are just a few more things I would like to clarify."

She sat. "Speak what is on your mind."

"How far is it to your domain?"

"For you, it is a two-day journey on foot. Our birds do not allow strangers to ride them."

Captain Brown nodded. "We have mounts of our own. When do you intend to leave?"

She looked surprised by the question. "We leave as soon as possible."

The captain smiled politely. "Then we will hasten our preparations. We should be good to go within..." He looked up at Sanchez.

"Two hours, sir. We've got enough fuel to get the trucks there if that's the case. After that, though... we gotta be real careful with our routing."

"Anything else?" asked the princess.

I saw Captain Brown hesitate, as though he wasn't sure he wanted to ask the next question. I was glad he did, though. It was eating at me, too.

"You said... you said that there are no males among your people?"

"There are not."

"And yet, you've lived for generations..."

Flower-Eagle looked right at me, and I grew redder and hotter the longer she spoke. "If a woman wishes to have a child, she is free to marry and leave the tribe. It is understood that any daughters she births are to be sent home. This does not always happen, but we have persevered. You will soon see. I should tell you that a great honor is being bestowed upon you. Of the eyes of men, few have seen what you soon will."

"Of the honor, I am sure of it," Brown said.

CHAPTER 17

"I do not like you going with the skull-faced bird-women," Epasotl said.

We were in the back of my mount, where I was searching for any additional NVG batteries to give to Sanchez, who would distribute them so everyone could keep seeing in the dark when we went to take on these "witches." Though Sanchez had specifically instructed me not to mention the *tlahuelpuchi* to anyone just yet. Even outside of Alpha, not everyone was happy about delaying our journey to what Clark had called "civilization," and Sanchez didn't want to give anyone additional reasons to grumble.

Word about the *all-women village* had spread, however. Quickly. There was no grumbling about that.

"You're talking like we're gonna leave you here, Epasotl," I said. "You're coming with us. We wouldn't abandon you."

"Yes, but Holy James and his people will look at me," she said. "I do not like it."

That was, unfortunately, true. Epasotl was not exactly welcomed by the Kuauchanejkej. They endured her, perhaps were even amused by her, but that was in large part because they were our guests inside Camp Arizona. Now we were going to their house, and that meant we didn't set the rules for what was or wasn't acceptable company. We assumed Epasotl was not.

The plan for that was to keep her with Alpha, who would be the last truck in the convoy. They would already be keeping an eye out for pursuers, and when we got where we were going they would post outside the village and serve as a QRF in case this was all some sort of trap by the SSG men. You know, a scenario where there really *are* male warriors and they sent their wives out to lure us in so they could kill us, eat us, and shrink our heads.

It's only paranoia if it isn't true, and while we all liked the Sugar Skull Gals, we kept our guards up all the same.

There was some debate about whether or not to have Alpha and the others make their way to the village later, but Captain Brown opted to have them stay and continue guarding the trucks. That made a certain amount of sense, but I also wondered if the captain just didn't trust Alpha to behave themselves. I know I didn't. I'd seen how they'd handled the Chaneque village, and I didn't want to see a repeat if St. James and his merry band of psychopaths decided they didn't like the Kuauchanejkej accommodations.

"Captain Brown or Sergeant Sanchez are riding back there too," I said to Epasotl. "They'll be watching out for you. It's for your own safety."

"I do not think Little Kahuna likes me," Epasotl said of Sanchez.

"He likes you just fine. He's just a grumpy old coot. We all value everything you've done to help us."

She hopped out of the back and watched me with her large eyes.

"Be safe, Ben-Ette," she said.

"I didn't know you cared."

"I care. We are friends."

Before I knew it, Wilson was standing next to me with his buff arms trapping me in a side hug. "Damn right, little sister. Slap me some skin!"

She smiled and obliged, then flashed me a shaka. "Hang loose, bro-ski."

"Epasotl's so rad," Wilson said. "I can't believe you wanted to kill her."

"I never wanted—" but then Wilson slapped me hard on the arm and went off to square away his own gear.

The lead element of the convoy was composed of nearly all of Bravo and Charlie Sections combined, with Sergeant Takahashi serving as team leader and Wilson as ATL. As the black sun rose over the horizon in the east, we formed up and rolled down the ramp exiting the hill fort. Goodbye, Camp Arizona. Sorry about the mess.

The princess and her riders formed a defensive screen around us as we drove out onto the open savanna. From my place in the turret, I saw that Flower-Eagle was riding her bird nearby. I'd voiced my concern about the wolf-vultures, but she assured me the predators tended to steer clear of her people's mounts. Hunting the feathered lizards was a sport for them, she explained, and her people could easily chase one down and spear it with their long lances if needed. Which, in fact, they soon did. We feasted on it that evening.

Thank goodness for those tiny little bottles of Tabasco sauce that came in our MREs. Flower-Eagle was less impressed with the stuff, though.

I wasn't the only guy getting friendly with some of the Sugar Skull Gals. Wilson kept up a cheerful banter with one of the warriors, a woman whose name translated as "Dressed-in-Stars." She was tall for her people and looked like she could snap any one of us in half with her bare hands. She had clearly taken a liking to the hulking, easygoing sergeant.

The drive was faster than if we'd have to hump, but I wouldn't call it fast. The terrain slowed us down more than we'd anticipated. There were a lot of hidden rocks and boulders beneath the waving savanna, and going too fast threatened to cause damage that we might not be able to repair. By nightfall, we were still a ways off from our destination. We made camp, and the warriors and their birds slept around us in a large circle, guarding us protectively inside their perimeter. Captain Brown had tried to impress upon Flower-Eagle how they would be safer letting our trucks serve as the outer perimeter, but she wasn't having it. Sergeant Takahashi kept a rotating watch all the same, with two of us always awake.

I was exhausted, but perked up when I realized that Flower-Eagle had a mind to keep watch with me. Well, not exactly *with* me, but she was keeping a watch of her own near her mount. Private Anderson was at his truck and I was at my own, our eyes opened wide in the darkness. We weren't using our NVGs since batteries were scarce and we'd need them later. *For the witches.* I wasn't particularly looking forward to that and was trying not to think about it too much. Maybe the whole thing was superstitious nonsense, but somehow, I didn't think so. Not after everything that had happened so far.

It was a moonless night, but the stars were bright enough to make out some detail, and I saw Flower-Eagle a short distance from her sleeping mount, just the silhouette of her, standing on one leg and leaning on her lance. Dredging up my courage, I approached her.

She acknowledged my presence with a slight turn of her head. She wasn't wearing the elaborate feathered headdress but was still dressed in the padded cloth armor they all wore. Her long, jet-black hair was tied back in a topknot.

We stood beside each other in silence for a time, watching the dark stretch of rolling grasslands. I always forgot how small she was until I was standing directly beside her. She had an imposing presence, but her build was more delicate than most of the other warriors. Not that she was delicate, of course. Anything but.

I was trying to think of something clever to say, but I'm not good at being clever or witty, especially around women. I settled for just being me.

"Still up?" I asked. "Something out there have your attention?"

She nodded. "There is a small flock of tlahuītequini that circles us warily." She meant the little lizard-things. "They come close, then dart away. They will not attack us tonight."

"Because of your birds."

"Yes," she answered, "and because they know us to be a danger. But they do not know your trucks, and they are curious."

"Are they smart animals?"

"Oh yes, very much so. They hunt like wolves, but with even greater cunning. Usually their flocks are small, but sometimes many flocks will work together to take down large prey or a herd."

I explained how we had found the remains of the Buffalo Soldiers. She nodded and said she knew of this band of Outworlders. One of the horse soldiers had escaped and had found refuge with her people. He was married to a Kuauchanejkej woman now, and she was expecting.

"I thought you didn't have men in your community?" I said, surprised.

She shook her head. "Few are to be trusted," she replied. "I mean no offense. And he does not live in our community. There is another village, far from our own, where men and those women seeking to rear children live. This man was found by our scouts. He was alone, his people slaughtered. He was… harmless."

I said that made sense. It also made some kind of sense as to why they didn't ask him or the other men of this—breeding village, I guess—to go after the witches. But not a whole lot of it. Why us, if they already had men? And if they had men, why were the women the ones doing the battle? Had Captain Brown gotten suckered into doing a hard job the locals knew better than to try? Were we the sacrificial lambs?

We lapsed into silence again, but despite all the questions in my mind, it wasn't uncomfortable.

"Where is the moon?" I asked after a time. I had asked Epasotl this before, but her answers always involved the feats and tricks of this god or the other. I was hoping Flower-Eagle could give me something more… substantial. "I haven't seen the moon since we arrived, and it's been over a month."

"I know only tales of the moon," Eagle-Flower said. "Legends say the sun swallowed it when Tezcatlipoca created this world. What did it look like?"

Well, so much for that. Still… we were talking.

This place was so weird, though. No moon. No moon, and a black sun. And constellations unlike any I'd ever seen before. Somehow it was the changes to the sky that hit me the hardest. These things were eternal constants that I'd always taken for granted as being… well, eternally constant. Until now, when they weren't anymore.

"The moon is a silver disk that lights the night sky," I said. "About the same size as the sun. Sometimes it's round and full, and very bright—though still easy enough to look directly at it—and other times it's a crescent-shape, like a fingernail." I explained how the phases worked and how it was really a great celestial object with steep mountains and deep valleys.

"It sounds very beautiful," she said, and she asked if anyone lived on it, and I said no, but my people had traveled to it and walked on its surface. I wasn't sure if she believed me, but she took an interest and began peppering me with questions about my world.

After I'd told her a bit about our modern age of fighter jets, television sitcoms, and VCRs, she frowned. "You come from a different world than Curly." At my look of confusion, she added: "The Outworlder who found my people."

Curly must be the name of the cavalryman who had escaped the slaughter of the Buffalo Soldiers.

"Same world," I said. "Different time. He comes from about a hundred years in our past."

"He has warned us not to trust the pale-faced Outworlders. But your warlord is painted, like Curly, and so are some of your warriors, and I sense no enmity. And Curly says only his father was painted, though his mother's face was not pale."

Painted was apparently her way of saying *Black*.

"Was Curly's mother Indian?" I asked.

"I do not know what Indian is. He said she was Navajo."

I nodded. "Where I come from, *when* I come from, we don't care about the color of a man's skin, only the content of his character. But Curly comes from a different time in our world, and he has good reason not to trust pale-faced people like me. His father's people were slaves once, and there was a great war between the, uh, pale faces, to free his people. The pale faces also treated his mother's people extremely unfairly. It was a sad time in our history."

Eagle-Flower thought about that for a while as she surveyed the gently waving stalks of grass under the starlight.

"How do you speak my language?" she asked after a while. "I have wondered much about that."

I explained about the two years I spent in Mexico on my proselytizing mission.

"So you are a holy man, like our Friar Bastía." She frowned. "Then you cannot marry. That is a great and unfortunate sacrifice."

"Oh—no," I said quickly. "It was only for two years. I do hope to marry and have a family." I felt my cheeks flushing, and was glad it was dark. "Uh, someday, that is. You said that your, uh, warriors marry?"

She seemed not to notice my embarrassment. "Some. When their fighting days are over. It is hard to fight well when carrying a child in your belly."

"And your men?" I asked. "I know they don't live in your village, but do they fight?"

"No. Our men do not make war. They are sworn to live a life of peace."

That struck me as odd, given how martial the women were.

"In the past," Flower-Eagle explained, "our men were great warriors. Greater than us by far. They bathed in the blood of their enemies and carried a lust for battle always in their hearts. The tribes raided and warred against each other constantly. Then an Outworlder came, a man much like Friar Bastía. He taught them the way of peace. He made the men bury their arms and swear an oath to never pick up a weapon again. Each generation renews that oath."

I wondered how it was that not even one of these guys broke their oaths. For a lot of men, fighting is as natural as breathing. "But you still need to protect yourselves," I said. "This land isn't a peaceful one."

"That is why we took up the responsibility," Flower-Eagle said of herself and the other bird-women. "That is why we live as a separate tribe and protect those who will not fight. Or cannot. It is a great honor."

"You are very... brave," I said. I almost slipped up and said "beautiful."

She gave a noncommittal grunt.

What the heck. I decided to risk it. "And very beautiful."

She laughed. "You have not seen me without my war paint. Perhaps I am hideous."

"I seriously doubt that, Your Highness."

"Your form of address is flattering, but it is not our custom. You may simply call me by my name."

"Siuapilxochicuauhtli, then," I said.

"My friends call me Xochi."

"Am I your friend?" I asked.

She smiled, and the starlight danced in her eyes. "I would like you to be."

***

We were completely unprepared for what we encountered when we arrived at Kuauchanko. We drove the trucks as far as we could into a forest of truly towering trees, but finally had to dismount and leave them to form a base camp. By that time, Jensen had died from his wounds. We stuck around long enough to bury him and say a few words. No one had really expected him to make it, and no one acted all that hurt about it as Captain Brown spoke a eulogy. Jensen was a popular enough guy, too. I think, after all we'd just been through, it was just getting easier to lose people. Like your mind just accepted it and moved on. That scared me a little.

I wondered if it would all come rushing over me like an emotional bill demanding to be paid later on down the road.

There was some debate over whether the other wounded—Douglas in particular—would be better off being carried on a litter to the village or left with the trucks. Doc had the final say, and his suspicious nature won out.

"We don't know what's waiting for us in this village," he told Captain Brown quietly. We were already scouting to be sure it was safe. "If you have to break or get in a firefight, I'm worried Douglas might get lost in the shuffle—or worse, sustain another injury. He's a tough SOB but he's not invincible. That'll put him in the grave. Right now, my gear is here and I have him stable. I'd like to keep it that way."

Brown said it was Doc's call, so that was that. Alpha Squad and Epasotl also remained in place with Doc and Douglas. Sanchez stayed as well. I think he would have liked to come, but he was doing his job and taking stock of where we stood on fuel and supplies after our sojourn. And maybe he was keeping an eye on Alpha, too. The rest of us got underneath our rucks and followed the Sugar Skull Gals through the woods.

After a hike, we finally saw the village... *above* us. Though it was large enough to spread over several acres, it was perched atop the boughs of trees. Or atop *one* tree, Flower-Eagle claimed. She explained that as the tree grew, its boughs threw shoots downward, and these shoots ultimately formed great trunks that supported its massive branches, each wide enough to form the avenues of the elevated community. The tree was named *Nantsin*, which meant "Beloved Mother."

All of us craned our necks upward to take in the spectacle.

"Righteous," Wilson said. I noticed that Dressed-in-Stars was standing with him.

"Marvelous." Captain Brown sounded impressed, but he was probably keeping his eyes open for ambushes and developing a plan to kill everyone as much as take in the beauty of it all in that Ranger brain of his.

From our vantage point down on the ground, I could see little apart from their "buildings," which were simple egg-shaped structures constructed of straw and woven branches, packed with hardened mud and decorated with bright feathers. They reminded me of the domed nests wrens built.

There was activity on the ground, too. Beneath the trees, I was surprised to see men hard at work tending to plots of corn, squash, and other vegetables. I was growing increasingly confused at their role in this society. Were they outcasts? Breeders? Or gardeners? They seemed cheerful, waving and smiling as Princess Flower-Eagle —Princess *Xochi*—and her entourage led us into their midst. If they were surprised or wary of us Outworlders, they didn't show it.

Xochi stopped before a solidly built man who was clearly waiting for us. He wore a loincloth and multicolored cape draped off one shoulder. Xochi introduced him to us as Sipaktli, her mother's chief consort.

Sipaktli knelt before us, bowed low to the ground, then scooped up some earth and kissed it. "You have tired yourself in coming," he said.

Captain Brown was unsure how to respond, and Xochi quickly explained that Sipaktli's gesture, which they called "eating of the earth," was reserved for honored guests and that we need only bow slightly in reply.

I was glad when Captain Brown voiced the question on my mind. "I thought there were no men in your village," he said.

"Sipaktli is no longer a man as you understand it. He is a eunuch. These other men that you see have traveled from the nearest village to see to our crops. The honor soon to be bestowed on you remains intact. You will dine with my mother the queen above the earth."

Apparently Xochi had misread Captain Brown's confusion as being insulted by the presence of other men.

"I took no offense," Brown clarified.

"Sipaktli will take care of you," she said.

"Does your mother have many… consorts?" I asked, unsure what the point of having eunuch consorts would be.

"Of course," said Xochi. "She is queen."

"And how does that work? I thought the women left when they wanted to have children."

"Yes, but she is queen. Our queen must remain among us. Her husband lives apart from her."

"Your father?"

"Yes, though I have never known him."

"Oh… sorry. About that."

She smiled softly. "The consorts are all fathers to me. Now, you must bathe, rest, and eat. But not too much! We will feast tonight."

Xochi departed, and Sipaktli motioned for us to follow him. He led us to a stone building below the village with a domed furnace set on the outside of one wall. The stones radiated with heat.

"This is the bathhouse. Please bathe," he said. "While you do, we will have your clothes cleaned."

The offer was gracious and hospitable, but I knew we also stank to high heaven, and I couldn't help but feel he had put a bit too much emphasis on the word "please."

As we looked to Captain Brown for his response, a middle-aged woman walked past us with a smile and a bow. She disrobed, entirely without shame, and then entered the bathhouse.

"Don't have to tell me twice," Wilson said. He was already stripping out of his gear with all the eagerness of a surfer taking off his shirt to go and catch a wave.

"We need to guard our equipment," said Takahashi. "García, Bennett, and Grant will go first."

"But there's a naked woman in there," I said.

"I was just about to say that," Wilson said. "Let me take Bennett's place, Tak."

"You can join him," Takahashi relented. "But Bennett goes too."

"It just seems… inappropriate, is all."

"Bennett, you stink," Wilson said. "Close your virgin eyes if you have to, but you're going in there."

"Yes, Sergeant."

I undressed down to my boxers and made to enter the bathhouse, but Sipaktli held out a hand and pointed to my underwear. I glanced at Wilson, who was already standing naked as a jaybird.

"When in Rome, trooper," he said.

Sighing, I slipped out of my boxers and tossed them on the growing pile of clothes, and then went inside with the others.

It was like walking into a wall of steam. A stone cistern set against one wall belched it forth constantly, but though the air was hot and incredibly humid, it was pleasantly scented with herbs. There was no bathing pool, as I had expected. The woman, whose eyes never met ours, motioned for us to sit in a small circle on mats woven from reeds.

Wilson stretched and sighed in contentment. García seemed relaxed as well. Grant gave me a questioning look, and I shrugged. I had no idea where Captain Brown was. Probably pressing anyone he could find for intel.

The woman picked up a bundle of grass, then walked along behind us, thwacking us with it. Not so hard it hurt, but not gently either. I wasn't sure what this had to do with getting clean, but it seemed important to her that we were all soundly thrashed. Next she filled a gourd with the steaming water and doused us each over the head and shoulders. I'd almost forgotten how good hot water felt after weeks of being in the field. I did my best to try and relax.

It was the next phase of her ritual that made me the most uncomfortable: the washing. She rubbed each of us down, not with a cloth, but with her bare hands—along with some scented powder. I protested while standing in line for my turn, but she was quite stern. When Wilson ordered me to obey, I endured the embarrassment like a good trooper.

It wasn't so bad, honestly. And it felt incredible to be clean again.

CHAPTER 18

I had thought we would get our clothes back right away. I was wrong. When our washing was complete, we were given loincloths and capes, just like Sipaktli wore. Just like all the men I'd seen so far wore, though the cape was apparently optional. The women had only a bit more variety: they wore a blouse and skirt with a sash, or a long tunic, or in some cases just the skirt and sash with nothing covering their upper torsos aside from intricate tattoos. The youngest children, I would soon learn, all toddled around completely naked. There were only girls here. The boys all stayed in the other villages until they were old enough to take a turn to help with the farming and then… catch a warrior woman's eye, I guess.

Sipaktli had to show us how to tie the loincloths while the second shift of bathers got scrubbed down. The cape was easier—it attached with a gold or bronze cloak pin—but Sipaktli had to demonstrate how it could be worn under the left arm and fastened over the right shoulder, cast back over both shoulders, or draped over the left shoulder. I felt mildly ridiculous in the getup, but it suited Wilson, who looked like a Greek god.

We had just finished dressing when Friar Tuck came waddling toward us with a great beaming smile. I mean Friar Bastía, of course, but the middle-aged rotund Franciscan would've fit into any production of *Robin Hood* perfectly. His hair was neatly trimmed and carefully tonsured, and his clean-shaven cheeks glowed. He wasted no time embracing each of us, whether we welcomed it or not.

"Peace be with you," he said, stepping back.

"And also with you," García answered. Apparently that was the proper reply.

"I have heard some of your story," the friar said, "but I would like to hear more. I meet so few people from my world. At least, I assume you are from my world. There are so many worlds. God is truly incomprehensible in the breadth of his creation." He waved us to follow him. "Come, come, join us. The feast is being prepared, but we can rest and talk. Yes, so many things to discuss."

I was about to protest that we needed to wait for the other bathers when Captain Brown, Takahashi, and the others stepped out of the bathhouse to receive their own native dress.

"I've been looking forward to greeting you," Brown told the friar.

The friar waited patiently for the rest of our team to get fitted and taught how to attach the capes—they had less trouble with it than I had—and as we stood there freshly scrubbed and in clean clothes, I couldn't help but think of Alpha, Doc, Sanchez, and Douglas still sitting back with the trucks.

Sucked to be them right now.

"Grant and Anderson, watch our rucks and gear while the other shifts bathe," Takahashi said once he was dressed. "*And* after, for that matter. No one touches anything. We'll rotate guards. The rest of you keep your rifles with you at all times."

"Oh, your things will be quite safe," Bastía said.

"All the same, Father, we'd prefer to keep an eye on it."

"Of course, of course. Soldiers are always the same, no matter when or where, always cautious. But you do not need to carry your *arcabuces*," he said. "That would be most impolite and offend your hosts. You are under their protection."

Takahashi looked to Brown, who nodded his approval. The sergeant grimaced but ordered us to stack our weapons.

We followed the friar as he waddled under the great boughs of the tree to a sort of ground-level village square, alive with activity. A wide pit of coals sat at its center, and several deer roasted on spits. Throngs of villagers were scattered about, some sitting in small groups while others worked to prepare some sort of feast. Most paused in what they were doing to look upon us with curiosity. I searched for Xochi but couldn't find her. I wasn't sure I'd even recognize her without her war paint.

The friar led us to a wooden platform and I could tell right away that it was some sort of elevator to the treetops. Ropes, each easily six inches in diameter, were connected to a series of pulleys overhead. "Come, come," he said, encouraging us all to step on before nodding to a man who attended a gear wheel.

The man whistled, and two teenage boys came running. The trio turned the wheel and we began to rise up off the ground.

There were no guardrails, and all of us kept to the center of the gently rocking platform. All except the friar, who held on to a stabilizing rope and looked unfazed, and Wilson, who was practically leaning over the edge and saying things like "Righteous" until Sergeant Takahashi had had enough and pulled him back from the edge.

"That's enough to give me a heart attack."

Wilson had a huge smile on his face. "Yeah, bro, me too."

The view was spectacular. We quickly rose above the canopy formed by the smaller trees and found ourselves in the domain of clouds and birds. From here we could see other mega trees like the one we were climbing, but they were spaced out and appeared like giants standing in a sprawling mist. I tried to get my bearings and look for some landmarks like the savanna or the fort, but it was just trees. A seemingly endless forest.

The wind blew a cool and comfortable breeze that carried a freshness rivaled only by ocean shores.

"You've been to the sacred village before, I take it?" Captain Brown asked the friar.

Bastía smiled. "I have, but not with the honor that you now experience. They don't see me as a man because of my vows. I am the same as one of their eunuchs. You must be careful—all of you—not to give the slightest offense. The reverence they have for this place is enough to make even the smallest indiscretion seem of great magnitude."

"I appreciate the warning, Father," Captain Brown said.

I swallowed. If the Gift of Tongues fell short, as it sometimes did, and I was asked to do any translating, I was going to have to be extremely careful not to cause an international incident.

After a two-minute ride, we came to a halt, stepped off onto a broad-planked boardwalk, and looked around. Everyone up here was female, warriors painted with the now-familiar skull face. They stopped and nodded respectfully as we passed them, but I could tell they watched us carefully.

Queen Skull-Dancer was on a dais off to one side, perched on the edge of a throne carved from a block of basalt. It must have been hell getting that thing up here. Three eunuchs attended her, and four warriors in full battle dress flanked her. The dais also held a low table laden with fruit, sweet corn mush wrapped in leaves, and several gourds. A young woman, almost a girl really, sat on one corner of the dais playing a clay flute.

Bastía took us straight to the queen, but we had to wait below the dais until a break occurred in a conversation she was having with one of her warriors. Only then did she smile at us and motion to the table.

"You have tired yourself in coming," she said. "Please, sit and be comfortable." She wore heavy gold earrings studded with rubies, and her hair was braided and piled atop her head, affixed with gold clasps. Her richly embroidered blouse and skirt were also threaded with gold, and a gold crucifix hung around her neck. It struck me that there was a lot of gold on display in the village.

She returned to her private conversation, and we settled around the table. Wilson reached for a gourd, but Takahashi held out his hand. "No drinking."

"Just wanted a taste, bro," Wilson complained.

"Your companion is wise." Bastía laughed. "Octli is strong drink. Moderation is a virtue." He took an overly large gulp from his own gourd despite his declaration. "So tell me, from whence do you come?"

Brown, who had been waiting to get to talking, answered. "We are from the nation of the United States, Father, in the year 1989."

"1989!" Bastía exclaimed. "I was wrenched out of New Spain in 1576."

"How long have you been in this world?" Brown asked.

"I stopped counting the years long ago, my son," Bastía said. "I was a young man then, barely just ordained. And now I've grown old and fat. But I am happy! God is great and has blessed me with a large flock to tend."

"Are all the Kuauchanejkej converted?" I asked.

"No, no, heavens no." Bastía laughed and then took another long drink from his gourd. "Some, yes, a goodly number, including the royal family—but not all. Many still cling to the old beliefs. But we coexist in peace. They wait for Quetzalcoatl's return, who they believe is their ancestor, but they don't worship the dark gods, thank the Lord. There is no human sacrifice or ritual torture here among the Kuauchanejkej, unlike many of the other peoples of this world."

"When you say 'peoples'..." Brown said. "Do you mean humans?"

The friar frowned. "Some are human. Descendants of Outworlders. The Kuauchanejkej are such. But there are also more savage types—what my people would have called barbarians. The cruelest and foulest abominations are the native species. Odd perversions of humanity. Little men mixed with cats and the like."

Wilson and I exchanged a look. The friar was definitely referring to Epasotl's race. I wondered how many more such "foul" races lived in this land.

"From your experience," Brown continued, "is this land, this world, occupied primarily by humans, or is it mostly these other races?"

"When it comes to the wider world, it is difficult for me to say. Around *here*, as you can see, the peoples are mostly human. There is even an entire city of Outworlders gathered in a city not many days' travel from here. A place of great wonders, much smaller than Paris or Rome, yet still fit for a king. But I assure you, you find yourselves among the best of humankind right here and right now."

"You flatter us," said one of the skull-faced warriors.

"Flattery in vanity. I strive to let my yes be yes and my no be no. It is the truth."

Sergeant Takahashi joined the conversation with a question of his own. "Friar, the Kuauchanejkej had a large army when they came to our rescue. This community doesn't seem large enough to sustain that many warriors."

"This village is but one of many," Bastía said. "It is special, because it is where the queen resides with her warriors, but I travel from village to village tending to my flock, which extends far across the land."

"All the warriors are concentrated here?" Brown asked.

Friar Bastía enjoyed talking and seemed to enjoy being questioned. He was, in general, a happy, agreeable man. It was clear to me that Captain Brown and Sergeant Takahashi were pumping him for military intel, but the friar either didn't notice or didn't care.

"That would be foolish, would it not?" he said. "No, there are warriors stationed among the villages and at outposts throughout the queen's realm. But they all come here when summoned! She is greatly loved." He shielded his mouth with his hand and added, "But not so much that *some* of those warriors stationed at the villages don't give up their duty to find pleasure in the holy sacrament of marriage."

He smiled and raised a gourd to the queen to toast her.

Queen Skull-Dancer smiled back at him. "Do not listen to the honey-tongued priest," she said. "I am a bitter old tyrant."

"But still as beautiful as when you rescued me from the cookpots of the White River People, my daughter," Bastía said with a wink.

"Your sight grows dim, Father," the queen replied, but her amber eyes sparkled like the gems in her hair.

***

As much as Captain Brown wanted to gather intel about Silver Eagle and this new world at large, the friar was the only one who seemed willing to talk. It was clear that, as far as the queen and her people were concerned, the feast needed to run its course before any business would be attended to. I did hear the captain ask about the Buffalo Soldier who had been taken in and married off. He desperately wanted to meet the man. But the friar was sad to inform Brown that Curly was in another village, according to custom.

"Only eunuchs, or those like myself who have proven their vow of celibacy, are allowed to remain long in such close proximity to this place," the friar explained. "Perhaps another time."

"I would like that," said Brown. "Very much."

Torches and lanterns were lit as the evening wore on, with music and dancing and far too much excellent food. The octli poured freely, and Sergeant Takahashi eventually relented and gave us the night off. Wilson found Dressed-in-Stars and wasn't seen again until the next morning.

But despite the honor of being in the boughs of the sacred village, and the satisfaction of eating real, mouth-watering food, after a time I felt there wasn't much else to do, so I took the rope elevator down to relieve Grant and Anderson.

I was perched atop our rucks, listening to the music and laughter from afar, when a young woman approached me carrying two steaming cups. Her hair was in long braids and she wore an embroidered blouse and skirt tied with a red sash. Her face would have been considered beautiful, if not for the terrible scar that ran from her right temple to the corner of her lip. The scar pulled at the side of her mouth, making her smile slightly lopsided. I noticed she turned her head as she approached to try and hide the disfigurement.

"They said you do not drink octli," she said shyly, "so I have brought you chocolate."

I recognized the voice at once.

"Xochi! I was looking for you."

"Were you?" she asked, sitting beside me and handing me a cup. She sat on my right side and kept her face turned so I couldn't see her scar.

"I was," I said. "I was hoping you'd join us. I met your sisters, but you never came."

"I am not welcome at my mother's table," she said.

I furrowed my brow in confusion. Wasn't she her mother's champion? I asked as much.

"I am not her champion. I am young and proving myself. As a princess I sometimes act as her representative. But as a daughter I am not in favor. It is complicated. Let us speak of other things. This night is not for talk of that kind."

"What would you like to talk about?" I asked before taking a sip of the chocolate. It was wonderful, much like I remembered drinking in the hill country in southern Mexico. Hot and thick, the bitterness offset by vanilla, with a slight kick from chili peppers. All it was missing was some cinnamon.

"I would have you tell me about yourself," she said, sounding regal just from the way she posed the request.

There wasn't much to tell, really, but I was pleased by her interest. Not just pleased. Her attention felt too good to be true. I told her I was the oldest of six children and that I'd helped raise my younger siblings when my mom was ill. I told her I'd been an Eagle Scout—that took some explaining—and talked about my two-year proselytizing mission. I explained that both my dad and grandfather had been to war, and I felt it was my duty to serve my country like they had.

"You have spent most of your life serving others," she remarked.

"I suppose," I said. "I never thought of it that way. It's never felt like an obligation, I mean. I guess it's what makes me happy."

"Did you leave other family behind when you were stolen from your world?"

"Oh, sure. I have more cousins than I can count, aunt and uncles, and my grandparents of course."

"No, I mean close family," she said. "A wife. Children."

"Oh. No. Well, I mean, almost, but it didn't work out." I sighed. "That's a long story."

"It is a sad story?" she asked.

"I guess. For me. Turned out well for her. I dunno. It was for the best, I suppose."

"Was she beautiful?"

I studied Xochi's profile. "Not as beautiful as you."

She faced me so I could see her terrible scar. "You are a poor liar."

"It's the truth." And it was. That was no practiced line. I found her beauty to be captivating. The scar only made her fit for mortal eyes. She seemed like a goddess to me.

I hesitantly reached up and ran my finger down her face, careful to be respectful and avoid touching the scar. She turned away, embarrassed.

"We all have scars, Xochi. Some you can see, some you can't. Our scars make us beautiful."

She turned again and her gaze met mine. I couldn't tell if it was hope or doubt that I was seeing in her eyes.

"I do not understand what I am feeling," she said softly. "You are a stranger from another world whom I hardly know, and yet I feel as if I have known you for many lives. It frightens me."

"It frightens me too."

Woodward, passed out drunk beside the pile of rucks, groaned and rolled over. "Shut up and kiss her already, Preacher."

So I did.

***

Xochi didn't sleep with me. Literally or figuratively. But she did stay up beside me until I was too tired to keep awake any longer. When I awoke, it took me a moment to realize that she was gone and it was Wilson who was shambling over to me holding his head with both hands in the predawn hours.

He noticed I was awake and looking at him. "Bennett, you got any aspirin in that med kit?"

"Sure, Sergeant, I'll get you some."

"Get some for me too," said García.

Soon all the guys in the detachment were up and surrounding me like supplicants. Even Sergeant Takahashi looked rough.

"I could use a saline IV too," Wilson said.

I laughed. "No can do, Sergeant. Gotta save what I got for emergencies."

"This hangover *is* an emergency."

"Sorry, Sergeant. You just need to hydrate and eat something."

At that moment Woodward turned green and stumbled a few yards off to heave into some bushes.

"Sergeant Sanchez would have us all running laps if he saw us," Anderson moaned.

"Then it's a good thing he's not here," Takahashi replied. "But remember, Captain Brown is. I said you could have the night off, not drink yourselves into oblivion."

"Look who's talking, bro," said Wilson. "You were the first one under the table."

"Can't help it," Takahashi said. "I'm Japanese, if you didn't notice."

"Really, bro? Never would've guessed." Wilson groaned and held his temples. "Damn, Dressed-in-Stars wore me out, man. For serious."

"Bennett got lucky too," said García.

Wilson's face lit up, his hangover momentarily forgotten. "*What? Bro! Really?*" He punched my shoulder. "With the princess! You slick son of a—"

"I didn't, no, it wasn't like that," I stammered, my face flushing. "We just talked. I like her, though."

"Guess you two chewing each other's faces off was just a prelude to some philosophical debate, huh, Bennett?" García remarked.

"It was just a kiss," I said. "Wait—were you watching us?"

"Had to take a leak," García said innocently.

Wilson punched my shoulder again. "A princess, bro. *Nice.*" He smiled, then sat down. "You're about to go from Hand Solo to Han Solo, Bennett."

The team laughed, but I didn't mind. I was feeling pretty good about the way Xochi was feeling about me.

"What were we drinking, anyway?" Anderson asked.

"Fermented agave sap, probably," I said.

"Tasted like sour yeast," said Grant. "But damn if it wasn't a kick in the ass."

The lower village was coming to life with the first signs of light. Four women approached us carrying baskets of their tortilla-like flatbread and steaming bowls of some reddish-white substance. They placed the food before us without meeting our eyes, then bowed and hurried away.

"Smells good," Takahashi said. "What is it?"

Pierce was already scooping the substance from the bowls onto a piece of flatbread. "Looks like some kinda eggs and salsa, Sergeant."

García grinned and joined him. "I hope so. Best hangover food ever, man."

Woodward took one look at the food and then went off to be sick again. After a time I got him to lie in some shade, and then I gave him an IV. Yeah, I know—emergencies only. But he was in a bad way and I felt that we needed to be presentable, given what we'd promised to undertake on behalf of these people. Eventually he was able to hold some food down.

We spent the rest of the morning recuperating. Our clothes were brought to us, clean and dry, and we lost no time getting geared up. Then Captain Brown told us the plan for the witches. Evidently, after I'd left the table and the others drank themselves into a stupor, Brown had finally gotten the briefing and intel he'd been jonesing for. In the late afternoon we'd follow a Kuauchanejkej guide to where the tlahuelpuchi were hiding out in the forest. Whether because of literal magic or just native superstition, we wouldn't be taking all of the men.

"Our allies are adamant that they will be able to detect us in advance of our coming if the war party is too large," Brown explained. "That said, I intend to position a QRF as close as is practicable. It's hard to tell how much is ghost stories and how much is real, but I'm informed that these witches…"

Captain Brown went on with his briefing, but I wasn't the only one who had trouble working up any serious concern about this mission. Maybe it was the lingering effects of the alcohol in the men —and the lingering effects of Xochi's kiss on me—but in the light of day, the witches seemed like a non-issue. Just a minor obstacle for big, bad Cav to roll over.

In hindsight we were far too cavalier about the whole operation, and that turned out to be a fatal mistake.

CHAPTER 19

Dusk was falling, the wan gray light barely filtering down through the canopy, leaving us in deep shadows as we moved cautiously and silently along the forest floor. This far into the jungle there was hardly any underbrush—not at all like the thick, tangled mess of vines you see in the movies. Here there were only rotting tree stumps interspersed with seedlings and the occasional hanging vine. It was dark enough that we probably would have donned our NVGs were it not for the scarcity of batteries.

Specialist Grant was on point, since he had the most tracking experience. Wilson was behind him, with Woodward and García following. I was next, with Sergeant Takahashi and Private Anderson behind me. Pierce was rear security. Alpha was still with the trucks with Sanchez hopefully keeping an eye on them, and with Doc keeping an eye on Sergeant Douglas, and Brown was with the rest, waiting for our return.

We knew the witches lived in a community of sorts—a "coven," the Kuauchanejkej called it. The Kuauchanejkej had given us a lot of intel to sort through, and Captain Brown had briefed us, but we didn't know how much was fact and how much was myth. They claimed that the tlahuelpuchi—the witches—began their lives as Kuauchanejkej in the villages throughout the region. As young children they were ordinary, indistinguishable from the "uncursed," but in puberty their powers manifested, at which point they would develop a thirst for blood. A thirst that was slaked in monstrous ways.

A Kuauchanejkej parent's duty to the queen required them to turn in such a child at the first signs of the curse. Occasionally a family would protect their child, hiding its true nature from the rest of the village, but eventually they were always discovered, usually because of some harm the young witch caused.

Discovered, and killed.

There was, apparently, no redeeming these children. Their hearts only grew blacker with time.

But sometimes the witches struck first, and a young girl well below the age of puberty, or more rarely, a boy, would simply vanish from a Kuauchanejkej village, stolen away in the dark of night. Some believed that these victims too were cursed, and that the witches had sensed the evil in them even before the curse manifested. The children's parents tended to disagree. But nothing could be done to recover these young victims, and they ended up joining the small covens like the one we were tracking.

More gruesome were the stories of disappearing infants. No one believed an infant could already have a curse within them. But the witches, you recall, have a taste for blood.

Some of this sounded plausible. Communities feared those who were different; that was as true in our world as it was in this one. And it was not uncommon for elaborate myths to develop to explain those differences, as well as to explain anything else that was hard to understand. The intel that was harder to believe had to do with the witches' alleged *powers*—and the belief that they could only be killed by men.

First the powers, though. They could change shape, the Kuauchanejkej had told us. Generally into jaguars or other predators. They could inflict festering wounds with only a touch. They could control the weather. They were almost always female.

The good news was being bitten by one didn't change you into one. Wilson asked about that specifically. Captain Brown told him he was getting witches mixed up with zombies. The Kuauchanejkej told him that didn't happen. But then they frowned at each other as if wondering about the possibility. I feared I'd just witnessed the birth of another tlahuelpuchi myth.

So now the second part, about how the witches can only be killed by men. Apparently, when the cursed children are brought to the queen, one of her eunuch consorts—who is still technically male—is tasked with the grisly job of snuffing out the life of the nascent witch. For me, that sounded way too close to human sacrifice than I was comfortable with. But Friar Bastía, who held his own strong Christian convictions, disagreed.

"The destruction of witches is only an abomination to the minds of those who don't believe such things exist. The tlahuelpuchi, I am afraid, are only too real. And terrible."

I wondered if the belief that only men could kill the witches had grown from the simple fact that, in their ritual, only men were asked to do so. But it was certainly possible that women warriors had tried to fight off grown witches and found the casualty rate was too high. I didn't ask, and if Captain Brown did, he didn't pass the information on. In the end, all that mattered was we had been given the job, and we aimed to complete it.

As the night grew, so did the darkness. We finally reached a point where the torch used by our Kuauchanejkej guide felt like too big a liability, and so Sergeant Tak had her extinguish it. It was so dark as a result that we were left with no choice but to use our NVGs and start using up those batteries. Our guide insisted that it wouldn't be much longer until we were at the coven.

She was right. A little while later we came across the first skeleton. Very small—a toddler, I guessed. More followed, mostly the odd small skull or scattering of bones, some even smaller than the first. Infants, possibly. This part of the ghost story was true, it seemed.

I'd never seen an infant's skull before. They were unnerving, like tiny grinning aliens glowing in our night vision.

Takahashi tapped me on the shoulder and signed for us to spread out into a wedge, I sent the signal forward. We were practically on the witches' doorstep according to our guide, but other than the bones, I couldn't make out any sign of a permanent settlement. Our movement slowed to a crawl, careful to be silent with each footstep.

Grant held up a fist and we all froze.

My heart was beating so hard I was sure it could be heard a mile away.

A few minutes later he waved us forward, only to signal another halt another ten yards on. This time we all took a knee and Takahashi crept forward to confer with Grant. Word passed from man to man: we had found the settlement, a cluster of half a dozen low mud huts with broad thatched roofs. But there was no sign of the witches.

Takahashi pulled us into a huddle and spoke in a low voice, almost subvocalizing. "We're going in to clear the huts. Stay low, stay quiet. Wilson and Bennett, you're our door-kickers. Take Pierce with you."

"Say again?" Wilson said. "Door-kickers? Dude. Remember that line from *Aliens*? 'We came here to destroy them, right?'"

The look of annoyance was visible on Takahashi's face even behind the NVGs. "What's your point?"

"So, like Ripley said, we nuke the site from orbit." Wilson patted his M203. "It's the only way to be sure. No need to kick in any doors."

"Negative," Takahashi said. "They steal children, right? There might be kids in there."

"Yeah, *cursed* kids." Wilson shook his head. "Okay, bro. Door-kicking it is. Bennett, you take left, I got right. Okay?"

I turned slightly from watching my sector and gave a thumbs-up.

We stood in a crouch and fanned out, slowly making our advance on the dilapidated mud huts while Pierce held the rear. Wilson and I stacked up on either side of the entrance to the first hovel. The doorway was so low we'd have to enter on our knees.

He gave a nod, and I swept the ragged cloth covering aside and swiveled into the hut, Wilson just behind me with his muzzle over my right shoulder with Pierce following. The others maintained security outside. The stench of stale blood that hit us as we entered was nauseating. But aside from several filthy old sleeping mats and creepy symbols made from tiny bones that hung from the ceiling, the home was empty.

As were the next three.

We were stacked at the fifth hut when Pierce called out "Contact!" and fired his rifle. He probably dumped half a magazine before yelling "Clear!"

Well, our stealth was blown. I tried to make out what he'd been shooting at, but it was too far away. He'd been firing toward the center of village, but I didn't see anything there.

Wilson snapped his fingers at me. "Focus, Bennett."

"Right, Sergeant," I said.

He nodded and I dropped to my knees to enter. This time the hut wasn't empty. Tied up in a corner was a naked little girl, no more than four years old. I knew she couldn't see us in the pitch dark, but she could hear us—and of course she'd heard Pierce. Her eyes were wide with fear.

"Shit," Wilson said.

I took my flashlight off my LBE, and after raising my NVGs I turned it on, shining it at the floor.

"It's okay," I said to the girl. "We're the good guys. We've come to take you home. Understand?" I did my best to keep my voice steady and soothing.

She nodded rigidly, still terrified. With all our gear and face camo we probably looked like the monsters she'd imagined in the dark. When I reached over to untie her, she flinched.

There was more gunfire outside, and the little girl cowered.

"We gotta di di mau," Wilson said. "Just pick her up."

I slung my rifle over my back and scooped her up in one arm. She couldn't have weighed more than thirty pounds. We crawled out and I was met by the sight of multiple muzzle flashes. I quickly stowed my flashlight and then lowered my NVGs. I almost wished I hadn't. Glowing figures were darting around everywhere. Some were human, some a hybrid of jaguar or wolf and human, all illuminated with a disconcerting aura in our night vision.

A woman with the face of a raven burst out of the next hut over, one we hadn't cleared yet, and charged right at us, crying shrilly.

Wilson hit her half a dozen times before she went down, and then kept pumping rounds into her until she stopped twitching.

"Mag out," he called.

I heard branches cracking above and leapt aside just before a naked, emaciated woman with clawed hands landed in a crouch right where I had been standing. She held her hands up against the glare of my NVG's IR illumination before pouncing. I guess she could see the beam. Witch powers or something. Our IR had probably made us just as conspicuous as keeping the torch going would have.

I turned my body to protect the girl, who was screaming now, and throat-punched the witch. She staggered back long enough for me to draw my knife, then she charged again.

Her mistake.

I drove the blade through a sagging breast and into her heart as she clawed for my face. Twisting the knife, I ripped it free, and hot blood sprayed me as I slashed her throat. Her screams turned into a sick gurgling sound, and she dropped at my feet.

Wilson was already engaging another raven-faced witch, but my gaze was drawn to the huge jaguar-man hybrid that was closing on Grant. The specialist fired until his mag was out and then drew his saber. The witch, or warlock, swiped down with a massive clawed hand and Grant jumped back, slashing down into the thing's arm. The jaguar-man roared as the wind picked up and thunder rolled.

I tried to bring up my rifle, but I was still holding the girl and worried that a one-armed shot would not only miss the witch, but potentially hit Grant.

In hindsight, I wish I'd risked it. For Grant's sake.

He pivoted and thrust his saber, impaling the warlock in the stomach, but the bestial man grabbed hold of both sides of Grant's head and ripped the specialist's throat out with his fangs. The warlock tossed the limp body aside, then pulled the saber from his belly and bellowed in defiance as the wind whipped us with branches and leaves.

At that point I set the girl down and brought my rifle up to take the abomination down.

"Mag out!" Wilson cried beside me.

There was another thunderclap, and a torrential rain began to fall.
I shot at the warlock, but the thing just vanished before my eyes. I
didn't know if I'd hit it or not.

A screaming witch, fully human, materialized before us and
swiped at Wilson, her claws ripping through his LBE and into his
chest. He fumbled his reload, dropping the magazine, and
backhanded her with his rifle.

The little girl was screaming again and I could see something
dark and shapeless streak toward her. I turned my body so my back
was between the girl and this… thing, then scooped her back up into
my arms. A witch? Something evil. Something that didn't deserve to
live. I knew that much. Shifting the little girl higher on my shoulder,
I drew my saber. The witch Wilson had backhanded was coming at
him again. I slashed her across the back. She howled, turning on me,
and I struck again. The sword cleaved her face in half. Wilson
slammed another magazine into his rifle and contact-fired into her
chest. She staggered back and fell into the mud.

Through the rain I saw García and Woodward converging on the
jaguar-man warlock, who had reappeared about fifteen meters from
where he'd vanished. They pumped rounds into him until he fell.
Woodward drew his saber and cut off the beast's head, just to be
sure.

Takahashi, Pierce, and Anderson were all firing at that dark,
shapeless thing that had rushed me and the girl. It was a witch, and
now it had gathered some friends. Anderson got tackled by two of
them, but Pierce was on them in a flash, knifing both savagely. I had
no idea he had that kind of violence in him.

Takahashi shouted for everyone to fall in. We needed to close up
our ranks and fight off the onslaught that was coming. The witches—
and I have no idea how many there were—had started to whip and
fly about the camp, gusting from here to there like shadows carried
by the wind, or turning into creatures and moving at an inhuman rate.
It was clear they were trying to isolate us and we needed to have one
another's back.

Wilson and I hustled to join the sergeant and had to skid to a halt
in our tracks as another of the raven-witches dropped down in front

of us. I thrust the saber into her stomach and she stumbled backward with a piercing shriek, pulling the weapon out of my grip. I fumbled for my rifle and fired from the hip, hitting her in the chest and putting her down for good. We continued toward the rally point, Wilson stumbling a bit beside me.

I saw Pierce and Anderson both shoot down witches of their own. Another large male witch, this one more wolf than man, leapt for Takahashi, but the sergeant smoothly rolled under the attack and delivered a savage kick, hitting the wolf-man right in the spine. The strike looked hard enough to have broken the warlock's back. It didn't. The beast turned and charged again, completely unharmed. Takahashi blended into the oncoming attack in a blur, rolling through the mud, and then snatched up Grant's discarded saber. He was on his knees as the wolf-man bore down on him, but simply twisted his body away from the gaping jaws and struck with such force that he cut the warlock clean in half.

He made it look easy. Effortless.

There was another thunderclap, this one much weaker, and the rain and wind abruptly stopped.

"Is that it?" Pierce called. "Did we get them all?"

"I don't see anything," said Anderson, still looking down his M16's sights as he surveyed his surroundings.

Wilson groaned and hit the mud face-first.

I set the girl down, told her to stay, then rolled the big sergeant over.

"I feel like shit, bro," he mumbled.

"Just hang in there, Sergeant. Let me take a look at you."

I pulled off his LBE, opened his blouse, and cut away his undershirt. The sight beneath was… foul. The witch's claws had raked deep into his chest, and the flesh there was putrefying and covered with boils. The necrotic stench made me gag.

"Is that smell me?" Wilson asked. "Ah, shit. It is, isn't it?"

"Afraid so, Sergeant."

"Wilson going to be okay?" Takahashi asked over my shoulder, his back facing me as he maintained security. We weren't entirely sure that we'd gotten all the witches at that point, although we'd soon find out we had. Our guide told us as much when she entered the space a moment later. None of us blamed her for not standing by us in a fight where she apparently could not kill, but only be killed.

"Was he bitten?" she asked of Wilson.

"No, just clawed," I told her.

"So what's the status?" Takahashi asked, clearly concerned.

I felt like everyone was talking to me at once. It dawned on me that Grant was probably dead, but maybe not? I needed to get Wilson squared away and then check to be sure. It was hard to think with everyone talking to me at once and Wilson moaning like he had a massive fever.

"Wound's infected, Sergeant," I reported.

The news seemed to rouse Wilson. "But you can fix it, right? Doc said he brought antibiotics, right?"

"Affirm," I said, but I wasn't about to make any promises.

***

The return trip brought us back through the village, rather than straight to Alpha Section and Doc. Our guide had run ahead while we carried our casualties. As a result, a *ticitl* was waiting for us. The title referred to men and women who were not only physicians, but also diviners, astrologists, and interpreters of omens. It was said they could speak with the gods.

"I would ask for the date of his birth," the ticitl said upon inspecting the wound even as we carried Wilson to her, "but he is an Outworlder, born under signs unknown to me, and I would not be able to create a horoscope."

"We have powerful medicines to fight infection," I said. "We just have to make the trek to our own doctor."

The old woman met my gaze. "So do we. But understand: the tlahuelpuchi has *cursed* him. Medicines will help with healing, but first I *must* counter the curse."

"This is bogus," Wilson mumbled. He was coming and going in what seemed like a fever, though he wasn't running a temperature. "So, what? I'm just going to rot away and die?"

I set him down in the middle of the village. We'd hooked him up to my last saline bag before moving from the coven. It was the best I could do for him. Now I needed to get to Doc.

"Without a proper horoscope it will be difficult to remove the curse, but not impossible," the ticitl said, not listening to what I'd had to say at all. "Do not set him here. Move him to the bathhouse. I will make a poultice to arrest the spread of the curse."

The commotion had brought Captain Brown and a host of others, including Xochi and an agitated Dressed-in-Stars, who paced back and forth.

"You said your doctor has powerful Outworlder medicines, yes?" she asked.

She was looking at me, and I nodded.

"On our fastest birds we could fetch him in no time," she said.

Xochi nodded. "It could be done. Go at once."

"Anyone know Morse code?" Takahashi asked, holding the PRC-77 in his hand. "Whoever's on the other end seems to be trying to communicate with it."

He had been trying to raise Doc on the radio the whole way back from the witch village, but the colossal trees were causing interference. He hadn't gotten more than snippets of voices distorted by static.

As an Eagle Scout, I stepped forward to help. Using the talk button on the handset I tapped out a radio check. I had to repeat it several times before receiving a weak response.

"I have comms with Sergeant Sanchez," I told Takahashi.

"Give him the sitrep," Takahashi said.

I tapped out a brief message: *Grant KIA. Wilson wounded. Strong antibiotics required ASAP. Riders dispatched to fetch Doc and drugs.*

I sent it three times before I got a simple dot-dash-dot in reply, meaning *Message received.*

CHAPTER 20

Dressed-in-Stars was seemingly back almost as soon as she'd left, but to my surprise, Doc wasn't with her. Evidently the birds were tricky to ride, likely to kill anyone unfamiliar, and lacked the ability to take a second rider, so Doc had given Dressed-in-Stars the antibiotics and was following on foot, which meant he'd be here in about two hours, judging by our earlier hike.

He'd hastily scribbled notes about what I should do with the extra bags of saline and vials of powdered Azactam he'd sent. Based on Dressed-in-Stars's report, he suspected the witches' claws carried a highly virulent strain of necrotizing fasciitis and recommended I start the administration of eight grams of the antibiotic that would continue over a period of twenty-four hours. He was also concerned about what the tribal physician's poultice might contain and included some notes on what to look out for. Top of the list were fecal matter, a favorite component in many folk medicines, and cocaine, which if combined with the antibiotics in the bloodstream increased the risk of methemoglobinemia, a blood condition that could lead to seizures and heart arrhythmias.

I stuffed the notes into my pocket and got to work.

The first vial I tried to reconstitute wouldn't dissolve properly and I had to toss it and try again. After some trial and error, I had the first two-gram vial prepared and ducked into the steaming bathhouse with my IV kit.

Wilson lay stretched out on a mat, and two women were thrashing him from head to toe with bundles of grass. Crushed leaves mixed with some kind of mush were smeared across his chest. The ticitl was there as well, inhaling from a pipe and blowing the resulting smoke into Wilson's mouth. All around them braziers filled with coals burned *copal,* a kind incense that smelled of pine and lemon.

My entrance agitated the old woman, who tried to shoo me out. "You are filthy and covered with blood," she admonished. "You cannot enter the bathhouse until you have been purified."

"Fine." I stepped outside, pulled off my boots and socks, stripped out of my BDUs, and removed my undershirt and boxers. Completely naked, but still just as filthy, I went back inside. "Better? He needs his medicine. *Real* medicine."

The ticitl scoffed. "What do you know about medicine? I have trained in the arts of healing for many decades."

Doctors, man. Always the same.

"He's an Outworlder," I said firmly. "He needs Outworlder medicine."

The old woman looked about to argue further, then relented. "First you must be purified."

"Great. Then let's get on with it."

I submitted myself to be thrashed, doused, and washed until the old lady was satisfied. While this was going on, I took the opportunity to question her.

"Why were you blowing smoke in his mouth?" I asked.

"There are three separate souls in the body," the old woman explained. "The omethi, the teyolia, and the ihiyotl. He suffers a malady of the ihiyotl, which resides in the liver. I blow the smoke into his lungs to purify his ihiyotl, which has been cursed."

"What are you smoking? Is that tobacco?"

"Of course."

"And what is this?" I asked, bending over to inspect her poultice.

"It is to heal and regenerate the flesh."

"But what is it made of?"

"Sap from the maguey, salt, chupiri, tletlematil, and other herbs."

"Any feces?" I asked.

The ticitl looked offended. "We are not savages."

"Just checking. And these crushed leaves?"

"Coca. For pain."

"That might be a problem," I said. "If it mixes in his blood with my medicine, he may have a seizure or heart troubles."

"It is only a small amount," the ticitl said, "and his pain is great. He is not intoxicated."

I frowned, but decided to risk the "small amount." I also made a mental note to use lidocaine as a topical anesthetic, which Doc told me was okay. I hadn't given Wilson any morphine, because, frankly, I didn't really have all that to spare and he was managing okay.

Once I was sufficiently purified, I moved around the women, sat near Wilson's head, and arranged the IV kit. He was sweating profusely, and whereas before his fever had come and gone, now he burned to the touch. Something was happening.

"How're you feeling, Sergeant?" I asked through the haze. The combined smell of burning copal, pungent herbs, tobacco smoke, and necrotic flesh swirling in the thick steam was dizzying.

Wilson opened his eyes and looked up at me. His gaze was clear —he wasn't "intoxicated," as the old woman had put it—but he was in obvious pain.

"Like shit, Bennett. How do I look?"

"The same as you feel. But your girlfriend must think otherwise. She raced like a bat out of hell to get an antibiotic from Doc. I'm going to pump you up to the gills with it."

"Really? Dressed-in-Stars did that for me?"

"Yeah. I think she's a keeper, Sergeant."

The ticitl watched suspiciously as I connected the saline bag and the vial of Azactam to the tubing and then started the IV. I hoped she didn't give me any more trouble; I'd need to administer a fresh vial every six hours until the full course of treatment was complete. For now at least, she said nothing, just resumed her position and once again blew smoke from her pipe into Wilson's mouth. If it bothered Wilson, he didn't complain.

Who am I kidding, he probably did this kind of stuff recreationally with his surf buddies before he joined up.

After a time, Dressed-in-Stars joined us, along with another Kuauchanejkej woman whom I later learned was the mother of the little girl we'd rescued. They both insisted on staying at Wilson's side, mopping his head and body down with cold water. The naked, sweating women surrounding me should've made me uncomfortable, but I was too tired and worried to even notice.

***

At dawn, Wilson's fever broke, and we moved him outside. I found Captain Brown waiting and looking worried. "How is he?"

"Better," I said.

Wilson's wound looked much improved. The ticitl carefully cut away the necrotized flesh with an obsidian scalpel, then one of the women attending her expertly sewed up the deep lacerations with some kind of thin fiber and a thorn needle. I had to admit, she did a much better job than I would've with my staple gun.

But something else was wrong. I could see it in the captain's face. Then it dawned on me. I'd been in that hut for a long time and nobody had come inside. There was one soldier, at least, who should have.

"Sir, where's Doc?"

The captain's look was grave. "We don't know."

"Sir?"

"He didn't arrive. Takahashi took a party to find him, aided by our new friends. There are no tracks indicating he came this way at all. However… we did find tracks leading *away* from our position. The tracks of the Humvees."

I couldn't quite believe my ears. "You mean Alpha took Doc and Douglas and Sanchez—"

"We don't know what happened," Captain Brown said, cutting me short, and in the process made me consider that there might be a scenario that didn't involve Alpha doing something dastardly. That was my own bias coming out. Not facts. "But we do know that three trucks are gone and the others have been busted up so bad it will take a miracle to get them running again. We've been trying to reach them on the prick, but nothing yet. Anderson is working with someone allowed up into the trees to see about running an antenna up above the canopy."

"What about Epasotl?" I asked. I didn't want to think about what Alpha would do to her if they'd gone off the reservation. Again, my own bias, not facts.

"No sign of her, either."

That was actually some relief. If they were going to kill her, I was sure they'd do it and dump the body as soon as possible. *After taking their trophies.* I shook away the thought. I couldn't help but feel guilty for leaving her. She had been worried about being left with St. James. She'd come to me with that concern. What if her fears were justified?

I forced myself to cut out the negativity. I was jumping to all sorts of dire conclusions and none of them would do me any good at the moment. I looked to the captain.

"I... I don't know what to say, sir."

The captain gave me a fractional nod. "I didn't tell you to get your opinion, son. I need you to know our situation and understand that, for the time being, you are it when it comes to platoon medic. So if any of the work being done on Wilson by the local healer is of value, it might be wise to pay attention."

It took my mind a minute to get in gear well enough to answer. "Yes. Of course. Yes, sir. I've been paying attention."

"Good." Captain Brown turned to leave, the weight of the world on his shoulders.

"Sir? Are we going after them?"

"Those trucks are beyond our reach on foot. I'm working with the queen to see what aid they can provide us. Might put us in their debt again, but there's nothing else for it. At any rate, we're on Kuauchanejkej time and not Ranger time."

I assumed that Captain Brown meant *Cav* time, but he was likely just as tired as I was. We had been bathing, feasting, and feeling good about our chances in this world not that long ago. How could things have gone this wrong, this fast?

***

The villagers buried Grant that same day, erecting a cairn over his body to memorialize his sacrifice. This was one of the things Captain Brown was talking about when he said we weren't on "Ranger time." The Kuauchanejkej felt that respects to the dead—which included the bones of the children who'd fallen victim to the witches—be paid before any departure would be authorized. I guess we all have our traditions.

Friar Bastía held a mass for his flock afterward. I had never attended a Catholic service before, and the rich liturgy and symbolism moved me. It was as different from the services I was accustomed to as night was from day. I wouldn't say I preferred it to my own simple form of worship, but it was beautiful in its own way.

Even then, riders weren't permitted to head out after Doc and Alpha. We were free to go out on foot by ourselves, but we'd already ranged as far as we could short of just walking after the tire tracks until we found where they stopped. That night, another feast was held—this time to celebrate our victory over the tlahuelpuchi. Queen Skull-Dancer gave a speech commending us on our bravery and thanking us for freeing her people from the plague of the witches. She lavished us with gifts: fine obsidian daggers, gold jewelry set with precious stones. But most importantly, she called us friends. Captain Brown was glad to hear it, and so was I, but our hearts remained heavy. We did our best not to show it, though. Captain's orders.

And he was right. Despite the circumstances with Doc and Alpha —and Grant, and Wilson, and Jensen and so many others—we had some reason to be happy. It was about time we had some allies in this dangerous land.

And I had another, personal reason to be happy. I watched for her constantly, but Xochi was absent from the feast. I guessed she remained unwelcome at the table. I didn't like that. As the evening wore on, I managed to slip away to seek her out.

I found her in one of the fenced-in corrals, tending to her war bird. It made a series of low piping notes as I approached, which I took as a warning to stay away. But Xochi saw me and smiled.

"Come," she said, beckoning me.

"I don't think it likes me," I replied.

"She would kill you. But you will be safe with me."

I've described the birds before—and my fear of them—but up close they are as beautiful as they are terrifying. They have small, flightless wings and long, powerful legs, and though at the withers they are about six feet tall, their muscular necks hold their heads aloft nearly ten feet from the ground. Their feet each have three toes ending in wickedly curved talons, but their most frightening weapon is their hooked beaks, eighteen inches long and thick. Those who saw the birds strike at the giants during the battle at Camp Arizona said the beaks moved with lightning speed and delivered horrifying wounds.

Hesitantly, I ducked through the rungs of the fence and approached slowly. The bird cocked its head to get a better look at me and made another of its piping warnings. Xochi gave a low whistling command, and the beast lowered itself to the ground, curving its neck protectively around her and eyeing me suspiciously.

"She is called Wind-Runner," Xochi said. "Come closer."

"I think this is close enough," I replied, stopping a few feet away.

Xochi laughed. "She will not hurt you. Unless I wish her to."

I smiled. "That's what I'm afraid of."

Xochi laughed again. It was a beautiful sound to my ears, like soft music.

"She's a magnificent animal," I offered.

"We were raised together," Xochi said. "We bonded when I was a child, and she was only a hatchling. She will accept no other rider. She is brave in battle, but stubborn. It was she who gave me this." Xochi touched the long scar running down the side of her face. "I was training her and she became obstinate. I grew angry and let down my defenses. She kicked me."

"I assumed you were injured in battle," I said.

"That would be a more honorable story. But it is not the true one."

"Are all the war birds you ride female?"

"Yes. The males are too aggressive. We keep a few for breeding, but that is all."

"I haven't seen any of these birds roaming free on the savanna. Where do they come from?"

"They were a gift to our people from our ancestor, the Wisest-of-Men."

"You mean Quetzalcoatl," I said. "He's your ancestor?"

The consensus we all had, and that included the friar, was that Xochi's people were descended from human Outworlders. Because physically speaking, they were human. But maybe Quetzalcoatl was, too. Maybe he was just the first Outworlder to arrive in this place.

"Yes. He is." I was about to ask more about this, but Xochi beckoned me closer. "Come here, don't be frightened. She won't harm you with me here. She is protective, but you are a friend."

Reluctantly I edged closer. Wind-Runner cocked her head to the side again, peering at me with one large yellow eye flecked with gold, the pupil dilating and contracting.

"Feel her head," Xochi said, demonstrating. "She loves to be scratched just so."

Gingerly, I reached out and ruffled the bird's head feathers as Xochi had shown me. The bird made a sort of *kuk-kuk-kuk* sound and closed her eyes.

"See? She likes you. That is good. She knows you are a friend." Xochi reached up and clasped her hands behind my neck. "Now kiss me."

And so I did. I felt a pang of guilt for enjoying it while there were people I cared about fighting for their lives, but this world and its troubles all melted away from me while I was in her embrace.

***

A new morning and still we weren't moving. I could tell it was grating on Captain Brown. Not just the delay, but suddenly finding ourselves so beholden to the Kuauchanejkej unless we wanted to go on foot with what little ammunition and other supplies we'd carried into the village in our rucks. It wouldn't last long. Nor would we.

There was some good news, though. Wilson was doing well enough to sit up and eat solid food. He was aided in this by Dressed-in-Stars, although it didn't seem to me her help was necessary. When he saw me coming to check on him, he said to her, "Give us a minute, babe."

She smiled, kissed the top of his head, and then walked away. He followed her with his eyes.

"You're looking much better, Sergeant," I said, squatting beside him. "How're you feeling?"

"Like shit," he said. He lowered his voice. "Listen, Bennett, we need to talk. *Mano a mano*. Not sergeant to spec-four. Just bro to bro. Brothers. You're like a little brother to me, you know."

"We're the same age, Sergeant."

"Okay, like the twin brother who came out last. Whatever. You're my bro, right?"

"Sure, Sergeant," I said, not knowing where this was heading but meaning it all the same. I liked Wilson.

"No ranks, bro. Just bros. We're two dudes having a chat."

"Okay," I said. "We're bros." I just wanted him to get on with this. Whatever this was.

"Bro, I need you to do me a solid," he whispered. "I'm asking you as a bro. I don't want to go back to the platoon, man. Don't look at me like that, bro. This isn't Panama. It ain't even the twentieth century. Whatever, whenever this is, we didn't sign up for fighting actual *monsters*. It wasn't part of the deal, and to just ride it out and pretend like everything's SOP, that's bogus."

He looked around. "But I *like* it here, bro. These are *good* people. We should *all* stay here. I don't know how we got to this psycho world, but we're here now, we're not getting out, and under this black sun, I'm pretty sure this village… this is as good as it gets. I know Captain Brown won't go for that, but it's true."

"Yeah, he won't go for that. Especially not after what happened with Doc and the trucks," I said.

Wilson looked at me in confusion. I filled him in.

"Shit. That's bad, man. You ask me, that's St. James going all Marlon Brando *Apocalypse Now* with his merry band of Alpha psychopaths." He thought about that for a moment. "Even so. You gotta help me, Bennett. I gotta stay here."

"Sarge, are you serious? Are you saying you want to desert?"

"You really want to put it like that, bro?" Wilson said. "I ain't no deserter. There's no Big Army here, man. No UCMJ. The platoon, bro, it's just a *bunch of dudes* now. What are they gonna do? Court-martial me? Send me to Leavenworth? It ain't *deserting* when you step away from a bunch of dudes."

I slowly shook my head. "I don't think Captain Brown is gonna see it that way."

"You said you were my bro, Nephi."

"I am, Dave." This was turning out to be an uncomfortable conversation. "I'm just wondering if you've thought this through. I mean, the rest of us are gonna go out looking for what I think are some legit deserters—not to mention kidnappers. You gonna let us go off on our own like that?"

"Yes." Wilson's face was dead serious. Then it softened and grew introspective. "I know how close I came to eating it after that witch scratched me. And that's gotten me thinking a whole bunch. We didn't get all the witches—that was just one coven—and someone needs to protect these people. Like an ambassador. A witch-killing ambassador. These are our allies, right? The only allies we've got. I'm taking one for the team here, bro."

I wasn't convinced. "I don't know if it'll work like that, Sergeant. From everything I hear, the Kuauchanejkej will just shunt you and your girl off to one of the other villages as soon you recover. You didn't see any sign of that Buffalo Soldier, did you? And they didn't ask him to take down the witches. That's because he became one of them—and their men don't fight. The same will happen to you."

Wilson shrugged. I could see his mind was made up and it was just a matter of getting me to where he wanted me to be. "Listen, bro. You don't have to agree. All I'm asking is for you to tell Tak and Brown I can't travel, not for a good while. Leave me my weapons and gear."

I tried another tack. "Don't you want to find a way back home?"

"That ain't gonna happen, bro. Besides, there's nothing waiting for me back in the world. Alimony to a stripper I shouldn't have married and child support for a brat I know isn't mine. E-Z payments at twenty-five percent interest for a damned Camaro IROC. What's to go back for? The real world sucks, bro."

"What about surfing? Dave, listen to me, you'll get bored," I tried. "You're always looking for the next thrill. What are you going to do here?"

"Dunno, bro. Make a life? Thrills ain't everything, cheah? Please, do me this one thing." He gave me a lopsided grin. "'Sides, there's gotta be choice breaks here somewhere. I'll find a way to keep carving."

I sighed and looked away.

"You owe me, bro," he said softly. "You know that, right?"

"What?" I turned back to him. "How do you figure that? I just saved your life. *You* owe *me*."

"Okay, dude, fair enough. Got me there. But I'm begging you. I do *not* want to go back. Just tell them I can't be moved for like a week or three. What's the harm?"

"The harm is, we got a major problem on our hands. That plus Sanchez, if he hasn't been shot and left in a ditch by Alpha, will smell right through it. I can't believe you'd really let us do this without you."

"There was never a scenario where all of us didn't eventually go our separate ways," Wilson said, his face returning to the resolve I'd seen earlier. "I'm cashing out now. You're either gonna help me, or you aren't. Look at me, Nephi, and be honest. If I hadn't asked you what I just asked you, and you didn't know what I want to do... do I *look* like I can hump it with you guys right now?"

Honestly… no, he didn't. So, yeah, I wouldn't be exactly *lying*… just kinda… stretching the truth.

I sighed. "I'll see what I can do."

Wilson grinned. "Hell yeah, bro. I owe you one."

"You already owe me one."

"Okay, so I owe you two."

"You do," I said. "And don't be surprised when I show up to collect."

It would be a long time until such an opportunity would come. Less than an hour after our chat, word came through that all of us—except for Wilson, thanks to the witches and thanks to me—were moving out after Alpha.

CHAPTER 21

We saw the carrion birds circling lazily in the sky and the plumes of smoke long before reaching the wreckage of our Humvees. I was part of a small scouting party that had left our main element pulling security farther back while we quietly moved to investigate the fires. Xochi sent her fastest rider ahead, and when she came back later, she was breathless.

"There was a battle," the woman said as she reined her agitated mount. "The giants found your mounts and laid waste to them."

"Are there survivors?" Captain Brown asked.

"I do not know. The tracks of one of your mounts continued on, but I know not how far. There were giants about, roaming, so I hurried back here. We must prepare for battle; I cannot be sure I was not spotted."

"We've got a choice that needs to be made, sir," Takahashi said to Captain Brown, almost effortlessly filling in the role usually played by Sanchez. "Do we haul ass and try to catch that Humvee that got away—if it got away—or do we check the wreckage?"

Captain Brown was chewing the inside of his mouth as he thought. "Wreckage first. Then we'll see if we can catch up with whatever vic got out. Xochi, can your riders form a screen, do some recon? I don't want us to be waylaid by giants."

Xochi nodded and gave a series of shrill whistles. She and three other riders spurred their birds and raced off ahead, while the remaining two wheeled their mounts around and moved to screen our rear.

Those of us who hadn't been fortunate enough to be raised side by side with a killer dino-bird formed a wedge and set off, alternating running and walking. It was grueling in the heat with our heavy rucks, and after the first two hours we were soaked in sweat and caked with salt.

When one of the riders came racing back toward us, we halted. It was one of the older warriors, a woman we called Rivers-of-Blood.

"Giants ahead!" she called to us, reining in her bird. "We will try to lead them away so that you can inspect the battlefield. There was a great slaughter of the giants there. Your men fought with honor."

"How many giants did you see?" Takahashi asked. "How far?"

"Twenty scouts encamped by a stream. Not far. Hold here."

She clucked, turned her bird, and sped off again.

"What are four riders going to do against twenty giants?" García asked.

"If the Sugar Skull Gals can bait them, maybe they can lead them out of our path," Pierce said.

"So, what? Do we just wait here?" Woodward asked.

"That's what the lady said," Takahashi replied. "Take a knee. Hydrate."

I noticed our remaining two escorts were pacing their mounts in a large semicircle about a hundred meters behind us. One of them abruptly spurred her bird, which leapt into the air with a shrill cry and then charged us.

"What the—" García cried before he was cut off by a wolf-vulture leaping out of the tall grass. Woodward and Anderson lit it up with their M16s as García dove to the side.

The charging rider blew by us, spearing another feathered lizard with her lance as she passed.

I felt something hit my ruck hard and I went sprawling face-first. I couldn't see my attacker, but I heard its talons and snapping jaws ripping through my gear. A hiss of a sword slashed through the air, and the wolf-vulture's head fell beside me, its jaws still moving.

Takahashi unceremoniously hauled me to my feet and pointed me in the general direction of the chaos. I shot one of the creatures off Woodward, and then another stalking García.

A sugar skull gal raced past with a wolf-vulture flailing on her lance. Another reined in near us, and her bird plucked a feathered lizard out of the grass and bit its body in half while the bird's rider hung halfway out the saddle and speared yet another one.

We'd formed a tight circle by then and were firing into the tall grass. Dark shapes rustled and raced around us.

"Mag out!" four voices shouted nearly at the same time.

Well, that sucks.

My bolt locked back nearly a second later.

"Mag out!" I cried.

We all raced to swap magazines. I'd like to say it was that smooth, automatic motion you read about in those books about SEALs and Delta Force, but it wasn't. It was a fumble. Pierce was cool enough to *almost* make it look pro, but the rest of us were rushing. Except for Captain Brown. The Ranger had no trouble.

What's the saying? Slow is smooth and smooth is fast?

The rest of us weren't smooth.

The wolf-vultures didn't wait for us to finish reloading. One leapt at Anderson, delivering a kick that sent him crashing backward into Woodward and García. Pierce was back in the action and shot two more charging beasts even as a fourth drove straight at García, who slammed his bolt home just in time to contact-fire into the thing's chest.

No, it didn't explode in a spray of gore. Come on. We're talking 5.56 here.

Takahashi and his saber carved one in half, then did some kind of crazy pirouette and impaled the one that had sent Anderson flying.

By then I'd gotten my magazine in, a round chambered, and was looking for more targets.

I got one and then that was it.

The riders made a hoarse, screaming *kee-eeeee-arr* sound that lasted for two or three seconds. Their birds replied with the same cry and then lazily walked around, picking at the dead creatures.

"Medic!" Woodward called out.

"Moving!" I replied.

Woodward was holding Anderson's head in his lap. The kid's face was contorted in pain, the front of his blouse torn and dark with blood. Pierce and García were leaning in to get a better look and I had to push them away.

"Give us some space, guys," I snapped. "Anderson, how you feeling?"

"Like hell, Specialist."

"Just hang on and let me look. Dude, you gotta move your arms so I can see." He was fighting me, not wanting to stop clutching his chest. Fighting him, I cut away his clothing and used a dressing to wipe away all the blood.

The feathered lizard had sliced him from nipple to navel in a long straight gash. It looked like someone had run a box cutter right down his chest.

I looked up at Woodward. "Hold him steady, okay?"

He nodded and tightened his hold on Anderson.

"All right, Cory," I said to my patient. "This is going to hurt. But you got this. It'll be over before you know it. Ready?"

And then I just stapled him up.

Anderson wasn't stoic about it like Wright had been. He screamed every time I shot the stainless-steel sutures into his chest and stomach. I was beginning to worry that if the reports of our rifles hadn't alerted the nearby giants, Anderson's screams would.

"Man up, Cory," Woodward barked.

Anderson ground his teeth and whimpered.

Truth is, he got lucky—the cut had been shallow. Much deeper and he'd have a punctured lung or his guts hanging out. Probably both. I dressed the wound and wrapped him in a poncho liner.

"Heads up, guys," Takahashi said. "I think we got trouble."

Xochi and her riders were returning, racing fast enough to send up a plume of dust.

"Why are you firing your rifles?" she cried. "We had them pursuing us and now they are coming for you!"

"Wolf-vultures attacked us, Princess," explained one of the riders who had been left behind.

Xochi saw Woodward and me by Anderson. "Is your man hurt? Can you still run?"

"Anderson isn't running anywhere," I said.

She looked around and cursed. "Then we must stand and fight."

"Against twenty giants?" I said.

"No." Xochi held up a handful of bloody hair and scalp. "Nineteen."

"You are incorrect," Rivers-of-Blood said, holding up another scalp. "Eighteen."

Xochi nodded. "They come!" she cried to us all. "Be ready!"

The ground began to tremble, and when I stood I saw them on the savanna, moving toward us. The riders divided themselves on either side of us, protecting our flanks.

"Form a line," Captain Brown ordered. "Remember, 5.56 won't penetrate their armor, so we have to hope we can bring them down with headshots. Aim small, hit small. Pick your targets. Don't rush the shot. Don't panic."

"They'll use their spear-throwers first, then charge," Xochi said.

Takahashi loaded a round of smoke in his M203 and launched it a hundred and fifty meters away. He fired two more, forming a smokescreen at our front.

We heard the spears before we saw them, a hissing-rattle raining down on us. Fifteen-foot-long projectiles as thick as my wrist slammed into the earth all around. The men and riders were spared, but one great spear impaled Wind-Dancer, sending the bird down screaming and throwing Xochi.

I made to rush to her, but García grabbed me.

"Stay in the line, Specialist. Shooting *is* first aid. *¿Comprende?*"

"Yes, Sergeant." I scanned the smoke, waiting for giants to materialize.

We heard the sound of shields clashing, and a few moments later the giants emerged from the smoke in a tight formation, nine men wide and two ranks deep. Their shields fit together almost perfectly.

"They're just going to steamroll right into us," Woodward said.

"Fire in the hole," Takahashi grunted.

I waved to Rivers-of-Blood. "Big fire! Boom! Get down!"

With a high-explosive, dual-purpose (HEDP) round in the M203, Takahashi stood and launched it straight into the formation. The round could penetrate two inches of steel. Whether it could penetrate the giants' shields, none of us knew. We could only hope these shields hadn't been blessed by their dark priests like the others had been.

I couldn't remember exactly what range was considered danger-close for a low-velocity 40mm HEDP grenade, but when I heard the shrapnel buzz overhead like an angry hornet, I was certain we were in it.

The explosion ripped a massive hole in the center of the shield wall. It had to have taken out at least a couple of giants. But the remaining brutes were unfazed, and quickly moved to close the gap.

Takahashi immediately fired another round, and this time I threw myself flat on the ground. He loaded explosive round after explosive round in his M203 until I was sure with each shot that he was out, but he kept firing his rifle rhythmically as he shifted his aim to pick apart the giants wherever they stacked together. He was forcing them to spread out, and when they weren't massed behind the shield walls they were vulnerable, individual targets for our guns and the Sugar Skull Gals' blades.

I scrambled back to one knee and brought my rifle up to my shoulder. The giants were separated, but still on the offensive. They were charging. They'd gained a lot of ground since I'd last seen them only moments before.

Breathe. Relax. Aim. Squeeze.

I centered my sights on the bridge of a giant's nose at fifty meters and felt the trigger break. A second later he froze, a look of surprise on his ugly face, stumbled, and fell.

I was already picking my next target.

Rivers-of-Blood shrieked a war cry, and the riders raced out to the sides and then curved back to hit the giants in the flank.

I was getting consistent headshots, but sometimes it took two, even three hits to bring them down. Captain Brown was showing off his Ranger training, and in the process showing all of us up.

"Mag out!" I cried.

I had a rhythm going now, and my reload was smooth, hardly interrupting my rate of fire. Not gonna lie. It felt badass.

Harassed by the Sugar Skull Gals, the giants on the flanks began to square off with them in close combat. That left a group of six headed directly for us.

Thirty meters.

Twenty.

Three giants had gone down.

Ten meters.

Only one giant left and he wasn't quitting.

The giant swung his oversized war club in a great horizontal arc meant to scythe us like wheat. I fell flat. I heard the hiss of the giant's macuahuitl passing overhead and then a deep, surprised grunt.

I looked up and saw that Takahashi had thrust his sword up under the giant's chin, through his head, and out the top of his skull. He'd had to jump *high* to make that strike. Like dunking a basketball.

Michael Jordan, eat your heart out.

The giant swayed for a moment, then teetered and crashed to the earth.

Nobody was calling for a medic, but I checked everyone out anyway. They were fine. Then the riders returned from dispatching their own giants without issue. Not a scratch. We were damned lucky.

Except for Anderson, of course.

And Wind-Dancer.

The bird lay in the grass making weak clucking noises, her head held gently in Xochi's lap. Tears stained the princess's war paint.

I knelt beside her. "Are you injured?"

Xochi shook her head.

"Can I check?"

"I am all right."

"I should check," I insisted.

"Leave me, please."

I nodded, got up, and backed away several paces.

Rivers-of-Blood came to stand beside me. "Half of her heart is dead," she said in a low voice.

Captain Brown joined us in our vigil. "Is the bond that strong?" he asked.

"Very much. Many birds perish from sorrow if their rider dies. Many warriors take their lives if their mount dies. They are one life, after all. How can you live when half of you is dead?"

Xochi drew her bronze dagger.

I started forward, but Rivers-of-Blood moved in front of me and held my arms. "You must not interfere. What will be will be. It is her choice."

Shrieking like a hawk, Xochi raised her dagger high. The bronze glinted in the red light of the black sun.

A cry strangled in my throat as she brought it plunging down… into Wind-Dancer's head.

The wind blew across the grass in a rippling wave, and then all was still.

CHAPTER 22

After a long moment during which I didn't dare breathe, Xochi reached up and sawed off her topknot. Then, with reverent care, she removed Wind-Dancer's saddle and bridle. She gave them to Rivers-of-Blood and threw her saddlebags over her shoulder.

When Xochi turned to me, the expression behind her tear-streaked war paint was a mask.

"It grows late," she said. "There may be other patrols. We must make haste."

"But what about—"

"Wind-Dancer is gone," she said coldly. "Only flesh and bone remain. She will be food for the beasts of the savanna, and the cycle of life will continue."

I wanted to say something more, something comforting, but I didn't know what.

Takahashi called us over to where the others were huddled in a defensive perimeter while Brown and Xochi discussed next steps.

"How many mags you got?" he asked me.

I had two, and he instructed me to give one to Woodward.

"Listen," Takahashi said to the group. "We're low on ammo, so if we have another engagement you need to make your shots count. No burst fire. Bennett, how fast can Anderson move?"

"He's barely held together with staples… So, not very, Sergeant," I said.

Anderson wasn't going to be running anytime soon, or even making double-time. At least not without ripping his stitches.

"Go tell that to Captain Brown," Takahashi told me. "And see if Anderson can get a ride on one of those birds."

"I'll ask, but if Doc couldn't ride one, I'm not optimistic about Anderson."

I hustled off to join the captain and Xochi. The princess wore an expressionless mask, her spark of laughter gone.

I reported to the captain first. "We can't move at more than a walk following Anderson's injury, sir."

Xochi spoke without looking at me. "At a walk, we will not reach your mounts until well after dark."

"How many hours after dark are we talking?" Brown asked.

"I do not understand *hours*," Xochi said. "Perhaps when the Old Mother rises above the western horizon."

"What's that?" he asked. "A constellation?"

I nodded. "It is, sir. Esapotl taught me that one. It should be visible at about twenty-one hundred hours."

The Old Mother was a cluster of stars that vaguely resembled Virgo. The story of the Old Mother was… disturbing.

"All right, men," Brown said. "Charlie Mike."

Anderson flinched visibly as he stood. "Got some morphine, Bennett?" he asked me.

"Later, Anderson. Try to suck it up for now."

"It hurts real bad, man."

"I only have enough for emergencies. *Real* emergencies," I said. "Try to suck it up."

"Come on, man," he whined.

"Just give him some already," García said.

"Sergeant, if I give him any it might make him sick and we'll have to carry him."

"Suck it up, Private," Takahashi said, and that was final. "Let's move out."

We continued to walk toward the rising smoke, and when the sky grew dark, we followed the path made by the stolen Humvees through the tall grass. It was slow going; Anderson kept complaining and we had to take frequent breaks. The rest of us followed him almost blindly, aided only by the stars. The Old Mother was well above the horizon by the time we got to the scene.

What we found there was ugly. The dead bodies of giants littered the landscape, chewed apart by the Fifty and the nineteen-mike-mikes. Spent brass was everywhere. The trucks had been overturned and ransacked, but there was no sign of anyone inside them, alive or dead. Alpha, Doc, and Sanchez had either escaped in the last truck together and alive, or they had taken the bodies of their dead with them.

Except one.

That was the most disturbing part. The now-ruined trucks were all parked around a pyramid of wood that looked to have been harvested from the Kuauchanejkej's forest. Lying on top of it was Sergeant Douglas. He was clearly dead. And not by an infection from his stitched-up stump or some war wound suffered in the battle. I think he was dead before the giants even hit the trucks. He'd been strangled, and the red marks around his neck stood out against his pale skin and blue lips.

"Looks like he's on a funeral pyre," Takahashi remarked as we gathered around our fallen comrade.

"No," Xochi said, her voice grave. "An altar. This man was to be sacrificed."

Captain Brown had been stalking through the wreckage, but he stopped on hearing that. "Sacrificed to what, exactly?"

"Mictlāntēcuhtli. To gain his favor, one is to offer a human sacrifice of both the living and the dead together. This one, your friend, was the dead."

Captain Brown stood glued to his spot. I think we all were. The giant attack was plain enough to comprehend, but the only ones in a position to set up an altar of wood made from the forest we'd just come from, and then surround it with our Humvees... was Alpha.

The captain looked around. "So who was the living? Diego? Doc?"

"That's two people," Takahashi said. "So they could try this again. What I don't get is why they would. It doesn't make sense.

Even for this place. Even considering"—he looked uncomfortable saying this—"how they've been acting."

Xochi had an answer. "The lure of Mictlāntēcuhtli is irresistible to those he has taken possession of. Some succumb quickly and exist in a living rot of deep hunger. Others… over time. He is a source of very dark evil."

Like I said. Disturbing. I had been worried about St. James and Alpha since the slaughter of Epasotl's people. But even I had never anticipated something like this.

"We need to keep moving," Captain Brown said, "but not before we search one more time. The grass is tall and this place is a mess. If Doc or Diego are here, I want to find them."

Everyone fanned out to take another look. It wasn't long before one of the Sugar Skull Gals hissed at a discovery and we all came rushing to her side.

"Defiled ground," she said, pointing to a stela much like the one Dee had touched. We could only see the top of it; it was almost completely buried and had been covered by the tall grass of the savanna. We wouldn't have seen it at all had we not been carefully combing through the tall grass.

"How did Alpha know this was here?" I asked aloud, giving voice to the question my train of thought had led me to.

It was Rivers-of-Blood who answered instead of Xochi. Perhaps she saw the strain of sorrow and fatigue that was on the princess's face. I doubted I was the only one who observed it. Xochi was clearly grieving.

"It is as my princess said. The lure of Broken Face is irresistible. The dark one led them here to make the sacrifice. Thanks to the giants, the ritual failed, but if two sacrifices remain, one living and one recently dead, they will try again."

Apparently Broken Face was another name for Mictlāntēcuhtli. Somehow that nickname sounded to me more like a character from one of the captain's comics than the literal lord of hell.

We didn't find Doc or Sanchez. Maybe they were alive and awaiting the same fate as Douglas. It occurred to me that we hadn't bothered to check Jensen's grave before we left in a hurry to catch

Alpha. Might they have dug him up for this? I wondered if he still counted as "recently" dead.

"Somethin's out there," García said.

We all snapped our rifles up and watched the perimeter. I dropped my NVGs and listened. If this wasn't worthy of using up some battery juice, what was?

There was a distinct rustling in the grass. It took me a moment, but I could see a slight displacement in the tall stalks in that direction. I motioned to make sure the others saw the same and kept the area in my sights. "Might be more of those lizard things," I warned the group.

"I am not a lizard."

I knew that voice. "Epasotl?"

"Yes. I will stand. Do not shoot at me."

Captain Brown gave the order, and a moment later I could see Epasotl's large eyes glowing a haunting green through my NVGs. I was glad to see her.

She entered our perimeter with her ears down, looking warily at Xochi and her warriors. Captain Brown seemed almost as relieved as I was to see her.

"Epasotl," he said. "I'm glad you're all right. Can you tell me what happened?"

She gave a low growl and then gave a hurried story about "Holy James" and the others that Captain Brown would ask her to repeat in more detail several more times over the course of the next few days.

According to Epasotl, Alpha had begun keeping strictly to themselves from the moment we left them behind. They would speak only to one another except when Sanchez spoke to them first. Almost as soon as we had left for the village, Alpha got busy gathering branches from the forest, collecting them with almost an urgency. At first they built them up as if they were fortifications, and Sanchez saw no reason to interfere. Epasotl said he approved, actually. No surprise there. But then, when Dressed-in-Stars came to get Doc after Wilson was injured, they inexplicably began to toss the wood inside the empty Humvees.

"That is when they became possessed," Epasotl said, her voice filled with disgust. "I could see the truth in their eyes. The deadness of one whose soul has been eclipsed by Mictlāntēcuhtli."

I thought back to the temple we moved through where Dee was consumed. It all flashed in my mind, how it happened.

"When Dee got… possessed," I said, "I asked everyone else if they'd touched anything. We all said no, but Bond and St. James shared a funny look. I pressed them on it, and Bond chewed me out over it. I didn't think anything of it at the time, but…"

Captain Brown patted my shoulder and then looked at the others. "And they were the ones who sabotaged our remaining trucks?"

Epasotl nodded, but her attention was divided as she sniffed the air.

Brown worried his brow. "What is it, Epasotl? Are the giants returning?"

She didn't answer, but instead darted off and disappeared into the grass again. I could hear her rustling in the dark, and then she sprang up again, perhaps thirty meters from our position. "I have found the little kahuna."

Sanchez.

We hurried to join her and found our platoon daddy a good distance off in the grass, bound and gagged with a bloody cut above his eye. He was pinned down beneath the mangled body of a giant. It took several of us to lift off the corpse, get him to his feet, and hold him upright while the circulation drove pins and needles through his body. He was loopy, practically dying of thirst, so I administered hydration and tended to his wounds.

Once Sanchez got his wits about him, he corroborated Epasotl's story up to where she'd left off and then told us that if we were going to find Doc, it wouldn't be here.

"At the camp," Sanchez rasped, "they started actin' real funny. Funnier than usual. So I went up to Bond and asked what he thought he was doing with the firewood. Bond got right up in my face and started jawin', and Wright comes over to do the same. That ain't happening. I'm ready to throat-punch the both of 'em when I get the sense that someone's comin' up behind me. I turned just in time to see St. James bringing the butt of his M16 down on me." Sanchez pointed to the cut above his eye. "Gave me this."

"What happened next?" Captain Brown asked, quickly darting his eyes to Xochi, whose warriors were graciously providing security and overwatch while we sorted through this nightmarish mess.

"Then… I woke up and we were rolling. They had me tied up and gagged, and knew to do it well enough that I couldn't get out. At least not easily. I started working on it. It was the sound that woke me, though. Like a struggle. So I lift my head up and McKee is driving and Bond and Evans are strangling Sergeant Douglas with a garrote." Sanchez's brown eyes looked downward. "He was kickin' and fightin' the whole way. But you can't fight your way outta something like that. Not tied up with one arm to begin with and against two men…"

Sanchez and Epasotl shared the storytelling duties from there. Sanchez wasn't alone in getting jumped. Alpha subdued Doc at gunpoint, then did the same to Epasotl. It was hard to tell in the dark at the time, but she'd taken a serious beating.

In time the trucks stopped, and the construction of the altar had begun, overseen by St. James. Looking at it now, I could see that it was the *exact* altar he'd ordered created for McCoppin. Was he, too, burned as a sacrifice? Were the Chaneques he'd slaughtered?

It looked that way now.

The Bible warned of angels of light coming with false messages meant to destroy. This was a good reminder to me that evil didn't always look like Dee. Sometimes evil is something you don't expect.

I didn't like Alpha, but this… It made me sick.

When the planned sacrifice to Mictlāntēcuhtli was interrupted by the giants, as Rivers-of-Blood had speculated, Alpha had to fight for their lives. They did so admirably, but were ultimately forced to consolidate into a single Humvee and go. Epasotl had chewed through her restraints and escaped at the very start of the battle, and had been moving in the direction of Camp Arizona, thinking we might come and find her there, when she heard our weapons fire echo across the plains and came back to find us. Doc and Sanchez had never been taken off the trucks to begin with—apparently

Epasotl had been selected to serve as the "living" sacrifice—but even in the chaos Alpha went to the trouble of consolidating their two remaining captives onto the same departing truck, no doubt seeing the two as a second chance to complete their sacrificial ritual.

Only, Sanchez managed to throw himself out of the truck just as they were taking off. The giants' pursuit was too close and Alpha wasn't about to turn around, but when a giant stumbled over Sanchez's body it was lit up by the fifty cal. The aftermath of that event was how we found our platoon sergeant.

Doc, however, was still captive. God help him.

I looked at the body of Sergeant Douglas on the altar. A tough man, and a good one. Like Jensen before him. And Grant. Shrimpton. Harris. McCoppin. Dee. And more, going all the way back to Arizona.

When we entered the Land of the Black Sun, we were a platoon of thirty-one men.

Now we were thirteen.

***

"As much as I'd like for us to return to the tree village and regroup," Captain Brown told us, "I'm not willing to do that without Doc."

Captain was certain Doc would escape the first chance he got—he *was* a fellow Ranger after all—and then he'd be alone in a wilderness infested with savage tribes, nightmare beasts, and the ravenous undead. And we all wanted to go get him. Not to mention make Alpha pay for what they had done to Douglas. He'd probably saved all of our lives at one time or another.

By this time the rear element had caught up to us, just in time to see Douglas buried. We had dug a grave for our friend away from the wicked altar and laid him deep enough that the lizards of the savanna would let him rest in peace. Captain Brown's speech was short. He looked at the grave and said, "I'm sorry."

It didn't feel like too little somehow, despite its brevity. We all knew what Douglas had done for us. Now he was gone. We were all sorry for it. That was that.

Death grew more familiar.

"We're dividing you into two teams," Sanchez said. "Gold Team will be led by Sergeant Takahashi and Corporal Stanley, with Cohen, Cameron, Lawrence, and Greene. Sergeant García and Corporal Bennett will lead Blue Team with Woodward, Pierce, and Anderson. Captain Brown and I will augment teams as needed. We'll get Wilson in the mix once he heals up fully."

It took me a moment to recognize the field promotion. To be honest I wasn't exactly thrilled at the prospect of being an assistant team leader. Pierce was more qualified if you asked me, but nobody had. Maybe it was just a time-in-rank thing.

We spent time going over the intricacies of the plan. Catching up to the truck would be hard, but not impossible. Sanchez figured Alpha would have run out of fuel not long after their escape. That meant they would be on foot and, unless they killed Doc, forced to march at the pace of a prisoner who would do everything in his power to escape or slow them down. Doc knew we'd be in pursuit. There was no leaving a man behind.

It would call for a hard and relentless march, especially for the wounded Anderson, who would likely have to stay back in what would pass for a meager rear guard and catch up during the lead scout's respites. But we would do it.

"I want to thank you all for your help," Captain Brown said to the Sugar Skull Gals, who had been listening from outside the circle of our fire and quietly consoling their princess over her loss. "Once again, we live because of your bravery. We will not forget this. We remain in your debt."

"You were promised a guide," Xochi said. It was the first time she'd spoken since we'd left her bird along with the rest of the battlefield wreckage, carrying everything of value that we could away from those Humvees. "I will go with you."

"My Princess, no!" Rivers-of-Blood exclaimed. "You cannot. Send me."

"I am no longer your princess," Xochi said softly. "The queen... my mother... I am disinherited."

That was news to me. Them too, apparently. A chorus of gasps rose from Xochi's warriors, and Rivers-of-Blood began protesting vehemently.

Xochi laid a hand on her arm. "There is nothing for me in Kuauchanko, sister. Wind-Runner is dead, and I am stripped of my privilege. I have cut my hair. See? I can no longer ride the path of the warrior. I choose a new path. I go with the Outworlders."

"Then we will go with you," Rivers-of-Blood said.

The other warriors murmured in agreement.

Rivers-of-Blood turned to Captain Brown. "We wish to join your... Cavalry. How might this be done?"

Brown rubbed the back of his head. You didn't have to be a genius to see that this was a complex social situation that involved our sole indigenous allies. And Captain Brown was more astute than most. "Your assistance would be invaluable. However, I am not yet fully familiar with the customs or expectations of your people. I do not wish to overstep my boundaries."

He looked to Xochi, who nodded her thanks back to him. She turned and looked at each of her warriors in turn.

"No, my sisters. Your duty is to our people and your queen. You know this. Do not defy your purpose. To do so would bring shame and vengeance upon the one for whom you intend to show only your love."

She was speaking of herself. And... she must have been speaking the truth. I could see tears welling in the eyes of Rivers-of-Blood. The rest of the retinue sniffled their sorrow openly.

"The sun will hide his face," Rivers-of-Blood said, her voice choked with emotion.

But Xochi remained stoic and regal. She may have been disinherited, but all I saw standing there was a proud, capable princess. "We will ride together again, my dear ones. If not in this life, then the next."

CHAPTER 23

"A barbarian like you could not track a giant turtle-rabbit across a muddy field," Epasotl snapped at Xochi.

We had followed the course of the last Humvee and had finally found it abandoned with no signs of life or death around it. We were able to grab some supplies and ammunition from it and add it to our already heavy loads, and since then the full platoon—puny as we might be—had been serving as government-issue pack mules. Epasotl and Xochi shared the duty as lead trackers, and both were doing a fine job in my view, despite their bickering.

The Humvee had been bone-dry on fuel as expected, which only encouraged us to pick up the pace as we continued after Alpha. Xochi said that Alpha was following the urges of Mictlāntēcuhtli, while we traveled with a noble purpose, and somehow in her mind this meant we would be swifter than them. I wasn't so sure about that, but as she and Epasotl discovered the tracks of quarry through broken trails of tall grass, it did start to look like they were wandering a bit, sometimes in circles.

Every man felt we would catch them, and every minute that passed without finding Doc's corpse made us believe we would rescue him.

But it would help if our native scouts reduced their mutual hostility.

"I can track a wolf-vulture across the savanna after a week with no rain," Xochi spat back. "And I can do it riding a warbird. I do not have to get down on all fours and sniff the earth like a savage beast."

"At least I can smell!" Epasotl shot back. "Your nose is clogged with dust, your eyes are fogged, and your ears are full of wax."

I sighed.

Alpha's route took them not back toward Camp Arizona, but slightly northwest across the plains, and despite our early optimism we didn't seem to get any closer to our quarry. Several days later we were still in pursuit, now deep into the jungle on the western side of the savanna, the black sun's wan red light filtering down through the canopy. Epasotl had taken point, as she could sniff out the trail Alpha had taken. It seemed that, in a jungle environment at least, she did prove to be the better of the two trackers. I wisely did not share this observation with Xochi.

In the end, however, when we finally did encounter a member of Alpha, it was Sergeant Takahashi who found him.

"Got somethin', Cap'n!" he shouted. "It's McKee."

Scouts and soldiers moved to the sergeant's voice. McKee was lying flat on his back with a badly broken neck. Ants were swarming all over him, streaming out of his mouth, nose, and eye sockets, making quick work of breaking down his flesh. It made my skin crawl, and I saw some of the others rubbing at their faces like they could feel the ants too.

"I'll bet my last bullet that Doc did that," Sanchez said upon inspecting the grisly remains. "Lifesaver *and* a lifetaker. Hooah."

"Bastard's rifle is gone," said James. "So's his ruck. I hope Doc took 'em instead them Alpha boys."

"And why could your proud nose not find this?" Xochi taunted Epasotl.

My Chaneque friend only hissed in response.

"Allow me to remind all of us that we're on the same team with the same goals," Captain Brown said to the group, though it was clear who most needed to hear the admonition. "Epasotl, this corpse tells us that you've led us along the right track. Thank you."

Epasotl almost purred with satisfaction. Her lips curled up into a singularly ugly smile. "The Doc went that way," she said, pointing in one direction. Then she pointed in a different direction. "Holy James and the others went that way."

Another fight between Epasotl and Xochi broke out over how best to read the faint tracks, or in Epasotl's case, faint smells. Never mind Captain Brown's gentle correction just a few moments earlier.

"That is *not* what the sign tells!" Xochi snapped. "They followed him."

"The dark one deceives your eyes, barbarian," Epasotl retorted with a threatening hiss. "My nose cannot be tricked. It is not Holy James who is now following Doc. It is others. They smell of death."

"The ravenous undead?" I said.

Epasotl nodded. "But he is well ahead. They came through recently. He departed before dawn. Alpha left in a different direction. The Doc must have fooled them into following a false path. He is clever."

"That will not matter," Xochi said. "If the Children of Mictlāntēcuhtli are pursuing, your friend is as good as dead."

"He's not dead until we find his body," said Captain Brown. "We follow."

"What about Alpha Section?" asked Takahashi. "Assuming Epasotl is right and we don't find them on Doc's back trail, I mean."

"We will deal with them later," Sanchez said. His tone made clear it wasn't going to be a happy reunion.

"So… these Children," I said. "What should we expect exactly? When Dee *changed*, he was incredibly strong."

"Yeah," put in García. "Are they like the Deadites in *Evil Dead 2*? Or the zombies in *Day of the Dead*? I mean, what are we dealing with? Are they fast or slow? Smart or stupid? Can they use weapons? How do you kill 'em? Do we need a chainsaw?"

"I do not understand most of what you ask," Xochi replied. "The Lord of Mictlān's children are as intelligent as they were in life, but possessed by an insatiable hunger for sentient beings. They move like the wind, employ weapons, and will not stop even when wounded grievously. Decapitation is the only way to destroy them."

"Decapitation kills everything," Takahashi said.

"Not *everything*," Xochi corrected him.

"Good to know," Stanley muttered, pushing his glasses up his nose.

"Lord of Mictlān?" Brown asked. "What is this Mictlan?"

Xochi looked surprised at his ignorance. "It is the Underworld, of course. Mictlāntēcutli is the lord of that realm."

"Can these creatures pass the curse on to others?" Captain Brown asked. "Are they contagious?"

"No," said Epasotl. "If they were, all the land would drown in a flood of ravenous undead."

"Right now all that's relevant is that potential hostiles, who are fast, deadly, and smart, might be pursuing Doc," Sanchez said. "Getting bitten or whatnot won't curse us too. Headshots and decapitation are the only way to stop them. That about sum it up?"

Xochi and Epasotl both nodded.

Sanchez threw a knife hand in the direction Doc had gone. "Then let's go get our man."

***

Our teams took turns on point, swapping every two hours, and moved in a modified wedge. Captain Brown positioned himself directly behind the leading team, and Sergeant Sanchez led the trailing team, with a twenty-meter gap between teams. We spread out as much as we could, while keeping within sight of our immediate team members. Lawrence and Anderson both carried radios and stayed close to Brown and Sanchez.

We set a pace that allowed us to move as silently as possible without reducing us to a crawl, but I was worried that Anderson wouldn't be able to keep up. The day before, I'd had to keep changing his dressings because the combination of blood and healing staples was causing blood to seep through and soak the bandages. He seemed to be doing remarkably well today though. I drifted over to him during a break, thinking he'd need another bandage change. The last thing I wanted was to find Doc only for him to chew me out for letting Anderson get gangrene.

"Let's take a look," I told him. "How you feeling?"

"Pretty good, considering."

I opened his blouse and inspected the wound. "Whoa. Who did this?"

Stuffed beneath the bandages were a bunch of green leaves that looked like they'd been chewed up and spit back out. The green juice had dyed the edges of the white bandage.

"Epasotl," Anderson said, smiling. "She found some kind of rare herb and said it would help me heal. Did this not long after your last bandage change."

I didn't like the idea of some unknown bit of flora mixing it up with a still-healing wound. Especially one as nasty as Anderson's.

"How's it look?" Anderson asked me after I'd stared at the wound stupidly for a few seconds.

I shook my head. "Amazingly well. As in, I wouldn't expect you to look this good for another week or more." I looked up from studying the wound to Anderson's face. "Rare herb, huh?"

"That's what she said, man. Said she'd been sniffing after whatever plant it is for a while and that's what kept her from recognizing McKee was there. Tell her thanks, the next time you see her."

"I will," I said. "And let me know if you see any more of that rare herb as we go. Might be a good idea to harvest some for later. I got a feeling we're gonna need it."

"No shit. You and me both, Bennett."

I hurried back to the front, hopeful for a chance to both thank Epasotl and also ask her what plant she used. My fears of Doc being angry at me once we finally found him changed to eagerness to tell him of our potential ability to replace some of our dwindling aid with natural remedies. But I didn't end up getting a chance to talk to Epasotl that day. She was tireless, bounding ahead and disappearing for long stretches of time as she scouted and tracked, while Xochi remained near the captain, making a good show of doing her own tracking, even though it always ended up taking us in the same direction in which Epasotl had already led us.

Dusk was fast approaching when we came across a dozen or so wattle-and-daub huts thatched with reeds. Everything was still and silent here, and it was obvious why: the bodies of dead Chaneques were scattered among the huts, badly mutilated and crawling with flies.

Captain Brown ordered García to send a three-man team into the village.

García looked at me. "Bennett, take Woodward and Pierce."

The village looked empty except for the corpses, but as I knew from prior experience, the Chaneques could be deadly enemies. And just because Epasotl was friendly with us didn't mean the others would treat us as anything but something to kill.

I assembled my team, double-checked that my rifle had a round in the chamber, and moved forward in a crouch. When we reached the first hut, Woodward staged himself on the left side of the doorway with Pierce on the right. I clapped Woodward's shoulder and we entered, disturbing a cloud of flies that had settled on yet another ravaged corpse. Huge sections of skin and flesh had been peeled off, revealing the bone underneath, and even the bone was scarred by deep marks, like something had been gnawing at it.

Despite the flies, the corpse was fresh enough that it hadn't begun to stink yet.

We quickly cleared the rest of the huts. Some were empty, others contained dead bodies. I waved an all-clear to García, and he and Anderson joined us, along with Captain Brown, Xochi, and Epasotl. Anderson looked strangely detached. Or probably just exhausted. We all were, and I shouldn't expect more from him despite whatever miracle drug Epasotl had given him.

"The ravenous undead," Epasotl hissed, stating the obvious.

"Well, I suppose we're on the right trail at least," García said.

"Yeah," said Pierce. "Behind them."

Captain Brown kicked at a pile of offal with his boot, sending up a swarm of flies. "Looks like they binged and purged."

"They do not *need* to eat," Xochi explained. "But their hunger can never be satiated."

The captain wandered around a bit, then turned a corpse with his boot so that it lay on its side. He squatted next to it. "This one's a Child of Mick."

We approached.

"It ain't a kid," Anderson said. "I thought they would be kids."

"It's an expression, like child of God," I explained.

"Yeah," said Greene. "Or in your case, Anderson, child of an overweight special-needs hoochie."

"Oh, Greenie, I almost forgot—screw you."

I tuned out the back-and-forth after that and looked at the body. The ravenous undead who was now… dead. It had been a man, and I noticed no flies were swarming over him. The back of his head was blown out and there was a small hole between his eyes, which were completely black, with no sclera or iris. His veins were also black, like Dee's had been, and his mouth was opened in a rictus that exposed sharp yellowed teeth. His skin was leathery and ashen, and the nails on his curled hands looked like claws.

"At least Doc has a weapon," Captain Brown said. "Or had one. Search the corpses thoroughly. See if he got any more. Or, worse, if they got him."

We all felt relief at not finding Doc as we searched the ruined Chaneque village.

"You think Doc was trying to make friends with the locals?" García asked. "I don't get why he wouldn't just go around the village. Unless someone else shot that zombie."

"We won't know until we hear it direct from the source," said Captain Brown, his resolve unfailing. "Let's keep up after it. I want to push on in the dark until we catch up with Doc. We'll save the NVGs. When it gets too dark to move safely, use flashlights. Red filter only." He turned to Xochi. "Can these creatures see in the dark?"

"Yes," Xochi said. "As well as they can in the day, but only for a short distance. It is said they are attracted to heat."

"Thermal-vision zombies," Pierce muttered. "This just keeps getting better."

"At least we don't need to worry about light discipline," I said.

"Cut the chatter," Sanchez snapped, perhaps still holding a grudge from our previous interaction. "You all heard the captain. Let's move with a purpose."

***

Epasotl's tracking led us down into a ravine choked with vines, with a stream at its bottom. I was on point, and as I descended the steep slope, the vegetation was so thick I had to hack my way through with my saber. The dim red light from my angle-head flashlight illuminated only the few meters in front of me. Then suddenly I splashed into the stream, and in an instant I was soaked up to my knees in cold water. The rest of me was already soaked through with sweat.

At least the mosquitos had finally gone to bed. It was just after midnight and my sleep-deprived mind was playing all sorts of nasty tricks on me. My eyeballs felt like they were coated with sand, and I was starting to see things in the shadows that weren't there— *hopefully* weren't there, anyway.

I hacked through another tangle and Epasotl pounced in front of me, holding a finger to her lips. I threw up a fist to halt the column and stood before her, panting.

She motioned for me to lean in close, which required squatting in the cold stream. That woke me up a bit.

"I have lost Doc's scent," she hissed into my ear. "But the Children have been here. Very recently. Their stench is strong."

All I could smell was the ammonia coming off my own body as my muscles broke down. I was just one big stinking, lumbering urinal.

I turned back to Pierce and sent word down the line that we'd lost Doc's trail and contact was imminent.

Epasotl tugged on my sleeve, and I turned back to her.

"I need a weapon," she hissed.

"Sure," I said, keeping my voice as low as possible. I handed her my knife, hilt-first. "Don't lose it."

"As if." She rolled her eyes.

"Should we keep moving?" I said, my eyes now peeled for more monsters.

I was alert. The adrenaline was back.

Epasotl sniffed the air. "The stream widens and is shallow ahead. It is a good place for an ambush."

"For us to ambush them or the other way around?"

"For them to ambush you."

"You're suggesting we walk *into* a zombie ambush?"

"We will probably die, but with great honor." Epasotl sounded happy about it.

Captain Brown had made his way up the column and crouched beside us. He didn't so much as flinch at the cold stream.

"Sitrep, Corporal?" he said.

I got him up to speed.

He frowned and played his flashlight over the steep, vine-choked banks of the ravine, then turned to Epasotl. "You said the Children keep their wits. So should we assume they still know how to set up an ambush? Maybe even use their weapons?"

Epasotl nodded. "They will ambush. Some use weapons. Others desire to use their teeth and hands. And they surely can smell you coming."

"And you can smell them," Brown said. "So you're sure it's not Alpha. How far away are they?"

"It is not the smell of Alpha. I told you, they moved in another direction from the Doc. As for these... I cannot say for certain. But if they are waiting where I would wait to ambush you, then... thirty of your meters ahead."

"Okay, listen close, trooper," Captain Brown said, apparently satisfied enough with Epasotl's report to formulate a plan and give orders. "When Sergeant Sanchez gives the word, you lead Blue Team quickly, and I do mean quickly, to this area Epasotl indicates. When you reach it, your team will form a line to draw them out. Do not advance farther. Sling your rifle and collect everyone's magazines. Strictly hand weapons only."

"And Gold Team?" I asked. I wasn't feeling good about this plan. It sounded an awful lot like we were being used as bait. And I didn't like the idea of going up against ravenous undead hand-to-hand. Not one bit.

"Leave Gold Team to me," he replied. "Just remember to form a line and hold. No firearms. I'll send Sergeant García forward with you. Relay my instructions to him. Now, what are my instructions, son?"

"Move forward like hell until the ravine widens, then form a line and hold our ground," I repeated. "No farther, and no rifles. Gather everyone's magazines just to be sure. Hand weapons only."

"Give 'em hell, son." The captain moved back down the line.

A few moments later García joined me, and I repeated the captain's orders.

"Okay," García said, sounding every bit as concerned with the plan as I did. It felt like Captain Brown—for the first time—was playing fast and loose with our lives. Maybe there was an issue of *X-Men* he was thinking of where this all worked out perfectly. I sure hoped so. "I'll lead the charge," he continued. "See to it you instruct each member of the team personally. I want everyone's mags passed up to me. You're responsible for making sure every weapon is cleared. When you're done, take the rear. Make sure everyone does their job and follows me."

"Yes, Sergeant."

"You first, Bennett."

"What? Oh, right." I handed him my magazine and then raked my bolt back, showing him the empty chamber. He nodded.

I slung my rifle behind my back and moved down the line, repeating the orders and clearing rifles as mags passed up the line to García. Finally, I took my position behind Anderson and made sure he was awake and had a knife ready.

Sanchez crept up behind me.

"Your team squared away, Corporal?" He spoke so softly I barely heard him.

"Yes, Sergeant," I subvocalized. "What now?"
"We wait."

CHAPTER 24

There was a muffled *thunk* from up ahead and a few moments later an intense white flare burst over the jungle canopy, sending erratic shafts of light down through the thick leaves.

"Move!" Sanchez clapped my shoulder, and I sent the order forward. We rushed along the stream bed. I heard another *thunk*, this one the sound of a grenade launching, and shortly thereafter a blast rocked the ravine somewhere ahead of us. García was shouting at us to follow him. I had to shove Anderson in front of me to get him moving, and he stumbled. I caught a strap on his ruck to heave him up and pushed him forward.

"On me!" García cried. "Form a line!"

Woodward and Pierce took positions beside García, sabers drawn and knives out. I manhandled Anderson into the formation and readied myself. Sanchez joined me on my right side. I didn't know where Epasotl was. Small fires were burning in the area where the ravine widened, and the vegetation was shredded and smoking.

"Hold steady, boys," our platoon sergeant called out.

Several moments of tense silence followed. Then bodies erupted from the thick tangle of vines on either side of the ravine.

The Children of Mictlāntēcuhtli.

The intense light from the flare, still strobing through the canopy as it fell swinging from its parachute, cast harsh shadows that made everything look surreal. We were facing more than a dozen enemies, maybe two dozen, men and women both, and they charged us with a fury, drawing their lips back against sharp yellow teeth. Some had primitive stone axes or war clubs, others bone-tipped spears. Most were completely nude, and their ash-gray bodies were emaciated, with large, distended stomachs. A few bore what looked to be grievous wounds from the grenade, but it didn't seem to slow them in the least.

M16s barked from high up on the left side of the ravine, the bullets slamming into dead flesh. A round hit one of the Children in the temple, blowing out the side of its head, and it rag-dolled. Another headshot sent a zombie dropping in place like a puppet with its string cut.

And then they were upon us.

We had to stretch out the line to give us room to work our sabers. In a fight like this a short, stabbing weapon would've been preferable to the long, curved blades we swung. I kept looking for an opening to get in a clean decapitation, but I was barely managing to parry and block their frenetic attacks.

Then Gold Team came swarming down the steep face of the ravine, attacking the Children from the flank and back. His order to stick to hand weapons made sense now, as did the precaution of gathering mags. A wise precaution at that, for Anderson was already falling back out of formation, rifle to his shoulder, pulling back on the trigger fruitlessly. If his weapon had been loaded, he'd have been shooting our own men.

Beside me, Woodward was fighting like a madman. He impaled one of the undead through the mouth with his knife. The monster dropped to its knees and Woodward kicked at the head to free his blade, then swung his rifle up to block a strike from a woman's war club. Another slash with the knife sliced the woman's fat belly open, and black intestines spilled at his feet, along with whatever her last meal had been. The sudden eruption of rotting meat made me retch, and I would've been skewered by a spear if Sanchez hadn't stepped in to parry the strike. With a quick flip of his wrist, he pivoted and slashed upward, his heavy blade cleaving deep into the zombie's skull and sending it flailing backward.

I used the moment's reprieve to haul Anderson back in line. His eyes were wild with fear, and I slapped him to get his attention, but he was insensible. He turned on me and slashed with his knife, totally consumed by fear and fighting for survival. It grazed my left arm, deep enough to draw blood but short of any muscle. Still, it hurt like a searing flame.

Without thinking I slammed the hand guard of my saber into his face, and his mouth and nose exploded in blood. He reeled back, dropping his rifle, and stumbled right into the claws of a Child, who howled and sank his teeth into the poor kid's neck.

Anderson went to the ground screaming, and the zombie fell on him. I lifted my saber and brought it down as hard as I could on the back of the creature's exposed neck, severing the head clean off.

Another zombie rushed me, but Epasotl pounced on it from out of nowhere and drove my knife deep into the back of its skull. She flipped off as it fell, landing lightly in front of me.

I caught sight of Xochi elsewhere in the melee, blocking attacks with her shield and striking at the undead with her war club. She took the heads of three Children in as many seconds. There was a beautiful efficiency in her precise movements, like a ballet of violence; she made the rest of us look like clumsy oafs. All of us aside from Takahashi perhaps, who at one point managed to decapitate two of the Children at once.

When the last enemy was down, we all stood under the light of a flare caught in a tree, panting ragged breaths. Combat is enough to make your heart beat out of your chest. Hand-to-hand combat makes you feel like every blood vessel in your body *is* a heart.

We watched for more of the enemy until the flare sputtered and went out. García and Takahashi started calling out names as flashlights came on, red beams stabbing through the darkness.

I got out my med kit and rolled Anderson over. The bite on his neck was savage, and I'd broken his nose, but he'd live.

We'd gotten out surprisingly well, all things considered. No mortal wounds, not even any serious ones… unless Anderson's bite became infected. Bites were always nasty.

García helped me bandage up my arm. It wasn't bad, but like any cut or laceration suffered out here in the field—especially the jungle—there was a chance of infection if you didn't stay on top of things. As he was wrapping me up, a voice called out from the darkness.

"Was wondering when you guys would show up!"

Half a dozen flashlights converged on a mud-covered man limping toward us, an M16 slung over one shoulder.

Doc smiled. "Took you long enough."

After a quick round of greetings, Doc went right to work as though nothing had happened. He was limping as he moved, and I could see that he'd packed some mud onto his leg.

"What's the story with that, Doc?" I asked.

"Just a spear wound. I packed it with clay. Not the best move, but I had to stop the bleeding somehow. I'll take care of it if you let me see your med kit."

"Kit's kinda sparse," I said apologetically. "Alpha must've taken your supply when they took you. Wasn't much left in the trucks for me to pack up."

He sifted through the contents of my bag with a frown. "Well, it'll have to do."

"Feel free to work while you talk, but I'd like to know just what happened out there," Captain Brown said.

Doc looked over at Sanchez. "XO probably already told you about Douglas."

Sanchez nodded. "Everything up through my escape. Got pinned under a giant or I'd've come after you."

"I'm just glad to see you're still breathing. I thought for sure you'd broken your neck bailing out like that."

Captain Brown gave Doc a look that said to get on with it.

"Yes, sir. After the truck ran out of fuel, we moved on foot. They intended to sacrifice me, only from what I could gather, they needed two, one living and one dead. They were talking over how to make it happen. Strange talk. It wasn't all English. Some of it was that language Bennett speaks."

Everyone was riveted by Doc's story. We needed to move on, set up a place to stay overnight. All that stuff. But at that moment, we had an even greater need to know what had happened. We'd all pushed ourselves to death's doorstep to find this man, and now our reward was hearing what had happened to him.

"They kept my feet free so I could walk faster. And I had worked myself to a point where I could get my arms free if I needed to. Ranger tricks." Doc winked at us. "I was biding my time, looking for the opportunity. It came when Clark started vomiting uncontrollably. I was away from them, guarded by McKee. He looked to see what was happening. It wasn't pretty. In fact, it pretty much sounds like what you described with Private Dee, Bennett. So I took the initiative, killed McKee, grabbed his rifle, picked up his ruck, and took off."

He looked thoughtful. "I should have shot the others. I kicked myself over not doing it, but my mind was set on escape."

"You did fine, trooper," Captain Brown said. "You might've just as easily gotten yourself shot, and we need you out here."

Doc smiled, not quite satisfied. "Just hope we don't all regret it someday."

"We found a zombie with a bullet hole in its head back at a Chaneque village," Sanchez said. "That was you, right?"

"You saw that mess, did you?" Doc gave a slow shake of his head. "The place looked abandoned, so I went in to see if there were any tools or food or the like. They were all dead and the creatures had all moved on. Except one. It saw me, I shot it. Then I left."

Takahashi looked around the battlefield. "So these things weren't chasing you?"

"If they were, I didn't know about it. I was already orienting myself to head east, figuring that Alpha was far enough away for me to try and link up with you, when I heard the gunfire and figured I knew who made it. Glad I was right."

Captain Brown shook our medic—our Doc's—hand. "So are we."

***

We encamped above the ravine, taking turns sleeping and holding security. There was a small fire for boiling water from the stream and for Doc to heat his knife, which he was using to cauterize superficial wounds.

He also tended to Anderson, who was worse off than I had first thought. The broken nose was of minor concern—Doc just packed it with gauze and bandaged it—but the kid was delirious with fever. We assumed it was from the bite. Doc complimented me on stapling up the kid's wound and I told him that Epasotl had been the bigger help there thanks to the poultice she'd made. The bite though wasn't looking too good. It was bleeding again and the edges of the wound were red and puffy. It was also starting to smell a little off and had developed a yellowish-white discharge.

I asked Epasotl whether she had any more of those "rare herbs."

"A winter plant only blooms in summer when the gods will it. Do not expect such a blessing again, Ben-Ette."

I took that as a no.

We were debating what to do when Xochi came to us and untied a small, stoppered gourd from her belt.

"For his wound," she said.

"What is it?" Doc asked.

"The sap of the maguey mixed with paste from coca leaves. It will help the infection and reduce pain."

"They used the same thing on Wilson," I said. "I don't know if it helped, but it didn't hurt. He seemed to recover quickly, but that could have been the antibiotics just as much."

"Maguey sap has been used for centuries as an antibiotic," Doc said. "The science is debatable, but yeah, it can't hurt. I'm not so sure about the coca leaves though."

"They will help reduce bleeding, swelling, and pain," Xochi said.

"Yeah, because it's cocaine," Doc said. "It's a highly addictive drug."

"Many of our warriors chew coca leaves, especially before battle," Xochi said. "It has many beneficial properties. But I will not use so much as to intoxicate him. That would be foolish."

Doc nodded his approval and watched with interest as she unstopped the gourd and dribbled a thick, viscous fluid along the cut. It was a milky, greenish color and smelled both sweet and earthy with a bitter undertone that reminded me of kerosene. She rubbed it in gently with her fingertips, and Doc applied a fresh dressing.

"Now your leg," Xochi said to Doc.

Doc looked uncertain.

"That goop is good enough for Wilson and Anderson, but not for you?" I said.

He chuckled. "Fair enough." He unwrapped the strip of cloth. "We need to flush it out first and clean it."

"No," said Xochi. "If you remove the clay plug it will begin bleeding again. Better to leave it in."

"It's fine," Doc said. "I'll clean it, repack it with gauze treated with iodine, and then we can smear some of your smelly goop on it and wrap it back up. Bennett, get me some boiled water? Preferably still hot."

I fetched a steaming canteen cup, and he irrigated the puncture before trying to dig out the clay with a pair of forceps. Sweat broke out on his brow and he gritted his teeth.

"Can't do it," he said. "Bennett, you need to get all that clay out of the wound."

"You sure?" I said.

"Just get it over with."

It took some doing, and a lot of cursing from Doc. I had to keep flushing out fresh blood to see into the wound, but after a while I was fairly certain I'd gotten it all out. I diluted some iodine and dipped the gauze in it before repacking the ragged hole. Xochi smeared her magic elixir over the wound, and we wrapped it with a clean field dressing.

"Feels better already," Doc said.

"Hurt me more than it hurt you, Doc," I said.

He laughed. "That's my line."

***

In the predawn of the following morning we trudged onward through the deep forest, dragging Anderson on a travois. We'd managed a few catnaps in between watches, but it hadn't done much for me; I felt practically asleep on my feet. We needed real sleep, but the captain was afraid the flare and gunfire from our encounter with the Children would draw unwanted attention and so we had to get some distance before circling the wagons.

Xochi led us. "Get us out of this jungle and back to your people," was all Captain Brown had told her. "I prefer to get us all somewhere safe where we can rest and heal up."

"Given how far we've already come, we could push on to Amoloyan," Sanchez suggested.

Brown shook his head. "Not without Wilson."

I pursed my lips and may have grimaced upon hearing that. I think the captain saw it.

Still, I liked the sound of the word "safe." At night, the forest had been full of glowing eyes reflecting the red light of our flashlights, and now in the daylight shadows flitted from tree to tree, following us. I'd lost track of what the date was back in the world, or even how long we'd been in the Land of the Black Sun. T-plus something; someone probably knew. Not that it mattered. I just wanted to sleep forever.

We didn't want to go back the way we'd come for fear of another ambush. Neither Epasotl nor Xochi had the slightest clue where those zombies had come from, but Captain Brown speculated there might be a "Mickey Mouse" temple nearby.

That was when Captain Brown's shortening of Mictlāntēcuhtli—first "Mick," now "Mickey Mouse"—really took on a life of its own. Eventually some of the guys started to refer to the ravenous undead as "Mouseketeers" and call the forbidden ruins—not to be confused with *our* Disneyland, the Disney Barracks at Fort Knox where we spent our time in OSUT—which, come to think of it, was its own special magical hell.

Xochi seemed to know where she was going. She said that she and her warriors had occasionally ranged this far, but the way was dangerous because of the Chaneques. These forests, after all, were their domain. Because of that, Epasotl stayed up front as well, using her nose and familiarity with the jungles to avoid trouble while Xochi led us to our destination.

After two days of humping it—at a slower pace now that we had Doc and with not-nearly-adequate-enough stops to catnap and gnaw on pemmican—we came upon the ruins of a city that was decidedly *not* Chaneque. Vine-entangled pyramids rose up above what appeared to have once been a vast complex of buildings, though now they were mostly crumbled and dilapidated stone walls almost completely swallowed by the jungle.

We ventured a few meters toward the mist-enshrouded discovery and came upon two massive clumps of vegetation covering what looked like some carved stone.

"Someone call Indiana Jones," Greene muttered.

I began to gingerly pull aside the vines with my saber.

"Careful," Doc warned me. "We might be at another Disneyland."

"Magic Kingdom locations in California, Tokyo, and now… hell on earth," said Pierce.

"There's one in Florida already," Greene shot back.

The vines revealed stone cut so precisely you couldn't fit a knife between the seams, much of it carved with motifs featuring jaguars who walked upright and held weapons, battling monstrous creatures that defied description.

I turned to Epasotl. "Relatives of yours?"

"My people are not *cats*," she hissed. "Why you Outworlders insist on calling us names like 'kitty' I do not understand. We look *nothing* like cats."

"You look *something* like a cat," I said.

"As if." She snorted. "Do I walk with backward-bended knees or have a tail? Do I have only two ears? You resemble a monkey more than I do a cat."

"This is a *Tlacaocēlōtl* city," Xochi breathed reverently, not bothering to hide her awe. "They are said to have been powerful sorcerers and fierce warriors with great skill in stone and metalworking. They were a great and enlightened people, before they became corrupted by dark magic in their thirst for power. But they lived in the days before the gods. Even their true name is lost to time."

"Before the gods? I thought Smoking Mirror created this world," I said.

"It would be more precise to say he *re*-created it. He subdued it and remade it in his own image. Songs tell of great battles between his armies and the Tlacaocēlōtls—although some legends claim it was the Tlacaocēlōtls who summoned Smoking Mirror here to begin with, seeking to bind and control him. In so doing, they brought about their own destruction."

Captain Brown was eagerly taking in all of this new intel. "Did you know this place was here, Princess?"

I thought I caught a flash of shame on Xochi's face, but if it was there, it went away quickly. "Yes. Not the exact location, but I knew it was somewhere close and because of its history, abandoned. An aged warrior I knew in my childhood—she married but was unable to bear children and so returned to her queen's service—claimed to have seen it once, but only a glimpse. I see now that her description was true and without exaggeration."

"How about you, Epasotl?" Brown asked. "Did you know of this place?"

She shook her head. "As I have said, we are well beyond my tribe's range. But even the tribes who live in this land will steer clear. Chaneques are not so foolish as to trespass into haunted places such as these. The spirits here are old, and restless."

"Tlacaocēlōtl… that means 'jaguar man,'" I said to Xochi, nodding to the motifs I had uncovered. "Is that meant literally?"

Xochi shook her head. "I do not know. They have been gone for seasons beyond measure. But some claim the Tlacaocēlōtls learned how to assume the form of men and live among us even now." She drew her bronze dagger. "This blade is a Tlacaocēlōtl artifact."

"They wielded daggers like our own, but they weren't human," Captain Brown said. "I wonder, then, how it was that this land came to be dominated by humans."

Epasotl took exception to this. "We are dominated by no one. Least of all by your kind."

"I meant no offense, Epasotl. You know that," Captain Brown said, and then, to my surprise, he tousled Epasotl's hair the same way I often would. She seemed to enjoy it, despite herself.

"The dagger," said Sanchez, who was standing nearby and listening. "How did you acquire it? Did someone find it? Did it get passed down?"

I got the sense that Sanchez might have thought that rather than disappearing, these people had eventually turned into the Kuauchanejkej.

"I took it as a spoil of war," Xochi said, not without a little pride. "It is said to have great power. I won it off the corpse of a giant I defeated in single combat."

"You fought a giant, in single combat, and survived?" I was trying to imagine her, a young woman under five feet tall, besting a man nearly three times her size.

"A large part of the victory is owed to Wind-Runner." A smile appeared on Xochi's face, but it did not reach her eyes. "But it was my lance that pierced his heart."

I let out a whistle. "It must have been an epic contest."

Captain Brown and Sanchez looked impressed as well.

"It was the first blood I drew as a warrior," she said proudly. "The warlord of the giants saluted me that day and ceded the field to us."

That little note caught Brown's attention right away. "Just like that? An entire battle decided in single combat?"

"Of course," Xochi said simply.

"Even barbarians fight with honor," Epasotl interjected. "Sometimes."

"As do savages," Xochi replied. "Sometimes."

CHAPTER 25

It began to drizzle, and the wind picked up as we moved cautiously through the ancient ruins. Epasotl did not like this at all—she had warned us to stay clear of the place, her ears laid flat—but Xochi told us that there was no need to trek around the abandoned city. That was fine with Captain Brown, so long as we were still heading toward the refuge of the princess's city among the trees. I for one was looking forward to another of those baths.

And at least the city gave us something to look at besides more trees. Some of the walls were unobscured by vegetation, and we caught glimpses of more reliefs like the ones I had uncovered, portraying the jaguar-men in battle, their figures now worn by eons of rain and wind. Other carvings showed portraits—probably rulers—or scenes of everyday life, or crowds of the jaguar-men worshipping a great feathered serpent whom Xochi explained was Quetzalcoatl. When I asked how that could be, if these people lived *before* the gods of her people as she had said, she simply shrugged and told me not to think so hard about such things or I might damage my head.

Aside from troops of monkeys who hooted in alarm and ran when we came near, the city was empty. There were no signs of habitation. No shelters, no fire pits... nothing. Captain Brown asked Xochi about it.

"How confident are you that no one inhabits this place? Epasotl's people have their superstitions, that I understand, but I wouldn't imagine the Children of Mick are quite as worried about ghost stories."

"They would not be, but there is nothing to feast upon here, you see?" Xochi motioned in a wide arc, taking in the expanse of the city with her gesture. "Nothing but the beasts of the forest haunt this dead city."

Captain Brown grunted. He didn't look convinced, but he didn't argue either. "If this place is as empty as you say and as defensible as it looks—and as a bonus, if it scares off the Chaneques—then I'd like to search for a location where we can lay up for a bit. As much as I'd like to push straight on to your village, my men have been marching for days. They need rest."

Xochi nodded and led us deeper into the maze of buildings. She didn't know this place any better than Epasotl or me and my fellow troopers, but we imagined she'd identify the more subtle types of trouble ahead of our point man, who happened to be me as the rain turned from a warm mist to a downpour. She went straight to one of the many pyramids, which on closer inspection turned out to be vine-encrusted ziggurats, and stopped before a steep staircase ascending to a wide opening leading into darkness.

"Clear it," Captain Brown ordered García.

"Bennett, you're up," García said in turn.

That meant I had the honor of being the first one in. Awesome.

Woodward and Pierce lowered Anderson's travois and bounded up the steps behind me. We checked our rifles and then made our entrance, Pierce and I first, followed by García and Woodward.

The doorway led into a hall wide enough to move two abreast, and the red light from our angle-heads bounced off stone as we continued forward. The floor was littered with leaves for the first several meters, but there was no evidence of animals. Every now and then a square ventilation shaft—or at least that was my guess—was set at the base of the wall on either side. They were big enough for a man to go down, thick with cobwebs, and sloped down into the darkness beneath.

The hall was long and straight, with no intersecting passages, and I was sure we had moved quite far into the structure before we even encountered the first chamber. It was a large room with a vaulted ceiling, and along all four walls hundreds of cubbyholes were stacked high to the ceiling. Dust lay thick on the floor, undisturbed for who knew how many centuries. At the center of the room a bronze brazier sat atop a stone pedestal.

"Looks like a crypt," Woodward said. "But where are the bones?"

"If this place is as old as Princess Sugar Skull says it is, they turned to dust a long time ago," García replied. "Let's keep moving."

We found a few more chambers identical to the first, and then we hit our first intersection. To the left stairs descended, there was a short hall of rooms to the right, and straight ahead another stairway led up to a small room at the very top of the temple, but the ceiling had collapsed and it was completely blocked off.

"Do we really need to clear this whole place?" Pierce said. "It's empty, Sergeant. No one's home."

García frowned. "Lemme check with Cap'n. Hold tight. Woodward, come with me."

As he and Woodward went back the way we had come, Pierce unclipped his flashlight and shone it down the stairs. "It may be empty, but it gives me the creeps."

"It's so quiet," I said. "Like too quiet, you know? I'd at least expect animals to shelter in here."

"Maybe they know something we don't and are smart enough to stay the hell out."

"Maybe. It's dry though, and warm. I could lie down and go to sleep right now just fine."

"You and me both," Pierce agreed.

We stood there in the silence for a long while, just listening. It was so quiet, I felt like I shouldn't talk. Like the sound of my voice was so deafening that it would easily allow anything—or anyone—to sneak right up on me. Pierce must have felt the same way, because he didn't try to make any further conversation either.

No wonder then that we both jumped when our sergeant finally came back.

"Bennett! Pierce!" García shouted from the first crypt. "Come back this way. We're all gonna set up in here. Don't get too happy, though, because we're still clearing the place."

Pierce and I edged away from the stairs, neither of us quite wanting to turn our backs on it. Finally, we laughed at each other nervously to break the tension and joined García and the others, who were already in the process of setting up shop. Some guys were already crashed against their rucks, snoring. Part of Gold Team was sent into the lower levels to make sure what was beneath us was clear. It turned out to be crypts lined with ancient sarcophagi— important people of the city, judging by the stone carvings. Other than the dead, it was sealed tight and empty, like Pierce had said.

With our place of rest secure, we went about the business of another night in paradise.

"I want guards watching the entrance and the hall," Sanchez said. "Two at each end. Make it happen. Just because we didn't find another entrance doesn't mean there isn't one."

"I need a volunteer," Takahashi said.

The first watch went to Gold Team. Stanley and Cohen got the entryway. Cameron and Lawrence got the hall.

Pierce and Woodward crashed beside me. Woodward was lights-out before his head hit his ruck. I for one wanted dry socks at least before I slept.

I only got one boot off before I passed out.

***

"Yo, Bennett, rise and shine," García said, nudging me with his boot. "You're up. Entryway. Pierce, you, too. Let's go."

"Moving, Sergeant." I'd been having a disturbing dream I couldn't remember, but the sense of dread it had awoken in me remained as I finished changing my socks.

Epasotl had curled up on the stone floor beside me, but now she raised her head. Someone had gotten a fire going in the brazier, and her eyes glowed.

"You can go back to sleep," I said, still groggy.

"The ghosts disturb my dreams," she replied.

"There's no ghosts. Even their bones are dust. Get some sleep."

She looked over her shoulder, and her ears flattened a little against the sides of her head. Xochi was approaching, my poncho liner pulled tight around her shoulders.

"Let your man sleep," Xochi said. "I will take the watch with you."

"It's your lucky day, Pierce," I said.

He drifted back into his ruck and mumbled something unintelligible that I think was a thanks before falling back asleep.

I grabbed my rifle, then stood and stretched. Epasotl gave a little hiss before lowering her head.

Xochi leaned in close and stood on the tips of her toes to whisper in my ear. "Your savage pet is most protective."

"She's not a pet," I whispered back, more angrily than I intended.

"I was only making a jest. Please do not take offense. She saved your life when we fought the Children. She has my respect."

"It wasn't the first time," I said as we walked out of the chamber toward the entrance. Two troopers were guarding the hall that led to the entrance, which had a single stairwell leading down in addition to a couple of small rooms that were either always empty or had been emptied before we ever got to them. Xochi called them treasure rooms, but all they held now was dust.

We sat just inside the entranceway and peered out into the rain and darkness. After a time, Xochi slipped her hand into mine.

It was nice. True, we were sitting in a creepy pyramid in the Land of the Black Sun, and I had no way home.

But it was nice.

After several minutes had passed, I asked if she would tell me what had happened between herself and her mother.

"Someday," she said, "but not now."

"I'm sorry, Xochi. I've seen what it's like to be disowned by family."

"It does not bother me. I care nothing for titles or privilege. Honor is earned; one is not born to it." She squeezed my hand. "And now I have you, no? I am content. God is good."

I squeezed her hand back, and she leaned her head against my shoulder.

"I'm not sure what kind of life we can have," I said after a time.

Talk of a life together might have seemed extremely premature to other men my age, but it wasn't to me. If anything, for me the question was why I hadn't already found a nice Mormon girl to settle down with after my mission. I knew my family had been wondering the same. But there were responsibilities I still had to meet. I was still a Cav Scout.

And even now, I hadn't made a decision to go native, like Wilson.

"You have to understand, Xochi, that I have a duty to my brothers," I continued. "I don't think I could leave them."

"I would not ask you to. I will walk your path and we will see where it leads. For now the future is alive with possibilities. *Lo que será será,* no?"

"What will be will be," I repeated.

I bent down to kiss her, but she laughed and pushed my face away. "We are on watch! What would your Sanchez say if he caught us distracted?"

I involuntarily glanced behind me, half expecting him to be standing silently behind us, like he does.

But I didn't stop holding her hand.

***

Captain Brown let us rest and recover the next day. There was a part of me that worried that we'd still have to do something, like take a full tour of this city. If that was the plan, the tropical storm that raged outside put a damper on it. I think some of the guys were a little disappointed by the weather, either because they thought it might be cool to try and find a bronze dagger like Xochi's or just because it would have been nice to sit in the sun without having anything to do. Instead we stayed inside, but at least we were dry.

***

Anderson's bite had improved a little bit, but not too much. Still, it wasn't getting any worse and that was good. He complained pretty consistently about bad dreams, and it wasn't long before the other guys mentioned that, yeah, they'd had some restless sleep, too. A few had nightmares so bad they woke up screaming, but it didn't happen on my watch, and I must've been in too deep of a sleep to have heard them, I guess. No nightmares for me. The guys who had them couldn't remember them.

Epasotl insisted it was the ghosts of this place haunting our sleep.

Despite the storm, the day went well. A few guys were tasked with getting into their ponchos and patrolling, because the captain and our platoon daddy weren't going to have us just sit dumb and blind inside a pyramid all day long. That was to be expected. Still, for the most part we rested, grabbing extra sleep and luxuriating in having feet and socks that stayed dry. Except for Takahashi and Gold Team, who had the fun of the rain-soaked patrol. But the fire in the brass braziers dried them out well enough once they trudged back inside.

The sun fell and the rain kept up. We would stay the night. I don't think Captain Brown wanted us to have to start our marching again in the kind of lousy weather that was soaking everywhere but our dry pyramid.

I napped and lazed about that second day, just like the other guys. Mostly just talking with Xochi. I might have been a little *too* inactive. That night I had second watch, but I was having trouble falling asleep. I felt wired. I could probably have just motored through it and passed out if I'd laid there long enough, but I noticed that I hadn't seen Epasotl in a while, so I got up to go looking.

I found her with Takahashi and Cohen, who were stationed to watch the hallway. Only they were watching the stairs that led to the lower levels of the pyramid. Her body was tense and her ears flat back on her head.

"Hey," I said. "What—"

Takahashi twirled around as if I'd startled him and then put his finger to his lips, telling me to be quiet. I shut up and stopped moving.

Strange, low howling sounds were drifting up through the ventilation shafts at the base of the stone walls. My mind told me it was probably the wind, but it made the hairs on the back of my neck stand on end.

"The ghosts come from down there," Epasotl mewled softly. "We have disturbed their rest and they are angry."

I whispered, "It's just the wind from the storm outside." I wasn't sure if I was trying to comfort her or myself. "Besides, what can ghosts do other than give us nightmares?"

It was more a statement than a question. I meant to ease her concern. I didn't believe in ghosts, not really, or her claim that they were haunting our sleep, but a lot of what we'd experienced already I didn't believe in either—until it happened to us. So maybe she was right.

"Doesn't sound like wind to me," Cohen said.

I looked at him. "You honestly think there are ghosts down there? We checked this whole place on day one. Empty. All of it."

"I do not know for sure," he said. "But all the hairs on my arms and neck are standing straight up when I hear it."

I frowned. "Mine too."

Takahashi smiled like he was going to laugh, but only shook his head. "You two Nancys need to man up. You had it right the first time, Bennett. It's the wind. And if it's the ghost of Jacob Marley or whatever, what's it gonna do?"

"I have suggestions," Epasotl hissed. "Steal our souls? Possess our bodies? We will need strong *naualotl* to defeat them. I must prepare."

The word meant *magic*, more or less. *Necromancy* might be more accurate. Witchcraft, perhaps? There wasn't a good translation.

"You know magic?" I asked. It was the first time she'd mentioned it.

"Of a sort," she said, and then rummaged through a pouch she kept to her hip. I didn't get a good look, but it looked like dried leaves and maybe some bone fragments. She checked it as she sidled past me. "Hopefully enough."

"That doesn't make me feel any better," Cohen said.

A blitz of lightning was followed by deep peals of thunder. The flash of light managed to reach us all the way down the long hallway deep in the pyramid, which told me the guys at the entryway must've felt blinded.

I blinked. The stairwell leading down was that much darker.

I don't know if there was a stronger gust of wind to accompany it, but the low howl from the bowels of the crypt, or temple, or whatever this place was, grew louder before dying back down.

Takahashi flicked on his flashlight and shone it down both stairwells. It went out, and he had to slap it to get it working again. There was nothing there.

"Bennett," Takahashi said. "Do me a favor and bring Sanchez or Captain Brown here. I want them to listen to this."

"Will do, Sergeant. But I thought you said I was right and that these aren't ghosts."

"You *are* right," the sergeant insisted. "But I don't wanna take anything for granted in this godforsaken place."

I couldn't argue with that.

CHAPTER 26

"What do you think, Captain?" Sanchez asked after the two of them had listened to the sounds that rose up from the dark, lower levels.

"I think it's the wind," Brown answered. "And if we were back home, I'd be willing to leave it at that. But we're not."

Sanchez grunted his agreement. "We can clear it again. Maybe there's some kinda breach we missed."

"Or a secret door," Cohen added.

Sanchez shot him a look that let him know his speculations on the issue weren't required. Cohen swore to himself and then focused on the dark stairwell.

"I'd like to avoid that if we can, Diego," Brown said. "We're leaving at first light regardless of the weather outside. We've rested up here for as long as I'm willing to. But let's play it safe. Get two more troopers on this stairwell and make sure they have the M60 trained on it."

It fell to me to spread the word, since Cohen and Sergeant Tak were still on watch. I got García and Woodward up. Neither was particularly pleased, but at least they weren't dead on their feet. The full day of rest had done wonders for all of us. I figured I'd better get some rack time, but Captain Brown found me and pulled me aside.

"Have you seen Epasotl?" he asked.

I shook my head. "Sorry, sir. She went off to prepare some kind of potion or something."

The truth was, I had no idea what she was doing. Making another poultice? How was that going to help with ghosts?

And yes, I had started to feel like she might be right about the ghosts. The sounds that I had written off as wind had taken on a major creepy vibe when I'd last heard them. They weren't any different, but the effect on me was. I have to admit I was freaking out a little.

"How about Xochi?" the captain asked. "Does she have a take on it?"

"I'm not sure she's heard the noises. I haven't talked to her since before I got up."

Brown nodded. "I'd like to get both hers and Epasotl's take on this. You mind staying up past your bedtime a little longer, Corporal? Xochi seems most comfortable when you're around."

"Yes, sir."

We found Epasotl in one of the empty "treasure rooms" and painted head to toe with strange glyphs and patterns. To my surprise, Xochi was with her, watching as Epasotl mashed a green-and-brown sludge inside an empty MRE pouch.

"Captain Brown," Epasotl said. "Your men should all eat this."

The captain wrinkled his nose at the contents of the bag as Epasotl held it beneath this face. I could smell its stench from where I was standing.

"What is it?" Brown asked.

"Protection against the necromancy that awakens in this place."

"I meant what's *in* it, Epasotl."

She rattled off a quick list of ingredients. It sounded to me like we'd need a necromancer of our own after we crapped ourselves to death.

"I'm sorry," Captain Brown said. "I heard you say *blood*. What kind of blood was that again?"

But Captain Brown had heard it right the first time, as had I. Menstrual blood. The other ingredients were no better, and some were worse if you can believe it. Nope. Not interested in this witch's brew.

"It is necessary," said Epasotl.

"I appreciate the offer," Brown said. "But I don't think our physiology is up to the task of keeping your potion down. If we have to fight, I don't want any of us to be sick."

"Sucks to be you, dude," she said.

She then filled the captain in on her species' view of the afterlife —namely the conditions required for the dead to come back and make a mess of things. According to Epasotl, this place was exactly the sort that met those conditions. All that was needed was a trigger.

"What kind of trigger?" Brown asked.

"The dead resent the living," she said, "and attack from malice. These have not yet done so, even though we are in their abode. Who can know what more will stoke their anger? To take what is not ours. To stay beyond their patience. There are many things that might provoke a restless soul."

I was listening to their conversation when suddenly Xochi was quietly whispering in my ear. "You are foolish to turn down this brew. The savages are powerful potion-makers."

I turned and gave her a look. Surely she hadn't already ingested some of that... filth. But I could see in her eyes that she had. And there was something else there, too. Something that troubled her and wouldn't come out until we'd left this place. A little spark to remind me that, perfect though she was to me, she was still human. And humans are... complicated.

It was Cohen's scream that got us all up and on our feet. That was followed by Takahashi's call of alarm. But nobody was shooting.

Captain Brown and I rushed to the commotion, followed by Epasotl and Xochi. We arrived to find a rare sight—a freaked-out Sergeant Takahashi. He was on his hands and knees, perhaps five meters from the stairs, shining his flashlight into one of the ventilation shafts and calling after Cohen. When he saw us, he got back to his feet.

"He went right down the hole!" Takahashi said.

"He climbed down?" Brown asked.

"I dunno! He—" Takahashi was cut off as another scream from Cohen carried up to us through the shaft.

"What's going on?" called García from the stairs.

"It is the ghosts," growled Epasotl. "We have angered them."

By then more of the troopers had geared up and were gathering to see what was next. Sanchez was among them.

"We're leaving," Brown said, loud enough that I wondered if he was trying to communicate to the spirits as much as he was to us. "But not until we get our man back. Diego, form up the teams. Doc stays with Anderson. I'll be on the prick, pulling security up top."

That wasn't a cowardly decision. Captain Brown was doing his job, and we would do ours. We quickly formed up and prepared to move down into the crypts by way of the one staircase. I was with Pierce, Woodward, and García. In the adrenaline build, as keening wails drifted up the stairs on a cold draft, I lost sight of Xochi and Epasotl.

I had assumed they would be with us.

At the bottom of the stairs was a dark chamber with a sunken floor that let out into tunnels on our left and right. The place smelled old and dusty, but dry. There was no mildew or rot to speak of. Our boots swished against the accumulated grit that coated the stone floor.

"Your NVGs, use 'em," Sanchez instructed us. "This is for one of us."

Cohen gave another terrified howl, as if he were being tortured. The sound seemed to come from all directions, as were the moans and wails that followed.

This was no wind.

"Teams of four," Sanchez said. "Split up. Find him."

I dropped my night-vision goggles down and let the IR strobe illuminate the darkness around me, wondering how long it would last. Sanchez sent us in different directions: Blue Team left, Gold Team right. I hadn't been down here before, but the guys who'd cleared said a series of rooms effectively formed a continuous hallway around the base of the pyramid. One room provided access to the interior, and things got a little more complicated once you moved toward the center, but it was hardly a labyrinth.

We made haste moving down the hall clearing room after room, always on high alert and always expecting something to jump out from the darkness to grab us. But nothing did.

As we went, Sanchez tried to keep contact with Gold Team. He had a connection for a little while, but then couldn't raise them and they didn't raise us. We kept moving.

"Clear," Pierce would call as we quickly scanned the four corners of each perfect square.

Next room it would be Woodward or García. "Clear."

Then me. "Clear. Where are we?"

"We're just shy of halfway around," said Sanchez, who was with our team. "Next room is the main intersection. There'll be another exit on the opposite side that continues the circuit, but also a side exit that goes to the center."

"Glad you can tell these rooms apart," Pierce said.

He was right. The rooms were basically identical, right down to the sarcophagi and the wall carvings of humanoid jaguar warriors. I say "basically" because both Xochi and Epasotl later told me that the script that adorned the sarcophagi had slight variations. Probably just the names of those entombed. It all looked the same to me. Apparently the gift of tongues didn't give us the ability to read ancient glyphs.

"Keep moving," Sanchez ordered. "Won't be long before we link up."

"You got them on the radio?" I asked.

Sanchez gave a quick shake of his head. "No. Just the CO."

That didn't make any of us feel better.

We hesitated before entering the next room for that very reason, calling out our position and doing what we could to avoid getting smoked by friendly fire. But the others weren't there. We couldn't hear anything, in fact, except for our own breathing and our hearts pounding in our ears.

Sanchez looked unhappy. Well, more unhappy than usual. "Maybe they already moved on to the center rooms. Bennett, you're up. Don't shoot any of our guys."

I took a deep breath and then scooted ahead of Epasotl. This doorway led not to another room but to a short tunnel that twisted and turned. Bronze scones lined the walls, but whatever oil or kindling might once have been stuffed inside them to light the way had long ago settled into dust at the base of the wall.

We stacked at the entrance to the next room, and then went inside.

"Yo…" Pierce said, letting the word trail off. "That's not good."

The rooms prior to this one had held one sarcophagus apiece. This room was large enough to hold four, and they were larger, obviously more important. Each was about four feet high and wide, eight feet long, solid stone, masterful engraving.

But what Pierce was commenting on was the sarcophagi lids. Despite looking like they weighed two tons each, they had all been pushed to the side and onto the floor.

Worse, the dust was unsettled. This was recent.

While we were mustering the courage to move and look into each tomb to confirm its inhabitant was still inside—I had my doubts about that—Epasotl and Xochi appeared from behind and raced past me. Xochi grabbed me and pulled me along.

"Bring us your light," she whispered in the darkness.

I could still see well enough thanks to what was left of my NVGs, but they needed me to shine my red beam for their eyes to see as well. That gave the three of us an up-close-and-personal confrontation with the final resting places.

"Empty," I reported. Somehow I wasn't surprised. "All of 'em."

García was looking around the room. "These lids came off, like, today. But there's no footsteps." He nodded to the opposite wall. "And those doors were open when we cleared."

The room had four open archways, not counting the way we came in, but facing the pyramid's center—or at least I thought that way was the center—was a pair of huge bronze double doors. Closed, as García has noted. Reliefs were cast in the metal, which was almost black with age, portraying grisly scenes of sacrifice, torture, and demonic beasts.

All at once, we could hear gunfire on the other side. It sounded almost distant through the heavy metal doors, but it was distinct and unmistakable. If you've ever been outside an indoor shooting range, you know the noise. This was a little quieter. We'd found Gold Team.

Sanchez grabbed the handset from Woodward and called the situation in to Captain Brown. After listening a moment, he cursed, gave the handset back to Woodward, and turned to face the waiting García. "Gold's prick is out of commo. Get these doors open but keep your heads down."

"Woodward, Pierce, get low and push the doors open," García ordered. "Bennett and I will be right behind you."

I moved behind Woodward and hovered my barrel over his shoulder. When I was set, I nodded to García, and he gave the order.

Woodward and Pierce shouldered the heavy doors and strained to open them. Xochi got beside Woodward and started shoving, with Sanchez on the other side by Pierce. There was a grinding sound and the doors moved a few inches.

Immediately the firing grew louder. Rounds pinged off the doors and I heard the crack of a bullet whizzing by my head. García and I both jumped back, and he swore.

"Stop shooting us, *gilipollas*!" García shouted through the crack in the doors.

I tried lifting my own voice above the din. "Hold fire, hold fire! Blue on blue!"

We heard Takahashi shouting for a ceasefire and the gunfire subsided. García waved his flashlight through the crack in the doors.

"Coming in!" he shouted. "Don't shoot!"

We heaved on the doors again and got them open enough to pass through. It was hard to tell how big the chamber we entered was. Wide enough that our flashlights didn't pierce much of the darkness to either side, and big enough to produce a decent echo.

We moved cautiously through the murky darkness and found Gold Team huddled by another pair of closed bronze doors directly on the opposite side of the room. Cohen sat on the ground with his back to the wall, staring off into space catatonically. He looked okay.

Much better than any of us were expecting or even hoping for. Stanley crouched beside him, whispering. Takahashi was kneeling beside Lawrence, applying a field dressing to the kid's arm, while Cameron was aiming his rifle at the open doors and muttering to himself. Sounded like the Lord's Prayer.

"What the hell happened?" Sanchez asked them.

"Some messed-up shit," Takahashi replied. "We're pushing through our side and we hear Cohen's scream. Real clear. Center of the pyramid. So we move that way. Next thing we knew the top of a sarcophagus blew open and there were jaguar specters everywhere. Like being in a whirlwind. Couldn't touch 'em. They drove us in here and those big-ass doors slammed closed behind us."

We all looked around for these apparitions, peering into the deep shadows. There was nothing there. Had it all been a hallucination? I had to hope so because none of us had Proton Packs and I didn't know how else we might bust any ghosts.

Sanchez tilted his head toward Lawrence. "I take it *they* can touch *us*."

"Actually, he got shot," Takahashi replied. "No idea by whom. Fire discipline went to shit in a heartbeat. Otherwise no one's hurt, not physically at least. Guys are all shook up pretty bad, especially Cohen."

Stanley had taken off Cohen's boonie to fan his face, and I noticed the kid's hair had gone from a chestnut brown to pure white.

Suddenly Epasotl raced to the heavy set of doors we'd just come through and began frantically trying to shut them by her tiny self. It might have been comical if she weren't acting so terrified. I'd never seen her like this before.

"Help me!" she cried. "Help me close it or we die!"

I rushed to her side, as did Xochi and the rest of Blue. Even as we ran, an echoing roar sounded in the distance, somewhere down the passage we'd come through. Sanchez barked for us to get the portal sealed, and Takahashi, Cameron, and Stanley ran up and added their own backs to the labor, leaving the wounded Lawrence alone to look after Cohen. We closed the heavy doors just in the nick of time. A spectral paw swiped through the crack at the last instant.

We leaned against the doors, and I could hear scrabbling on the other side. I wasn't sure how doors were stopping ghosts, but I wasn't going to question it.

Epasotl was now stalking around, both pairs of ears erect. She stopped abruptly, folded her ears back, and hissed at the darkness. The glyphs and patterns she'd painted on her body began to glow.

Xochi shifted the balance of her war club in her hand and raised her shield. "Be ready," she warned.

I was about to ask what we needed to be ready for when all our NVGs went out. Just like that. Every dang one all at once. My flashlight was dead, too.

We were all plunged into the deepest of darks.

And then, from the center of the room—the room we had just sealed ourselves inside—came a growl.

Sanchez snapped a chem light and hurled it into the darkness. It landed about twenty-five meters away, its green glow illuminating a massive, bronze-armored jaguar standing erect and wielding a curved sword.

Cohen started screaming again. Those same tortured screams we'd heard when he first went missing.

"Oh, hell no," Sanchez said.

The *thunk* of his M203 echoed through the chamber, and his projectile hit the cat-man in the gut, below his breastplate. The walking statue took one step forward before a blinding red light burst out of his stomach and he went up in flames like an old Christmas tree.

Sanchez had fired a flare at the thing.

At that range and in that level of darkness the flare was… well, it was like looking into the sun. For the first time we could see the whole chamber at once, all of it bathed in a harsh, eye-watering glare.

The armored jaguar wasn't alone. There were six of the— mummified jaguar-man guardians? Yeah, that works. Six jaguar-man-guardians in a line, one currently ablaze. They roared a challenge and charged us, all of them, including the one lit up like a twenty-thousand-candlepower torch.

Epasotl thrust her hands forward and—bear with me, I know this is going to be hard to believe, but remember, we're fighting jaguar-man-mummies, so things have already gone beyond weird—a visible wave of blue force rippled through the air, knocking two jaguars down and tossing the one on fire into the far wall.

All of us troopers hit the deck at the sudden, unexpected kinetic outburst. When Epasotl said she knew magic, she really meant *magic*. Like Gandalf magic. Or Palpatine. What the hell kind of poop-and-blood potion was that stuff?

Then she lit up in a blue-white flame and fell to the ground.

Everyone started firing at once, the rounds ripping into the bronze armored guardians with no apparent effect beyond making little 5.56-powered holes. Thankfully Lawrence had anticipated what was coming and had gotten himself and a still-screaming Cohen off to one side and out of the way, because even when our shots were on target they went right on through. Sergeant Sanchez was shouting something, but I was deaf from the echoing reports of our M16s firing simultaneously.

My bolt locked back, and I ditched the rifle just as a particularly pissed-off-looking guardian bore down on me. I got my saber out just in time to deflect a jab that would've skewered me through the chest, and then I leapt back and ducked, hitting the wall as the strike transformed into a sweeping arc meant to take my head from my shoulders.

The bronze sword scraped across the stone, throwing sparks. I tried to roll away, but the guardian pivoted and slammed his free hand—or paw; something in between, really—into my chest, pinning me to the wall, his claws cutting right through my LBE and into my flesh.

Xochi swept in and lopped the arm that held me clean off with her war club. Then she pirouetted, leapt up, and slashed through the jaguar-mummy's neck. She got her shield up as he went to punch her in the face with his sword-hand, but the force of the blow sent her flying backward. He was turning to finish me when his head sort of wobbled and then fell off his shoulders and his whole body exploded in a shower of choking grave dust.

"Xochi!" I cried, feeling my way along the wall. My mouth was dry and tasted like two-millennia-old ash, I couldn't see well, and my chest burned excruciatingly where the mummy-guardian's claws had pierced me. Were these undead warriors like some ancient honor guard buried alive that we'd now accidentally awoken?

Another guardian's silhouette came blurring into view, and then I saw Xochi. Or rather, I saw the blue-white flaming outline of her. Both she and the guardian were both just shapes in my hazy vision, circling each other, striking and feinting, dodging and parrying. She was lightning-fast, faster than I thought possible. But the mummy was even faster, driving her back, relentless.

He roared, and it sounded like thunder. She responded with a shrieking war cry that made the very air shatter like glass. My ears and nose began to bleed.

She blocked a thrust with her shield that should've pierced straight through it, then delivered a sweeping strike with her war club that took the mummy's sword-arm off at the shoulder. He responded by catching her by the neck and lifting her off her feet.

I dove forward, half-blind, and struck at his thigh, gripping my saber with both hands. The steel cut deep, and the mummy faltered, stumbling as his bronze-wrapped leg gave out under him.

Xochi raised her war club, even as she dangled in the air, and brought it down hard, slicing down through the mummy's head from scalp to shoulders. He toppled, taking her with him, and burst on the ground in a billowing cloud.

"Xochi…" I gasped, fighting to breathe, stumbling, reaching out. She caught me and eased me down to my knees.

"I am here," she said, her voice a haggard rasp. "Stay with me, my love."

I coughed spasmodically and tasted rancid bile. "I think… I think I'm dying, Xochi."

It felt like my body was drying up from the inside out. My tongue was stuck to the roof of my mouth and my throat began to close.

"You have been cursed by the ancient ones," she said. "Please, be strong. Stay with me. Nephi. Stay with me."

I tried to reach out to her, but she was too far away. My vision tunneled and everything went black.

***

I awoke to the sound of rain beating off a poncho that Xochi had pulled over the two of us. She cradled my head in her lap and was pouring something into my mouth. It smelled sour and unpleasantly earthy and tasted even worse than the ancient ashes I'd been gargling before I lost consciousness. I gagged.

"No, no, you must," she said, her voice harsh and raw. "I know it is foul, but you must drink it. Epasotl prepared it. The last of her precious herbs."

I heard boots splashing in the mud and someone lifted a corner of the poncho.

"How's he doing?" It sounded like Doc.

"Awake," Xochi said. "Awake and alive. Thanks be to God."

"Thanks be to whatever that concoction is Little Miss Kitty made."

"How is she?" Xochi asked.

"Alive," Doc answered. "I don't know anything about her species, but her vitals seem good. She's—I'll spare you the technical jargon—let's just say she's in something like a coma."

"I do not understand *coma*."

"She's in a deep sleep she can't be woken from."

"Ah, yes, I understand."

"I've never seen anything like what happened to Bennett," Doc said. "He looked like an old dried-up corpse."

"It is necromancy," Xochi said. "A curse. Though I have never heard of a curse such as this one. It is terrible dark magic."

"At least we have a cure," Doc said. "Do you need anything?"

"No, thank you."

Doc left and Xochi continued to make me drink Epasotl's disgusting potion. I kept gagging on it, but somehow I managed to keep it down.

Xochi stroked my forehead, and I looked up at her. Her face was drawn and there was a horrible mass of bruises around her neck.

"Where are we?" I asked.

"Safe, for now."

"What happened?"

"We fled the temple."

"What about the… ghosts?"

"Hush. You are too weak to be asking questions. Be still and drink."

I did so and then closed my eyes, feeling an immense fatigue settling over me. I felt her stroke my hair and drifted… drifted.

"Be still," she said, her voice a quiet murmur. "Be still and listen. To my confession."

I was going in and out of consciousness. What she said next was like a dream. I don't know if she truly meant for me to hear it. I don't even know if I should write it down.

"There are many ways to lose the favor of the queen my mother, and few to regain it. The lost city… I led you to it. I knew it was here, somewhere. I did not expect to find it, but I hoped. And when we came upon its forgotten pyramids, I felt the hand of God guiding me to restoration."

I felt her fingers in my hair. I could almost *see* her words, as though she were fashioning a vision in my mind through speaking. Or maybe it was the potion. But she was telling me what to dream. It had never happened before, and it hasn't happened since.

"That race was a dark one. Their evil left an imprint that lasts to this day, though they are dead and gone, vanquished long ago. But if I could walk through the valley of the shadow of evil and return to tell the tale… such a tale would be told and retold. The bravery of Siuapilxochicuauhtli would be known. There would be no shame then for me, and no shame for my mother the queen to return me to a place of honor. For I would be one to have led warriors through the city of the dead and lived."

She squeezed my hand. "Nephi… Nephi. Had I *known*. Had I even suspected that what we found could be so black and so strong and wicked, I…"

She went quiet for a long time.

"I am sorry, Nephi. Forgive me."

I did forgive her. Of course I did. But I said nothing.

It seemed better, for her sake, that she think I hadn't heard her at all.

CHAPTER 27

It was Woodward who later told me what had happened. Xochi had banished the ghosts temporarily with the powers she had gained from Epasotl's brew, and we fled the temple, carrying our wounded, which included me. By some miracle no one had died, but I had been cursed with what Woodward was calling "Mummy Rot." I'd survived, but the side effects... well, I had to see it to believe it. I'd aged ten or fifteen years. It was only Epasotl's potion that kept the aging process from turning me into a desiccated corpse until I ended up as dust. Or so Xochi said. Who was I to argue?

It was worse for Cohen. After those things grabbed him and pulled him down the shaft, they performed some kind of spectral torture on the guy. He was talking, and had his wits together well enough to recount what happened, but he was badly shaken... and he was blind. Not full-on blind, but his eyes were clouded and he said he could only make out light and dark and a few shapes. Doc couldn't do anything for him, but we held out hope that Epasotl might know a trick... once she woke up.

She had remained comatose from the moment she'd collapsed in the fight.

We were in bad shape, and not only physically. Most of us were black on ammo and the pemmican was running low. About the only thing we had in abundance was water, thanks to the monsoon we were caught in during our two-day respite in the city.

There was a bit of good news in all this. Anderson's fever had broken, and he was ambulatory. Which was all the more fortunate as now Epasotl needed to use his travois.

The plan was still to make for Xochi's people again, regroup, and then… I didn't know. I assumed Captain Brown still intended to link us up with the mysterious Special Forces colonel who was located in Amoloyan. But all that felt distant to me. No one said it, but I think the consensus was, "if we make it that far."

All I wanted was that bath and the feeling of security that would come from being among the Sugar Skull Gals. Wilson had been right about them: they were good people. And so was Wilson, even if I was still upset with him for staying behind. He was my friend and I knew talking would help. Talking about… everything. Everything that had happened starting with Arizona.

It sucked. All of it.

No, I take that back. Xochi was a bright spot. She made taking care of me her personal mission. She was kind to the other guys, too. I knew that she was taking the blame on herself for what had happened in the pyramid, and I supposed she had every reason to. She hadn't exactly led us into the crypts, and she'd had no way of knowing just how deep the evil was that still inhabited what the rest of all thought was an abandoned city, but still… things had turned out the way they'd turned out.

I didn't mention it.

We all have our burdens.

We made slow progress over the next three days. We moved by day and camped at night. Our flashlights had begun working again as soon as we were out of the pyramid. The NVGs were still dead.

It was a relief to all of us when Epasotl woke on the third night, weak and disoriented. She had become like a little sister to the entire platoon, and now she was the little sister who knew actual magic and had saved all of our asses from certain death. She remembered almost nothing of the encounter in the temple. I explained that her potion had saved us from a grievous curse, and apologized for not taking it when she offered. Captain Brown did the same.

Epasotl gave a weak smile and called us fools for not listening to her, but said she was glad we were still alive. "If you had drank, you would not have been cursed. But you look better older, Bennett. Less a child."

I wasn't so sure about that. There was gray around my temples and lines around my eyes. Xochi said it made me look noble, so I guess it wasn't all that bad.

We were still pushing out of the jungle to reach the plains again when we ran into the next installment of what had been a long string of trouble. I was on watch. Staring into the darkness for a long time can start to play tricks with your eyes, so you can't fixate on any one thing. I was scanning slowly, watching for movement in my peripheral vision, and had my jaw open slightly to hear better, but there wasn't much to see or hear. It was dark, *really* dark, with only a couple stars shining through gaps in the canopy. Every so often there'd be a rustle or a smear of shadow on shadow as the nocturnal animals went about their business.

I had a ringing in my ears, and I popped them to try and stop it, but it persisted. The ringing had been occurring on and off ever since the temple, and I assumed it was caused by all the gunfire in a closed space. It was especially noticeable when it cropped up in quiet times like this.

Woodward tapped my shoulder and got close to my ear, subvocalizing. "Did you hear that?"

"Hear what?" I asked just as quietly.

"Sounded like footsteps."

"Where?" I asked.

"Four or five o'clock."

I swung in the direction he'd indicated and peered at the trees.

"Don't see any—" I stopped. There was a shadow about twenty-five meters away where there hadn't been one before. "Might have something." I raised my rifle to my shoulder.

The shape was motionless. It might be a man, a small one, or maybe a child, crouching; maybe my eyes were playing tricks on me, and it was a tree stump that had been there the whole time.

"Got movement. Three o'clock," Woodward said. "Distance twenty meters."

"Possible movement. Six o'clock," I replied. "Fifteen or twenty meters."

Something was out there. More than one something.

I was about to call out that we had contact when Woodward abruptly pushed me over and buried himself beside me as he shouted, "Grenade!"

There was a blinding flash and an earsplitting bang followed immediately by another. The ringing in my ears rose to a crescendo. Then someone grabbed my arms roughly behind me, and zip ties closed around my wrists. I tried to look up, but a knee dug into the back of my neck and rammed my face into the wet soil. I might have heard voices shouting through the ringing, but I couldn't be sure. My mouth and nose were full of dirt, and I couldn't breathe.

I felt a sharp crack against my skull. The second blow put out the lights.

***

When I came to, I had the worst headache imaginable. I moved up onto my knees, my hands still tied behind my back, and vomited.

It was still dark, but I could see the shapes of my teammates kneeling nearby. Epasotl was standing, however, and she was arguing with someone. It took my brain a few moments to make out the words through all the buzzing in my ears.

"... have no honor. You walk in shame! You are nothing but playthings of the Outworlders."

A voice from the darkness replied, even and controlled. He spoke with a sibilant hiss like Epasotl, but with a deeper pitch. "You're one to speak of shame, little sister. Did these Outworlders capture you, as I have now captured you? How long have you walked, dead among the living? Shall I give you an honorable death? Would that please you?"

"I stand unafraid," she replied. "I am a warrior, not an assassin like you. Let the ordeal begin, and I will show you how a true warrior dies."

The voice made that staccato hissing sound that I had come to recognize as Chaneque laughter. "No, I think not. I think the All-Father would prefer you alive, bearing my cubs for the rest of your days."

Epasotl hissed and spat and lunged forward. A shape materialized out the darkness and swung something that cracked against her head, sending her sprawling. She twisted on the ground, mewling softly.

The shadowed Chaneque man spoke loudly to the platoon. "Who's in command here?"

He spoke English perfectly, or at least as perfectly as a Chaneque mouth could form English words.

"Amos Brown, Captain," our CO replied.

"I'm Milo," the Chaneque said. "So now we're friends. When are you from?"

When, not where. Interesting.

The captain didn't answer.

Milo made a sound between a sigh and a growl. "No need to be stoic, Captain. Please answer the question."

Captain Brown remained silent.

A second Chaneque man stepped forward from the darkness and grabbed Cohen's head by the hair. I could tell it was Cohen because his white hair practically glowed in the dark.

"Okay," Milo said. "Let's play a game. I'll ask a question. You'll answer. If you refuse, one of your men loses something. An ear, a nose, maybe an eye. I'll let Felix decide. That work for you, Felix?"

"Yes, sir," said the Chaneque holding Cohen's hair.

Cohen whimpered.

"So, Captain," Milo said, "when are you from?"

The captain repeated his name and rank.

Milo sighed. "Felix, remove the man's—"

"Nineteen eighty-nine!" Cohen shrieked.

Milo didn't hesitate. "What unit?" he asked.

"Red Platoon," Cohen said. "Alpha Troop, Second Squadron, Ninth Cavalry Regiment, attached to Seventh Division."

"Are you scouts?"

"Yes."

"How long have you been here?"

"Two, three months. I—I don't know exactly."

"Felix, jog his memory," Milo said.

"No! Two and half months? I stopped counting. The days all run together!"

"You know what, Felix?" Milo said. "I think I'll let you decide."

"I don't like his ears," Felix growled.

"Excellent choice."

"Sixty-two days," Woodward said, his voice cracking. I thought he was going to cry.

"See? This *is* a fun game," said Milo. "Now, what are you doing in my forest?"

"We're only passing through," Captain Brown said.

"Ah! So you *do* know more than your name and rank. For a moment I thought you an imbecile, Captain, but it seems you're simply stubborn. Felix, show the captain what we think of stubborn prisoners."

Cohen suddenly screamed bloody murder, and I knew then that the one named Felix had cut off the poor guy's ear.

Captain Brown lunged to his feet, but five more shapes darted into our midst and held some kind of stubby firearms against our heads, mine included.

"Unwise, Captain," Milo said coldly. "Do that again and someone dies. Back on your knees."

"You bastard," the captain growled.

"*On your knees.*"

Brown swore under his breath and knelt.

Cohen was blubbering.

"Americans. Late twentieth century. Cavalry Scouts," Milo said softly, as if reciting the facts to himself. "'Passing through.' Twelve men plus two indig females: one human, one Chaneque. Say again? … Roger."

So, he wasn't talking to himself. He had a radio.

Milo raised his voice. "You, woman, what tribe are you from?"

"I am Kuauchanejkej," Xochi said proudly.

"What are you doing with Outworlders?"

"I am their guide," she replied.

"Are you their captive?"

"No, they are my friends."

He relayed her response. His radio must've been jacked into some headphones, because I couldn't hear the other side of the conversation at all, not even static or squelch.

Then something he'd said jolted me. He'd reported twelve of us. But there were thirteen. Who was missing? I tried to search the faces of my companions, but it was too dark, so I began eliminating possibilities based on size and shape. After a while I realized I figured out who was missing: Sanchez.

Had he escaped undetected? Or had they already killed him?

"How many of you arrived here, Captain?" Milo asked.

"Thirty-one," Brown said.

"Including yourself?"

"Yes."

"That's a lot of dead men." I think Milo would've whistled ironically just then, but the Chaneques can't make that sound. "You haven't been doing so well."

Captain Brown didn't respond.

"Do you know about Amoloyan?" Milo asked the captain.

"Rumors," Brown admitted. I could tell he was being cautious, but he was interested.

"What kind of rumors?"

"We were told by indigenous assets that there was an American presence holding the city."

Milo started speaking softly into his radio again. "Prisoners claim limited intel. Continue interrogation? … Roger. … Confirm last? … Roger."

Something about the way Milo was talking bothered me. He was speaking with a certain level of military discipline, but there was an edge of menace in his voice. I couldn't be sure if that was intentional or just by virtue of him being Chaneque.

"Can my medic attend to my trooper's injury?" the captain asked.

"Of course," Milo replied. "We're not savages."

Brown's voice was defiant. "Could've fooled me."

Milo only laughed in response.

A figure stood and moved to Cohen's side. "I need my hands free."

Doc.

Felix moved behind Doc, and I heard zip ties being cut. Doc knelt and shined his flashlight on Cohen, who by now was only softly whimpering.

"I need someone to hold my light," Doc said.

Felix took the angle-head while two other Chaneques moved up to cover him.

The red light was enough for me to make out our captors, though I tried not to be obvious about looking at them. I counted twelve Chaneque men surrounding us, all dressed in dark camouflage. They wore advanced-looking load-bearing equipment tailored to their small statures, possibly armored, and all held suppressed MP5 submachine guns.

I also saw no sign of Sanchez's body. I told myself that meant he had escaped, not that he had been disposed of off in the brush.

"Where's his ear?" Doc said. "I can sew it back on."

Felix growled.

Milo shrugged. "What can I say? Felix likes his souvenirs."

"Damned savages," Doc muttered. He stood, towering over Felix. "Give me the ear."

The two Chaneques who'd been covering Felix jammed their suppressors into Doc's chest. He didn't even flinch, just stared at Felix. The little Chaneque squared his shoulders and rose to his full height—all four feet and whatever spare inches of him. Doc was easily a foot and a half taller. Felix's ears folded back, and he bared his teeth.

"You're all about honor, right?" Doc said. "So fight me for it. Just you and me. Warrior against warrior. You like knives? I *love* knives. What do you say? Hmm? First blood or to the death? I'm cool with either. What's it gonna be, man?"

Felix's eyes darted over to Milo, who didn't look particularly happy. He was muttering again, giving a play-by-play to whomever was on the other end of the transmission. He must have had some sort of tiny headphone, because I couldn't hear the other side of the conversation. He said "Roger" a whole lot, then he tapped something on his chest and said, "Stand down, Felix. Give him the ear."

Felix didn't look happy to hear the order. He snorted, pulled something out of a pocket on his LBE, and held it out to Doc. Then he dropped it and laughed in that special Chaneque way.

"Dick," Doc said. "Just hold the damned light so I can see what I'm doing."

Doc got Cohen to lie down, gave his "This'll hurt me more than you" line, and got to work.

Cohen wasn't stoic about the process at all. It was a little embarrassing, to be honest. But then again I've never had my ear cut off and sewn back on, so who am I to judge?

When Doc was done, the Chaneques made us all stand and shoved us into a rough line.

"Start walking," Milo ordered.

"Where are you taking us?" Captain Brown demanded.

"Wherever I want," Milo answered menacingly.

"We can't see for shit," Doc said after nearly tripping over a fallen branch. Felix had turned off the flashlight and hadn't given it back.

"Don't worry," Milo said. "If you leave the path, we'll shoot you."

CHAPTER 28

They marched us north through the night and into the next day. They'd stripped us of everything except the boonies on our heads to keep the sun off. We marched through the brush until we were standing at the edge of a massive pit, and I got the terrible feeling that we were about to be tossed down however many feet existed between us and the bottom. In this instance, Cohen was lucky to be blind.

Instead, they began to toss in all of our weapons and equipment. Rifles, sabers, knives, everything. They fell out of sight and clattered as they landed somewhere down below.

It soon became clear that this was for show. Milo looked at us benevolently and said, "If All-Father likes you, you'll get better gear. If he doesn't, you won't be needing it."

"And who is this 'All-Father'?" Captain Brown asked.

Milo gave an ugly, hissing smile. "You have the honor of soon finding out."

And then we were marching again. I had hoped we would be allowed to rest, even at that portal to the center of the earth—or whatever planet this was. But no. We kept moving and were prevented from talking. I tried to get a sense of how Xochi and Epasotl were, but they were kept well away. I might've worried about how Xochi would be treated, but the Chaneque had made it clear that to them she was as ugly as Epasotl was to us.

As for Epasotl, honor, or what passed for it, seemed to keep her safe from their predations.

So we marched. I saw no sign of Sanchez and began to worry that he was dead after all. There was no one I could ask about it and you couldn't read anybody's faces for clues on the rare occasion that I saw something other than the back of the next guy's head. We were all looking defeated.

My head was pounding, and my mouth was bone-dry. It was all I could do to keep putting one foot in front of the other. Around noon, guys started falling out. The Chaneques hauled them back up and made them keep walking.

Finally, Doc had had enough.

"We need water at least," he said. "Or are you planning on just marching us to death?"

Milo signaled a halt and made us sit. He had Xochi's hands freed and ordered her to give us water from our canteens.

"Are you all so very tired?" Milo asked us, mockingly. "Don't worry. We'll be hooking up with a truck that'll take you the rest of the way. Shouldn't be more than another three hours of humping it. Then you can ride in style. Cav ain't made for walking, are you?"

If his proficiency in English was interesting, his use of American speech patterns fascinated me. To hear him talk you'd think he'd grown up back in our world.

Not only that, his Chaneque troopers behaved like trained military. They didn't slouch or mill about. They didn't engage in idle chitchat. They split their numbers between covering us and watching the perimeter. They did their jobs.

"I want to check my people," Doc said. "We have wounded, and they need attention."

"Then check on them," Milo said.

"I need my hands to do that."

Milo ordered one of his men to cut Doc's bindings. As Xochi gave us water, Doc went down the line.

When he got to me, he checked my eyes and pulse, then shook his head. "You geniuses gave this man a concussion. He can't be walking in this heat."

Felix growled his displeasure at our medic. "Then carry him, if you're that worried."

"It's okay, Doc," I said. "I can make it another three hours. How's Cohen?"

"He'll live," Doc said. "It's Anderson I'm worried about. The fever's back."

"I said you could check on them, not talk them to death," Milo snapped. "Hurry it up. I'm on a schedule."

Doc stood and spun on Milo. "I got a man with a fever and another with a concussion. Half of them are showing signs of heat stroke. You keep pushing us like this, they're not going to make it."

"Then they aren't worthy of meeting the All-Father," Milo said. He raised his voice. "Break's over. On your—"

Just then we heard the telltale *crack* of an M16, and Felix's head snapped back in a cloud of red mist.

Milo's men started shouting and moving for cover. Doc yelled for us to hug the dirt even as he tackled the closest Chaneque. A wickedly curved blade appeared in Doc's hands, and he used it to slit the guard's neck before cutting the submachine gun's sling.

I had no idea where Doc's knife had appeared from, and I was even looking at him when it happened. They had searched us— thoroughly, I had thought. But not well enough apparently.

But then, Doc was always special.

Another two cracks echoed through the trees, and two more Chaneques fell. Doc took out three more with the submachine gun as he bolted into the jungle for cover. Bark and wood splinters flew from trees as the remaining Chaneques returned fire.

Xochi also had her hands free, and she didn't just stand there gawking. She snapped a Chaneque's neck from behind and then, using his body as a shield, worked his weapon across two more soldiers, ventilating them.

If I wasn't in love before, I was now.

Sanchez was our sniper, of course. He materialized behind Milo and jabbed his Beretta against the Chaneque's head. "Drop your weapon and get your hands up."

Milo let the gun dangle on its sling and complied.

The only remaining Chaneque ran into the trees. We heard a couple short bursts of suppressed automatic fire, and Doc re-emerged a few moments later unscathed.

"Always loved the MP5," he said.

Captain Brown was with Sanchez and our new prisoner. "Takahashi, García, collect their weapons and ammo and see if there's any food in their assault packs. Get a security perimeter set up."

Xochi and Doc went through the lines and untied us. One of the fallen Chaneques groaned, only to be pounced upon by Epasotl, who tore his throat out with her claws and then spat on the corpse. Doc moved on with her to make sure the others were dead as well.

We got busy collecting gear off the dead and stuffed our pockets and LBEs with magazines, fraggers, and flashbangs. The assault packs contained the standard packing list for a three-day patrol, including MREs. They were definitely US-made, but the recipes were different from what I was accustomed to. They looked like they might even be edible.

It took me a minute to figure out the sling on the submachine gun. It was an ingenious two-point design that let the weapon sit in a low ready position across the chest, freeing your hands, and could be cinched up or let out rapidly via a pull-tab. Brilliant. Why didn't *we* have those?

The weapons were only about twenty inches long with the stock folded, including the integrated suppressor, with a twenty-five-round magazine and a fancy-looking red-dot sight. I'd never used one before, but it seemed simple enough. Just point and shoot. But they were *quiet*. Not as quiet as the mouse farts you hear in the movies, but close enough for me.

All in all, the differences in the gear were slight, but the impact on us was significant, because we all understood what it meant. These weapons, this gear—the radio, for certain—it was better than ours. More advanced.

It was from the *future*. Post-1989.

We had known for weeks now that Smoking Mirror was ripping people out of different time periods in our history, but somehow in all that time it had never occurred to me that some of those people would be not from our past, but from our future. I couldn't help but wonder just how far into the future. How advanced some of them might be. And how vulnerable that made us.

Were we the Buffalo Soldiers now?

I mulled this over as I got behind some cover and settled in with a packet of Southwest Beef and Black Beans. It actually smelled good. Didn't taste half bad either, which was fortunate because my head was still killing me, and I was still getting hit by frequent waves of nausea.

Xochi proudly approached me, carrying one of the deadly little MP5s in her hands.

"It suits you," I said, and she gave me a savage smile that melted my heart. If there's anything more beautiful than a woman with a firearm, I haven't seen it.

After Milo's men were deprived of the last threads of life left in their bodies, Brown addressed the sudden turning of the tables with the sole survivor of that unit. He had taken Milo's weapon and had just finished a long inspection of the radio setup. "Your daddy gives you nice toys, Milo."

To me the radio looked like a science fiction walkie-talkie, and was wired into a headset. It seemed to have a range extender which looked a lot like a future generation version of our own pricks. It was slick. And much easier to take with you. Captain Brown and Doc said it looked a lot like something called a SINCGAR, but smaller. I'd never seen one of those—not high-speed enough to catch glimpses of the new stuff—so I wouldn't know.

Milo wasn't talking. He looked down, his Chaneque features somehow making him look both angry and dejected at once.

Epasotl stalked past us. Her left eye was black and swollen shut, and the skin was split on her cheek. She strode up to Milo, and then looked up at Sanchez.

"May I have a word with my kinsman, Little Kahuna?" she asked politely.

"Be my guest," Sanchez said.

She struck Milo in the face with her claws and then spat on him.

"Thank you, Little Kahuna," she said before turning and walking away. "I have said my piece."

Sanchez actually… chuckled. Yeah, you read that correctly. Consider my mind blown.

"Okay, Milo," Captain Brown said, rubbing his wrists. "Now it's your turn to play a game. I think you know the rules."

"You're all dead men walking," Milo said. "You know that, don't you?"

The captain ignored him. "Who's the 'All-Father'?"

Milo laid his ears back and hissed.

"How many ears has he got, Diego?" Brown asked.

"I count four, sir," Sanchez replied.

"Damn, this game could go on for quite a while," the captain said. "Somebody, get me a knife."

"It is no use, Big Kahuna," Epasotl called to him. "You will only grant him an honorable death. Send him to the underworld in his shame."

Brown leaned in close to Milo. "Is that the deal, Milo? You think you can handle an honorable death?"

Milo bared his teeth. His face was bleeding badly from where Epasotl had raked him with her razor claws. The cuts ran deep to the bone.

"Wait one," Captain Brown said. "Doc, take care of this asshole's face before he bleeds out on me."

Doc stepped in and inspected Milo's face before pulling out his staple gun. "This is gonna hurt you a lot more than it hurts me."

To his credit Milo didn't make a sound, not even a mewl.

Captain Brown picked up the radio he'd taken from Milo's Chaneque-sized chest rig. I wondered how such modern-looking equipment had been sized for someone as small as Milo. I had seen some short, small soldiers in my time, but nothing like him. But the more I thought about it, the more I believed that future armies had just figured out how to make things smaller. Like going from records to cassettes, you know?

Brown mumbled something to Sanchez, who gave a quick nod.

"Since you're not interested in answering my question, Milo," Brown said, "and since I have no other use for a coward who had the shame to be captured by his own captives"—Milo winced at this; Captain Brown knew how to twist the knife—"we're going to use your radio to put a call in to your All-Father directly. Cut to the source. Tell him he needs to find better help than the likes of you."

Again Milo winced, but remained silent.

Captain Brown cupped one of the headphones to his ear and angled the mic to his mouth. He moved away from us and started pacing. "This is Captain Amos Brown, Ninth Cavalry Regiment. United States Army. I wish to speak to the 'All-Father.'"

"Captain Brown!" came the reply. "Thank God you're all right. This is Chief Baker, United States Army. I'm a pilot. I take it you've neutralized those psychotic little Chaneques."

Captain Brown was clearly taken aback. The voice on the other end of the line was concerned, American, and professional.

"I need to know why you were receiving intel from them, Chief," Brown said.

"It was a one-sided conversation, Captain. The only time I spoke up was when trying to save your lives. I'm American, like you. Those Chaneques don't have anything to do with us. Not anymore." Chief Baker didn't sound defensive so much as eager to explain. "See, we tried training the Chaneques to serve in combat, only the little bastards didn't take to it. They killed their advisors, stole the gear you saw them with, ambushed whoever we took out and more than a few other men sucked into this godforsaken world like yourselves. Milo was the worst. He used the radio to taunt me, act like he was out on duty, a loyal soldier in the jungle. However you got the drop on him, I thank you for it—we never could catch the slick son of a bitch. But there may be more of them out there. Captain, it might be best if you come my way unless you've got an existing safe haven somewhere nearby."

"And where are you?" Brown asked.

"A small outpost near the eastern side of the jungle. Got me a pair of Hueys and not much else. Still, you can't miss it. I don't know your position, but if you're in Milo's usual stomping grounds, we're north of you, maybe an hour or two at a fast walk."

"Whose outpost, and who is 'we'?" Brown pressed.

"Colonel Dietrich—the indigs call him Silver Eagle. He's a Green Beret—Special Forces. The Americans in this place have linked up under his command, most of them anyway. There's a lot to explain, but this isn't the place. I really think you need to keep moving before more of those Chaneques come sniffing around. Come find me and I'll tell you everything I know."

Brown looked at Milo, who was snarling fiercely now. The captain had disconnected the earphone jack and we were all hearing what was being said.

"There's still one of them left," Brown said, staring at the savage little Chaneque. "Milo."

"Kill him," Chief Baker said over the radio. "God knows he deserves it. Then get your asses out of that jungle, because there are a whole lot more like him and his ilk. Godspeed. I'll be waiting. Call me anytime, brother."

"I'll let you know," Brown said. "Out."

Captain Brown hung the radio headset at his belt and lifted his weapon. "Diego. Release the prisoner."

Sanchez let Milo go and took a step back. Captain Brown sent a burst of fire through the Chaneque's head. The little devil pitched forward and bled out his brains into the scrubby ground.

Epasotl walked up to Captain Brown. "You gave him too much honor."

"Just got tired of looking at him," Brown said, and then called to all of us. "Everyone! We have a decision to make."

CHAPTER 29

It was a decision that would irreparably impact the courses of all our lives. Either we would go and meet up with Chief Baker, the American helicopter pilot, or we would push our way out of the jungle and cross the savanna again to return to Wilson and Xochi's people.

My vote—not that it was up for a vote, just a discussion—was to go back to the village. I figured we could make contact with Baker another time, but for now, we needed to rest and recover. I was in the minority.

"We need to consider the technology apparently available to this group," Doc had said during our group discussion. "Fuel. Flight capabilities. Food and, based on what those kitties had with them, better medical equipment than anything we have left to us. I have sick and injured men, and serious concerns about Anderson's ability to survive a long trip. If we're right on the doorstep of an American outpost, we have to take advantage. I vote we at least see what Chief Baker has to say."

There was a general murmur of agreement. Woodward was the loudest of these, and he soon made things personal.

"I've got a wife and kid back home," he said. "Bennett might enjoy the way his life is shaping up here with his new girlfriend, but I thought the plan was to get back home. A helicopter and civilization sound a whole lot nearer to that than going back into the Land of the Lost to live with the native girls."

"I wasn't saying we should give up and go native," I protested. "Only that going back to the tree village would give *everyone* the time we need heal up. Not to mention link up with Wilson. Or were we going to just leave him here once we found our way home?"

Okay, so that was a little cheap. Wilson *wanted* to be left here. But I was feeling wounded that Woodward went after me directly when all I did was say what I thought would be best for everyone. Getting home is great, but no one wants to do it in a body bag.

In the end though, it was Doc's assessment of Anderson's condition that settled the matter, even for me. When things quieted down, all eyes went to Captain Brown.

"I promised I would get you men home," the captain said to us. "That can't happen if we don't survive long enough to get the chance. We'll move to Chief Baker's outpost, but we're not going to just waltz in and put all our trust in a stranger. If after recon it looks good, we'll make contact. After that, I'll consider how best to recover Wilson. A functioning Huey could go a long way into making that trip easier. Doc, I'd like to be there before sundown, but you make the call to move out."

Our medic nodded. "Then let's move."

***

The black sun was low in the sky when Cameron, who was on point, reported that our destination was just on the other side of a rise. Captain Brown made us halt below the military crest and went forward with Sanchez to observe.

It wasn't long before Brown and Sanchez were back.

"They're human," Brown said, "but if they're all Americans, it looks like they've been here for a while."

"Their gear looks good," Sanchez added. "Better than what we arrived in this world with. What bothers me is the uniforms. Same kind the kitties that ambushed us were wearing."

Takahashi shrugged. "If the kitties are killing patrols from this base, it would make sense they'd have their uniforms."

Captain Brown gave a nod. "I raised Chief Baker on the radio. We saw him talking to us from a parked bird inside the outpost. So that checks."

"What's the word, sir?" García asked.

"We'll make contact," Brown said. "But not all of us. Doc, Sanchez, the wounded, and a security team—that's your boys, Takahashi—will stay back out of sight. I'll take the rest and we'll go to the gates. Gonna let Chief Baker know to roll out the welcome mat first, though."

While the captain made his call, I gathered up my gear. My ruck, like everyone else's, was taken from the Chaneques. I would leave it with the group and just bring my canteen and extra ammo.

"Am I to accompany Big Kahuna?" Epasotl asked.

"Pretty sure you're included with 'everyone else,' Epasotl," I said. "Captain Brown will want you there to fill him in on anything that doesn't smell right."

"Much of this place does not smell right," Epasotl replied. "The humans guarding the gate reek. I began to smell them long before now."

"I'm going too," Xochi said, and then checked her weapon. I was impressed with how easily she had picked up the function of the submachine gun. It only took a brief tutorial from Doc and she was carrying with all the confidence of an expert.

We moved down from the rise toward an outpost straight out of Vietnam, complete with sandbags, a tower, concertina wire, and two old Hueys sitting in a dirt field. Only, the birds didn't look particularly old. All that was missing were a couple of Gis smoking pot with their chinstraps dangling like in *Full Metal Jacket*. Instead, the post was guarded by thirty or so half-naked humans with spearthrowers and stone axes. I figured they were indigs, though they could also have been ill-equipped soldiers from who-knows-when. There was a machine gun in the tower, though, and a handful of the indigs wore BDUs with the same odd blocky camouflage pattern the Chaneques had. They carried a stubby version of the M16, some sort of carbine, and wore what looked to me like skateboard helmets.

Six men in camo were standing at the gate, waiting for us with their carbines hanging on their slings. They watched us approach the whole way and to my eyes looked a little twitchy. It wasn't until we got within ten meters that we realized these weren't Americans. They were natives.

"Close enough," the leader of the group called out in broken English. "Put weapon down."

I glanced up and saw the tower's machine gun trained on us.

"That's not the deal," Captain Brown replied. "Where's Chief Baker?"

"New deal." The man pointed to the ground. "Put weapon down."

The five men behind him had their hands on their weapons now. A couple of them even had fingers on triggers.

"What's this Mickey Mouse shit?" Brown barked. "We're keeping our weapons."

"No Mickey Mouse. No shit. I big man here. I say new deal." He pointed to the tower. "Or you big dead."

A lanky human in a flight suit stepped out from a sandbagged building, chewing on a cigar. I saw Captain Brown relax a little bit. That must be Chief Baker.

"You trying to pull a fast one again, Maololi?" the chief shouted.

The man who was trying to get us to surrender our weapons turned and shouted back, "No fast one, Chief. This my outpost. I say no weapon inside."

"I wonder how long this outpost of yours'll last if I stop making supply runs." The man clamped the cigar between his teeth and swaggered over. He passed by Maololi with a shake of his head and extended a hand to Captain Brown.

"Nice to meet you in the flesh, Captain Brown. I'm Chief Baker." He looked around. "This everyone? That little demon Milo made it sound like there were more of you."

Maololi and his men backed off and returned inside the compound. Captain Brown watched them suspiciously, and then held that suspicion on his face when addressing the chief.

"This is all that I was willing to bring up to start with. In case of something like *that* happening."

"Hell, I'm sorry, Captain. I truly am. I can only imagine what's going through all of your minds right now. I know I was in a *state* when I first flew in here. 'Course, the advantage of being in flight when I was transported to this place is that I could see my way to the city right away. So I avoided the horror stories that most of you who go through the wilds endure."

The chief quickly went around and introduced himself to all of us. He was polite to Xochi and Epasotl alike. I figured he might be a little hesitant about our Chaneque guide, given the way he talked about Milo, but he didn't seem perturbed.

Captain Brown must have wondered the same. "This outpost. It's to protect against the Chaneques?"

"Them and the undead," Baker confirmed. "Those guards you met are the local indigs. They're learning civilization, but it's a slow process. There are outposts like this set up all throughout the jungle. Sort of an early-warning network to keep Amoloyan free from trouble."

"You don't seem bothered by Epasotl," Brown pressed. I think he was suspicious that maybe Milo and his crew were connected to this outpost, and Baker was lying about it to cover for their treatment of us.

"That's because I'm not," Baker said. "Look, with the Chaneques, they're either your best friend or your worst enemy. I see this one here walking peacefully with you, I know she's in your debt. That's no problem. But if she weren't, she'd try to kill you and me every bit as much as the ones you escaped from would. Only thing unique about those boys was they got some training on how to use our kit and lived long enough to make us regret it. If you don't believe me, ask her."

"No need," Brown said, a slight smile on his face. "Epasotl has let us know plenty of times that she'd kill us if it weren't for her honor. Although I'm hoping that will change in time."

"It will not," purred the complicated little thing.

I smiled despite myself. I hoped there wasn't some kind of jubilee where her shame would wear off after a while, freeing her to kill me in my sleep.

"Speaking of the radio," Chief Baker said, "I take it you left it with the others."

Brown nodded. "They're waiting for my order to move forward. I figured if things checked out, I could call them from your bird."

"Well," Baker said as he turned and pointed his cigar toward the outpost's interior, "let's go make that call. There's still enough light that I can take you to the city tonight. That's the plan."

"Is it now?" Brown said.

Baker laughed. "I made some calls in between our talks. Amoloyan is like Saigon, if you take my meaning. It ain't America, but it's got enough to make you feel at home. Your wounded will be better taken care of there, as well."

We filed inside the compound and past Maololi and his men, who parted for us but were still looking twitchier than I liked. I glanced up at the tower again and saw the machine gunner leaning on his weapon, looking bored and perhaps a little disappointed. Sorry, bro.

"Would I be wrong to assume that you were a pilot in the Vietnam War before you were transported here?"

"Right timeframe, wrong country," Chief Baker confirmed. "Guatemala, October fourth, 1965. That was my last day home."

We strode toward the Hueys for Captain Brown to make his call.

"Looks like something out of *Platoon*," García said.

Chief Baker stopped. "You're probably the fourth guy from my future who's mentioned that picture to me. But I wouldn't know. When are you boys from? Milo whispered something about you being from… 1989?"

"That's right," Brown confirmed. "Different jungle than yours, though. Panama. George Bush is president and the Oakland Athletics are World Series champions."

"I know about the presidents okay," Baker said. "You guys are going to elect a freaking draft-dodger in a few years. But I appreciate the baseball update. The Athletics were in Kansas City last time I was home. Anyway, here's the bird. Mostly I just fly sorties out of Amoloyan to the jungle outposts—keep them supplied and operating. You want help working the radio?"

He got Captain Brown set up, and while the captain communicated with the rest of our team, Sanchez quietly led a discussion with Baker. We all listened in.

"Your crew come here with you?" Sanchez asked.

"My co-pilot was DOA—dead on arrival. Commie rebels got him. My gunner, well, rebels didn't get him, but this place sure as hell did. Flying over the wild lands ain't exactly safe. Some of them crazies can send a spear up into the sky pretty good."

Sanchez nodded toward the second Huey. "So, who brought this one in? Friend of yours?"

"Nobody," Baker said. There was a slight, coy smile on his face. "We made this one from scratch."

"How's that?" Captain Brown asked, climbing out of the Huey.

"The colonel, he's got something of an artifact. It gives what you ask it to. Folks that grew up here call it a gift from the gods. I call it the only thing that's kept us alive."

"What do you mean, 'gives what you ask it to'?" Brown asked.

"I haven't actually seen it myself," the chief clarified. "But I'm told that if you tell it what you want—bullets, rations, helicopter parts, radios—it gives it to you. Sometimes it takes a while. This Huey was built out of almost nothing, but it works identical to mine, the genuine article."

That sounded too good to be true. But given everything we'd already seen in this world, I didn't question it.

The captain did. He turned to Epasotl and Xochi. "Have either of you ever heard of anything like this?"

They hadn't.

"You're gonna get your chance to ask about it directly if you want," Baker said. "There'll be people who know the things I don't once you arrive in the city. I don't ask a lot of questions. I'm content to fly."

"You don't want to go back home?" asked Pierce.

The chief eyed him. "Whose home? Yours or mine? Besides, you say that like it's an option. It ain't. There's no going back."

Another pilot came over, a woman, along with a pair of door gunners. There were no co-pilots, apparently. Before long, the birds began to spin up.

Epasotl tugged on my sleeve. Her eyes were big as saucers.

"Yeah, we're riding in them," I said. "Don't worry, it's fun."

"I do not want to fly in the belly of a dragon!"

"They're called 'birds,'" I said, "and trust me, you'll love flying." She didn't look convinced.

"Just got a few things to check and then we'll take off as soon as your crew arrives," Chief Baker told us.

Captain Brown decided to use that time following the chief around and asking him questions. He instructed Epasotl and me to follow him, probably because he wanted our guide to hear what was being said and inform him of anything she might view as out-of-place. But Epasotl was so jumpy around the helicopter that I wasn't sure she was even aware of the conversation.

"I take it this one hasn't been with you long?" Baker asked.

Brown shook his head. "Long enough to be a good guide. Saved us more than a few times."

"They're a weird bunch. We've almost managed to turn some into capable soldiers. Most are just savages, though."

"Did this 'artifact' you mentioned also create the supplies to build this post?" Brown asked. "Concertina wire doesn't grow in the jungle, last I checked."

Baker winked. "Welcome to the *real* Land of the Black Sun. Now then, your men are here and I don't wanna burn any more daylight."

We loaded Gold Team and Captain Brown on Baker's bird, and the rest of us boarded the other. Our pilot was a woman named Yaretzi. She spoke in the same heavily accented English that the post guards had used, so I took that to mean she was an indig. The door gunner might have been, too, but he didn't speak. The man just leaned on his minigun as we got in and gave a lazy salute.

Yaretzi parroted the classic commercial airline hostess schtick about tray tables and flotation devices before taking us into the air. I think Army regulations require all pilots do that.

We lifted off, and the bird shook like it was going to fall apart any second. I looked over at Epasotl to make sure she was doing okay. To my astonishment, she was loving it. I had to keep a firm hold on her because she kept leaning out into the wind. It was Xochi who clutched tightly at my arm and smiled uncomfortably when I looked her way.

"Beautiful, isn't it?" I shouted to her.

"Yes, very loud," she yelled back.

***

The flight lasted perhaps a half hour. We traveled mostly over jungle, and though I tried to crane my neck behind me well enough to catch some familiar landmark to indicate where we had been, it was just endless trees. Before I knew it, we were racing along what looked like a hamlet of thatched houses spread out among farming plots.

Then we came into sight of the city itself.

Amoloyan was larger than I'd expected. It was carved out of a vast area of jungle, with hundreds of buildings radiating out from a massive ziggurat that loomed like a mountain. The sight of it brought back memories of the haunted jaguar-man ruins we'd encountered in the jungle, and I felt a slight chill of apprehension. But it soon passed. From the air at night the city looked like a reflection of the stars. The pilots gave us a brief tour, circling the pyramid once before setting down on a flight pad illuminated by electric lights.

Yes, I said that. *Electric.*

A medic crew with a stretcher ran out to greet us and quickly loaded up Anderson. Doc took Cohen by the arm and waved for Lawrence to follow. They went in one direction, and the rest of us ducked under the rotor wash as the birds spun down and headed for a small detachment of indig soldiers led by an officer who looked like a short Viking raider.

The officer saluted Captain Brown as we approached. They shook hands, and he introduced himself as Lieutenant Bergstrom, formerly of the SAS. He was stocky, with a mop of blond hair and an impressive beard.

We made introductions, then Bergstrom led us into a stone building and down a long echoing hall strung with more lights. His men followed us.

"You have electricity," Captain Brown stated.

"Yes, sir," Bergstrom replied in a rough British accent. Cockney maybe? I dunno. "Let's get you and your men settled in your quarters. You can grab a hot shower, get some real food, and then sleep in an actual bed. I'll see to it you get fresh clothes and toiletries."

"I was hoping to speak to Colonel Dietrich," the captain said.

"Let's get you all settled in first, sir. The colonel's tied up right now—business with the indigs, you know how it goes—but he's eager to meet you." He stopped and pointed out some doorways. "That's you and your platoon sergeant. Hope you don't mind sharing. These two are for your men. That one over there's for the females. Latrine and showers are down this hall, to the right for males, left for females. I'll have to respectfully ask you to remain in your quarters unless escorted. My men will be posted in the hall— they'll get you anything you need."

"So we're prisoners then," Sanchez said sourly.

"Not at all," Bergstrom replied. "You can keep your weapons, although we ask that you take out the magazines and leave them empty. It's simply a security precaution. You know how it goes."

"Thank you, Lieutenant," Captain Brown said.

Bergstrom clicked his heels, saluted, and gave Sanchez a nod before marching away.

His men took up positions outside the doors of our quarters. They were all armed with the carbine versions of the M16 we'd seen at the outpost and stood at parade rest, eyes forward.

"All right, men," the captain said. "Get settled in your new quarters. Take the LT's advice and get yourselves a hot shower and a meal. Then get some sleep." He addressed one of the indig soldiers. "I'd like to get word about my men in the infirmary as soon as possible."

The indigenous man snapped to attention and saluted before speaking into a handset clipped to his shoulder.

"Yes, sir!"

I wasn't crazy about being separated from Xochi or Epasotl, but I wasn't gonna be the guy to cause trouble. We filed into the rooms Bergstrom had indicated was ours, one for Blue Team, one for Gold. They were windowless and lit by electric lights strung from the ceiling. Bottles of water were lined up on a side table, along with a bowl of fresh fruit. There were six beds made of wooden frames with rope under the mattresses, which felt like they were stuffed with cotton. I couldn't resist trying one out and nearly fell asleep the instant I lay down.

"I know we're all exhausted," García said, "but I've been smelling trooper funk for nine weeks and I'm sick of it. Let's hit the showers."

We stripped out of our BDUs, which at this point were stained with blood and worse, and could probably get up and walk by themselves. Each bed had a folded towel with a bar of soap at the end. It was surreal seeing things like that and the water bottles... like we'd just woken up from a bad dream. I almost wanted to sneak out past the guards to see if Epasotl was in her room, or if the whole thing had been a figment of my imagination.

A hot shower after all this time in the jungle should have been magical. But I'd been spoiled by the baths of the Sugar Skull Gals. Still, I was clean, and that alone had me feeling good.

When we got back to our quarters our clothes were gone, replaced by neatly pressed and folded uniforms in the same camo pattern all the soldiers here wore. New undershirts and boxers too. And boots. That might have been the best part. My boots had been falling apart and smelled like something had died in them. And these new boots were a far cry from what the Army issued us. They even looked comfortable.

Woodward picked one up, turned it over in his hands, and gave a low whistle. "Look at these," he said in wonder. "Synthetic soles and uppers. Gotta be waterproof. These are *really* nice. How do you even make something like this?"

García shook his head. "A couple days ago we were fighting freaking ghosts and sword-wielding jaguar-mummies... we've met cat-people, giants, hot babes with voodoo skull faces, ancient ruins and soldiers from outside of time. But you? You're getting your mind blown by *boots*. You're a weird kid, Woodward."

***

Colonel Dietrich didn't see the captain that night, or the next day, or the day after. In fact, a whole week passed before the colonel met with him. We were all getting a little stir crazy by that point, and Captain Brown was clearly frustrated. Bergstrom said we weren't prisoners, but it was starting to feel like it. I think we would have been agitated if we weren't so dog-tired. We got three square meals a day and hot showers, so there was that. But as the week dragged on, we started bitching.

We were Cav, after all.

Doc told us that the medical treatment probably saved Anderson's life. Cohen's vision was improving as well, and by the end of the week both of them were back with us. Lawrence had returned the first day, after confirmation that his arm wasn't infected. That made our bunkhouse feel a bit more crowded, but they were alive and that made us confident the captain had made the right call in coming here instead of trekking back to the tree dwellers. Some of the guys did wonder out loud when and how we'd get Wilson back, and whether he'd recovered by now or not. I just kept my mouth shut. I knew Wilson would be as bummed as bummed could be if we all showed up.

During the day, I spent a lot of time with Xochi and Epasotl, both of whom said they were being treated respectfully by the guards. I got the sense that neither of them was crazy about city living. I told them that it was a lot more enjoyable once you were freed from house arrest.

So, a week in and we were clean, getting our strength back, and growing restless. Then Captain Brown got the invite to speak with Colonel Dietrich—just the captain—and we all waited for his return. I was talking with Xochi when Sanchez interrupted to say Brown was back.

"NCO meeting in captain's quarters. Xochi, too. Epasotl is already there. Let's go, Bennett."

Here was a meeting I was actually eager for. I got right up and moved to the captain and platoon sergeant's quarters.

"Grab a seat, Bennett, Xochi," Captain Brown said as I entered. His room was a small barracks, like ours.

The rest of the NCOs were already present. Xochi and I found a place on the empty beds in the room as he paced. Finally, the captain stood at parade rest and cleared his throat.

"Here's the situation, men. It reminds me of a story arc in *X-Men* issue one hundred and—you know what? Forget that. It was before your time, and I don't feel like explaining."

That was a new one. He always seemed to enjoy explaining the wisdom of his Uncanny friends.

He then told us that Dietrich had been a colonel leading a Special Forces A-Team in, get this, the year *2008*, along with two CIA operatives they were working with in Latin America. "And George Bush is president again—only this time it's his son."

We all smiled and gave quiet laughs at this, but Captain Brown was serious. We quieted down when we realized he wasn't telling a joke.

Brown continued. "Despite the fact that he's from our future, he claims to have arrived here twenty years ago. Obviously, time here doesn't work the way we understand it. From the colonel's perspective, we just showed up on Tuesday."

The men chuckled, but it was an uneasy laugh, as much to relieve the tension over what we were hearing—all those new, blossoming questions—than anything else.

"When Dietrich arrived, a warlord was in control of Amoloyan, exercising a brutal dominion over a variety of human tribes living in this region. He and his cohorts united and then trained the local tribes to overthrow this warlord and assume control. Xochi, Epasotl, I know this place is well beyond your usual roaming, but I wonder if you know of anything that could corroborate or refute this claim."

Epasotl snarled in displeasure. "I knew stories of savages—humans—beyond our forests. They knew not to enter. Some would. They died. That is all."

Xochi shook her head, unable to add anything further. "Uncivilized tribes live beyond the plains. There are always some who would venture beyond, and that is where the rumors of the Silver Eagle spawned from. But these were the words of savages and we did not fully trust them. I am surprised to see these people take on the trappings of civilization here. It is not what I expected."

She had told me much the same in our discussions. I got a sense that the glimpses we had gotten of the city, the buildings, the technology, didn't impress her. Though her dwelling place was more primitive, it was also much more beautiful and peaceful.

Captain Brown kept his face impassive and unreadable. "Colonel Dietrich is an American, but this place is not a democracy. He says he tried that at first, but to continue on would have been to replicate the errors of the State Department in the Middle East. Apparently we get caught up in a forever war over there not long after our time, so warn your children when we get back home. His point being, the tribes did not want an equal voice or to 'Rock the Vote' or anything else. They wanted to be left alone and to live in a system of government they understood and trusted. The result is a sort of feudal governance, which has grown in the past two decades to a sizable collection of fiefdoms. It's a kingdom, as it were. Colonel Dietrich controls lands to the west and south and has established trade with other nations, both indig and Outworlder."

"So how does that all play out?" García asked. "On a map, I mean? Does any of this look like Panama? Does it look like South America, or something else entirely?"

"The colonel and I," Brown said, "and I assume all the Outworlders who come here, have had similar questions. There's a map in his quarters, but not the sort you're thinking of, and it's incomplete, going only so far as his men have personally been able to verify. There are fuel limitations for the Hueys, and patrols, even armed ones, don't make it far. You'll remember our difficulties.

There's a coastal region to the west, however, and then a few islands and an endless ocean. As far as anybody knows."

"Can we trust this man, sir?" García asked. "Because all I can think about is *Apocalypse Now*."

Brown softened up and gave the mildest of smiles. "He's not Kurtz. The colonel's exceptionally intelligent, cunning, and yes, ruthless, but he's not insane. Not so far as I could tell anyway. I don't claim to be a psychologist. But he's established a successful feudal military junta, and that's no easy task.

"I don't mean to suggest he's a dictator, either. The people call him… *Tlahtoāni?*" Brown looked to Xochi and me for confirmation that he'd pronounced the word correctly. We both nodded. "The rank is similar in many respects to a shogun in feudal Japan, but it's somewhat of a figurehead position in this government. A council of the surviving men who arrived here with him make the actual decisions."

"That explains the system of government, but what about technology?" Doc asked. "Where is all this infrastructure coming from? It's so different from what we've seen thus far that it feels otherworldly."

Brown nodded in appreciation at the question. "I did ask about the machine that Chief Baker mentioned. How it worked, where it was located, things of that nature. He confirmed that it does what Baker said, but told me further details are best discussed between friends, and we're still strangers. I can understand his guardedness. If I possessed technology that can do what this machine does, I'd keep it a close secret too."

"So is he the good guy or the bad guy, sir?" I asked.

"It's best to avoid dichotomies, Bennett. I'd recommend approaching this situation from a dialectical angle."

"Begging your pardon, sir," said Stanley, "but can you translate that into English?"

"Avoid thinking in terms of black and white," the captain said. "There's a lot of gray in this new world. We must adapt to the situation, as we've been doing since we arrived."

"And just what is the situation, sir?" Takahashi asked. "You've given us the background, but where do we stand?"

Captain Brown nodded at Sanchez, who stepped forward.

"The colonel is at war with a rival faction of Outworlders," Sanchez said. "We are being asked to join in that fight. We are to assemble before Colonel Dietrich and he will share the proposal given to the captain. Dietrich is a busy man, but Captain Brown insisted that you men have the opportunity to hear it directly from him. And we will do so—*respectfully*. He brought us here, has treated us well, and has provided the medical necessities required to save Anderson's life and get Cohen on the path of recovery. Captain Brown feels we should listen to what he has to say, and so do I."

CHAPTER 30

We found that Lieutenant Bergstrom had been patiently waiting outside of Captain Brown's barracks and sitting in a chair, hat in lap, far enough away from the door that no one could accuse him of eavesdropping. As we filed out of the room, he stood up and re-donned his cap to greet us.

"Good to see you men again. Please understand that we are at war, and Colonel Dietrich has only come to the city as a show of good gratitude to fellow Americans." Bergstrom puffed out his chest. "He does the same for any Brits who find themselves cursed to this land as well. Good man. Now, follow me and you'll get a closer look at the city in all its splendor."

"Where is the colonel quartered?" asked Doc.

"You noticed the central ziggurat on arrival?" Bergstrom asked over his shoulder. "The natives insist that their leaders live there. And so, when in the city, the colonel uses it as a military headquarters." He stopped when he saw Epasotl and Xochi filing in with the rest of us. "I'm not sure the invitation extends beyond your team of Outworlders, Captain."

"The colonel will be aware from our conversation that we view Epasotl and Xochi as valuable team members," Brown said. "I'm sure he will have no problems. Any decision we make impacts them as well as us."

"Right."

I got the sense that Bergstrom didn't agree, but it wasn't something he would fight over.

He led us past saluting guards and then out of the compound and onto the street. There a small, motorized flatbed truck with guardrails and wooden benches on either side of the bed waited for us. We all climbed in while Bergstrom went into the cab to sit up front with the driver. Sergeant Sanchez helped to pull Epasotl and Xochi up onto the back. They sat on either side of me, and we began to slowly drive through the streets. Our driver would periodically beep the soft horn at anyone lingering in the roadway.

Amoloyan reminded me of some of the old cities I'd seen in my mission trip. It was a settlement full of wood and adobe buildings with cut-out windows and brightly painted shutters. The tallest building by far was the pyramid, with nothing else rising up beyond three stories. The streets were a sort of cobblestone, but less uniform. Still, there were gutters and raised stone sidewalks that were crowded with people—indigs I assumed—who were living life much the same way I imagined they had prior to Colonel Dietrich. Some sold wares, fruits, vegetables, and meat in little stands. Others sat outside their buildings and ground corn and wheat into flour or meal.

The people all looked friendly enough, though the strain of poverty and hard living kept them generally lean and grimy with hard lines in their faces. Only the soldiers, who seemed to move through the city in pairs, armed with submachine guns that hung on slings, looked like what an American would call healthy. Nobody was fat. The soldiers dressed in what I was thinking of as Dietrich's camo, and the citizens wore brightly colored sarapes or light-colored linen shirts, dresses, and trousers.

Interestingly, I saw far more women than men out and about. There was no vagrancy of any kind. The streets were clean, and simple electric lights hummed inside the shops and buildings we drove by. Children played games of running after the truck, and we smiled and waved at them as their little legs ran out of steam and they were forced to fall behind.

It seemed like a good place, and I was feeling better about going to meet with Colonel Dietrich than I had been when we first left our barracks. This was civilization. If not for the black sun above—and the sight of Epasotl beside me—I could almost have forgotten we were in another world.

Our ride came to a stop on squeaky brakes right in front of the pyramid. There were several entrances on the base level, and central stairs led up to a second level with additional openings before continuing up a long way to the pinnacle, which had just one final entrance. Every entryway was guarded by what looked like Outworlders, wearing a sort of dress version of the same uniform we'd seen on all the others.

I called them Outworlders mainly because of their physiognomy. You could only really be sure if you heard them talk. Otherwise, these were blacks, whites, Hispanics, and a few Asians, all looking like they could have been pulled out of any American city. Contrast that to ones I saw as indigs, who tended to be darker and looked more like the unreached or lost tribes deep in the Amazon. Of course, this was all assumption on my part, perhaps influenced by too much American media, but in time I would find that the assumption was largely correct.

Bergstrom led us up to the steps to the top level without speaking. We didn't talk to any of the guards we passed along the way, and they probably wouldn't have answered if we tried. They stood ramrod straight, always staring straight ahead, like an honor guard or the—what're they called, Beefeaters? The guys who guard Buckingham Palace. Only these guys wore combat helmets instead of those Flintstones-style tall woolly hats.

The top entrance was just below the apex of the pyramid, and the lieutenant stepped aside to bid us enter. We followed Captain Brown through the opening into a single room that took up the level. The place was ancient stone and antique-looking furniture of polished wood. There were bookcases filled with tomes, and shelves with various pieces of art—little statues, some looking classical and straight out of ancient Greece or Rome as well as objects that looked like they belonged to this world. Soft, yellow electric lights glowed in sconces set up on bare spaces on the walls.

Woodward tripped and had to take a couple of quick steps onto the oriental rug that Dietrich's great mahogany desk sat on top of.

Colonel Dietrich stood from his chair. "Sorry about that."

Woodward mumbled a thanks and then turned around to see what his foot had caught. It was a trench or trough of sorts carved into the stone floor.

"This room was once used for human sacrifice," Dietrich explained. "The blood of victims would flow through these trenches, out the four entryways, and down the steps of the pyramid on each side." He knocked on his desk. "Replaced the altar with this desk. Carved up the altar's stone to block up the other three entrances."

I looked to where those entrances would have been, dead center of each wall. The space directly behind the desk was covered with bookshelves, but on either side you could see some of the mis-colored stone still visible behind the room's decorations, which I now saw included an assortment of mounted rifles that looked a lot like our M16s but smaller, newer, and tan on one side with an American flag with gold frills on the other.

Colonel Dietrich bent down at his desk and opened a file cabinet drawer. "I'd offer you a seat, but lugging enough of them up here would be hell."

We all chuckled at the joke.

He brought up a finely carved wooden box and placed it on the desk, then opened the lid and turned it so we could see inside. "So let me offer you men a cigar instead."

Captain Brown was quick to graciously decline.

"The hell with that," Dietrich said. "You don't have to smoke 'em if you don't want to—maybe you shouldn't; I hear they pull in a nice price in barter. But don't insult me. Every one of you dogs, reach a paw in here and pick one out. Keep me from dying of lung cancer that much longer."

The captain relented and then we all followed, each of us reaching in and giving our thanks like an amoebic mass of arms before settling back.

Dietrich came around from the desk with a Zippo lighter and assisted everyone who even *remotely* looked like they wanted to smoke, encouraging and cajoling each man until the guys who really wanted to light up did so. I put my cigar in my pocket, but Xochi, to my surprise, puffed away expertly. Epasotl made a face like the cloud of blue smoke filling the room was going to make her sick.

Finally Dietrich sat back down behind the desk, lit his own cigar, puffed on it, and examined its ash as he let out a long exhale. He held that pose as he moved his eyes from the cigar to us.

"This nation is at war. It's a war against other Outworlders, same as you and me. Americans, even, if you can believe it. I tell you that now so you won't feel like I'm trying to pull one over on you in the event you accept my proposition, which you're under no obligation to do. The cigars are free, gentlemen."

Again we laughed. I got the sense that a lot of the guys were warming up to Dietrich right away. Maybe that made me feel a stronger need to be wary. I don't know.

"When I came here, twenty years ago, there were Outworlders here, but not in the sort of numbers there are now. In carving out some of what you've seen of Amoloyan, it was pretty much myself and two fellow operators, who unfortunately are no longer with us. But more allies came in time, and we were able to, at the very least, beat back the savagery native to this land and give some sense of peace and stability to the region. Albeit, not using the forms of government we are most familiar with."

He glanced at Epasotl and then Xochi. "I'm glad you have made friends with some of the indigenous peoples. I understand from your captain that neither of them were aware of what we've done here in Amoloyan beyond a few rumors. That is because our war is not a war of conquest, but one of self-defense."

Colonel Dietrich paused to enjoy his cigar again. "Damn fine cigar." For a moment looked lost in his bliss.

"About ten years ago a small island nation of no account off the western coast of this continent began to raid coastal shipping lanes. Their fleet was sizeable. A few of what we would consider to be modern boats, and some older boats that we would more easily place in the days of high seas piracy and oceanic exploration. Enough firepower for them to establish a beachhead and take a coastal city that rivals this one in size. We made it clear that we saw them as no threat and hoped they would do the same. We departed in peace.

"But almost the second we did so, they began pushing out, gaining territory. They are now operating in the mountain range that separates us from the sea. There's no further they can go that doesn't involve direct conflict with my forces. I have helicopters, as you've seen, and from aerial reconnaissance we see that they are preparing for a major offensive. I could use experienced scouts like yourself to assist my troops in locating and identifying these enemy forces."

A silence hung thick in the air.

Colonel Dietrich smiled. "I know. Laid it all on you at once. If you've got questions, I have time to answer them, but my time is not inexhaustible, gentlemen. I don't mean to be rude, but that's the reality of holding together the first lasting peace this world seems to have ever known."

Sanchez took up the offer. "All due respect, sir—we've seen that you have Hueys. Why not have them do your scouting?"

"Because they're hard to come by and easy to shoot down. Our best results are achieved through cavalry, like you men."

Captain Brown took a deep breath. "Our goal has been to find a way back home."

"Understandable. I've had a twenty-year head start on that and I haven't found a way, son. Getting home—whatever that looks like for so many of us from different periods of time—is, of course, Mission Priority One. If you all find a way, I hope you'll tell me. If I find a way, I'll certainly tell you. But after twenty years... let's just say I'm not holding out as much hope as I once did."

None of this was news to us—we'd heard as much from Chief Baker, and we already knew Dietrich had been here for twenty years —but to hear the words straight from his mouth with no sugarcoating... it still rocked us all hard.

Doc, who'd been standing quietly in a corner, spoke up. "All due respect, Colonel Dietrich, but we might not be quite ready to take your word for it. Joining you, even if your cause is just, would put us under a chain of command that might directly fly in the face of our own objectives."

Dietrich considered before answering, which I appreciated. I've seen a lot of officers who see the end of someone else's sentence only as an opportunity to say what they were going to say anyway. "Your captain and I discussed that. I am not seeking to assume you into my military. You would be operating as allied forces for our mutual benefit."

"Permission to speak freely, sir?" Takahashi said.

Colonel Dietrich looked to Brown.

"Granted," Brown said.

"I can see how this would be beneficial to the colonel. However, I'm not sure I see how it benefits us."

"In this way, Sergeant," Dietrich said. "On your way through the city, you may have noticed a distinctive lack of able-bodied men in the streets. This is because every man in this city is engaged in some sort of useful work. They are either too young to be asked to fight, too old to be asked to fight again, or they possess a skill vital to the community. Those that do not possess such skills are *not* given handouts. There are inns, taverns, and the like, but there is not charity. The people here do not know charity. Recall, they're a generation removed from killing their own children with stone knives and weeping tears of joy at seeing the blood flow down these steps. The indigenous people, when they find a man of fighting age not employed in skilled labor, they take that man by force, remove him from the city, and put him in the infantry."

We all looked at one another, none of us liking what we'd just heard.

"You're threatening us with conscription if we don't join you?" Captain Brown asked.

"No, Captain, I am not and I *would* not. Ever. That said, I also will not disrupt the tender cultural balance we've achieved by stopping them from taking your men. You cannot be, nor do I suspect you would desire to be, permanent guests consuming limited resources for nothing in return. But you have those cigars and will be granted a month's local pay regardless of your decision. A gift to fellow Americans. You can use that to attempt to set up here and show a skill that the town elders appreciate, or you can move on and try your luck elsewhere. The decision is yours alone."

Colonel Dietrich stood. "I have to be moving on, gentlemen. I understand that this is something you need to consider before making a decision. Whatever that decision is, inform Lieutenant Bergstrom. He'll take it from there. I'd like to stay and swap stories, but I have to be leaving."

He strode out with confidence. We watched him go, not speaking, and when his shadow left the temple's pinnacle, all the questions I wished I had asked came flooding to me all at once.

Doc spoke first. "What we're talking about here… is being mercenaries. Selling our services."

Captain Brown took in a deep breath and then slowly let it out. "It sounds a lot like selling our services to a foreign nation, I agree. I think I'd be more alarmed if Colonel Dietrich had tried to sell this all as some continuation of America, but he's been very clear about the realities of this world. I think we need to consider those realities as well."

"So what does that mean?" Takahashi asked. "We took an oath. Does that end now that we're in another world?"

Sanchez was quick with an answer. "We represent the United States of America in this godforsaken place."

Brown nodded. "As far as I'm concerned, we're still bound by the oaths we took. Whether this helps us get home or not still remains to be seen."

"Assuming that's even possible," Stanley muttered.

"I wanted you to hear everything from Dietrich's own lips, but here's my decision," Brown said. "We act as scouts for Dietrich. In our earlier discussion, the colonel explained that this comes with pay, supplies, and munitions. We'll be scouting where and when asked, but will obtain a status that allows us free movement throughout this 'kingdom' once we're through. Assuming we don't blow it all and get ourselves conscripted."

A few guys smiled, but nobody laughed.

"If the terms were in any way different, if we were to be rolled into a larger army or split up—and that includes separating us from

Epasotl and Xochi, who I consider a part of our autonomous unit—I would have refused them outright even before bringing you to see the colonel. Similarly, if I didn't believe we could use this as a means to better understand the world we're in and determine a subsequent course home, I believe we'd already be on our way. But right now, this is our best option for the future. It's not perfect, but neither is it permanent. That's my decision."

"I think we should have a say in this, sir," Doc said.

Brown didn't look angry. "And if you did, what would your vote be?"

"I don't know," Doc admitted. "I'm worried that this might be a step into something none of us can get out of."

"I mean, it's not like we haven't stepped into some serious shit multiple times already," García said.

"I know that all you men would prefer a guarantee," Captain Brown said. "So would I. That's something I can't give you. So…" He motioned to the entryway. "There's the door. All of you are free to walk through it with my blessing. Consider your term of enlistment over. Doc, you at least have medical skills that can likely earn you as comfortable a life as anyone else in this city."

Doc crossed his arms. "I'm not leaving these men any more than you are."

"Screw it," Takahashi said. "Let's do it and see what happens."

A cascade a similar surrenders to fate followed until I found myself saying, "Yeah, okay. Let's do it."

I couldn't quite read Captain Brown, but I thought he was either proud of us… or relieved.

He looked to Xochi and Epasotl. "You are also free to go as you please. We will endeavor to send you wherever you may wish to go."

"I do not wish to go fight for the Silver Eagle," Epasotl said flatly. "But I must and so I will."

"Epasotl," I said. "Let it go. You don't have to—"

She stuck out her tongue and made a face like she was going to barf. "Spare me the lecture, dude. I will live by honor."

Xochi was quiet, so Captain Brown asked her point-blank. "Do you wish to continue on with us, Xochi?"

She nodded. Later she would tell me, "I will stay with you, Nephi."

"That settles it then," Captain Brown said. "I'll tell Lieutenant Bergstrom and we'll see what's next."

But the lieutenant was already in the doorway. "Personally, I think you've all made a very wise decision. Now, let's get you outfitted and familiar with our forces."

CHAPTER 31

We had a lot of questions that day, but there was little time to ask them, let alone find someone willing to answer them. Lieutenant Bergstrom wanted us outfitted and in fighting form as quickly as possible. It didn't feel like there'd be much of a honeymoon period. The week of rest and recovery we'd had while confined to barracks was all that we would have before training ramped up to a feverous cadence. Captain Brown went off to do officer things with Bergstrom while the rest of us were handed over to a certain Chief Rossi.

The man looked and spoke like a Bronx gorilla. He was broad-chested and hairy, and his long arms swung as he strolled in front of us, but he was practically effervescent as he chattered on about his armory, giving us the tour.

"Given the threats in this world, we like to pack a punch," he said as he motioned to a rack of big, sleek-looking carbines with odd accessories along the wall. "Gentlemen, meet the FM SCAR-H. 'H' is for 'heavy.' You probably noticed five-five-six doesn't do much against a lot of the nasties out here. Well, *these* girls here are fully modernized *battle* rifles. Holographic sights, IR lasers, they got the works."

"Lasers are sweet," García said.

"Where'd you get all these from?" Woodward asked. "They look brand-new. Did a supply train get sucked into this world or something?"

"Nope. Made 'em out of thin air," Rossi said.

"With that machine we've been hearing about?" Sanchez asked. "How's that thing work?"

"Yeah," the chief said. "It's like a… like a replicator, you know? Like from *Star Trek*. The newer one. *Next Generation*. Was that on the air before you guys got sucked in here?"

Pierce guffawed. "I mean, not like I watched it, but yeah."

"I watched it," García said. I gave him a look, and he shrugged. "What? Troi is a babe."

"When are you from, Chief?" Sanchez asked. "After the new *Star Trek* show, I take it."

"Yeah. I got sucked out of the year 2002. Been in country for going on eight months now."

It could hurt your head if you thought about it too hard, how people from our past or future could somehow arrive in this land ahead of us by a few months or twenty years, despite having lived untold decades in our past or future.

"So what you're saying, Chief, is that this thing can make anything?"

"*Any*thing!" Rossi held his long arms out, as if embracing the whole armory. "You give it a sample of something, and it'll spit out an exact copy."

"So, this machine," Sanchez said, clearly angling for some intel or answers that the captain would want to know if he didn't already. "What's the story behind it? Did some grunt from a couple hundred years in both our futures bring it with him?"

We'd already heard that Colonel Dietrich was supposedly from 2008, which had us wondering if others had come from even *further* in the future. Might we come across some Space Marines or Starship Troopers or something?

"Nah, nothing like that," Rossi answered. "This is a native artifact. They used it to make shiny trinkets for the rulers, useless things like that. Once the colonel got it, he saw how it could make a whole lot more than jewelry, and he started putting it to use to win wars. The only constraint is, you have to have an example of the thing you want. Gotta be careful not to use up your last anything or you ain't gettin' more. Which is why we've got a warehouse full of stuff that don't get used just in case. Insurance policy. And the boss offers huge bounties for any Outworlder tech that we don't already have one of. So keep your eyes open for that."

"So, it's a magic copy machine," I said. "But for stuff."

"Basically. We can tweak things a *little* bit, like different sizes is easy. Reconfiguring the base SCAR model to a precision rifle for sniper teams was a bit more challenging. Don't get too excited, though—the copy process takes some time, so we only use it for stuff we really need and can't get anywhere else. Like the things you see on the wall. Although a few of us have put together a petition asking Dietrich to brew up a pallet of Heineken… if we ever get a sample brought over with us. You guys didn't happen to…?"

"Nope," Pierce said. "Ate my last Pop-Tart weeks ago, too. Woulda hung on to it if I knew."

"Big-D practically industrialized the whole operation," Rossi continued, hiding any disappointment at the lack of beers to replicate. "Now it's running full tilt, making arms, munitions, hell, even the clothes you're wearing down to your boots."

"Well, at least the Great Boot Mystery is now answered," García said. "Happy now, Woodward?"

Woodward ignored the jab. "What powers it?"

"No clue," Rossi said. "It's an artifact, kid. It's magic. You been out in the bush long enough to know that means something around here. Anyway, I don't run the thing and I ain't never seen the thing. All I know is the priests can make us whatever we want. Most of its output is for the military, but we produce exports too."

"Why?" Woodward asked.

"Why what?" Rossi said.

"Why make exports?"

"For trade, obviously." Rossi looked confused.

"But what do you need to trade for if you can just replicate anything?"

"Ah, right. Well, a few reasons. One, like I said, we've gotta use it judiciously. We've only got the one artifact, and it can only make but so much. Especially if we're talking huge volumes. Took years to stock up this armory. Second, the boss hates being dependent on the priests, who can get uppity I hear, so he's been working on making us more self-sufficient. We got mining operations, smelters, smithies, machine shops, distilleries…" He grinned. "We also make our own ethanol for the generators. Frankly, we could operate at roughly a mid-eighteenth-century level without the replicator at all."

That was all fine and good—fascinating even—but my big takeaway was that everyone in Amoloyan seemed to have completely given up on any thought of going back home. Everything they did was about the here and now. Life in this Land of the Black Sun.

I worried that it wouldn't be long until we all thought the same way.

***

When we linked back up with Captain Brown, he had an excitement that was difficult to miss. With his meetings came a clearer picture of what was in store for and expected of us. Part of that would be combat operations, which suited our former Ranger captain just fine. Only we weren't Rangers. We were now what he called "dragoons."

"Job One is still reconnaissance," he told us. "But we're a *fighting* unit now. Don't forget we're raiders as well as recon. We will find the enemy—and destroy them if required. We'll be mounted, but typically fight as dismounts. That's how dragoons operate. Move swiftly, strike fast, and fade away. It's all about speed, mobility, and shock value. Our versatility will be our strength. Reconnaissance in force."

"Sir?" García held up a hand. "What will we be mounted in? Humvees again?"

"No." The captain grinned broadly. "Horses!"

"Horses…?" García said. "Sir, most of us don't know how to ride."

"You'll learn. The colonel's wranglers and Xochi will see to that. We'll be going where vehicles can't go, and there's no supply chain for refueling anyway. Horses are ideal for our mission parameters."

That was an interesting twist. We were Cav, so we had to ride something, but given the magical mystery machine that was spitting out all the weapons, I'd just assumed we'd have Humvees—or at least Jeeps. Then again, who was to say that ours weren't the only Humvees on this planet? And last time I saw them, they weren't in such good shape. But horses suited me just fine. I'd always had an affinity for the beautiful creatures. I wasn't an experienced rider, not by any stretch, but being in the saddle felt natural to me, like I'd been born to it. I was the descendant of pioneers and ranchers. Horses were in my blood.

In addition to the new mounts we'd soon be meeting, Sanchez saw to it that Chief Rossi issued us all battle rifles, except for Cameron, who was issued an M240 machine gun. Additionally, Sanchez, Stanley, and Woodward got FN40GL grenade launchers, which were mounted under the barrels of their battle rifles just like an M203 on an M16. Cohen was assigned as Captain Brown's radio man and was issued a shiny new radio called a SINCGARS, which was head and shoulders above a prick.

As I was the only designated marksman who wasn't a team leader, Captain Brown assigned me to lead our new sniper team, which was rare for Scouts, but he felt we needed snipers in our modified role as dragoons. The assignment made me a team leader, but the team was me and Pierce.

So I was a team leader... of Pierce.

Captain Brown christened us *X Team*. With our departure from Blue Team, Greene and Cameron were moved over from Gold to take our place.

As the trigger-puller on our team, Pierce was issued an M24A3, which was essentially a Remington 700 with a twenty-seven-inch barrel chambered in .338 Lapua Magnum. He not-so-secretly wanted a mammoth rifle called the Barrett M82 that fired fifty-caliber rounds and apparently could reach out and touch someone at something like one and a half *miles*—at least that's what Chief Rossi said the record was back when he came from—but I reminded Pierce he'd have to hump the thirty-pound monstrosity, and after that he said the M24 would do just fine. Besides, it's not like Lapua Magnum didn't pack plenty of boom.

Being Pierce's backup and spotter, I got a "recalibrated" SCAR-H with a two-stage match trigger and a twenty-inch barrel. I wasn't about to complain.

The captain didn't leave Xochi and Epasotl out. Rather than have them unofficially attached, he swore them in as the first female 19Ds from another dimension—and in Epasotl's case the first non-human—in US Army history. Or at least that we knew of. He assigned Epasotl to the headquarters element, in exactly what role was unclear, but apparently "Little Kahuna" SFC Sanchez had taken more of a liking to her than I'd suspected. PFC Epasotl kept the suppressed MP5 we'd captured—anything else was too big and bulky—and Xochi, who Brown decided to make his intelligence officer and swore in as a CW2, was issued an FN SCAR-H like everyone else, which surprised me given her size; something lighter than a battle rifle seemed more appropriate. But Sanchez didn't want one trooper fielding different ammunition from the rest of the platoon, which made sense. Chief Warrant Xochi didn't seem to mind, although firing the heavy 7.62 rifle on full auto was no joke. Then again, she's stronger than she looks.

Cohen's eyesight was still iffy, and we wondered if he'd recover in time to deploy with us, but as it turned out he'd probably have time to do just that, because despite our day one hustle of getting equipped and outfitted, we were going to be staying in the region for a while to undertake additional training.

"You and Pierce will be sent to a seven-week sniper school," Sanchez informed me as he set up his office inside our temporary headquarters. Epasotl sat in a corner, balancing on a stool. "You leave tomorrow."

I must have worn my concern on my face, because Sanchez followed up with the ever-dangerous question, "That a problem?"

Seven weeks? I was feeling protective about Xochi and didn't like the idea of leaving her. It wasn't like we were a… thing. Officially. But we had a… I guess you could say an understanding. There was a togetherness between us that we both felt would turn into something. Eventually. Hopefully. She was a warrant officer now though… and there are rules about fraternization. I wasn't sure how much of a stickler Captain Brown would be about that.

"No, sir, not a problem," I said, knowing better than to reveal my tender heart to him. "I'm just surprised to hear that there's such an extensive school."

"Apparently it was founded and originally instructed by Colonel Dietrich himself. Getting assigned there is a big deal among the indigs and his army."

I nodded. "Anything to help the team, Sergeant."

Sanchez grunted, and I was dismissed.

Epasotl stuck her tongue out at me to say goodbye.

***

That night was our first inside the city with any freedom, and it also had to be my last with Xochi for a while, "fraternization" or no. We stood on a veranda just outside what was to serve as our training barracks, which was a lot fancier than where they'd put us the first time. More like a hotel, with all the rustic charm of a pre-modern Mexican resort. In fact, it offered us a wonderful view of the local promenade, with a glittering pool at its center. The sky was calm and cloudless, with a warm breeze that ruffled her blade-shortened hair.

"I am sad that you will be gone for so long," she told me. "And worried."

"If it's about me, you don't need to," I said. "I'll be fine. I'm more worried about you. Not that you can't take care of yourself or anything. Just… don't have too much fun while I'm away."

I winked at her, and she laughed.

"You are without reason to be jealous, Nephi. I look forward already to your return."

I let out a deep sigh. I felt the same way. But I was still worried about her. More particularly, I was worried about how she'd mix in with the guys. One guy in particular hadn't bothered to hide his wolfish looks when it came to Xochi.

"Just watch out for Corporal Stanley," I advised.

"Stanley is a *coyametl*, but men are often that way, no?"

I didn't recognize the word and asked her what it meant.

"You know, smelly creatures who root in the mud and are always rutting."

"Ah, pigs," I said. "Yeah, that would describe him."

"It is nothing."

"*I* don't think it's nothing. I don't like the way he looks at you."

She smiled. "You *are* jealous."

"I'm not jealous," I said. "I'm worried. Worried about your safety. He looks at you like—"

"Like a starving animal," she said, serious now. "Yes, I know. I have eyes. Your concern is noble." Xochi entwined her fingers in mine. "But I am a warrior, no?"

"You're half his size."

"Do you doubt my skill? I have killed giants in battle. True giants. I can handle a lone... pig? Even one"—she made air quotes —"twice my size."

I didn't know where she'd picked up air quotes. It was cute though.

I sighed and stared across the pool, which reflected the lanterns and electric lights of shops and vendors. The waters were ringed by palm trees, and at their center was a marble fountain capped by a larger-than-life gold statue of Colonel Dietrich dressed as a Mesoamerican king, his war club held high to the heavens. Around him bronze warriors knelt in obeisance while nude maidens poured water out of jugs.

It hadn't escaped my notice that similar monuments dotted the city.

Our guides had explained that this wasn't his own doing, but rather the way the locals demanded they pay homage to Dietrich. The statues that stood now were merely replacements of statues from the previous ruler; the next warlord or whatever always received the same. Denying the natives their custom would only accelerate that next changing of the guard and usher in unnecessary bloodshed.

I still wasn't crazy about it.

"Your mind dwells too much on what might be," Xochi said, "and very often on what was, instead of enjoying that which is before you *now*."

"I take that as a very not-subtle way of telling me to shut up and kiss you."

"Then you are wrong. I don't want you to kiss me. Later, maybe —if you stop being rude to me—but not right now. Right now, I want you to be still and just *listen*."

"I wasn't being rude," I said, placing my palm across my chest to feign being wounded. "But for you, right now, I'm all ears. Talk to me."

"Not listen to *me*. Ugh. Sometimes you have no head. Listen to the *city*. What do you hear?"

I cataloged the usual night sounds of the city. Horses and carts, the occasional truck, people walking past in conversation, the chug and hiss of a steam engine in a nearby factory, dogs barking, street vendors, music...

I raised an eyebrow. "Music? Is that what you want me to listen to?"

"Yes! The music! I have heard it every night since we first came to this city. I have never heard anything like it before."

"Sounds like a bluegrass band," I said, the oddness of such a thing only dawning on me as I spoke it.

She tugged at my hand. "Come, take me to it."

Despite her request, it was Xochi who led me at a trot down the promenade around couples walking slowly and groups of soldiers who whistled after her. We wove through bright streets and dark alleys. Her laughter was pure and clear.

The source of the music was a tavern with warm light glowing from its doors and windows. Musicians had set up on the veranda and played as men and women danced in the street.

Xochi clapped. "That!" she said. "That is what I want you to do with me."

"What? Dance?"

"Yes!"

"I can't dance."

"Tonight, you will learn," she said, dragging me into the crowd.

***

Sniper school was a ton of math and a lot of sitting or lying prone, motionless, for hours, but by the end of it, I was in tremendous shape and shooting farther and better than I would have thought possible. Apparently Pierce and I were the holdup, because our arrival back to the unit marked our last night in the city; we were told we'd be heading out first thing the next morning. A lot of the guys seemed to have trouble saying goodbye, which I understood, especially those who had found the comfort of a woman. All of them drank liberally that night.

I was just glad I'd be back with Xochi again.

While the rest of the men were out for a final night of carousing, I found her alone in the stables brushing her horse. It was sleek and as black as the face paint she'd once worn. Xochi's gorgeous amber eyes widened when she saw me, and she rushed over to tackle me in an embrace. I leaned my head down and she met my kiss with a ferocity that quickly grew more intense than either of our religious convictions allowed. She pushed away hands that had begun to roam just a little—okay a lot—and laughed at me as she retreated and put the horse between us.

"Sergeant Sanchez had me help the wranglers train the men how to ride the horses," she said, focusing intently on her brushing as color rose on her cheeks.

"They shuffled me away to sniper school so fast I didn't even see my horse," I said.

"Oh! You must meet him. He is a magnificent animal." She ducked past me, dodging with a laugh as I grabbed at her waist, and took my hand purposefully. I let her drag me down the stalls until we came to a stop before a tall gray stallion.

"This one is meant for you," Xochi said. "He is Duke. His previous rider was killed in battle. You will fare better."

I smiled, not exactly thrilled at hearing the fate of Duke's previous rider. "Hey, Duke."

The horse snorted at its name but looked at me warily.

Xochi went to a bag of oats and pulled out a handful. She offered it to me. "They love this. You should feed him so he will love you."

I did. Duke was a little nervous, I think, but he was a trained war horse and didn't shy away for long. Soon he accepted handful after handful, his huge velvety lips smacking against my palm wetly.

"You spoil him," Xochi teased. "But... he will remember you tomorrow morning. Your first ride will be easier now."

Duke let me pat him, and then Xochi led me back to her own mount.

"This is Lancer." She made a series of soft clicking sounds, and Lancer stepped back two paces, then turned around full circle.

"You taught him that?"

"It is a beginning," she replied with a grin. "I was told these horses are all named after the mounts of great warriors from your world. Do you know a rider of Duke?"

"Yeah, that's the name of the horse General Sherman rode in Atlanta."

I doubted Xochi had any idea what that meant, and I suspected that her asking me about Duke was so she could ask about her own, which she did.

"And Lancer is also named after a great warrior's mount?" she said.

"Well, I don't know if he was a great warrior exactly, but General Custer is certainly famous."

"What is this Custer famous for?"

"Dying, mostly, and getting a lot of troopers killed in the process." I laughed. "That's a long story. He was a complicated man."

"All people are complicated."

I blew out my cheeks. "Truth."

"Did you miss me?" she asked.

"Terribly," I admitted.

"Good!"

"Did Stanley behave himself?"

She shrugged and waved her hand dismissively. "He has to salute me now and call me 'ma'am,' which amuses me because he hates it so."

"And the others?" I didn't mean to sound protective or jealous, but that was probably how it came out.

She didn't seem to mind all that much. "They treat me like 'one of the guys,'" she said, and I knew it wasn't a complaint over some lack of special treatment. A warrior through and through, she wanted nothing less than to be seen as a part of a fighting machine.

And a fighting machine was exactly what we'd become.

Tomorrow we'd be going to war.

CHAPTER 32

Pierce and I were perched on a shelf protected by a screen of bushes that overlooked a road about four hundred meters to our northwest. Well, "road" might be generous. It was a wide track through a pass in the Blue Mountains. At this altitude the jungle had given way to pine and oak, but it was still hot. The horses were tethered farther back up the mountainside in a dense thicket.

"Sun's getting low," I said in a soft voice. "It'll be dusk in an hour."

"Longshot, this is Nightcrawler," García transmitted, as if he was reading my mind.

"Go for Longshot," I replied.

Captain Brown had christened me with my new callsign. He made a point to explain who the guy was, what issue he first appeared in, and other various bits of trivia, all in great detail. It didn't matter. I loved the name and was still basking in the glory of hearing it over our new, hella-sweet AN/PRC-126 radios. The things were small enough to strap to your plate carrier, and we had earpieces with little boom mikes. I felt like some sort of high-speed future soldier.

"Pull out and link up with us after dusk. We'll lead you in with lasers."

"Roger, Longshot out."

"García and his lasers," Pierce grunted. "He could just use an IR strobe."

"Lasers are more fun." I sat back and cut open an MRE. "Mmm. Chicken chunks."

"Chunks of *something*," he said. "Tastes like chicken at least. Aw, man. Got another vegetarian one. Who put this crap in my assault pack?"

"What is it?" I asked.

"Cheese tortellini in tomato sauce."

"That's not half bad. Trade you?"

"Nah, keep your mystery chunks."

"So, I gotta wonder," I said after my first mouthful. "If the replicator makes these, is the meat really meat?"

"No, that's why they're mystery chunks."

"But the pork's good," I said.

"Roger that. I'd trade my left nut for a maple pork sausage patty right now. Hey, you seen the 2013 issue of *SI* yet?"

"No, who's on the cover?"

"Some chick named Kate Upton. Smoking hot, like fry-your-eyeballs hot. She's on the deck of this boat wearing a parka. Just the parka, that's all, and the caption's like 'Kate Upton Goes Polar Bare.' Get it? Bare? Cracked me up."

"Where'd you get your hands on that?"

"They actually replicated a stack of them to give out to the troops. Morale thing."

"She better than Kathy Ireland?" I asked.

"Damn, that's a hard call, man, but get this: this Upton chick was born in '92."

"Oh, dang. So she's not even alive yet." I wrapped another chunk of mystery meat in a tortilla. "They should've replicated the '89 issue. That'll always be the best one."

"No lies detected," Pierce said.

"Sanchez has the '89. They could sample his."

"Yeah, but the pages are all stuck together, and it would replicate *that*, too."

We'd been talking low, almost subvocalizing, and I had to bite my tongue to keep from laughing out loud. Then I almost choked to death on a chicken chunk. Silently though. Because, OPSEC. What can I say? I'm a professional.

"Twelve hours sitting here looking at that empty track," Pierce sighed. "Gotta love recon."

"Should get exciting once we make it through this pass and get back into the jungle," I replied. "Venomous flying snakes, for crying out loud."

"I already hate snakes enough as it is," Pierce grumbled. "Whose idea was it to give them wings?"

"Flying other things too."

"Oh, you mean Batman."

"Bat-*men*," I corrected. "*Camazots*. The description Lieutenant Bergstrom gave in the ops brief was insane, eh?"

"Would've said he was full of shit, except"—Pierce waved an MRE spoon around vaguely—"after seeing those vampire-witch-werewolf things, I'll believe just about anything. Shit just gets better and better."

I shuddered involuntarily. I still had nightmares about the *tlahuelpuchi*. In fact, I'd been having a lot of nightmares lately, even more so since we'd arrived at Amoloyan. Nothing much I could remember, but the dreams left me feeling… off.

Other things felt off to me too. Little things, like our new gear. My clothes were… I don't know… uncomfortable, and my rifle never seemed clean no matter how often I cleaned it. It looked fine, but it just felt… dirty. Come to think of it, *dirty* was a good word for what I was feeling.

Even the MREs with the upgraded menus didn't taste quite right —but then again, they're MREs. They never taste right.

"You ever get the feeling something's… weird about all this new gear?" I asked. "Like all the replicated stuff is… not quite right somehow?"

Pierce cocked an eyebrow and pointed his spoon at me. "You worry about the weirdest things, Benn—*Corporal*. This gear is choice beyond words."

"Sanchez isn't around," I said. "Don't 'corporal' me, man."

He laughed softly. "But seriously, Nephi, we got bigger things to worry about. Like venomous frigging flying snakes."

"And bat-men."

"Yeah, and Batman."

***

Navigation in the Land of the Black Sun had always been problematic not only because there was no magnetic north, but because for most of our time in this world we'd had no maps. We'd long ago found ways to deal with the first problem, and now we'd solved the second. The maps we were provided weren't the topographical type with grids like we were accustomed to, but they had major geographical reference points and we were told they were accurate. It was still difficult to communicate positions, especially to other units, but by orienting off the geographical features—say, a mountain peak or two—you could get by.

Plus, we were always all right so long as our favorite Chaneque was with us. Epasotl had long ago taught us how to find north using the constellations and tracking the shadow of the sun, but she herself didn't seem to need these tricks; she had an almost preternatural sense of direction. Somehow she always knew if we were off course. It wasn't like she could point and say, "That's north," but if you gave her a direction, she'd stick to it. She was indispensable as our living wayfinder and usually buddied up with whoever was on point. Her enhanced senses didn't hurt in that role either.

Our headquarters was FOB Cincinnati, where First Battalion was stationed. It was part of a line of outposts stretching some hundred miles across a ridge that ran along the western side of the Blue Mountains. The base to our north was FOB Detroit, home of the Second Battalion, and FOB Atlanta was to the south, home of the Third. Interspersed were various smaller outposts and forts. From what we were told, these smaller locations were mostly manned by indigs, with Outworlders selected by Dietrich making sure things didn't fall to pieces.

Altogether, this line of outposts comprised the entirety of the Fifth Regiment, which was commanded by an Outworlder named Colonel Gutierrez, who was our boss, I guess. He was a conquistador out of the sixteenth century, apparently, which was cool in a way, but also strange. We hadn't met him yet.

It was a lot of territory to cover, doubly so because all the indig conscripts traveled on foot fielding war clubs and spears, and because we were in the tail end of the rainy season, which was called the Season of Farming. Soon it would be the dry season, the Season of War, and Colonel Gutierrez's forces would sweep down the west side of the mountains in an attempt to push the enemy into the sea.

But first we had to find them. That was *our* job.

"I just got off the radio with Chief Baker, and he reported a company-sized element in this valley," Captain Brown said, pointing to a map spread out on the ground. "From what he observed, it's an indigenous unit, but he only got a glimpse before they scattered under cover, so their size is only a rough estimate."

Sanchez, Takahashi, García, and I were squatting in a loose circle with the captain. We'd been scouting the narrow valleys for days without any direct visual on the enemy. The few villages we'd encountered had been friendly enough, if wary, but not exactly forthcoming with information. You got the impression they were playing both sides, which under the circumstances made sense: there was a noticeable lack of military-aged males—no doubt from forced conscription on both sides—and defenseless people caught between two sides of a war are probably always going to make nice with whoever happens along, just hoping to keep out of the crossfire. We weren't necessarily comfortable with "our" side stealing young men from villages to fill the ranks, but that was how the game was played in this world. To tell an indig chieftain or commander that they *couldn't* build their forces in such a manner was the same as asking them to join your enemy and fight against you. Or so the veterans told me.

"First Battalion is set up there," Sanchez said, pointing to another place on the map, "which leaves this pass over here completely unprotected." He pursed his lips. "If that unit Chief Baker spotted cuts across southward, they'll have a straight shot through the mountains, unless FOB Atlanta can get the Third in place, and that'd be tricky, given their position. Frankly, sir, none of the battalions are deployed ideally to prevent an incursion along that route."

"I've already pointed that out to Colonel Gutierrez," Brown said, "and he assures me he has his reasons, although he hasn't seen fit to tell me what those reasons are."

"I'm no strategist, sir," put in Takahashi, "but frankly *none* of the battalion deployments make sense."

"No, Hachirō, they don't," Brown replied. "But strategy is Colonel Gutierrez's job. *Ours* is to tell him where the enemy is, and to do that we need eyes on that element Chief Baker spotted this morning." He drew his finger in a line along the map. "We need a screen along this spur."

Sanchez gave a low whistle. "That's a lot of ground for fifteen scouts to cover." He began stabbing his finger at different points along Brown's line. "We could put observation posts here, here... here, and... ideally here, but we'll be well out of radio contact with each other, and I don't like that one bit."

"Neither do I, Diego, but we don't really have a choice. Once we get eyes-on and know where they're headed, we can consolidate the platoon. We'll have to rely on dispatch riders to communicate." He met each of our eyes in turn. "This is strictly a recon gig, boys, so avoid engagement like they're one of those zombie stones. Clear?"

We all nodded.

"Good."

***

Duke snorted softly, his hooves squelching in the thick mud of the streambed while we climbed the draw. Insects trilled and birds flitted between the tall pines towering overhead. Pierce and I had been sent out to establish OP Echo at the far northeast of Captain Brown's line. We'd been working our way up the spur that divided two valleys for over four hours now, and it'd been hard going most of the way. My BDUs were crusted with salt stains and still felt damp from the rainstorm two nights ago. Sweating in this heat didn't help. My thighs were chafed from riding in wet clothes and my butt was killing me.

Up ahead, Pierce threw up a hand to halt, and I rode up beside him.

"I think we're going to have to make the rest of the way dismounted," he said, turning to me. He looked as exhausted as I felt.

"Roger that." The draw was only getting steeper, and the ground was becoming too treacherous for the horses. Sooner or later one of them would slip, and that could end up being a fatal disaster. "We'll picket them here then."

I dismounted and tried to rub some feeling into my backside, hobbling bow-legged around Duke to take off his tack.

Pierce laughed softly at me. "You're moving like an old cowpoke," he said, keeping his eyes and rifle trained up the steep slope.

"You don't look so great either, city slicker."

"Ain't that the truth." He tried to peel his pants away from his thighs with one hand. "Bro, I'm chafed in places I didn't think could *get* chafed."

I grunted, setting Duke's saddle off to the side. The horse nudged my shoulder with a soft nicker as I rummaged for his nose bag. "Yeah, yeah, I'm getting there, Your Grace."

Once I had his tack off, I rubbed him down while he contentedly munched his oats, then I took Pierce's place on watch so he could deal with his own horse, Shiloh. For short, dismounted jaunts we'd leave their tack on, but this could turn into an extended OP, and the last thing we needed, or wanted, was for them to develop saddle sores.

Pierce joined me a few minutes later and handed me my ruck. I shrugged it on and tightened the straps, and we set off, boots squelching and slipping on mud and scree. Soon our rifles were dangling on their slings as we climbed, relying on our hands as much as our feet. We were both in good shape—better in fact than ever before in our lives, due in no small part to the rigors of a life deprived of Humvees—but by the time we'd reached the crest, we were panting.

"Aren't you glad I talked you out of the Barrett?" I gasped, waving at Pierce to take a knee with me. "Can you imagine humping that thing up here?"

"Oh, hell no." Pierce rolled his eyes and patted his M24 sniper rifle. "Sybil is just fine by me."

"Sybil?" I asked in a low voice as I scanned the trees.

"You know, *Sybil*, man."

"Doesn't ring a bell."

"'Don't Make Me Over'?"

I shook my head.

Pierce grunted. "Typical."

"Typical what?"

"Bennett, you're so white you glow in the dark."

"You dissing me, homie?"

"Just… don't even, man. Your kook Utah ass can't slang worth shit. You sound like Mr. Ruzicka in Pre-Calc, trying to be a brother and all."

"Got me there," I admitted, flashing a smile.

"Cheah." Pierce grinned back. "Got you there."

"Well," I sighed. "Up and over? See if we can't find a good hidey-hole?"

The crest was rocky, but thick with trees. Pierce nodded and we advanced at a slow crouch, clambering over boulders and around patches of loose rocks. There were lots of good hiding places, but none with much visibility. We crossed over the crest and moved carefully as the ground sloped down in front of us. Ahead and to the right the trees thinned out somewhat and then suddenly dropped away into nothingness.

I got on my belly and crawled the last few yards to the edge of the stone shelf. I was glad not to be on my feet when I arrived— ahead of me was a sheer drop of a few hundred feet right into the valley below. Lying flat on my belly with as much of my body hugging the ground as possible felt like a *much* safer viewing position.

Pierce wormed up beside me and clucked his tongue appreciatively. We didn't have much cover, but it was a great perch with an amazing view. "Oh, this should do nicely," he whispered.

"Not much concealment," I muttered.

"Only from above, and they don't have any air cover, right? No one down there's going to see us."

That was true. So far, only Dietrich's forces had helicopters or any other type of flying machine. His was an extremely small force… but he did have air superiority.

Pierce extended his rifle's bipod and got comfortable behind the 10x40mm scope. "I got this, man. Why don't you get some chow. Switch off in thirty?"

"Solid plan," I said, clapping him on the shoulder before I scooted backward on my belly and into the cover of the trees. I tried a radio check, just in case, but García and Xochi in OP Delta must have been out of range for the handhelds, just as Sanchez had feared. All I got was pops as it scanned and failed to find anything.

***

The black sun was a fire in the western jungle foothills, setting the drifting cumulus clouds alight in brilliant hues of red and purple. I couldn't see the ocean from our perch, but snatches of wind carried the unmistakable scent of salt. Over three hundred feet below me the narrow valley stretched out on a northeast-to-southwest axis, thick with pine and scrub oak. It would be difficult to catch anyone down there, but my powerful spotting scope helped to even the odds. When the light eventually fell, I had a night-vision monocular I could attach to the scope's eyepiece, but I wouldn't need that for a while yet.

Pierce and I had been keeping up a constant rotation, swapping off every thirty to forty minutes behind the glass. Spend too long staring through optics and your eyes get fatigued, not to mention it was crazy hot lying prone on the shelf of rock we were set up on. I wiped sweat out of my eyes and willed the sun to set faster as I pivoted the scope on its tripod mount, scanning up and down the valley. We'd divided the observable area into zones, and I was just about to move on to the next one when I caught movement and zoomed the scope's powerful 12-to-40x magnification to get a better look.

"Contact," I whispered over my shoulder.

Pierce low-crawled beside me and set up his rifle. "Whatcha got?"

"Multiple contacts. Definitely an indig war party. Size unknown. They're moving in zone four to the northeast. Wait… got a dude in tiger-stripe cammies. Caucasian. He's got some kinda submachine gun." Pierce got busy jotting down the details in a notebook. "More indigs. Mostly armed with spears. A few war clubs. Wait… got another dude in tiger cammies. He's got a submachine gun too… and… dang, looks like a bazooka."

"Bazooka?" Pierce said.

"Yeah. Some of the indigs have backpack frames loaded with spare rockets."

Pierce gave a low whistle.

We continued to track them as they moved up the valley in the fading light. There were a lot of them. It was a fair bet this was the company-sized element Chief Baker had flown over in the morning. In all we counted at least eight Outworlders, two bazookas, and a heavy machine gun humped by indig porters.

"Think we should pull out and report it to the captain?" Pierce asked.

"Soon," I replied.

"It's not getting any lighter, Bennett. And I don't like the idea of riding down that draw in the dark, even with NODs."

A dark shadow blurred overhead, and I wrenched my head up. "What was *that?*"

"What was what?" Pierce asked.

I searched overhead and glanced back over my shoulder. "Not sure… thought I saw someth—"

Another shadow swooped over the trees before plummeting straight toward us. It was huge, about the size of a man, with leathery outstretched wings that blotted out the dark gray sky. Red eyes blazed from a hideous bat-like face as it dove, its taloned, grasping feet reaching out for me.

So this was what a camazot looked like. Or as Pierce preferred: Batman.

Pierce snatched his rifle and rolled onto his back as I fumbled for my own weapon. A crack like thunder sundered the dusk, and Pierce's round tore a jagged hole in the horrific creature's wing. It veered, its talons flashing inches from my face, and the wind of its passage kicked up a blinding whirlwind of dust and small stones. I had to blink the grit out of my eyes as I tracked it with my rifle for a few moments before squeezing off a couple of rounds, but it twisted in the air and dived.

So much for avoiding engagements.

"Back to the trees!" I shouted.

Pierce worked his bolt and fired at another shape plummeting out of the gathering darkness before rolling to his feet. One of the flying monstrosities corkscrewed out of the sky and grabbed him by the drag handle on his plate carrier, lifting him off the ground. I fired a shot center mass, and when the thing shrieked I knew I'd at least caught something. But the camazot didn't let go of Pierce, and I could only watch as the creature and Pierce went over the edge of the cliff and tumbled out of sight.

CHAPTER 33

I shouted for Pierce in hopeless desperation and then ducked as another camazot swooped overhead. Bringing my rifle up, I swung around and fired, giving it a decent lead in my sights—it was moving *fast*. It bucked in the air for a moment before dropping into the trees like a rock. I moved back to the edge of the rock shelf carefully and peered down into the darkness, trying to suppress the feeling of vertigo. My heart was in my throat, and blood pounded in my ears.

Something far below belched flame, and I stared dumbly as a blazing point of light rocketed up toward me. It took what felt like an eternity for me to register the threat and hit the deck. The bazooka rocket flashed overhead and arced into the trees, where it exploded with a deafening roar.

"Bennett!"

"Pierce!" I shouted back, surprised at the rush of relief that crowded in with the fear, anger, and every other emotion I was feeling at that moment. I scrambled back to the edge of the shelf, praying I wasn't about to eat a faceful of rocket. I could see Pierce about a meter below, clinging to the rocks like a lamprey. "I can't reach you! Can you climb?"

He grunted and then swore in horror as a chunk of cliff ripped free and tumbled into the darkness below. I tore my eyes away from him to scan overhead for any more of the terrifying bat-men. We were in the clear, but for how long was anyone's guess. Not to mention… bazooka rounds.

"Gotta hurry, man," I urged.

"Working… on it…" he grunted, searching for another handhold.

He found purchase in a fissure with his fingers and heaved himself up another couple of feet, enough for me to reach his hand and haul him up. There was another flash of fire from the valley below as I dragged him over the edge.

"Incoming!" I cried, throwing myself down.

The rocket hit just below where he'd been moments before, and the whole shelf lurched. Pierce swore again and we crabbed away from the edge, the ground crumbling beneath our feet. He slipped and I caught him by his drag handle and pulled him after me. Somehow I had the presence of mind to snatch my spotting scope too. We got to our feet and made a mad dash for the trees as a third bazooka rocket whipped overhead and exploded, igniting a tree and sending razor splinters of wood whistling in all directions.

"Eff you, asshole!" Pierce threw a middle finger back at the darkened valley.

"Come on, man," I gasped. "We need to get out of here, *yesterday.*"

"Shit, you okay?" he asked, noticing my limp as we scrambled for cover.

"Dunno," I said. My right leg felt wet and wasn't working properly.

"Shit." He threw my arm over his shoulder and helped me as we raced into the trees and scrambled up the crest before half running, half sliding down the mud and scree to the draw where we'd left the horses.

By now my leg was burning and I was starting to feel dizzy. Duke and Shiloh both snorted in alarm as we approached. I collapsed next to my saddle, and Pierce got out his flashlight and ran its red glow over me.

My pant leg was shredded and dark with blood. There was a splinter of wood the size of a combat knife sticking out of my thigh.

"That's not good," Pierce said.

"No kidding, genius," I replied through gritted teeth.

"Longshot, this... Xavier." Sanchez's voice was faint and distorted in my earpiece. "Do... read me?"

Pierce ripped open a field dressing.

"Don't pull it out," I warned. There was always a chance the huge piece of tree in my leg was blocking an artery and I'd bleed out if it was removed.

"Duh," Pierce said, wrapping the dressing around the wood fragment. "I took Doc's refresher like everyone else."

"Xavier, this is Longshot," I transmitted. "Read you weak and distorted. OP compromised. Pulling out. One wounded."

"Say again?" Sanchez transmitted.

I grunted as Pierce tied off the dressing.

"Your leg's torn up pretty bad, man," Pierce said. "I don't have enough bandages."

"I'll live," I said. "Get the horses tacked up."

I hit the IR strobe on my plate carrier and keyed the radio again. "Xavier, this is Longshot. Repeat: OP compromised. One wounded but mobile. Pulling out. No sign of pursuing tangos."

Hopefully it would stay that way. I didn't want to even think about collecting any more camazots in pursuit. I was less worried about those bazooka-happy people in the valley below; they'd have a hell of a time climbing up after us.

"Roger, Longshot," Sanchez replied, this time stronger and far less distorted. "I have visual on your strobe. Hang tight. The cavalry's coming."

***

"He needs a doctor, a *real* doctor," Doc said to Captain Brown. "Even if there isn't an artery involved, I can't repair damage like that, and he'll probably die... later if not sooner. Barring another field amputation."

Brown looked at my wound with a stark sobriety that had me thinking the man had completely shut down all of his emotions and was operating on pure reason and logic, like some fantastic, dark-skinned, deep-voiced Ranger Vulcan. "You saw their medical capabilities more than I did," he said. "You think Dietrich's people can save Bennett's leg?"

Doc had me laid out in the middle of a hasty assembly area deep in the forest on the other side of a long spur dividing the two valleys. He let out a sigh and gave a slight shake of his head. "Even with a real doctor he still could lose the leg, but at least he'll have a chance. It's that bad. Can we get an evac?"

Epasotl furrowed her brow in concern under the red light from Pierce's flashlight and glanced back and forth between the medic and officer. Doc had taken her under his wing, and she was proving to be a natural as a combat medic, which wasn't a surprise considering she seemed to be some sort of amateur black magic witch doctor in her own right, specializing in making incredibly nasty potions.

"No guarantees, given how few helos they have," the captain replied. "But I'll make the request."

There had been more sightings of the camazots flying in low search patterns. From what little I'd gathered in my pain-induced haze, Captain Brown was convinced they were working with the enemy as aerial scouts, which was a new development. We'd been briefed only about their existence; Bergstrom had said nothing about them reporting to the opposition. If the captain was right, the bad guys now *did* have an air force.

"How long do you think Bennett can hold out?" Brown continued.

Doc pinched the bridge of his nose. "Another day? If we can hang tight in the meantime. I don't want to move him; he's already been jostled enough. And it could be less. Depends on whether there's arterial damage, which I won't know until the foreign object is removed, and if I do that before getting him to a surgeon…"

"Big Kahuna, there is… another way," Epasotl said, holding up a small hand.

"What's that?" Captain Brown asked.

"I know of a… poultice that can heal such wounds. I have the ingredients."

"You might have mentioned this before," Brown said. "That would've been useful information."

"It is only used in grave emergencies. One of the ingredients is… expensive." The captain quirked an eyebrow, and Epasotl elaborated, reluctantly. "For the magic to work, the healer must infuse part of herself into the poultice."

"Part of…" the captain said. "You mean more menstrual blood?"

"No, a living part of herself. To bind her life force with the *naualotl.*"

I finally had to speak up. "I don't like where this is going, sir," I told the captain, lifting my sweat-soaked head to better see everyone before getting lightheaded and dropping it down on my makeshift pillow again. I wanted Xochi to be there, but she wasn't.

"Neither do I," Brown agreed. "Epasotl, could you be a little more specific?"

"It would not have to be much," she said, considering. "The tip of a finger or ear should be enough."

"Absolutely not," I said. "You're not carving off pieces of yourself to heal me."

"It is better to sacrifice part of an ear or finger than lose a leg, Ben-Ette. The trade would be…" She made a small throwing-away motion with her hand.

"Nobody's losing any legs," I said firmly. "I'll be fine."

"You might or might not be fine," Doc said somberly. "And you may or may not lose that leg. Depending on what we find in there, even a surgeon might not be able to fix it. And we don't know how advanced the facilities at FOB Cincinnati are or how good their doctors are."

"First let's find out if that's even an option," Brown said, snapping his fingers to get Cohen's attention. The specialist ran over with the SINCGARS. "Tim, get me Chief Baker."

"Yes, sir," Cohen replied.

Doc bent down to inspect the wound again, probing gently under the red light.

"I appreciate the offer," I told Epasotl. "I sincerely do. But I can't let you mutilate yourself for me. Especially when we have doctors that can fix me up good as new."

"It would be shameful to refuse to make the sacrifice," she said. "*Especially* for a slave."

I rolled my eyes. "You're *not* a slave. Not mine, not anyone's. You're a free woman. And it's not necessary."

"I don't know about that," Doc said warily. He was eyeing Captain Brown, who had stepped away to take the call to Baker. I followed Doc's gaze. It was hard to make out the captain in the darkness, and he was talking in a low voice, but his body language wasn't encouraging. I saw him give Cohen back the handset and then call Sanchez over, which was even *less* encouraging.

"I'd get the poultice ready, Epasotl," Doc said in a low voice. "Just in case."

"No—" I began.

Doc cut me off with a knife hand. "Not your call, Corporal. Lie down and shut up."

Captain Brown strode back into the red puddle of light around me, this time with Sanchez at his side. Sanchez's nostrils flared momentarily, which coming from him was the equivalent of a full-on screaming session.

"Negative on the evac," Brown stated in a cold voice. "Too much of a risk with RPGs in the area. Not to mention the other aerial threats."

Doc squeezed his eyes shut and pinched the bridge of his nose. "So, they're cowards. Great. We have a wounded man here, sir. Potentially *mortally* wounded."

"You sure about this 'poultice'?" Sanchez asked Epasotl.

"Yes, Little Kahuna," she replied.

"I'm not going to let—" I began, but Sanchez shot me a look that shut me down instantly.

"Do what you can," Brown said.

I lay there for a while longer while everyone else came and went. Captain Brown stayed by my side most of the time, and I appreciated that more than he knew. But Xochi... I didn't know if she'd been ordered to stay away or what. I guess I wouldn't have disobeyed a direct order not to go see her if our situations were reversed.

When the whole gang—Doc, Epasotl, Brown, and Sanchez—gathered together, I knew some kind of decision had been made and my fate was decided.

"We're going to try to remove the object," Doc informed me. "If the artery is okay, we can at least get you bandaged up and ambulatory. If not..." He let that thought die away and asked me if I wanted anything extra for the pain.

I shook my head. The adrenaline dump had worn off a long, long time ago and my leg was on fire, but I wanted to stay sharp.

"You will live," Epasotl said.

"Okay, Bennett," Doc said. "This is gonna hurt you more than it hurts me."

Brown came over, took Doc's light, and held it in place.

"Just get that thing out of my leg," I said.

"Don't say I didn't warn you."

Doc produced a tourniquet and fixed it high up on my leg, next to my groin. I suppressed a yelp as he tightened it.

"On three," Doc warned, taking a firm grasp on the dagger-sized splinter. "One... two..." He pulled gently but firmly, and I suppressed another yelp and the urge to swear profusely, despite my upbringing. The sadist hadn't even gotten to three yet.

"That's no good," Doc said calmly, ever the professional, as blood poured from the wound. "Give me more light, Captain."

I gritted my teeth and fought the tears forming behind my eyes as he probed the wound. Doc's frown grew deeper, which seemed impossible.

"Yeah, it's as bad as I feared. Whatever you're gonna do better work, Epasotl, or Bennett's a dead man."

"You need to work on your bedside manner," I croaked.

"It *will* work," Epasotl said emphatically.

I don't think anyone disagreed. We'd been around the block a time or two under the black sun, and magic was as real here as anything. Also, she had more than come through back in that abandoned city. By now we'd learned to trust her magic, although this was a far cry from curing an infection or a... curse.

Epasotl drew her knife, and I wanted to look away but couldn't. She calmly took her lower left ear between her fingertips and neatly sliced off the tip without so much as a grimace. Then she *put it in her mouth*, chewed for a moment, and spit it into the MRE packet she'd mixed her horrible-smelling poultice in.

"That doesn't seem very sanitary," I said numbly.

"Trust me, Ben-Ette. I'm a professional."

She scooped out the nasty concoction, and I gritted my teeth as she shoved it into the wound with nimble fingers. I watched the whole process with as much clinical detachment as I could muster… which wasn't much.

Then things got weird.

Okay, weird*er*.

Epasotl closed her eyes and placed both hands over the wound. She chanted slowly in a dialect I couldn't understand, and I felt a chill flowing through my veins as her hands began to glow with an icy blue light. She slowly moved her hands up and down my leg with a feather touch, and I watched transfixed as slivers and splinters wormed their way out of my flesh.

Brown inhaled sharply and Doc swore softly.

As she continued, the pain was replaced by a tingling numbness that's hard to describe. It wasn't exactly pleasant, but it was certainly a far sight better than the burning had been.

After a few minutes Epasotl sat back on her haunches and swayed a little. Traces of the strange blue light played over her hands for several seconds before flickering out.

By now a few gawkers, guys who weren't pulling security, had come in close, and there was a low buzz of hushed amazement.

"Well, now I've seen everything," Doc said in awe. "There isn't even a scar."

Brown played his flashlight over where the deadly wound had been and gave a low whistle. He nodded at Epasotl. "Well done. That was impressive." I think he meant *frickin' mind-blowing*, but officers are known for understatement. "Although I still would've liked to have known about the… full extent of your medical talents earlier."

Epasotl inspected her palms, turning them over to look at the backs of her hands, and then unsheathed her claws experimentally. "I have seen it done... once, but I never attempted such healing myself." Her big eyes were half closed with exhaustion, and her ears, one of them now with a piece taken out of it, hung limply. "I had never succeeded in wielding *naualotl* before the crypt. My mentor thought I was a... how do you say? Shubie?"

Brown raised an eyebrow, and Sanchez sighed irritably at Wilson's corruption of her vocabulary.

"Wannabe... sorta," Pierce translated for the surfing illiterate, rocking his hand from side to side.

Doc blinked and then frowned, stabbing a finger at Epasotl. "Wait a minute—you said you were *certain* this would work. You lied to us? He could've died! Do you understand that?"

Epasotl laid back her ears, exposing her sharp white needle teeth with a hiss. Inch-long ivory claws sprouted from her fingertips, and her eyes flashed like agates.

"Stand down, Epasotl," Sanchez said softly.

"I *was* certain it would work," she growled at Doc, her muscles coiled to pounce.

I held my breath. Doc didn't know how close he was to getting his *own* arteries severed. Then again, the man was pretty hardcore himself.

"I said *stand down*," Sanchez repeated. Our XO wasn't in the habit of asking twice; Epasotl must have had him wrapped around her deadly little finger to get this much of a warning out of him.

She sheathed her claws and relaxed slightly, glancing up at Sanchez. Her ears were still flat against her head though, and her eyes were flint-hard, but she forced a smile. Or tried to, anyway. She never could get that expression quite right. Doc had questioned her honor, and she was out for blood.

But then... Doc wasn't exactly wrong, either.

"We good here?" Captain Brown asked, sweeping his gaze between Epasotl and Doc. "Because I don't want some native blood grudge happening between what apparently are my two best medical professionals."

"Yes, Big Kahuna," Epasotl said. Her tone was neutral, but it didn't fool me. I could tell she was anything but *good*. I don't think it fooled the captain either.

"Yes, sir," Doc echoed.

"I *was* certain," she repeated, flashing a glance at Doc.

He puffed out his cheeks and regarded her sternly for a long moment. "All right, I believe you."

She regarded him coolly, and her flattened ears twitched. Chaneque honor was a touchy thing at the best of times, and they had long memories for insults. Doc seemed to get the message, and he held out his hand, which she looked at with disgust.

The corner of his mouth quirked. "You did good."

Which was probably the closest thing to an apology she was going to get from the sergeant. I cleared my throat, and when she glanced at me, I flicked my eyes over to Doc and his outstretched hand. She took the hint at least, and slapped his palm begrudgingly.

The guys clustered around us were all still staring at me, and I realized uncomfortably that I was lying there basically naked from the waist down.

"Uh, can someone get me some pants, please?"

CHAPTER 34

There were a lot of pats on the back for me once I started to move about our makeshift camp. It was Epasotl who should have received their kudos; all I did was survive a wound that probably had my number. Epasotl seemed… relieved that I was all right, despite her insistence to Doc that she had *known* it would all turn out okay. I thanked her profusely, but she wouldn't accept. What else could be expected of a slave?

I hated that, after all we'd been through, she still thought of her relationship with me and the rest of the platoon that way.

Then again, she *was* a PFC now… so "slave" wasn't all that far off the mark.

Greene clapped me on the shoulder as we crossed paths in the middle of camp. "Hey, Bennett, glad you're okay."

"Thanks," I said, stopping midway and turning to ask a question that had been on my mind. "Have you seen Xochi anywhere?"

Greene nodded. "Yeah… on the east end of camp." He motioned vaguely in the direction.

"By herself?"

"Guess so."

I gave my thanks and changed directions. A thought gave me an uneasy pause. "You seen Stanley around?"

Greene shrugged and kept on to wherever he was going.

A nervous pit formed in my stomach, and I began a light jog east. Visions of Stanley finding Xochi alone morphed into other thoughts of all the ways that that could go badly. I hated the way that guy looked at her, and I was starting to hate him for it. Everyone else in camp, it seemed, had gathered to watch my ordeal, the surgery and the latest magic potion, not to mention Epasotl's parlor trick of cutting her ear off—okay, maybe it was just the tip, but still. If Stanley had it in his heart to do something to Xochi, would there ever be a better time?

I picked up the pace, careful not to flat-out run for fear of making the guys think there was an attack.

Given what I'd just been through, my leg should have been killing me, but it felt fine. Actually, better than fine—it felt refreshed, like I'd just gotten a deep tissue massage that worked out all the knots, kinks, and tension that had built up through marching, riding, stalking, and, yes, impaling. Even if the leg hurt, though, I'm not sure I would have noticed the pain anyway—I'd convinced myself that something bad had happened to Xochi.

Why else wouldn't she have been there earlier?

I found her kneeling by the base of a tree—alone. Her head was bowed and her hands were clasped in her lap. I was sure she'd heard me coming; I was breathing heavily on arrival.

"Xochi," I called, soft as I could. "Are you okay?"

Despite no sign of Stanley or any other trouble, I was still a little worried. Or maybe it was just insecurity I felt.

She turned and gazed at me over her shoulder. I thought she was smiling, but it was just the way the scar on her cheek turned the corner of her lip up. But soon a genuine smile formed on her face as she crossed herself before springing up to embrace me. The sudden flurry of little kisses to my face and neck drained whatever dread I'd been feeling a moment before.

Yeah, I know. Fraternization. We skirted that rule as much as we thought we could get away with.

I still wondered why she hadn't come to see me when I was getting the treatment. Everyone else had. Did she not know? As our S2, she was supposed to know things, right?

I decided not to ask her directly, asking instead, "What were you doing?"

She looked up at me. "Praying for you, Bennett. So that you would not die."

Someone might think that's a funky thing to say. Like, how can prayers be more useful than her being there holding my head in her lap while I faced a swirling drain, wondering if Doc and Epasotl could get it stopped before my life slipped away?

But…

I grew up differently. Prayer meant something to my family. You expected that something would come from it. Maybe not what you wanted, but something firm and meaningful. I used to feel that way about it myself.

Looking at Xochi at that moment, I could see that she still felt it. Felt it completely. For her, knowing that Doc and Epasotl were doing everything they could… for her, coming over here and pleading for my life was the most constructive and powerful thing she could do.

"Thank you," I told her. "Don't stop. Don't stop praying for me."

"I haven't since I first knew you would come," she said.

I gave her a look—what did that mean?

She didn't elaborate. "Another time. Takahashi and Stanley should be back soon. I need to hear their report."

Ah, so *that's* where Stanley had been off to. Right.

I felt just a little foolish in retrospect.

***

Takahashi and Stanley's little scouting expedition confirmed that the group in the valley who'd engaged Pierce and me with the bazooka were indeed Baker's "company-sized element." Furthermore, they had solid evidence as well that the bat-men were working with them —aerial reconnaissance in force, or something like that. So, that was… less than encouraging.

"Now is the time where we prove ourselves as assaulters—as dragoons," Brown told us as we took a knee in a loose semicircle around him. "I've seen the way you men fight. You've slain giants and vanquished very real nightmares. If you lack renown, it is only because you have left no survivor to tell of your feats. Today, command is gonna learn that we're not just here to sneak and peek. We have teeth… and the bastards who tried to snuff out Pierce and Bennett are going to learn that the hard way."

Led by Sanchez, Brown's comments drew the requisite number of *hooah*s. I sound like a smartass about it now, but at the time, I was ready to run through a hail of gunfire for the man.

Brown continued. "Here's how it's gonna happen…"

The plan was to push out ahead of the hostile force and arrange an ambush. Xochi and Brown had aerial photographs at their disposal, courtesy of Chief Baker and his crews, and other scouts had verified navigable routes that would get us around the ridge where Pierce and I were hit and into position to lay the hate on those guys.

I was getting excited. Not going to lie. I was ready for some payback.

Sergeant García had a question. "How do we know they won't try to scale that ridge and come right out of that valley?"

It was a valid point. Brown and Sanchez exchanged a look, which told us that they weren't exactly thrilled about the forthcoming explanation. Then the captain said, "Commo with Chief Baker indicates that our intel of the enemy's location allowed a friendly indig team to get eyes on the target. They're moving in a westerly direction now, following a river back toward the coast."

Indigs. From what we'd seen of them so far, that was a real mixed bag. Some were capably trained, but those were mostly operating hand-in-glove with experienced soldiers who kept them in line. The few indig-only patrols we came across were more like the guys who tried to shake us down at Chief Baker's outpost way back when. You couldn't count on them to be professional.

"It's up to us to make sure those indigs don't screw up the ambush," Sanchez added. "So… don't screw things up, hooah?"

We broke with an answering "Hooah!" and mobilized, pushing ourselves under the cover of night. It wasn't easy going thanks to the terrain, but our night vision helped. We kept to the trees as much as possible, but never got sight of any more bat-men flapping through the night sky. That didn't convince me they weren't out there somewhere.

Shortly before dawn we reached the valley floor and dug in on opposite sides of the river in a sort of T-shaped ambush position. The vertical line was away from the canyon walls; we figured that anyone with half a brain wouldn't march in between a river and a canyon. There were woods out beyond the river, but they were gnarly—lots of drop-offs, slopes, boulders, and other uneven and difficult terrain. If these guys were interested in making any kind of time, they would move along the riverbank.

Out in those woods were our indig forces, who had commo with Chief Baker, who in turn called details into the SINCGARS that Cohen humped alongside the captain... like a game of telephone. I wasn't sure why we couldn't just connect directly to them, but no one asked me about it either way. The indigs had briefly lost the enemy target before spotting them again. Last report was that they were heading in our direction and would most likely arrive with the rising of the sun or shortly after.

It turned out they were early.

Pierce and I were set up on the far side of the T, just outside the main line dug into the tree line. Right now, the river was at that main line's back, and we were the containment line for anyone who might try to push their way through what was coming for them. A similar containment line was set up on the opposite side of the river, just in case our prey crossed the lazy, shallow stream before reaching us. The main firing line could hit them on either side, and whatever containment line was on the wrong side of the water would cross and then add their guns once they were in position. Sergeant García's team with the M240 would be the main muscle of the ambush; the rest of us were there to drive the enemy force into the machine gun's fire and deal with any squirters.

Visuals showed a lead indig element serving as scouts, still carrying spears, but they were interspersed with the troopers in tiger-stripe fatigues. These were definitely the guys who'd hit us last night.

We let them move into the kill box. They were spread out decently, but we were well hidden; when the time came, they were going to have a bad, final day.

The patrol—our target—kept moving deeper into our trap. I figured it would be any moment before Brown or Sanchez had Cameron and Greene go live with the M240, accompanied by the FN40GL grenade launchers that Stanley, Woodward, and Sanchez had mounted on their rifles. Sure enough, Sanchez's order over our handhelds to "Execute, execute, execute!" was perfectly timed, and within a heartbeat all of us were dumping rounds on our hapless targets.

A perfectly executed ambush feels a lot like murder.

Hostile indigs and armed soldiers had little choice but to stand and get holed, or throw themselves down in a search for cover. The scouts had kept them too close to the water, and our guys in the woods were absolutely shredding them. A few indigs attempted to run across the river and make for the cliffs, as though they might climb their way out of the kill zone. But these we cut down in the water, leaving them to bleed out downstream with the current.

I was moving from target to target with my SCAR-H when I felt Pierce knocking on my shoulder. It was loud as hell, and I couldn't hear what he was saying.

"What?" I shouted.

He pointed at something in the kill zone, and I looked. Did one of our guys mistakenly edge out there for some reason? No. Nothing stood out. Whatever Pierce saw, it was over, because he went back to it. I did the same.

The calls for cease-fire gradually spread among our platoon as the barks of our rifles subsided.

"Dude, did you see that?" Pierce was in my ear almost immediately.

"No, man. See what?"

"Marines!"

I scanned the tree line. Did Dietrich have a Marine recon team in the area? All I'd heard about was an indigenous force, and since I wasn't seeing them, I started to wonder if maybe the message got garbled.

Or maybe… maybe I didn't want to believe that we'd just wasted a bunch of fellow Americans. Even if they were Marines.

Pierce confirmed it anyway. "Not out there, Bennett. In the column. We wasted them."

"How do you know they're US Marines?"

"Uniforms," Pierce said. "Look—see? Their camo is different. Remember those guys in sniper school? The Marine Recon dudes from the future? Well, *our* future. They wore a different camo pattern than what we were issued. MARPAT or something they called it."

He pointed to some bodies out among the dead and dying strewn in the river and on its bank. I couldn't believe my eyes—those certainly looked like post-2005 US Marine uniforms.

I felt sick.

"Hang on," I told Pierce. "I need to call this in." I keyed my handheld. "Xavier, this is Longshot. We got a possible blue-on-blue here."

To be honest, the situation was a little gray—I mean, these Marines were on the "other side," but they were our guys too, right? Maybe it was more of a… green-on-blue? I wasn't sure what to call it. It was bad-on-bad, anyway.

Sanchez made his way over to me with the captain in tow, and I pointed out the Marines. The bodies weren't obvious at first; there were only three of them, and they seemed to have been traveling among the tiger-striped soldiers spread out along the riverbank. "Specialist Pierce identified individuals wearing US Marine uniforms among the enemy element," I said. "I count three down."

Brown and Sanchez's eyes both snapped to where I indicated further downstream.

"Shit," Sanchez said, and then squinted. "One of 'em is still moving."

I don't know what possessed me, but I sprinted out along with my med bag, readying it as I ran. All I could think about was that a fellow American—maybe someone from my own time—was lying there wounded.

I heard Captain Brown yell something, not a recall, more like orders to cover me. Someone else called for Doc, and I soon heard him splashing behind me.

The Marine had been crawling in the river, but he turned over and propped himself up on his ruck when he heard us coming for him. Right away I could see blue-black spider-veins on his face, rising from his neck and onto his cheeks before circling his eyes. It was the same look Dee had had when he started to turn after he touched the stela.

Only this guy, whose helmet was cast off farther upstream to reveal wet, dark chestnut hair, didn't have the same distant, ravenous look in his eyes that Dee did before he tried to eat Wilson's face. His eyes were as blue as the sky back home in Utah.

And they were frightened.

That's what struck me. The fear in those eyes. Doc's trained vision probably picked out whatever wounds the man had taken. But mine, mine were fixed on the guy's eyes. They softened when he saw me. Like… he felt safe because of us.

He opened his mouth and said, "Ameri—"

I was maybe three meters from the guy when his chest erupted in a violent puff of blood. Both Doc and I dove into the water. When I raised my head, I saw the guy tilt over, those blue eyes now lifeless as his mouth streamed blood out into the river.

A couple of shots sounded. Then our guys were yelling, and the shots ceased.

"C'mon," Doc said as he hoisted me up from the water. "Something's goin' on back by the woods."

I took another look at the dead Marine and then followed our medic back toward Sanchez and Brown. They were talking with yet another Marine, a sniper like Pierce and me, only he was carrying an M40A1. And this one was a friendly. I found out later that he was part of Dietrich's element—the "indigs" who had been following the force we just ambushed. Except there were no indigs; this man *was* the other element. Just a lone sniper who operated over vast swaths of country.

Which… why would Chief Baker lead us to believe there were indigs instead of a Marine, and several troops instead of just one? Did Captain Brown just misunderstand? That wasn't like him.

"You boys didn't get too close, did ya?" the sniper asked.

"You saw how close," Doc said, his displeasure evident.

"Gotta be careful with the infected."

Brown raised an eyebrow. "Infected?"

"Yep," the sniper said. "Sometimes it takes a long while, sometimes it's fast as lightnin', but they always turn eventually. Sure as the sun rises. First they go all psychopath on ya, then the next thang ya know, they're tryin' to eat your face."

"The ravenous undead," Brown said.

"As good a name for 'em as anything. Believe you me, sir, I did that man a favor… and you too."

After that… Doc, Brown, and Sanchez worked out cleanup. There were no other survivors. The sniper slipped away without anyone so much as noticing. I think Captain Brown would've liked to have asked more questions.

My mind kept going back to the look on that Marine's face. I'd seen Dee up close when he became possessed. This guy was different. There was a *soul* behind those eyes. And his words… when Dee spoke, it was like an evil being was speaking through him. Not so with this guy. This guy seemed like…

I don't even know what to say. None of it made sense.

All I can do is put it out there.

When I was near that Marine, I felt like he was… good. Like he'd overcome a great evil and still bore the marks of it, but it hadn't consumed him. In fact it was the sniper who gave me a dirty feeling. That same dirty feeling I had from my rifle and gear.

The Marine in the river, he was infected. Clearly. No doubt about that. But he hadn't *turned*. He'd been corrupted, but he'd fought it. And won.

And it made me wonder if there might be hope for Alpha, if those guys were still alive out there somewhere. Maybe not Wright—he'd been a psychopath to begin with—but maybe Clark and Bond. Maybe even St. James.

More than that, though, it made me wonder how we'd gotten ourselves into a situation where killing other Americans was par for the course, even if they *were* on the "wrong" side of whatever turf war this was between Dietrich and whoever these Acálan guys were.

I didn't think Captain Brown liked that.

I knew I didn't.

CHAPTER 35

"I thought this was supposed to be the *dry* season," Cameron groused as water poured down the front of his boonie. He draped his poncho further over the M240 machine gun he carried across his saddle and scowled at the downpour.

"It's a dry rain," Greene quipped.

"Could be worse," García observed. "Could be *cold* and wet."

"A warm flood is still a flood, Sergeant," Cameron replied. "Anyone see a dude around here building an ark? We might need one."

"You boys will have a roof over your heads soon enough," Captain Brown said, moving his big Friesian nearer to García's team to be heard over the rain. "Just as soon as this column passes by."

We'd all pulled our mounts off to the side of the road—river of mud rather—that led into Forward Operating Base Cincinnati to allow First Battalion to pass by. The half-naked indig conscripts looked like they'd had one hell of a battle, and our captain was inclined to let them and their wounded go first while we waited in the downpour. It's not like we could get any wetter; it'd been raining like this for a solid week now.

FOB Cincinnati was a large, sprawling base perched on a small rise in the saddle between two towering mountain peaks. A killing field had been cleared out to five hundred meters from the sturdy fifteen-foot-tall palisade of tree trunks that had been erected on a mound encompassing the base's perimeter. Fronting the wall was a sizable ditch that was now partially flooded, and we could see concertina wire poking up above the murky water. The killing field outside the wall wasn't completely empty though; ramshackle huts leaned against one another and butted up against the edge of the ditch. The small shantytown stretched at least two-thirds of the way around Cincinnati's perimeter, and naked children raced in between the dilapidated structures.

A young man rode out of the gate, forcing his way through the line of soldiers, and cantered over to us through the mud.

"Crazy Horse Platoon?" he shouted to us when his horse had drawn near. He spoke with the precise, affected accent of the finer English boarding schools.

"That's us," Brown answered.

"Captain Brown?" the young—*very* young—lieutenant asked, glancing past the captain to search our faces for Crazy Horse's commander, who, presumably, couldn't be the very large black man looming right in front of him.

"The same," Brown said dryly.

"Ah! Yes, sir. Colonel Gutierrez's compliments, sir!" The officer saluted. "The name's Atkinson. I've the pleasure to escort you and your men."

Captain Brown returned the salute as his eyes wandered over the column of soldiers struggling past. "Just waiting for these men to get through the gate."

"Oh, don't mind the sepoys, sir. I'll clear you a path through the riffraff."

"These *men* have wounded," Brown replied with a frown. "We can wait."

"Uh, very good, sir"—the lieutenant hesitated—"but the colonel was most insistent I fetch you right away. 'Post haste.' His words, sir. Wouldn't, ah, want to keep him waiting, eh, sir?"

Brown bit off a sharp reply and simply nodded.

Atkinson wheeled his horse and made for the gate, flicking at soldiers with his riding crop and shouting for the "bloody wogs" to make a hole.

The captain's shoulders bunched as he spurred his horse, coming alongside the lieutenant and leaning in close. I'm not sure what he said, but the kid went ash-white and nodded vigorously. From the look on his face, I didn't doubt the young man found himself the sorely chastised owner of a brand-new second butthole. Frankly, I was surprised his head was still attached to his body.

We rode through the mass of grim-faced indigenous men standing aside, trying to kick up as little mud as possible, and entered the base. Inside we found a reasonably well-ordered arrangement of low, thatched, clapboard buildings laid out on a grid. Atkinson led us across the wide central parade ground and up to a large two-storied structure. He dismounted and whistled.

A crowd of young boys came running.

"These—" Atkinson checked himself. "These, uh, *young men* will see to your horses, sir."

Brown gave a slight shake of his head. "I prefer my men to take care of their mounts."

A huge, gruff-looking sergeant with a scarred face had emerged from the building. He was deeply tanned and had a crooked nose that looked like it'd been broken more than once and never healed right.

"Stablemaster's a mite particular, sir," he called out to Brown over the downpour. "Best to let the boys earn their keep." His deep bass voice sounded like gravel pouring down a coal chute. He turned to Atkinson. "Colonel's waiting, sir."

"Thank you, Sergeant," Atkinson said. Then to Brown: "If you'll follow me, sir. Master Sergeant Escarra will show your men to their quarters."

"Right," Brown said. "Xochi, with me."

She dismounted and quickly moved to his side. Atkinson looked uncomfortable.

"Uh, the colonel requested officers only... for just now that is, sir." He waved his hand in a vague gesture as he tried to figure out what role Xochi had in our platoon. "You won't require your... uh..."

The corner of Brown's lip quirked. He seemed to be enjoying making the little prick squirm. "Chief Warrant Xochicuauhtli is my intelligence officer," he stated flatly.

"Ah, naturally. Quite right, sir." Atkinson looked flustered. "Very good, sir. If you'll follow me…"

The livid scar on Sergeant Escarra's muscular jaw twitched. Probably from suppressing a laugh if I had to guess. He exchanged a knowing look with Sanchez as Atkinson led Brown and Xochi away. Then he caught sight of Epasotl perched behind Sanchez and cocked an eyebrow.

Sanchez dismounted and held out a hand to Escarra. "PFC Epasotl is my apprentice in Sneaky Pete mayhem—in addition to being a passable assistant medic. She's… mostly harmless. Mostly."

"Heard you men had a tame Chaneque in your outfit," Escarra rumbled, taking Sanchez's hand.

"Oh, I wouldn't call her *tame*," Sanchez replied as Epasotl bared her teeth in a rictus smile. She hopped down beside them and held out her hand. Her head barely reached Escarra's belt buckle.

"How's it hanging, Master Sergeant?" she said, managing in her special way to convey innocence and respect instead of life-threatening chutzpah.

Escarra took her tiny paw in a shovel hand and grinned, then looked toward the rest of us. "Right, then. How about we get you boys out of the rain and find some hot food for your bellies."

***

"What was Gutierrez like?" I asked Xochi. We sat with Epasotl under an awning outside our barracks fronting the parade ground. Overhead, Dietrich's dagger-and-thunderbolt flag snapped in the hot breeze as conscripts drilled in muddy earth that was quickly baking under the black sun.

Xochi tore off a piece of her fried unleavened bread and chewed thoughtfully. "Gutierrez is a hard man, I think," she said after a moment. "His eyes are like a serpent's."

That could be taken literally here, I thought with a shudder, and asked her as much.

"No." She laughed. "Not like that. He has cold eyes that do not blink. It is unsettling. He came from the same time as Friar Bastía, but he was not a holy man. He was a great war chief in your world. A —how do you say—onquistador?"

"Conquistador," I corrected.

"Ah yes. A conquistador. Friar Bastía told us many stories of those warriors. They were hard men, greedy and zealous. Soldiers of fortune who raped the land and the people in it. They made slaves of those they conquered." She waved her bread, encompassing the base. "He has done the same thing here."

"Slaves? You mean the conscripts?"

"Them, but also the women and children who live in the town outside the walls. The old people too. All the servants you see here are slaves. He called them something different. 'Indentured.' But it means the same I think."

"More or less." I snorted. "Captain would have a thing or two to say about that."

"He is not pleased with the arrangement, no, but it is not an uncommon practice in this land. One people conquers another and enslaves them. It is the way of the world. At least the colonel does not sacrifice them to Smoking Mirror. My people were the same, before Friar Bastía." She paused thoughtfully. "No, not the same. We had slaves, but we never worshipped Smoking Mirror. We did not make human sacrifices or partake in ritual cannibalism."

"Then you are foolish," Epasotl cut in. "The sun must rise, no? My people have no love for Smoking Mirror, but he must be appeased, or the land would be eternally dark."

"That is a false superstition, my savage friend," Xochi said, not unkindly. "Smoking Mirror has no power over the sun. God controls its movements. The Word of God says 'he makes his sun rise on the evil and the good.'"

"Your Outworlders' holy book is full of nonsense, my barbarian *friend*," Epasotl countered. "Everyone knows the greatest giant of them all tallies the sacrifices to Smoking Mirror each morning before he casts the sun into the sky."

"Actually, the sun doesn't really move across the sky at all," I said. "The world spins around like a top. It only looks like the sun's moving."

They both shot me a pitying look like one would give a slow child.

"Your jokes are always terrible, Ben-Ette," Epasotl said. "If the world spun, we would all be dizzy."

"She makes a good point," Xochi agreed. "But the giant does not count sacrifices, Epasotl. He obeys God's command, not a demon like Smoking Mirror."

Epasotl shrugged. "Perhaps, but why take the chance?"

"Nice try," I said, "but we're still not going to sacrifice and eat you."

She scowled and leaned back, folding her arms across her chest as she let out a feline hiss.

"Anyway," I said to Xochi. "Colonel Gutierrez gives you the heebie-jeebies, eh?"

"I do not know what that means," Xochi said. "He is certainly not a pleasant man."

"Means he gives you a bad vibe—bad feeling. Speaking of which, do you have any more thoughts about that Marine?" I asked.

We'd spoken about this before, so she knew which Marine I meant. Not the sniper, but the other guy. The one who was infected but hadn't turned into one of the ravenous undead. I continued to be bothered by the look in his eyes. And by his death.

"It is perplexing," Xochi said, pursing her lips. She glanced at Epasotl, who simply shrugged.

"You two have discussed it?" I deduced. "What did you conclude? You're the experts. I'm just visiting."

Xochi frowned slightly at my little joke, and I felt bad for saying it. "We have talked about it, she and I, and we do not know what to make of it. As I have told you, I have heard no stories of such a thing happening."

"Unless he was a virgin," Epasotl pointed out.

"That is only a legend," Xochi said.

Epasotl shrugged again.

"Wait, what?" I asked.

Xochi made a shooing motion with her hand. "It is a silly legend. Some believe a virgin cannot be turned."

"Whew." I mocked wiping my brow. "Guess I'm safe."

"Me too." Xochi laughed.

"Wait—" Epasotl's eyes widened. "You have not mated yet?"

I felt my cheeks flush. "Uh, no. It's… er… you know. We can't, you know, because she's a warrant and I'm just a grunt. Fraternization and all."

"Frater…?" Epasotl asked, puzzled.

"I think we have already bent that rule," Xochi said with a wink. "Several times. But Bennett is making excuses. That is not why. God forbids it."

My face was flushed and racing into beet-red territory.

"So does Sanchez. That's why we have our… little blue chaperone now." I motioned to Epasotl with my chin.

Xochi laughed.

"I would not tell anyone," Epasotl said seriously. She stood and peered through the window. "It is empty. If you want to mate, I will make sure no one interrupts you. If the gods bless your mating, you will produce a cub."

I had now moved right past beet red and was barreling into cardiac-arrest-by-embarrassment. Xochi, by contrast, couldn't stop trembling from quiet laughter.

Epasotl regarded us impatiently and put her hands on her hips.

I took a deep breath. "We can't, Epasotl."

"Because of dumb soldier rules?" she asked. "Or because of your"—she made air quotes with her fingers—"God?"

I opened my mouth and closed it a few times. I *hated* talking about this kind of stuff publicly. Which, of course, the guys all knew and exploited, just to watch me squirm.

"The wrath of Sanchez and Brown will probably land on us first," I said. "But the bigger thing is…"

"It is forbidden by our religions," Xochi explained, wiping tears from her eyes. "We are not married. *Yet.*"

Awkward pause time.

"I… didn't know we were engaged," I finally said. Not that the thought hadn't crossed my mind… as a possibility. Maybe even a *good* possibility, but we still didn't know each other all *that* well.

"You took too long to ask," Xochi said with royal hauteur. "So I have made what Captain Brown would call an 'executive decision.'"

"There's still the 'dumb soldier rules,'" I pointed out.

"Details." She waved her hand airily. "Captain Brown will agree with me when I explain to him. He is not a stupid man, and he is not without reason. He knew of our feelings for one another *before* I was formally made your superior."

"My superior, huh? You've taken to being an officer, all right." I winked to let her know that I wasn't serious. But I wasn't so sure that we could count on Captain Brown just being cool with fraternization.

Sanchez appeared from out of nowhere, as he does, and I jumped to my feet. He sniffed and gave Xochi and me a critical glance before turning to Epasotl.

"These kids haven't been fraternizing, have they?" he asked her, and I wondered what he'd overheard.

"Not even a little, Little Kahuna," Epasotl said, sounding disappointed.

"Good." He walked past us and into the barracks. "NCO meeting in five, Bennett."

***

The meeting turned out to be priority orders to escort a shipment from FOB Cincinnati to an outpost. So much for our promised R&R. We were to leave immediately, providing security for a couple score of native porters overseen by an officer named Lieutenant Saitō, who was an honest-to-goodness samurai, or maybe a *ronin*, technically. I wasn't clear on the details. Anyway, he had the two swords and topknot and everything. He told us he'd come here with Colonel Gutierrez—*Adelantado* Gutierrez at the time, which was a noble rank of some importance, I gathered—all of which seemed incredible. It was Sergeant Takahashi who explained to me that yes, Spanish conquistadors indeed hired Japanese mercenaries back in ye olde Hernán Cortés days.

"Learned that in my Intro to Japanese History class before I figured an AA wasn't gonna make me be all that I could be and signed up," Takahashi explained. "Just in case you get it in your head that everyone with a Japanese last name is an exhaustive encyclopedia of facts about *Nippon*."

So *that's* the stuff you learn about in college. The more you know.

We set off that very afternoon. It was hard to leave behind the actual beds we'd been able to enjoy for one whole glorious night, despite the promise that after this "one last mission" we'd get some time off for real. I frankly wasn't holding my breath. We'd been running ops nonstop for weeks. Why change the tempo? Besides, a break would just give some of the guys an opportunity to get into trouble with the local corn beer and "indentured" prostitutes, despite the alleged poor quality of the former and Doc's warnings about the latter.

The porters were all older men, but not old, and carried the crates on large litters, five men to a side. I wondered why they weren't using horses and wagons until we encountered the first real rough patch in the route. This mountainous country was not conducive to wheels in the least.

Dusk fell quickly, and we made camp after only a few hours' travel. Before long I was sitting with my usual crowd, minus Xochi, who was busy with Captain Brown and Sanchez sitting a ways off, engrossed in conversation with Lieutenant Saitō.

I looked over at them and then turned to Epasotl. "I'd like to be a fly on that wall."

She paused from eating from her MRE, made a face, and stuck out her tongue. "Why would anyone want to be a fly? They are weak. They carry sickness. And even if you were so cursed, there are no walls near them."

The other guys around us chuckled. Epasotl smiled, making me wonder if she'd really taken me literally or was just playing. It could be tough to tell with her. She'd come a long way, but she could still be maddeningly naïve at times.

"I just mean, I'd like to know what they're talking about."

"Officer things," she said around a mouthful of Chicken a la King. "Probably how to make our lives more difficult."

"No doubt," Pierce agreed.

Stanley snickered at me from across the fire. "You're pathetic, you know that, man?"

I whipped my head around. "Excuse me?"

"You, Preacher. You're pathetic," he said. "The way you're always staring at the princess like a lovesick puppy. Pathetic."

"Shut up, Stanley," I said, maybe a little more stone-faced and angrier than I needed to be.

He shrugged. "All I'm saying is a real man would do something with a royal piece of ass like that."

"I said shut up."

"Just saying." He pushed his glasses up on his nose and grinned. "If you don't hit that, someone else will. Course, they'd have to put a bag over her face because of the scars…"

Pierce shot me a glance and shook his head.

"Stay away from her," I told Stanley, with a voice of liquid nitrogen.

"Whatever, Preacher. She ain't gonna wait around forever, you know. Soon enough she'll start looking for a real man."

"Too bad for you, Stanley," Epasotl said, totally ambivalent as she licked the last bits of Chicken a la King from her fingers.

That might have been enough to lighten the tension and let things clear out. But I wasn't willing to let it go. This had been a problem for too long, and I wasn't going to see it get any worse. "I'm warning you, Stanley."

"And I'm literally shaking." Stanley stood and slung his rifle. "What're *you* gonna do, Preacher?"

I started to rise to show him, but Pierce put a hand on my shoulder and pulled me back down. "Not worth it," he muttered.

Stanley laughed and shook his head before walking away with Lawrence and Anderson, leaving us alone. I gritted my teeth.

"So, *so* not worth it," Pierce said in a low voice.

I stared laser beams into Stanley's back as he walked away. "If he touches her, I'll—"

"He's not *that* stupid."

"You have to have seen how he looks at her."

"Sanchez would have his balls for breakfast."

Epasotl looked between us and frowned. "Little Kahuna would eat Corporal Stanley's testicles? This would give him great fertility."

"Wouldn't put it past him." Pierce chuckled. Then to me: "Just chill out, man. Stanley's a pig, but he's not gonna do anything. He's just yanking your chain for his own personal entertainment."

I settled back into the circle. "I'm not so sure… I got a real bad feeling about him."

"Course you do," Pierce said. "He's Stanley. He's a dick. Always has been."

"I do not think you need to be jealous, Ben-Ette," Epasotl said. "Xochi would not mate with him. Even if he forced her into marriage to appease her God."

"I'm not *jealous*," I snapped, my agitation showing. "I'm *worried*."

Epasotl frowned and then she laid her ears back. "You are afraid he will—"

"Yes," I said sharply.

"Do you want me to kill him?"

"Whoa!" Pierce held his hands up. "I did not just hear that. She isn't serious, is she?"

"Like, totally serious," Epasotl said in a way that made me miss Wilson.

"She's serious," I said, shaking my head. "No, Epasotl, I don't want you to kill him."

"It would be easy," Epasotl snarled. "I would make it fast. Like an animal. He does not deserve to die with honor. I understand if you wish to gut him yourself. It is your honor he has insulted."

"Absolutely not," I said firmly. "No one's killing anyone. Are we clear? Maybe just… I don't know… help me keep an eye on him."

"For sure," Pierce said, patting me on the shoulder.

Epasotl regarded me with narrowed eyes and nodded slowly.

"No killing," I said. "Are we clear on that? Let me hear you say it."

"Clear," she said.

"Promise?"

She held three fingers up by her shoulder, palm facing outward. "Scout's honor."

"Scouts don't have no honor," Pierce quipped.

"*Boy* Scouts," I corrected.

"Oh, right," Pierce said. "Yeah, those kids are okay. Forgot you were one of those, Mr. Dudley Do-Right."

Epasotl showed her teeth in a Cheshire grin. "Wrong. He was a *Mountie*."

Pierce rolled his eyes and shook his head. "Whatever. I bet neither of 'em sold anything that rivaled them Girl Scout cookies. Which one was your favorite, Bennett?"

Epasotl raised her ears inquisitively. "Girl… Scout… cookies?

Pierce was animated. "Oh, man… they got so many different kinds, and…"

…and the night went on.

CHAPTER 36

"Well, there it is," I said. "Bigger than I expected."

"That's what she said," Pierce muttered, unable to restrain himself.

Outpost Hotel-Romeo lay a klick below us in a lush green valley. It was a rambling collection of outbuildings scattered around a tall pyramid overgrown with vegetation and scattered among other crumbling, overgrown ruins, all fenced in with a triple-stack of concertina wire and walls of sandbags. The outpost was divided into different sections, some filled with equipment and crates, others with housing for the workers and soldiers, and still more stuffed with people—refugees or, more likely, prisoners. Several machine gun towers loomed over the grounds.

"Looks like a cross between a warehouse and an internment camp," I said as I peered through my spotting scope. We were doing a standard bit of recon, just to make sure that what we marched toward was still friendly and we weren't blindly moving into a trap. Everything looked legit, but I couldn't for the life of me make out what the purpose of this place was. So I started to think out loud by talking with Pierce. "What the heck are they all doing here?"

"POWs?" Pierce asked.

"There *are* some military-aged men," I confirmed. "More than a few. Some even look like they're Outworlders. But there are a hell of a lot of women and old people. Not only humans. There are Chaneques too. And children."

"Any more Marines?"

"Not that I see."

Pierce took out his shooting notebook and a pencil. "Okay. Let's get down how many. Captain will wanna know."

I scanned again, dividing the different groups of people into smaller units, made a count, and then multiplied them back together. "Hmm… rough estimate? Two hundred and sixty. Maybe a fifth of them MAMs. The men and women are segregated. And the humans and non-humans. Not many Chaneques. Maybe two dozen."

"Probably not a POW camp then. Collection point for slaves? I mean, 'indentured servants'?"

I was looking through the scope, but I was pretty sure Pierce made air quotes.

"Could be. Doesn't look like they have permanent housing for the prisoners. This is a supply depot, after all. I wonder what went down that got all these people out here then. Refugees, maybe?"

"From what I've seen so far, Bennett, the people around here are just more supplies. That's the vibe I'm getting anyway."

I lowered my scope and looked at my friend. He'd touched on something that had been bothering me as well. "Yeah."

Pierce chewed on the end of his pencil. "Some indentured workers at a place like FOB Cincinnati—even the pleasure girls, whack as that is, I can still see—but way out here? Like what's the purpose? This is miles from *anything* of value. Why march people all the way out here unless there's a city or a base or something nearby that can use them that we don't know about? Hell, even a plantation or something."

I nodded. Everything Pierce was saying made sense, which is to say, the existence of all these people in the middle of nowhere *didn't* make sense. At least not to this lowly specialist. There was nothing here. We were too far from Amoloyan or any major base for it to serve as a depot. There weren't any major routes nearby. If they were being held for shipment somewhere else, this was a really inconvenient location. It was completely isolated.

"And if they were here to work," Pierce continued, "like, say, to expand the outpost, they'd be working. Only I don't see any major projects underway. There's nothing to work on."

I shook my head and went back to my scope. "Yeah. I don't get it either. They're just being kept here, penned in like animals."

Pierce spit off to the side. "Super rotten, bro. Super."

I continued studying the outpost through my glass. The guards in the towers seemed to be paying as much attention to the prisoners as they were to the perimeter.

"They're not taking very good care of these slaves, either," I said. "A lot of them look sick and malnourished. I see signs of mistreatment too. Physical abuse."

Pierce grunted. "Like I said, man—slaves are just expendable goods, right? Work 'em till they're dead and then replace 'em."

"Ugh. Ever get the feeling we're on the wrong side?" I asked.

"Who says the 'other' side is any better?" Pierce countered. "Those Acálan pricks could be just as bad. I rather we weren't on *any* side. We need to be finding a way home, not getting involved in a turf war between assholes living like kings off the locals."

I sighed and started to think about Epasotl. Slavery came naturally to her mind, right from the moment we'd captured her. It was her sense of that being the "honorable" way of things that had motivated her to save my life way back when all this started.

But there was nothing honorable about it. And if you're stuck in a world where slavery just *is*, what do you do about it? I mean, seriously, what? Was our purpose here to start an abolitionist movement among people who already should know better? It could take lifetimes to reprogram this place from what they'd been doing for generations before Outworlders ever showed up.

I realized that Pierce was looking at me sharply.

"What?" I asked.

"You don't *want* to go home, do you?"

I returned the man's gaze, intent on giving my friend an honest answer. "I don't know, man. Sometimes, maybe. I miss my family, sure. But…"

"But the princess," Pierce said.

"Yeah. The princess."

"You got it that bad for her, eh? Gonna run off and go native?"

I shrugged.

"Betcha that's what Wilson did," Pierce continued. "He didn't look so bad to me last time I saw him. Bet he figured out a way to stay behind with that Amazon he fancied. Draped-in-Stars or whatever her name was."

I almost choked. Pierce was right on the money. If he'd guessed it, I was sure Captain and Sanchez had as well.

"Dressed," I said. "Her name was Dressed-in-Stars."

"Yeah, her. She was a little too buff for my tastes, but Xochi... I might even want to stay in this hellhole myself for someone like that. Maybe someone a little taller though. She's hella short, like you."

"I'm not short."

"Hell you aren't."

"I'm a perfectly statistically average height," I protested.

"Maybe in Munchkinland."

"You aren't a towering giant yourself, man."

"Couple of inches makes all the difference," Pierce said with smug satisfaction.

"That's what she said."

Pierce laughed.

"Come on," I said. "We need to get this intel back to the captain."

"You just want Xochi to *debrief* you."

I shot him a finger gun. "Can you blame me?"

***

"—plus five machine gun towers sporting two Fifties and three RPDs between them, and at least two dozen guards armed with AKs. Also about"—I double-checked Pierce's notes—"fifty men armed with spears and macuahuitls. That's what we could see, but there could be more in the buildings. The barracks could easily house twice that number."

"And two hundred and sixty prisoners?" Xochi asked.

"Best guess, yes." I saw Captain Brown, who was riding on Xochi's other side, raise his eyebrows and then catch my eye. "Ma'am," I hastily added. The formalities of rank seemed a bit superfluous to me, especially at this point, all things considered, but Brown ran a tight ship. Or enjoyed making my romantic life difficult. Both, I guess.

"Seems like a lot of security, sir," Xochi said, turning in her saddle to face the captain.

"Perhaps, Chief," Brown said. "Depends on the true purpose of the outpost and the threat assessment—both internal and external. Anything else to report, Nephi?"

"No sir."

"Thank you, Corporal," my girlfriend said formally. "Dismissed."

"Saying things like 'Dismissed' isn't something you can do, Chief, but you get an A for effort." Brown's lips quirked. "That'll be all, Nephi."

He was having way too much fun with this nonsense. I let my horse fall back beside Pierce and shook my head. I would've had to salute her too, if we weren't in the field.

Pierce just laughed softly before saying, "Not the debrief you were hoping for, I bet."

"Just, don't even," I muttered.

"Guess we know who wears the spurs in *your* relationship, *Corporal*."

"Har har." I sighed. "I swear the only reason Captain made her a CW2 was to spite me."

"He's just protecting your innocence."

"Hello, life of permanent celibacy. Maybe I should go back and see if Friar Bastía can swear me in on all the right vows."

"Hey, having a virgin in the platoon could come in handy." Pierce chuckled. "Captain's thinking ahead. Might have to sacrifice you to a dragon or something."

I forced a laugh, thinking back to what Epasotl had said about virgins being immune to being "turned." But that was just Chaneque superstition, which meant it had about as much legitimacy as Pierce's joke about dragons.

***

The first thing that struck me as we approached the gate of Outpost Hotel-Romeo was the overpowering miasma of unwashed bodies, excrement, and fear. The entire camp smelled absolutely horrible. Clearly sanitation wasn't high on the list of priorities.

The second thing was the brooding sense of wrongness.

I don't just mean the moral injustice of seeing stricken faces peering at us from behind the wire. This feeling ran far deeper. As if the land itself was cursed by a deeply entrenched evil.

The source of that evil became immediately clear as we entered the grounds and I caught sight of the first squat black stela. I realized with nausea and shock that the outpost had been built around not just any ruined pyramid, but an ancient temple of Mictlāntēcuhtli. Why would anyone do something so foolish as to build an outpost in the middle of unholy ground—especially one as dangerous as this? It would be like making camp in a Superfund site. Worse than that, because radiation and toxic chemicals didn't turn you into the ravenous undead.

A sergeant of the guard waved us over to a corral as Lieutenant Saitō led the porters farther into the outpost.

"Welcome to Hotel-Romeo." The squat man spoke with a pronounced Spanish accent and had the broad features and swarthy complexion of a Yucatán native. "You can leave your horses here. We have quarters for you to spend the night."

Spend the night? I didn't want to spend another minute here, let alone stay overnight.

"Thank you, Sergeant," Captain Brown said, apparently not feeling the heavy dread that I did. He turned in the saddle to address the platoon. "You heard the man. Dismount and see to your horses."

I rode over to him and leaned in close.

"Sir," I said in a low voice, "these ruins—the stelae, the pyramid, everything—they're the same as the place where Dee was turned."

"Are you sure?" he asked in an equally low voice, his face revealing nothing.

"Can't you feel it? The Lord of Mictlān was worshipped here. It reeks of evil even stronger than where we lost Dee."

"It certainly reeks, and it's certainly evil," Brown replied. "But there's more than enough human misery concentrated here to explain that."

I opened my mouth to reply, but he cut me off with a curt wave of his hand.

"Not now," he ordered. "We'll speak later."

"Yes, sir," I said before turning Duke and leading him into the corral.

Xochi caught my eye, and I could tell she was thinking the same thing I was. This was, as Wilson would've said, some seriously bad mojo.

I tried not to think about it as I took off Duke's tack and fed him some grain. Xochi moved beside me as I was brushing him down.

"Mictlāntēcuhtli." She crossed herself as she said the name, like it was a curse.

"Yeah," I replied, glancing furtively around. "No doubt about that. Captain doesn't seem convinced though."

"He is not a stupid man. He knows." Her eyes darted over to the posted sergeant lazily watching us care for our horses. "It is best to exercise discretion."

I nodded thoughtfully. Probably wise not to make a scene about it, not until we had a better grasp of what was going on.

Another man entered the corral. He was tall and pale, with sharp features and a hawklike nose. He strode over to Captain Brown and saluted.

"Lieutenant Arnaud, sir," he said with a sharp French accent. "I'm Captain Yolotli's XO. It is an honor to meet you. I will have your gear and tack taken to your quarters, with the CO's compliments. He invites you to join him for dinner."

Brown returned the salute and then shook the man's hand. "Pleasure to meet you, Lieutenant. I'll see to my men first, if it's all the same."

"Not to worry, sir. They will be well taken care of. Food, women, whatever they desire." He snapped his fingers and the sergeant who had been watching us snapped to attention. "Sergeant Tadeáš, see to the captain's men," the lieutenant ordered. "See that they are well fed and… *warm* for the night."

"Yes, sir!" the sergeant barked with a salute.

Brown frowned. "Food, yes. Women won't be necessary."

Arnaud sniffed with injured pride. "I assure you they are clean, sir."

"My statement stands, nevertheless."

Arnaud composed himself. "As you wish, sir."

"I presume my staff is also invited?" Brown asked. "This is Sergeant Sanchez, my XO, and Chief Xochicuauhtli, my intelligence officer."

"But of course, sir." Arnaud returned their salutes before shaking Sanchez's hand affably. Then he took Xochi's hand and kissed it. "If you will come with me?"

Frenchmen. Seriously.

Once they'd left, Takahashi introduced himself and the rest of us to Sergeant Tadeáš. It turned out both Tadeáš and his CO were Mayan rebels from the Caste War of Yucatán in the late nineteenth century, as were several others of the Outworlder contingent manning the outpost, though most of the guards and even a few of the noncoms were indigenous. Lieutenant Arnaud had served under Napoleon III in Mexico a few decades earlier. The lieutenant had been in-country for a year now, Tadeáš and the Mayan rebels for an entire decade.

"Do not worry about your tack and gear," Tadeáš said casually. "That is what the servants are for, no? Let us get your men"—he glanced at Epasotl—"and your… *pequeña amiga*… something to eat. You must be tired and hungry."

"Won't say no to a hot meal," Takahashi agreed with a broad smile.

I think a lot of the guys' rumbling stomachs outweighed everything else happening around them, but I couldn't say the same. Between the smell, and the suffering, and the cloying blanket of *evil* permeating the camp, I'd completely lost my appetite.

We filed out of the corral and followed Tadeáš past another stinking pen of prisoners—this one full of emaciated, blank-faced Chaneque women and children. Epasotl growled in disgust—whether over the dishonor of their capture or the captors themselves, I didn't know. The sergeant led us past a line of clapboard buildings, mentioning in passing that one of them would be our lodging place for the night, and into a broad, dusty square dominated by a huge arch made of great blocks of basalt. Each block was carved with intricate designs and polished to a mirror shine. It seemed out of place, disconnected from the other ruins and serving no apparent architectural purpose besides being simply very large and bold.

"Sergeant Tadeáš, what is that?" I asked, pointing to the arch.

"You have not seen a portal before?"

I shook my head. "A… portal?"

"Ah, then you men are in for a treat!" he replied. "It is *muy espectacular*. If you don't mind waiting for a few minutes, I believe it is scheduled to open soon."

"Open?" I asked, perhaps a little dumbly. I could tell the men around me were curious as well, though.

"*Sí*, the parts you escorted here are a priority order from *El Señor* himself! His Majesty is most anxious to get them into production. As I am sure you are."

Takahashi quirked an eyebrow. "We are?"

Tadeáš gestured to us. "I assume you would wish to have new vehicles, no? We have already produced the fuel." He motioned to a stack of fifty-gallon drums and grinned proudly.

"Wait!" Woodward said excitedly. "This… portal… it's the *replicator*, isn't it?"

"*Sí, sí*," Tadeáš said, the smile still in place. "I have heard others from your time use this term."

From somewhere unseen a gong sounded three times, and the servants and laborers who'd been bustling around the outpost dropped to the ground in genuflection.

"Ah, here we are," Tadeáš said in a hushed voice. "The priest comes now."

A procession emerged from a building facing the square. It consisted of an honor guard of six soldiers, armed with macuahuitls and dressed in quilted armor and elaborate headdresses of eagle feathers, escorting a bent old man wearing a loincloth and sleeveless vest embellished with fringe. The priest's headdress was even more elaborate than the guards', and he carried a fuming incense burner. One of the honor guards held a conch shell, which he blew at regular intervals as the group made their way into the square.

Once under the arch, the guards moved to either side of the span, and the priest stood under the rise and waved his burner in the air, producing a thick cloud of smoke. The unseen gong sounded again, and the priest drew a bronze dagger which he proceeded to draw through the air in a complex pattern.

My jaw dropped involuntarily as lines of energy appeared in the air from the dagger's tip, forming an elaborate series of pictographs that hung in the space before the priest. The small cloud of smoke from his incense burner thickened and grew like a thunderhead, slowly filling the entire space of the arch. The cloud coalesced, spinning and flashing with lightning, before abruptly blinking out of existence.

Except now the arch led into… somewhere not *here*.

Ash and the stench of sulfur floated forth from the portal, and through it I could see a black stone road leading into a dark realm permeated with the flickers of raining embers. A wave of evil thrummed in the air, almost palpable in its malevolence, and nearly brought me to my knees. It was overpowering, suffocating, and I found myself praying silently with a fervor I hadn't felt for many years.

"Mictlān," Epasotl hissed beside me in a voice meant only for the two of us. Her ears were laid back and her pupils were the thinnest of slits as she raised her face to meet my gaze. "It is a road to the Underworld!"

CHAPTER 37

I heard the sharp crack of a whip and snapped my head around to the sound.

From across the square Lieutenant Saitō came riding, leading the porters with their litters of crates. Guards armed with AKs and whips flanked the sweating men. They looked frightened—the porters, that is. The guards had the same bored, impassive look I'd seen on truck drivers cruising down the highway. This was nothing new to them.

Saitō rode his high-stepping horse into the portal without showing a trace of apprehension, as if riding into the bowels of Hell was just another Tuesday. Whips cracked, and the reluctant porters followed. Then the priest and his honor guard assembled and trailed after them into the darkness.

With a *whoomph,* a sharp wind stirred up dust devils in the square, and the portal vanished. The arch remained, but it was now just an arch, with nothing through it but the other side of the square. Even the smoke was gone.

All the servants and laborers who had been genuflecting stood and returned to their business. Sergeant Tadeáš clapped his hands in a one-man applause and smiled.

"Impressive, no?" he said to us. "Of course, one gets used to it, but the first time I saw it my face was much like yours."

We were all stunned speechless for several moments before Doc cleared his throat and spoke. "Very impressive. So this is where you… 'manufacture' everything?"

"One of many such places." Tadeáš waved his hand dismissively. "We are but a small outpost in a great network, but we take pride in our work. And such work makes a man hungry, no? Let us eat!"

He waved us forward to the mess hall.

As my comrades shouldered past me, I gave a long, apprehensive backwards glance at the great, sinister arch.

The doorway to Mictlān.

The road to Hell.

Food was the last thing on my mind.

***

"'One road, but many gates.' That's how Captain Yolotli described it," Xochi told me as she sat down on the edge of her bed.

We were having an impromptu NCOs meeting in the four-person room that had been assigned to Captain Brown, Sanchez, Doc, and Xochi. With Takahashi, García, Stanley, and me all present as well, it made for a tight squeeze. The heat of the waning day and the fact that all of us were on the riper side didn't help my feeling of claustrophobia. Then again, maybe that sense of the walls closing in was just because of the sheer evil oozing out of the ground in this outpost. It made my head hurt.

"So the replicator is located in Hell, more or less," Doc said. "That's awesome. What could possibly go wrong?"

"Oh, it gets better," Sanchez said. "Ma'am?"

Xochi rubbed her eyes with the palms of her hands and then looked to the captain, who stood against a wall with his thick arms folded against his chest.

He nodded at her. "This is your briefing," Brown rumbled gently.

"It's about the prisoners," she said finally. Her voice was weak, on the verge of cracking. "They're…" Her eyes looked harrowed and brimmed with tears. "The fact is, they're…"

She made a small choking sound and buried her head in her hands.

"They're what powers the artifact," Brown continued for her in a dispassionate voice. "The prisoners are sacrifices. They're fuel. Souls in exchange for goods."

"Souls?" Takahashi asked.

"Souls. Energy. Life essence, call it what you will," Brown said. "The artifact draws its power from their deaths."

"Wait," García said, plucking at his uniform. "So our clothes, our gear, our weapons, everything we've been issued… it's made from souls?"

"Essentially, yes," Sanchez said.

García looked at his rifle like it was a viper and crossed himself. "Is all our stuff *haunted*?"

"I don't think that's how it works," Brown said. "But I don't know."

No wonder everything we had felt off to me. Call it intuition or spiritual sensitivity, but it had made my skin crawl even before I'd heard this bombshell.

"Uh, sir, how did you get this intel?" I asked. "Why haven't we heard anything about this before?"

"Because Dietrich wanted our service," Xochi mumbled, her head still in her hands.

"Captain Yolotli was very forthcoming," Brown answered. "Surprisingly so. Or at least he was once I guessed at the basics. But I believe Xochi is correct—Dietrich had to have known that upon hearing how he made use of his little 'replicator,' we wouldn't be particularly keen to support him."

"How did you manage to guess at it, sir?" I asked.

"It wasn't that hard to put one and one together," Brown said, holding up one hand, palm up and cupped like he was holding something, followed by the other. "A portal to Hell and a camp full of slaves. Do the math."

No mental arithmetic in my brain would've added up to that sum, but then again that's probably yet another reason why he was the captain and I was just an E4. And also maybe there was an *X-Men* story arc that gave him some special insight into infernal manufacturing techniques. In fact, there probably was. But now didn't seem to be the time to ask.

"Jesus," Takahashi breathed. "What are we going to do, sir? We obviously can't keep operating for these psychopaths."

"No, we can't," Brown agreed. "But what we are *not* going to do is make a big show of our distaste. This is likely a test, sending us here. I assume we're being observed, and how we hold ourselves might mean the difference between walking out of this outpost or being sent through that portal as the next sacrifices in line."

"You serious, Captain?" García asked.

"A man holds slaves, commits human sacrifice for personal gain… Sergeant, when someone shows you who they are, believe them."

"So we just play along like we're cool with this?" Doc asked, his tendency to get a little hot under the collar flaring up. "Do whatever these bastards tell us to do?"

"Not at all. We're done taking orders from Dietrich or his people. But they don't need to know that—yet. They'll find out soon enough… when we complete our new objective." Captain Brown let the silent anticipation hang in the air. "That artifact, replicator, soul-eater, whatever you want to call it… we're taking it out."

Before any of us could reply, Brown went on. "For two reasons. First"—he held up a meaty thumb—"because it's the right thing to do. And second"—he held up his index finger—"because this should further our mission to find a way home."

Sanchez nodded, but none of the other NCOs seemed to follow Captain Brown's thinking. It was García who admitted it first.

"I'm not sure I follow, sir," García said. "The second point, I mean. I totally agree it's the right thing to do."

"Think you can take this one, Chief?" Brown asked Xochi.

She nodded, wiped her eyes, and took a deep breath. "Mictlāntēcuhtli is… think of him as Smoking Mirror's top lieutenant. We—that is, Captain, XO, and I—we think that destroying the artifact will draw Smoking Mirror out. And Smoking Mirror is the key to getting you all home, not to mention freeing the people of this world from his rule." She smiled weakly. "So it's a win-win."

"What about that Quetzawhatever dude?" Takahashi asked.

"Quetzalcoatl," I said.

"Yeah, him," Takahashi said, nodding to me. "I thought *he* was the key to taking Smoking Mirror out. I mean, we *are* still talking about fragging a god—two gods now, actually." He forced a laugh. "We're gonna need more C4."

"Extra-dimensional entity," Brown corrected, stressing whatever distinction his *X-Men* comics had taught him. "*Not* a god."

I agreed with the *not a god* part. In my mind, we were dealing with demons. The thought didn't exactly give me the warm and fuzzies. Maybe thinking of them as extra-dimensional entities would be easier, come to think of it.

"Yes, sir," Takahashi agreed in a tone that conveyed respect for an officer yet also somehow managed to mean "whatever" to the rest of us lesser mortals. It's a skill you learn when you become an E4 and sticks with you throughout your career in the ranks.

"We don't know how to locate the Wisest of Men," Xochi said. "But yes, he would be a most valuable ally if we only knew how to find him and enlist his help."

"Which is why Quetzalcoatl is Plan B," Sanchez said. "Plan A is destroying the artifact, and yes, we could *always* use more C4."

"With respect, sir," Stanley said, speaking up for the first time, "there's only fourteen of us. How're we supposed to pull this off? There's enough guns in this outpost alone to flatten us all."

"Sixteen," I corrected, and yeah, I was being petty. Dude deserved it. "There are sixteen of us."

Stanley glared at me and sneered. "Okay, *sixteen*. Still… we're not *operators*. We're just scouts. Raiding isn't in my job description."

"It is now, son," Sanchez said sharply.

"My people will help," Xochi said, squaring her shoulders. "We will return to Kuauchanko and gather the warriors. There is an outpost near our lands with another of these 'portals.' I saw it marked on the map in Captain Yolotli's office. Outpost Kilo-Charlie."

Stanley rolled his eyes and was about to say something when Brown cleared his throat. The pain in my rear end snapped his mouth closed, proving that the jerk had at least a few functioning brain cells.

"And all these portals take us to the same place?" Takahashi asked.

Xochi nodded. "'One road, but many gates.'"

"But we don't know how to open the portal," Doc pointed out. "That's a problem."

"Epasotl watched the priest carefully," Sanchez said. "She's assured me she can replicate the operation. If not, we'll just have to *convince* the local priest to open it for us. But I believe she can do it."

"Thankfully," Xochi said, holding up her bronze dagger, "we have a key."

***

With the meeting adjourned and all of us knowing what was expected of us—if not exactly what to expect when it came to raiding an underworld—we racked out and then linked back up with Lieutenant Arnaud in the morning. I hadn't slept at all, and had a migraine; the rest of the guys looked like they'd had a rough night as well. All except for Stanley maybe. I bet he'd slept like a baby.

Arnaud took us to an equipment yard filled with stacks of crates and shelves of auto parts and other machinery. I walked with Sergeant Sanchez. As we passed one of the cursed stelae, I nodded at it and whispered, "You'd think people would be turning here, Sergeant, into, you know, the ravenous undead."

He shrugged. "Captain Yolotli told us his priests have 'deactivated' those things."

"Deactivated?"

"Something like that. Can it, Bennett, the lieutenant's talking."

"—so we have all the parts we need now to build your vehicles, your… what do you call them?" Lieutenant Arnaud was saying to our group.

"Humvees," Captain Brown supplied. I could tell from the tone of his voice that he was surprised to hear what these porters had been carrying. That was quite the coincidence, and clearly Brown hadn't been filled in until right now.

What was the deal with that?

"Ah, yes. Humvees. Strange name for a horseless carriage."

"It stands for High Mobility Multipurpose Wheeled Vehicle, sir," I offered.

Sanchez gave a little groan and Stanley rolled his eyes. Arnaud repeated the acronym to himself and then nodded to me.

"Of course it will take months to get all the parts produced and to assemble them," he continued. "However, we recovered something of even greater and of more immediate value from the equipment you were forced to abandon." Arnaud led us to a large table in the center of the yard, where something was sitting under a tarp.

The lieutenant's eyes twinkled as he swept the covering aside with a flourish, revealing a brand-new MK-19. "We've been seeking one of these models for a long time. The tlahtoāni is a very happy man. This is a, how do you say, 'game changer.' Normally it would take some time to generate the weapons and ammunition in sufficient quantities to deploy them in the field effectively, but fortunately for us an auspicious time is coming when the output of the artifact will be multiplied greatly.

"The locals have two calendars, as you may already know," Arnaud went on, looking quite pleased with himself. "The first, the 'year count,' follows the solar cycle, and the second, the 'day count,' tracks a two-hundred-and-sixty-day ritual cycle. Together they form a fifty-two-year 'century.' The day in which the two calendars align, which they refer to as 'The Binding of the Years,' is most auspicious. On the eve of that day, the priests and people will all participate in the New Fire Ceremony, which they believe staves off the end of the world."

"It is true," Epasotl said. "The woman Tzitzimime, who lives in the stars, will descend and devour the world if the rituals are not observed."

"It is a false superstition," Xochi muttered.

"What rituals?" Brown asked Epasotl.

"There are many, Big Kahuna, but chiefly, all fires are extinguished and then a new fire is lit in the heart of a sacrificial victim. It is stoked into a great bonfire, and from it runners carry torches throughout the land to relight all other fires, from temple to hearth."

"More to our purposes," Arnaud said, "on this day the artifact will produce a great bounty like none we have seen before. So the priests promise us anyway. No one knows really, since the last Binding of the Years was before any of us were here—at least, any of us that we know of." He made a motion encompassing the outpost. "Which is why we have assembled so many captives."

He spoke in a matter-of-fact tone, like he was discussing the workings of an ordinary machine and not a diabolical artifact that was powered by living souls.

"And when is this… binding?" the captain asked.

"In twenty-one days," Arnaud replied. "And then… game changer." He smiled and swept his hand across the MK-19 one final time. "But come, you must depart for FOB Cincinnati and you have not had breakfast yet. Forgive me the delay. I was eager to see you enjoy the fruits of your arrival."

And I'm eager to see you enjoy yours, I said in my mind, wanting to put an end to all this. It wasn't right.

Captain Brown gave a polite nod. "It's been enlightening."

I felt a jab in my side and looked to Sanchez, who'd landed his elbow against my ribs. He pointed to his face and I immediately understood. I had been scowling, letting my emotions get the best of me. I did my best to rest my face into something more impassive and less *I want to kill you.*

The lieutenant hadn't seemed to notice. He strode from the equipment yard briskly, motioning for us to follow, and we fell into step behind him.

On the way to the mess hall, we passed by a group of human male prisoners. One of them fought his way to the front of the wire.

"Captain! Captain Brown!" he called.

The man was disheveled and malnourished but still powerfully built. He was of perhaps slightly above average height, with a mop of sandy hair and an auburn beard. His blue eyes looked frenetic. And… somehow he knew Captain Brown.

Brown stopped dead in his tracks and spun to face the man. The captain's face lit up with recognition. "Mitch!"

"Captain! What are you doing here?"

"I was about to ask you the same thing," Brown replied. "You look like hell, son."

"I've been better, sir."

Brown turned to Lieutenant Arnaud. "I know this man. Release him."

The lieutenant hesitated. "He's from Acalán. A prisoner of war, sir."

"I don't give a damn who he fought for or against in this hellhole," Brown said in a cold, flat voice. "He's an officer and one of my men in the *real world*. I'm responsible for him. Now get him out of that cage, Arnaud."

CHAPTER 38

Captain Yolotli hadn't been keen to release Lieutenant Whitlock, but Brown's persistence had won out. Now we were heading back to FOB Cincinnati, officially at least.

Captain Brown called a halt that evening, and we set up to talk away from prying ears and eyes. But we spoke of nothing of substance, nothing relating to what we had seen or what we planned to do, until night fell. Perhaps we needed the psychological effect of the night to begin to speak of the double dealings and danger we all knew had come upon us.

We sat around a campfire under the trees in a small valley.

"I've been here two years now," Lieutenant Mitch Whitlock said. He'd been one of Brown's platoon commanders back in the Ranger Batts and looked a hell of a lot better now that he'd gotten a real meal, a fresh change of clothes, and a chance to clean up.

Brown shook his head. "You were with First Battalion at Torrijos in Operation Just Cause, right? So same timeframe as us, and we've only been here a few months. You'd think people grabbed from the same time period in our world would arrive at the same time."

Whitlock shrugged. "There's no rhyme or reason to it. People come from all over history and get dumped here *whenever*. I've met guys from our future who've been here a decade or more and dudes from centuries ago who've only been here a few months. There are more Outworlders in this shithole than you might think."

"What happened to the rest of your team?" the captain asked.

Whitlock shrugged. "I don't know if they even came along with me for the ride. The last time I saw any of them was Panama."

"Did you get separated?"

"I didn't think so. But… I dunno. Must have."

"Tell me more about Acalán," Brown said. "I know it's an island off the coast, but other than the fact that it's at war with Dietrich, there hasn't been much intel about the political or social situation. Unchecked expansionism is the reason Dietrich has given for the war, but given what I saw at that camp, my willingness to believe the man is low."

"The population is mostly native, plus some of us," Whitlock said. "By 'us' I mean us from the real world, not just Americans." He raised one hand, palm up, and then the other. "American, not American, frankly it doesn't really matter here. Both sides have Americans. They're still trying to kill us and we're still trying to kill them. Anyway, in Acalán we Outworlders mostly serve as advisors. The city-state is run by a council of natives and Outworlders together, representing the factions holding power on the island. It's not a democracy, but it's not oppressive either. The whole government was set up by pirates, believe it or not, and has a sort of corporate structure. I mean real pirates, by the way, 'Yo, Ho, Ho, and a Bottle of Rum.'"

I noted that the lieutenant didn't go into the reasons for the war, which was where I would have expected him to begin if Acalán was going to be presented as the good guys. It felt like he was avoiding something.

Brown pressed him on the same point. "And Acalán *is* expansionist? Looking to conquer Dietrich's lands?"

Whitlock waved a hand dismissively. "Not remotely, sir. We—I mean they—don't care about his land. They only want to control the artifact. That's the real power of this place."

"You should want to *destroy* it," Xochi cut in. "Only evil people would want to control and use a tool of the Devil like that."

"An artifact fed by souls is… unnerving at first," Whitlock admitted. "But what if you only fed it *evil* souls, eh? Criminals and assholes like Dietrich's officers. I don't see a moral quandary there. We execute criminals back home. Same here, only you can get a lot more out of it."

"A soul is a soul," Xochi countered. "Each is created in the image of God."

My girlfriend was Catholic all right.

"You're conflating terminating a life with sacrificing a soul," Brown told Whitlock. "Assuming there is a distinction in that—"

"There is," Xochi insisted, and then remembered herself. "All due respect, sir."

Brown gave a fractional nod and continued. "So what happens to the souls the artifact consumes? Are they destroyed? Enslaved? Dooming an immortal soul isn't to be taken lightly, and I don't know I'd trust anyone to be the judge of who is sufficiently 'evil' to face that fate."

"That concern only applies if you believe that such a thing as an immortal soul even exists," Whitlock countered.

"Metaphysical questions on souls notwithstanding," Brown said, "human sacrifice is wrong, plain and simple. No two ways around it."

Whitlock remained silent. He didn't look convinced, but he wasn't going to argue. It probably wasn't lost on him that if not for Captain Brown, *his* soul would have been among the next in line for destruction.

The captain took in the measure of his men. "We have less than twenty-one days to prevent a minor holocaust. If we ride hard, it will take us at least that long to reach Kuauchanko, perhaps leaving us no time to gather their warriors. We may have to consider assaulting the outpost alone, despite our numerical disadvantage. Potentially a *substantial* disadvantage if the outpost receives reinforcements in preparation for this 'Binding of the Years.'" He spread his hands. "I've been considering the problem carefully, but I want all of your input."

said with a wicked grin. "What if you had a faster mode of transportation?"

Brown arched an eyebrow.

"I know the location of a cache you might find useful," the lieutenant said. "A few fast attack vehicles and light off-road motorcycles. Fueled and armed."

Brown looked skeptical. "You, a captured prisoner of war, just *happen* to have an undiscovered cache of exactly what we need right now?"

I felt a little uneasy about it, too. Like it was too convenient. If sending us to the outpost and giving us a glimpse of what was *really* supplying Dietrich's operation was a test, who was to say that Lieutenant Whitlock wasn't another test? A plant placed just to see where our loyalties lay.

I lingered on that thought, wavering between paranoia and shrewd judgment and unsure which side to land on.

"You got me wrong," Whitlock answered. "I said that I *know of* a cache, not that it's mine. It belongs to the guys you're working for. I was part of a scouting team that found it. Only we never linked up with the rest of our group. My buddy was killed and I was captured. But it should still be out there, I should think."

Pierce and I exchanged a look. We were both wondering whether the team Whitlock had been reporting back to had been the same team we had ambushed. For all I knew, this guy might have fired a bazooka at our faces.

"What do you think, sir?" Sanchez asked.

The captain showed his teeth, and his eyes glinted in the firelight like a predator.

"You've never let me down yet, Mitch," he growled. "Game on."

CHAPTER 39

"Oh, hells yeah," Pierce said as he helped me drag the camo netting away. "Now *that's* what I'm talking about, man."

We stood gawking at a pair of rugged coyote-brown dirt bikes that were so ugly, they were beautiful.

Pierce got down and started inspecting one of them. "You ever heard of Christini?" he asked.

"Never," I said.

"Well that's who made these, whoever that is. Looks like a four-fifty thumper." He got up in the engine's face. "Check out this drive chain, bro. These Bettys are all-wheel drive."

"No kidding." I got down beside him. "That's sick. Didn't think you did anything on the beach but surf."

"Whatever," Pierce said. "Couldn't surf all the time, brah. Dad had a ranch out there and I would hit the trails on my KDX. Did some competition riding too. I ain't no squid. You ride?"

"Honda CR500. Never did any MX. Just me and my brothers tearing it up out in Moab."

"Braaaap!" Pierce laughed. "Look at you, Richie Rich. Man, these girls here have four-stroke engines. I bet they go like a bat out of hell."

While Pierce and I were admiring the bikes, the rest of the platoon was uncovering the other prizes in Whitlock's cache. In total it held three Chenowth fast attack vehicles, which were militarized four-man dune buggies, and five of the Christinis. The FAVs were armed to the teeth, sporting an M2 machine gun in addition to two M60s and a pair of AT4 recoilless guns. The cache also had ammo. Lots and *lots* of ammo.

"X Team gets the bikes, obviously, because we both know how to handle them, like legit handle them," Pierce said. "Ain't that right, Sarge?"

"Affirmative," Sanchez said. "Doc and I get the other two."

"I call dibs on the fifth," Greene said.

"Negative, PFC," said Sanchez. "Lieutenant Whitlock's already claimed it."

"Bogus," Greene muttered. "Army promised us motorcycles. It was in the commercials every Saturday morning and everything. That's the whole reason I became a Scout."

"If that's the worst lie your recruiter told you, you got off easy, man," Woodward said. "I was promised Airborne School."

"Now why would you want to jump out of a perfectly good airplane?" García asked.

"Because chicks don't dig legs, Mr. Dope on a Rope," Doc replied.

"My love life was just fine, thank you kindly," García said. "Before we got dumped here anyway."

"Don't see how it's changed much." Doc's grin was savage. "You still got your right hand."

García punched Doc's arm hard as he walked past toward one of the FAVs. "Come on, Blue Team," he called out over his shoulder. "Let's get our mount ready. Greene, check in with the captain. You're his new gunner."

"I don't even get to drive, Sarge?" Greene whined.

"Hell if you'll be driving *my* mount, kid," García called back. "Not when I got Woodward."

Greene muttered something under his breath and shuffled off to Brown's FAV.

"Epasotl riding with you, Sergeant?" I asked Sanchez.

"That's an affirmative," he replied. "You and Pierce get the bikes squared away. We're burning daylight."

"Yes, Sergeant. Oh, what about the horses?"

"What about 'em? Cut 'em loose."

"Right, Sergeant."

That was a bummer. I'd grown attached to Duke, and I wasn't sure how he'd fare out in the wild. Horses seemed to be a rarity in this world; Xochi had never seen one before Amoloyan. She'd heard of them, but her people thought they were some kind of giant stag. I had a feeling wild horses didn't last long against the indigenous predators. Nothing to be done about it, though; it wasn't like we could take them with us. With luck Duke would find his way back home. I swallowed the unexpected lump forming in my throat and got with Pierce to shake the bikes down and get ready to move.

Captain Brown saw that the men were loaded up, then came to Pierce and me. "I want you two to stay back here as a rear guard. We left that outpost on good enough terms, but let's not assume they still think of us as part of one big human-sacrificing family. Wait thirty minutes, then move to follow. If you spot a patrol, do not engage. Contact us by radio and then slip away and rejoin when you can."

"Yes, sir," I said.

Pierce gave a "Roger, Cap'n" a split-second behind me.

Brown nodded and departed with the rest of our column. Destination: Kuauchanko. The land of the Sugar Skull Gals.

Wilson was going to be so pissed to see us show up.

"So whatcha think?" Pierce asked me.

"Let's cover up the bikes and set up an observation post."

"Yeah, no shit, Sherlock. I mean about the outpost and Dietrich and all that. You think they'll be pissed? Think they'll come after us? I mean, it's not gonna take long for them to realize that we didn't return to Cincinnati. If they check this cache and see it raided... they're not dumb, Bennett."

I pushed my bike behind a broad-leaved bush and looked for some branches I could set over the top to fully obscure the ride. Pierce was at my side, doing the same with his own bike.

"I don't know what they'll do, but things weren't gonna stay friendly regardless, bike theft aside. I mean... how much can you be friendly with someone who's good with sacrificing souls for personal profit?"

"Yeah, sounds like corporate America, man. You can't trust 'em." Pierce lowered his voice. "Which is why I don't trust Captain Brown's Ranger friend, either. Dude had himself convinced that when *they* used the soul sucker, it was all good. I hope Cap'n knows what he's doing, man."

"Well, if Whitlock has a problem with it, he's had plenty of time to bug out. He knows the plan, same as the rest of us. He hasn't, though."

"Huh. Still. I don't like it."

"I haven't liked much of anything since we first got here. Looking forward to seeing Wilson again, though. You all set?"

"Yeah, I'm good, man. Mine's a bit more visible than yours, but it should do."

I looked at Pierce's ride. The bush he'd found was a little shorter than mine, and you could just make out the seat rising above the fronds.

"Actually, that gives me an idea." I unslung my ruck and set it on my bike, then took off my boonie and placed it in the bushes.

Pierce squinted at my handiwork. "Kind of undid your hide there, bro."

"Yeah. Since yours is gonna be at least a little visible, I thought maybe we could work that to our advantage. You remember that sniper?"

The Marine sniper who had been following the unit we ambushed had never really left my mind. There were a lot of things off about that whole situation. First, we were told that an indig unit had been shadowing our targets—but if those guys were out there, we never heard or saw them. Then this guy shows up, conveniently when we need him, and he somehow bugs out when we're not looking. I had the feeling his real job was to keep tabs on us.

"Okay," Pierce said upon hearing my reasoning. "So?"

"So, I set up my ruck and hat as a decoy. If that sniper is still following, and if our actions have angered Dietrich enough that we're dead men walking, maybe he'll fall for the bait. If a standard patrol comes after us, we should hear and see them coming, and we can just bug out."

"Gee," Pierce said sarcastically, "sure love your optimism, Bennett."

We found cover behind a rotten log and fell into quiet, keeping still and watching our surroundings. Periodically one of us would pop up to take a look, keeping my spotting scope on hand in case we saw anything that warranted a closer inspection.

Pierce had just finished taking a scan when something bit on our decoy. Only, it wasn't the one I'd set up on the bike. The snap of a round impacted against the log, sending the spotting scope Pierce had accidentally left sitting on the log flying and showering us with deep red rotting timber. The only explanation I can think of is that the sniper caught sight of the lens in his scope and decided to put one through our eyeball.

The fact that he was shooting at all was bad, though. At best, he thought we were hostiles, but my money was on him following us with orders to kill if the opportunity arose.

Which it now had.

"Shit!" Pierce said, dropping low next to me.

My heart was pounding in my ears, making it hard to hear anything else. I strained... nothing. "You think it's just the one guy out there?" I asked.

Pierce shrugged and waggled his hand in a "maybe" motion, saving his voice for the radio report he was sending ahead.

"I think it's just the one," I said, my suspicion about that lone sniper feeling validated. "One of him, two of us. We need to flank him."

"No shit, Sherlock. But I'm nice and cozy right where I am."

I blew out my cheeks and nodded. "Okay, I'll go." I raised my head quickly and then ducked again. Another round buzzed overhead followed by the rifle's report. "See that good-sized tree to the right, past the bikes about twenty yards? When I make for it, give him something to think about. Radio check?"

I heard him key his radio twice in my earpiece and gave him a thumbs-up. "Count of three," I said. "One... two... three!"

I rolled to my right a couple yards and then sprang to my feet in a sprint, dodging undergrowth and skipping over logs. I heard the report of Pierce's rifle behind me, and another angry hornet nearly clipped my ear. My time on the short shuttle when I played football in high school was pretty fast, not NFL or even collegiate fast, but fast enough. It still felt like it took an eternity to reach the tree. I hugged my back against the trunk and gulped air.

My guess was the sniper would be waiting for me to appear on the right side of the tree, and he'd be leading his aim. I pivoted low around the *left* side of the trunk and squeezed off a couple rounds, then returned to cover and keyed my radio twice. I heard two clicks in reply, and when Pierce's rifle barked again, I bolted ten yards to my right before hitting the dirt and proceeding to low-crawl through thick ferns. I rolled to my left twice, paused, and then leapt to my feet and pumped my legs like I was making for the end zone.

Pierce's rifle thundered behind me.

I dropped to the ground and scrambled on knees and elbows behind a rocky outcropping. Before I could pop out to take another shot, Pierce's voice came over the radio. "Alpha Mike Foxtrot! I got him. Someone, get a body bag. You okay, Bennett?"

I checked myself and then propped up on one elbow to see the bikes. I'd nearly been shot back there, and a round had hit the pack I'd set up as a decoy. I could see a huge, ragged hole in my assault pack leaking something wet. "Roger," I replied. "Pretty sure he killed my franks and beans though. That's gonna be a joy to clean out."

"I think we now know what old Silver Eagle thinks about us," Pierce said. "Better catch up with the boys."

"Yeah," I said. "Wanna check that sniper first, though. Dude owes me a scope."

CHAPTER 40

The debrief and report resulted in mixed feelings. I had checked the sniper—it was indeed the same Marine from before—and had taken a lot of his gear. Without Dietrich's support, we were back to having to conserve everything, just like when we first left Panama. Captain Brown pointed out that the sniper might have simply believed that Pierce and me were a pair of enemy soldiers who'd found their cache, but I didn't think so. For the first shot, maybe. But he had to have had a good look at me while he was sending bullets in my direction. And he kept firing.

Plus, there was no doubt that he'd been following us. It was far too big a coincidence for him to randomly show up at the cache twenty minutes after the others departed. I could think of no good reason for him to do that. No friendly one, anyway.

After five days of hard driving—with Xochi serving as a scout, now that we were closing in on her little corner of this-messed up world—any doubt that Dietrich's forces weren't after us evaporated with the sound of beating rotator blades moving in our direction.

"Two birds inbound," Pierce said. "You think they're here to talk?"

It had once again fallen to Pierce and me to serve as rearguard, this time atop our bikes.

One of the Hueys flared and then turned to reveal a waiting door gunner taking aim. That answered that question.

Pierce and I peeled off in opposite directions, looking to reach a stretch of trees ahead. Spires of dirt spit up into the air in gouts as the gunner's aim attempted to catch up with Pierce's speeding motorbike. We reached the woods and saw that there were far fewer trees in front of us than it had looked like—I could see the other side no more than a hundred and fifty yards away.

The Hueys raced over the treetops and hovered on the other side of the shallow woods before beginning to slowly send their skids down to earth.

"Looks like they're gonna put some feet on the ground to come after us," I told Pierce as our bikes found one another.

"I got this," Pierce said, leaning against a tree and peering through his scope.

I looked at the guy in disbelief. "You can't take out a bird with *that* rifle."

"No, but I can get the pilot."

I returned my gaze to the Hueys. They were hovering about three meters off the ground when half a dozen motorcycles launched out of the sides of each bird. Motorcycles ridden by *Chaneques*.

I didn't have time to even begin to wrap my head around that new bit of insanity. "Time's up!" I snapped, shoving my new spotting scope back into my assault pack. "We gotta split."

"Just a moment…" Pierce mumbled. He took a breath, exhaled, and then his rifle bucked against his shoulder with a deafening crack. I whipped my head back to the Hueys and my jaw dropped as one of them shot up in the air a dozen meters before pitching onto its nose and rolling into a dangerous dive that sent it careening into the trees. The second bird pulled up and back, narrowly missing its flailing sister. The sound of cracking trees and tortured metal split the air, followed by a jet of flame and a colossal, oily black mushroom cloud.

Pierce slung his rifle and hopped on his bike, firing up the engine. "Told ya," he said with a smug grin before racing off into the woods. While shallow in the direction we wanted to go, the thin stretch of trees went on to the side for a while. I could already see the

Chaneque team entering the trees, and I revved my throttle and took off after him.

The line of trees we followed quickly began to move downhill amid rocky terrain. The pucker factor of riding at high speeds through a forest down what suddenly felt like a mountainside was dialed up to eleven with the Chaneques in pursuit. Fortunately, they weren't shooting at us; handling firearms on a dirt bike isn't so easy as they make it look in the movies—which is to say, it's nearly impossible—but they were gaining and trying to flank us. And they outnumbered us six to one.

Maybe with some luck, the main element would hear the Hueys —or at least the crash—and come back around to investigate, but they wouldn't get here in time to help. Pierce and I would have to work our own way out of this mess.

I raced off a shelf of rock, flying a good fifteen meters before I executed a rough landing that bottomed out the shocks. I heard one of my pursuers crash epically—and probably fatally—behind me as I proceeded to slalom through the trees and jump deadfall. Branches whipped my face and tore at the bike and my clothes.

My mom back home would have a stroke if she knew I was riding a dirt bike like this with just a boonie for a helmet.

I could see one of the Chaneque riders approaching in my peripheral vision. He was closing fast on my right, trying to herd me off into a steep gully. That wasn't going to happen. I pulled the clutch and let go of the throttle so I could draw my sidearm and squeeze off three quick rounds in his general direction. I didn't hit anything, of course, but it distracted him from seeing a log in his path in time, and the little blue rider suddenly did an endo and flew over the handlebars. As the bike flipped in the air and went somersaulting through the undergrowth, it managed to catch his flailing body in its path.

I barely holstered my pistol and got my own bike under control fast enough to avoid wiping out myself. A quick downshift and blip on the throttle brought my front wheel up and I hopped over a rocky outcropping, fishtailed, and pinned it through a small clearing.

But that maneuver had caused me to slow down enough that another Chaneque angled in from my left. To my shock he jumped his bike and performed an aerial dismount, flying toward me and tackling me from behind. It's easy to forget how acrobatic those little things are. His sharp claws dug painfully into my arm and shoulder, and I could feel his hot breath on the back of my neck.

I felt my flesh tear as we flew from the bike and then slid and tumbled through the ferns. We stopped with me ended up with my face in the earth with him straddling my back. I felt the impact of something—probably a knife blade—scraping against my kidney protector.

Bucking my hips, I twisted under him to throw him sideways. He was big for a Chaneque male, at least ninety pounds of compact, agile muscle, but I still had a good eighty pounds on him, and by this point not an ounce of it was fat.

Still felt like wrestling with a mountain lion.

I'd managed to turn myself around, and we were on our sides, face to face, his ears laid back and his needle teeth bared as he hissed and spat. He got in a couple of snake-fast body blows, each of them slashing across my chest plate, before going for my unprotected neck in a strike meant to slit my throat from ear to ear. I caught his wrist and twisted hard, and he swiped at my face with his free hand. The razor claws slashed through my right cheek like a brand of fire. I pivoted on top of him and slammed my elbow into his throat, turning my face away from his claws and bearing down with all my weight. His slit-pupil eyes bulged. I was pretty sure I'd crushed his larynx, given the shade of blue he was turning.

Well, blu*er*, anyway.

His lips frothed and he weakened enough for me to wrench the knife out of his hand and drive it up into his ribs. His pupils dilated suddenly and then went glassy as he gave a last, shuddering breath.

Blood was pouring freely from my cheek and splashing down onto his contorted, ugly old-man's face. I could hear more bikes approaching swiftly, and I pulled myself off the corpse, taking a knee and bringing up my rifle as the next biker bore down on me.

A quick double-tap sent him rag-dolling, and the riderless bike tore past me before careening off into the forest. I took down a second rider before the third ditched his bike and took cover behind it about thirty yards away and started firing at me with short, controlled bursts from his suppressed MP5.

The memory of Chief Baker talking about how they'd *tried* to train Chaneques came to mind. Looks like they'd discovered the secret formula after all, and had decided to test it out on me. I found myself hoping that Baker was the pilot Pierce had popped.

Dirt and shredded vegetation kicked up around me as I hit the deck, pulling myself behind the dead Chaneque for whatever cover he could offer, which wasn't much. There was a pause in the barking chitter of the submachine gun, and I grabbed a grenade out of my pouch, pulled the pin, and tossed it overhead. I heard a brief yowl of surprise, and then the sharp crack of the grenade detonating in a flash that lit up the forest.

I lay there for several moments, breathing hard, when Pierce's voice came over the radio.

"Bennett?"

"Still here, bro. You?"

"Only because the cavalry arrived. I ended up driving these biker kitties right into Gold Team's fire. Six KIA. You have any hostiles breathing?"

"Don't know, wait one."

I lifted my head over the corpse cautiously and peered into the forest beyond. Nothing moved. The engine of one of the bikes was still running. Bringing up my rifle, I raised myself into a crouch and eased forward, scanning for where the last Chaneque had been. The side of my face hurt like heck, and blood was dripping down my neck and into my clothes and plate carrier.

I saw the twisted and flaming wreckage of his bike first, and then I saw him. Parts of him, anyway. Whatever was left. There wasn't much.

I vomited, then wiped my mouth with the back of my hand and keyed my radio. "Yeah, I think I got them all."

"Where are you?" Pierce asked.

"Don't know, man. In the woods somewhere downhill."
"Hang tight. I'll circle back for you. Glad you're not dead."
"Glad you're not dead too."

CHAPTER 41

"Well, you can kiss your career as a Hollywood heartthrob goodbye," Doc said as he knotted the last of the stitches. He shrugged. "But who knows? Chicks dig scars."

I winced as I worked my jaw. "Thanks, Doc."

"I have to patch you up more than anybody else, Bennett. I don't know if you've got such bad luck that the men should stand clear of you, or you're the luckiest man alive for not being dead yet."

Once Doc stepped aside, Xochi—who was present this time and watching the entire procedure—flouted all fraternization rules and embraced me fiercely.

"I was so worried when I first saw you," she said. "Your face was a mask of blood. And your clothes…"

"Told you it wasn't as bad as it looked. I'm a bleeder."

Xochi touched her own scar and laughed self-consciously. I knew what she was thinking: now we matched.

I kinda liked that.

Sanchez, Epasotl, and Captain Brown crossed the assembly area toward us. We'd stopped in the eastern foothills of the Blue Mountains to spend the night, and most of the guys were out pulling security. There hadn't been any further signs of Dietrich's forces, or any other hostiles, but we weren't taking any chances.

"So much for the late Chief Baker's cock-and-bull story about the Chaneques working for Dietrich all going rogue," the captain said as he approached. "You holding up, Nephi?"

"Yes, sir."

"Get some rest," Sanchez said. "No point in debriefing you while you're loopy from painkillers. We've already spoken with Pierce. Just came over to make sure you're okay."

"Oh, he hasn't had any morphine, Sergeant," Doc said. "I tried to talk him out of it, but he's stubborn."

Sanchez quirked an eyebrow.

"That was unnecessary," Brown said to me. "Trying to be macho isn't going to win you any points, son."

"I wasn't... it's not like that, sir," I stammered. "It's just... I thought we should save it for when someone *really* needs it. We might never get a resupply."

Not that getting a couple dozen stitches in the face didn't hurt like heck. Not gonna lie. It's just... pain is temporary, right? And I have a thing about drugs and not being in control. Besides, Doc gave me some Motrin. I'm not some kind of masochist.

"We'll have to keep a close eye on it for infection," Doc said as he packed up his med kit. "I don't have any antibiotics, but Epasotl can probably handle anything that comes up. Ain't that right, PFC?"

Epasotl threw a lazy shaka sign.

"And like Sergeant Sanchez said," Doc continued, "you *do* need to get some rest, Bennett. Doctor's orders."

"Roger, Doc." I turned to the captain. "Pierce probably already told you all that's worth telling, sir. I can't add much other than I'm just lucky to be alive."

"It was more than luck, son. You did good. You can give your report to the chief," he said, nodding to Xochi. "When you're feeling up to it."

He slapped my shoulder and then he and Sanchez strode away, leaving Epasotl with Doc. She gave my face a close look and grunted in approval at his handiwork.

He smiled at her reaction. "I do fine needlework if I do say so myself. Gonna be a nasty set of stripes, but shouldn't be too hideous.

I'll want to take another look at it in the morning." He looked over at Xochi. "Make sure he gets some rest, ma'am. I'm serious."

Xochi nodded and then smiled at me when he left. "The scars will suit you. They go well with your face. A weathered warrior."

"You mean an old man." I didn't think about the fallout of what had happened in the jaguar temple often—only every time I looked in a mirror—but I knew I looked old. At least thirty-five. Older than Sanchez, and he was practically geriatric.

"You do *not* look old," Xochi scolded, her amber eyes twinkling. "Just… rugged and experienced. I like it. I can't wait to show you off once we reach my people."

Epasotl rolled her eyes. "Get a room."

***

Our route took us back into the plains, which now felt familiar. This land was becoming a home away from home, and I had a sense of excitement as we neared that last leg of our journey. My mind remembered the treetop spectacle that was Xochi's village, and I thought longingly of the banquet table… and even the bathhouse.

All those thoughts bubbled up as we waded into that sea of golden grass. We pushed for a few kilometers underneath an overcast black sun. By midday, things had cleared and we could see afar.

"That looks like smoke," Pierce told me. He had come with Epasotl and me to scout ahead.

Epasotl sniffed the air. "Yes. Far away. I can, like, barely make it out."

I pulled up my spotting scope. A blurry, vaguely green swath at the end of the grass sea appeared at maximum magnification—the forest dwelling place of the Sugar Skull Gals. Rising up behind them somewhere were pillars of smoke.

"That looks bad," I said, not exactly sure if the stretch of trees was Xochi's village or not. Forest fires happen, but I had a feeling this was something worse.

"Maybe they got hit by those giants?" Pierce said. He was thinking the same thing. Maybe we just had gotten used to having bad luck. It just didn't seem likely that there would be a fire in that forest and it *not* be a portent of disaster.

"Or our friend the Silver Eagle. Either way, let's call it in. We might have to burn the last of the fuel in our tanks to reach it quickly, but I bet Captain Brown wants us there yesterday. Crap, Wilson…"

I let the troubling thought die on my lips.

"Wilson probably helped them kick whoever's ass came knocking," Pierce said as we remounted our bikes.

We reached our main element in a blur, but the subsequent trip toward the trouble was a cautious one. We knew hostiles of one sort or another were near Kuauchanko, and there was no telling if they might be lying in wait along the great plains as well. Still, the route proved to be absent of all life. Epasotl kept peering up in the sky, scanning for a helicopter, but none appeared. It was as if we were the last people left in the world.

"You know why, right?" García asked me during a break to refuel. We were pulling security together, with Pierce nearby, perched on a flat stone boulder that rose up from the grass and looking through his scope for trouble.

"Why?" I asked.

"Because there's nobody left."

I looked at my friend and then went back to watching my sector. "What are you talking about?"

"It makes sense if you think about it. Replicator Christmas is comin' up, right? And to take full advantage, Colonel Dietrich needs all the sacrifices he can lay his hands on. The Sugar Skull Gals aren't the type to be domesticated as slaves, so normally they aren't worth the battle. But now… that's changed. He's snatched 'em all, I bet. If they aren't being marched to meet a priest right this minute, it's because they're already dead."

***

We found the first bodies along the edge of the grasslands, where the terrain shifted and the trees began to shade the ground. Bullet wounds and empty casings told us what we'd pretty much all come to accept. Amoloyan had declared war on the Kuauchanejkej.

The bikes had the ability to travel through the forest in a way our Humvees didn't back when we were here the first time, but we stashed our vehicles and went in on foot anyway. The motors would only draw attention if there were still hostiles in the woods.

By the time we reached the forest, those pillars of smoke had grown thin. As we pushed into the woods in search of the magnificent treetop village, the number of dead bodies subsided, then disappeared. But there were still signs of destruction—blood splatter on rocks, fragments of clothing, discarded swords, things like that.

Captain Brown called a halt.

"Why are we stopping?" Xochi asked him in a way that was a lot more princess than it was subordinate officer.

"Because I want to avoid an ambush, and if memory serves, we're coming up on a stretch that would do well for one. You're welcome to scout ahead with Bennett and Pierce, provided you do *not* press on to the village without the rest of us. Clear?"

She gave a quick nod, turned, and then led Pierce and me into the woods. And by *led*, I mean *ran*. Somehow she did it without making a sound. Pierce and I had way too much gear to match her pace without making more noise than we'd like. I gave Pierce a "sorry about her" apologetic smile as we did the best we could.

We pushed into the trees, barely keeping sight of Xochi as she moved through a place so familiar to her that she could probably have made the same time while blindfolded. Eventually it was too much for us and she got out of our sight. I figured we wouldn't catch up to her unless we pushed all the way to Kuauchanko, never mind the captain's orders, but I was wrong.

We found her standing still, her back to us, shoulders slumped and arms down at her sides before a mound of earth and stone.

Pierce and I hastily scanned our surroundings as we slowly moved to join her.

"Xochi," I subvocalized. "You okay?"

She turned with tears in her eyes. It was then that I saw the small wooden cross on top of the mound... and her mother's necklace hanging from it.

"My queen is dead," Xochi said, trembling. But she quickly steeled herself and wiped away the tears. I knew that the last thing she wanted—even if she badly needed it—was a tender moment inside what might still be hostile territory.

Just then something moved in the trees ahead, rustling a branch and sending all of us to the dirt, weapons aimed at the disturbance.

"Dude, do *not* shoot."

I lowered my rifle barrel and rose to a knee. "Wilson?"

"Yeah, dude, it's me. I'm coming out."

The friend who emerged from the trees with his hands up was a sight for sore eyes. Apparently the sight that met *his* eyes was something less familiar.

"What the hell happened to you, brah?" Wilson said to me. "You look like my old man."

"Long story," I said. "What happened here is more important right now."

Wilson shook his head. "Bad juju, man. *Seriously* bad juju."

CHAPTER 42

I expected to have a hard time getting Xochi to come with us back to where Captain Brown and the others were waiting, but she came along the moment I asked. Her compliance came with a certain emotional distance, though, and I knew that her thoughts were far from the rest of us.

Wilson hadn't been roaming out there by himself. He had with him a man named Curly, the Navajo scout Xochi had mentioned on our first visit here, who'd escaped the slaughter of the Buffalo Soldiers and had come to live with the Kuauchanejkej. I had an abundance of questions, about everything, but we needed to stay sharp as we moved through the foliage. The time for a debrief would come soon enough.

The moment we linked back up with the others, Xochi went off to be by herself. I wanted to go after her, but Sanchez made it clear that he wanted me present for the debrief. So I followed Wilson, who nodded and shook hands with the boys, the reunion less happy than it should have been. Everyone could see from the look on the jacked surfer's face that he'd been in a tough spot.

"It's an honor to meet you," Captain Brown told Curly when the two men were standing face to face. "I'd hoped to have done so when we were last through this part of the world. I wish it were under better circumstances."

Curly didn't talk much; he'd barely said a word on the way back, other than to introduce himself. He seemed impressed by the size and stature of our captain, but said only, "A pleasure, sir," and shook the offered hand.

Brown turned to Wilson. "Welcome back, Sergeant. Nice to see you on your feet and in good health." Something about the way he said it must have cut through, because Wilson turned his head and flashed his eyes at me as if to ask whether I'd spilled his secret.

He turned back to face the captain before I could shake my head or otherwise defend myself. "Thank you, Captain. I wish the platoon had been with me when this all went down. Would have been a different story."

"It's a story I need to hear regardless," Brown said. "What happened?"

Wilson's face looked haunted as he recounted his experience. It was nothing we hadn't expected. Dietrich's men had raided the villages, killing anyone they couldn't take captive. The assaulters took losses of their own, but their numbers were overwhelming.

Wilson glanced at Epasotl. "They had Chaneques with them too, except these guys were all kitted up, complete with body armor. And some other indigs, real savage types, like cannibals in some bad movie. There were a few of our guys, too. Americans, I mean. At least they looked American."

"We heard of giants involved in some of the attacks too," Curly added, "though we didn't see them ourselves. If the Quinametzin are allied with the Knife and Thunderbolt people..." he spread his hand helplessly, "this is a grave situation."

Brown explained what we had learned from the outpost, and what lay in store for those taken into captivity.

"We came here to collect an army to put a stop to it," he said. "I'm sorry we didn't arrive earlier."

"There are still fighters enough, sir," Curly said, an eager edge in his voice. He stuck out a lip toward Wilson. "Dressed-in-Stars has been organizing the survivors. Some warriors remain."

Brown looked to Wilson. "What is the state of the warriors? Are they combat effective?"

Wilson blew out his cheeks. "They are, and there's a good number of them. There's a lot of villages that weren't hit, and the warriors are gathering at Kuauchanko, or what's left of it. The problem is, they lack leadership. The queen is dead, the new crown princess was taken, and the queen's other daughters…"

"Didn't survive their abuses," Curly finished for Wilson. "The men want to fight too, after what happened. Even if it means breaking their oaths. I'm sure as hell going to fight. I almost didn't get my wife out in time, and no oath is going to stop me from protecting her. She can't fight, not carrying our child, as much as she wants to, so it is only right that I fight in her place."

"There's another thing, sir," Wilson said. "And… you're not going to believe this, but I saw St. James. Except he was all black-veined, you know, Bennett, like Dee was? But he wasn't trying to eat anyone's effing face. He was still himself, still… lucid. Giving orders. Overseeing the burning."

Sanchez frowned, his arms crossed. "He was infected but hadn't turned." He exchanged a look with Brown.

"Sure, I guess so, I dunno," Wilson said.

Well, so much for the virgins-can't-be-turned theory. Or at least the *only*-virgins-don't-turn theory.

"What's your influence among the indigenous people, Sergeant?" Brown asked Wilson. "You mentioned Dressed-in-Stars stepping up to lead. Can we count on her working with us to provide us with whatever warriors remain?"

Wilson tilted his head noncommittally. "She's been doing a bang-up job, sir, but she lacks legitimacy. They need their queen." He gave me a look. "Or a princess."

Brown picked up on his meaning. "My understanding was the queen disinherited Xochi," he said.

"That won't matter, sir. Not anymore. The warriors want to take the fight to Amoloyan. They'll accept her leadership."

"Sounds like you already have a plan," Sanchez said. It was clear he didn't approve.

"Assaulting Dietrich's main settlement isn't a sound strategy," Brown said. "Not as the primary objective, although it could serve as a diversion. I have another plan." He turned to me. "Nephi, go fetch the chief while I bring Sergeant Wilson and Mr. Curly up to speed on what our intentions are."

"Yes, sir," I said, rising to my feet. I ducked out from beneath the low-hanging branches that had formed a sort of teepee around us as we talked privately. Other than a few security teams, most of the men were resting up after the long, breakneck drive to get this far.

As I set off in search of Xochi, I was surprised to spot the silhouette of the great warbirds tethered in loose groups between a copse of trees. When Greene came running by, I held out a hand to stop him. "What's going on?"

"Sugar Skull Gals just got here for a visit," Greene said, barely slowing down and hustling past me. "Goin' to tell the captain."

I moved toward the birds, following a hunch that I might find Xochi nearby. Sure enough, she was sitting in a small circle with several other women. I cleared my throat to announce myself as I approached.

She looked up at me through red-rimmed eyes.

"Captain Brown asked for you," I said softly.

Dressed-in-Stars had arrived and had been comforting the princess before I came. She shot me a sharp look. She and the other warriors were dressed for battle, and their sugar skull war paint gave them an especially frightening aspect in the streaky light of the forest.

Xochi laid a hand on Dressed-in-Stars's shoulder and forced a smile, then stood to come to my side. We walked slowly toward where the captain waited.

"I'm... so sorry," I said. "About your mother... and sisters. Your people. I have no words."

"There are no words to say," she replied.

"I know things were... not the best between you and the queen when you saw her last."

She stopped short and looked into my eyes. "Do you know why it was so?"

"You never said."

The corner of her lip twitched. "It was because of you. She was angry that I chose you, an Outworlder, and rejected my betrothed."

"Your betro—you were engaged?"

"Of course. I am a princess. It was decided when I was only a child. The marriage would not take place for many years—I am a warrior, no?—but it was decided nonetheless. Only… I learned in time that he was not my destiny. I saw my destiny in a vision. A powerful vision. A *true* vision. I saw you in the spirit before I ever met you in the flesh. I saw what we would accomplish together. I have known since then where my path would lead, but my mother could not accept it. She grew angry when you came. Angry that the vision I had was true."

Xochi laughed sadly. "She was such a stubborn woman. Very, very few Outworlders have been allowed to live among us. For a princess to bind herself to one was… unthinkable."

Xochi looked back to the circle of warriors, who watched us without shame. "Dressed-in-Stars told me my mother's heart softened after I left. She felt… regret. My mother said she wished she and I could be reconciled. Now, that cannot happen. Not in this life." A tear rolled down her cheek and she wiped it away with a sniff. "I knew she would feel that way, in time. She believes in her own visions, after all."

I was dumbfounded, barely able to ask, "What happened… in this… vision?"

Xochi stood on tiptoes to kiss my uninjured cheek. "That is for another time, my love." She bit her lip and gazed at me thoughtfully. "I knew before we met that you would be mine, but I have never thought to ask how *you* feel. For me it is a sure knowledge, but for you… perhaps you are still deciding? Have I been too bold to assume you would want me?"

I stared into her golden eyes and saw strength and sadness, determination and hope. And for perhaps the first time, I saw fear.

I also saw my future.

"No, you haven't been too bold," I said after a long moment, and I took a deep breath. "I don't know if I believe in destiny, but I believe in *us*."

"But do you *want* me?"

"You know I do."

"No, Nephi. I do not. That is why I ask."

I took her hand and held it to my chest.

"Your path is my path. Your heart is my heart. You are my soulmate. Yes, I want you, Xochi. You and only you, forever and always."

***

The royal village of Kuauchanko was barely recognizable. The great and ancient tree Xochi's people referred to reverently as their Beloved Mother, which spread across many acres of the jungle, was blasted and charred. The nest-like homes in its strong high boughs had burned away like so much kindling. The Kuauchanejkej's seat of power for scores of generations was now reduced to smoldering ruin, its treasures ransacked, its peoples carried away to feed the insatiable hunger of Dietrich's artifact. Dozens of warbird had been slaughtered too, and their bloated carcasses stank in the heat as survivors climbed numbly through the wreckage, searching for the curled, blackened corpses of loved ones.

All the softness and warmth in Xochi's soul froze instantly at the sight of the ruined tree, to be replaced by a hardness and chilling cold I'd never witnessed in her before. Her eyes, once the color of warm honey, were now the flint-hard eyes of a bird of prey, and her scar was a livid purple, writhing like a living thing along the side of her face as we held our council of war. It plucked at the corner of her lip gruesomely, giving her a permanent sneer.

"And why should we not burn Amoloyan to the ground and salt the earth with the ashes of its people?" she asked in a voice of regal determination.

"Because, speaking frankly, Princess, an assault on Dietrich's fortress would be suicide," Captain Brown answered calmly. I'm not sure what the rules are for warrant officers who are also the de facto rulers of nations, but the captain apparently felt her place now was leading her people, not serving as his S2, and he deferred to her noble rank.

"Then we will die avenging our people," Dressed-in-Stars cut in.

"You will die, yes," Brown said, "and you may avenge some of your fallen, but you will not save those he took captive, and you will doom the survivors of this attack to death as well. Dietrich will undoubtedly retaliate, and when he does, the Kuauchanejkej will cease to exist. He will make sure of it, and your people will be wiped off the face of this world. He has the manpower, the technology, and now, apparently, he's cut a deal with the giants to the north. We spoke about this before coming to this place, Princess, and you agreed with my plan at the time."

"That was before—" Xochi said.

"Yes, that was before you saw Kuauchanko for yourself. But it changes nothing," Brown said firmly. "You are angry, and understandably so, but you cannot let your thirst for vengeance cloud your vision. You yourself know that in two weeks something will happen with the artifact that will give Dietrich a force multiplier we can't begin to calculate. We have to take out the artifact *now*. That is how we weaken him. Without it he cannot expand his power base. It will give you time to strengthen your own forces and form alliances against him."

"Alliances with whom?" Dressed-in-Stars asked skeptically.

Xochi had already guessed the answer and motioned with a hand toward Epasotl without taking her eyes off the captain.

"With the Chaneques?" Dressed-in-Stars cried. "Never! We would *never* ally with those savages. They aren't even *human*. They would betray us at the first moment it became convenient. They were among those who carried out the slaughter! They cannot be trusted!"

"Those were not *my* people. *My* people do not betray their word once it is given," Epasotl said with force and surprisingly little rancor. "Our oaths are more sacred to us than life itself." It looked like she wanted to say more, probably about how humans were the oath-breakers if I had my guess, but she held her tongue.

For a change.

"I do not see how we could broker such an alliance," Xochi said, with the emotionless practicality of a ruler. "Epasotl certainly cannot be an emissary; she is dishonored and dead to her people."

"There are ways for the dead to speak," Epasotl replied vaguely.

"Cryptic replies are not helpful, Epasotl," Brown said, giving her a frown.

Epasotl sighed. "It is hard to explain, but I can try."

"Later," Brown said. "The specific details of *how* are a future concern. Given the political situation, an alliance against Dietrich would benefit both parties, and I'm confident the two nations will find a way to put aside their differences against a common enemy. But our *immediate* concern is securing the portal at Outpost Kilo-Charlie and using it to destroy the artifact. To that end, a diversionary assault on Amoloyan *will* be launched—but it will be a feint, *not* a suicidal charge for vengeance. There will also be simultaneous assaults on other outposts in the area, but the main thrust will be Kilo-Charlie. To that end, we will be sending a small team to reconnoiter the objective. Meanwhile—"

Captain Brown continued to lay out a plan. By the time he was done, even the most ardent of the Sugar Skull Gals seemed to at least tacitly be nodding their heads. I know I was.

Even better... the band was getting back together.

***

Wilson thumped my shoulder. "I can't get over you looking like an old fart now. Those jaguar mummies sound sick as shit. You get to say goodbye to your girl yet? Come to think of it, you seal the deal yet?"

"None of your business and no... she's been busy."

Wilson laughed. "Don't look so glum, bro. We won't be gone long. Just a couple days for a quick sneak and peek. In and out. It'll be a walk in the park. Just like old times."

"I don't know about that, Sergeant," Pierce interjected. "Old times didn't involve giants and Mouseketeers."

"Mouseketeers?" Wilson asked.

"Creatures like what Dee turned into," I explained. "Children of Mictlāntēcuhtli. Captain started calling the Lord of the Underworld 'Mickey Mouse,' and it kind of went from there."

"Yeah, I get it," Wilson said. "I'm more interested in getting after those Chaneques. Not a good combo, kitties with gear and weapons. I'm hoping to get lucky and dust some of 'em."

"If we're *lucky*, no one will see us and we won't have to fire a shot," Lieutenant Whitlock cut in, joining us and signaling that we were now cleared to move out. "That's our objective. What kind of *scout* goes looking for a fight anyway?"

"This one, sir," Wilson said, thumbing his chest. "What kind of Ranger *doesn't* go looking for a fight?"

"This one," the lieutenant replied. "Least not when my CO tells me to be like Greenpeace and leave no trace."

"Spoilsport," Wilson said.

"That's what us officers are for." Whitlock laughed. "God knows we aren't good for anything else."

"You said it, sir. Not me." Wilson gave Whitlock a fist bump.

Curly, the fifth member of our recon team and our guide, frowned as he watched the two men. Wilson caught his look.

"Don't mind the LT and me," he said. "We go back. If I caught either of these pukes givin' him any disrespect, I'd have their nuts for a necklace."

"You knew each other back in the world?" I asked. This was news to me—news that put me a bit more at ease with our new lieutenant. Whitlock hadn't yet entered my full confidence, no matter what Captain Brown thought about the man.

"Pathfinder School," Whitlock supplied. "Then there was that scuba trip to Maui."

"Way I remember it, we spent more time chasing tail than diving," Wilson said.

"I'm surprised you remember anything, the way you were drinking."

"Cheah, I don't remember much, but I remember Chloe."

"Oh, her. Yeah. She was…" Whitlock trailed off.

"… flexible," Wilson finished.

Whitlock coughed and then grinned at us. "Of course, we were both NCOs at the time, so it was all kosher. Mostly."

"Why'd you go mustang anyway?" Wilson asked.

"Remember Captain Nguyen?"

Wilson gave a low whistle and waggled his eyebrows.

"Had to get around the fraternization rules somehow." Whitlock shrugged. "Heavy price to pay, but it worked."

"No shit? You put a ring on that finger?"

"And a bun in the oven." The lieutenant smiled, but it quickly faded. "'Course, that was two years ago now."

"Maybe to them it was yesterday," Wilson said soberly. "We don't know how this works. We'll get you back to them, Mitch."

Whitlock nodded. "Well, if anyone can make it happen, Captain Amos Brown can. I've seen that man work miracles. Speaking of making things happen…?"

Wilson nodded and turned to us. "The bikes ready?"

"Yes, Sergeant," Pierce answered. "Ready to rock and roll."

"My man," Wilson said, flashing him a shaka sign. He clapped his hands and turned to Whitlock. "All right then. I think we're good to go, sir. We got beans, bullets, and rad-looking *motorcycles*."

"Roger that," Whitlock said. "Let's mount up, gentlemen."

I gave a last look back at Kuauchanko as we started up the engines, hoping to catch a glimpse of Xochi, but to no avail. Then we were off, racing into the jungle.

CHAPTER 43

"I don't see how we're supposed to assault that," I said, handing the spotting scope to Pierce.

He gazed through the glass for a minute, chewing on his mustache thoughtfully. "Take out the machine gun towers with AT4s and blow a hole through the wire with forty mike-mike would be my guess."

"There'd be a lot of collateral damage," I said. "They have the prisoners penned up along the perimeter. It's a human shield."

"Not if we hit the southeast corner. That's just an equipment yard."

"There's still the machine guns."

Pierce sniffed and tugged on his nose to dislodge whatever was in there. "Can't be helped. People are going to die, Bennett. Hate to break it to ya."

His words sounded harsh, but I knew he didn't like it any more than I did. It wasn't our call anyway. Captain Brown would define the tactics of storming the outpost, he and the senior NCOs. I knew they wouldn't waste innocent lives needlessly, but they wouldn't risk *our* lives by being squeamish about collateral damage either. And it wasn't going to be easy. Outpost Kilo-Charlie wasn't as big as Hotel-Romeo, but it was well fortified.

The outpost sat on a rise in the jungle, and like Hotel-Romeo, it had been built right smack in the middle of an ancient temple complex. About the only thing we had going for us was that the kill zone around the perimeter had become overgrown, so we could get closer without being seen. In fact, Pierce and I were only three hundred yards from the eastern side, close enough to catch a good whiff of the human misery every time the wind shifted. Still, it'd taken us two hours to crawl to our position, and any attackers would have to do the same, because the whole area leading to the outpost was one big booby trap. We'd already counted a dozen punji pits and one tripwire leading to a claymore mine.

"Wish we could get a better look inside the wire," Pierce said. "Hard to recon a place from downhill. You any good at climbing trees?"

I glanced back behind us. The nearest trees were about two hundred yards to our rear.

"With the elevation of the outpost, I don't know if we'd have much of a better view, and no, I'm not."

"So what do we got? Three machine gun towers on this side, the same on the other, two rows of triple-stacked concertina with a ditch in the middle, and about a million places to step into a hole full of sharp spikes or get blown up."

"Don't forget the giants," I said. I'd taken back the scope and was watching a patrol of the lumbering creatures coming over the lip of the rise, walking the perimeter.

"Yeah. How could I? Awesome. At least these assholes aren't friends with Batman."

"That we know of," I said. "Guess we should count our blessings."

"You know what I don't figure?"

"What's that?"

"All these people penned up here, you can smell 'em from forever. Why aren't the Mouseketeers flocking to this place like flies on shit?"

It was a good question. I frowned and gave a thoughtful shrug.

"What if they're allies?" Pierce asked.

"You're thinking about what Wilson said about St. James."

"Yeah. If they're not totally mindless feeding machines, then they could make a deal, couldn't they? Or maybe the priests can control them or something. These priests, they've all gotta be mixed up with Mickey Mouse anyway, right? Why not use his kids as foot soldiers or scouts or whatever?"

"Maybe," I said. If the Children could be controlled, organized, *weaponized*, we'd be in a world of hurt. "But we haven't seen any evidence of that. From all we've seen, the Children just wander around the jungle in packs, eating people. If they were an *asset*, you'd think we'd know about it by now. I mean, we covered a lot of ground working for Dietrich and never saw anything like that."

"Because he didn't *want* us to see it," Pierce said. "Like he didn't want us to know about the artifact devouring souls."

My radio clicked three times, and I keyed it twice in reply. That would be Lieutenant Whitlock checking in. After such a long stretch of our only officer being Captain Brown, it almost felt odd to work like this again.

I glanced at the sun. We had a few hours until dusk.

"Point taken," I agreed. "Captain will be interested in your theory, if he hasn't thought of it already."

"Bet he has."

"Yeah, probably." I grinned. "Or Chris Claremont did. *X-Men* issue number zombie-armies-from-hell."

We finished up our observation, sketching out everything we saw and taking notes of troop and prisoner concentrations, patrol patterns, whatever might make our next task easier. Then we made the long, patient crawl back to the others.

***

"These sketches are really good," Lieutenant Whitlock said in hushed tones from under his poncho. Faint red light leaked from beneath the poncho's edges.

"Thank you, sir," Pierce muttered.

Whitlock killed the light and emerged from under his cover. "They're art, really. You should be an architect."

It was dark, the jungle canopy blotting out even the stars, and I could barely make out Pierce and him as dark shapes. Shadow on shadow. I sat leaning against a tree, hoping for a little sleep to find me before it was my turn to pull security. They kept their voices low, almost subvocalizing.

"I'll think about it, sir. GI Bill can put me through school." Pierce paused. "If we can get back home."

"Don't give up hope." Whitlock laid his hand on Pierce's shoulder. "We'll get back."

I heard a faint shuffling in the undergrowth. That had to be Wilson, because Curly was dead silent when he moved. It was unnatural.

"Sir," Wilson hissed. "Something's out there. Multiple somethings. Couldn't get a good look, but whoever or whatever they are, they're not friendly. We're being stalked."

"Roger," Whitlock murmured. "Get everyone ready. No firearms if we can help it. Use your knives. We need to maintain noise discipline if we can."

Wilson confirmed and then moved over to me. "You hear the LT?"

I flipped down my nods as I gave him a thumbs-up. Wilson had his IR illuminator on, and it gave enough light to see his hulking form clearly in front of us. He scowled under his night-vision goggles, making him look like some kind of froggy beast man, especially with his non-regulation bushy beard.

"Curly has the twelve o'clock and I've got six," Wilson said. "Pierce, you take three, and Bennett, I want you on nine."

"And the LT?" I asked. Whitlock was proving himself to be likeable, but I still couldn't bring myself to fully trust him. The guy had straight-up said he'd be happy to use "bad guy souls" to feed the machine. Further, from everything I gathered his island boy allies hadn't made attempts to get home. Now he was being Mr. Encouragement about it, telling Pierce not to lose faith.

It all felt... I dunno... staged, I guess. A little phony.

But he was an officer, and Captain Brown had put him in command of our recon team. Wilson gave me the reminder I probably deserved.

"He'll be wherever he needs to be. Now get moving."

I gave another thumbs-up and slipped into position as silently as possible. Despite my efforts it sounded to me like I was making an unholy racket, but everything sounds louder at night. At least the insects and tree frogs were active enough to give us some auditory cover.

I activated my IR illuminator and then took a knee behind a clump of ferns as I drew my knife, balancing it lightly in my hand. The six-inch hawksbill-shaped blade I'd been issued as part of the standard set of kit we'd received in Amoloyan was a fine weapon, but at the moment I wished I had something bigger, a *lot* bigger. Like the saber I'd lost when Milo and his gang of psychopaths threw all our old gear in the pit.

I thought again about the encounter with Milo, and Chief Baker's story about that Chaneque team being a failed experiment, its members gone rogue. In hindsight, that was obviously all a lie. Probably should have seen it for the lie it was at the time, too. I think we were all just so relieved to see friendly faces—not just humans, but *Americans*—that we weren't thinking clearly.

And that pit. It was probably a collection point for "samples" for the soul-eating artifact.

A tap on my shoulder nearly sent me jumping out of my skin. Taking a deep breath to calm my nerves, I turned my head to see Whitlock beside me. The man moved as quietly as Curly. It was hella creepy. He held up two fingers to his nods and then flashed a hand with three fingers extended, holding down his pinky with his thumb, before holding his hand in an inverted finger gun and sweeping it in an arc around us. I nodded, and he shot me a thumbs-up before moving off behind me.

So, six bad guys. At least six that he knew about anyway. Coming from all directions. My mouth was dry, and I could hear my heart beating in my ears. Something with too many legs crawled across the back of my neck and I resisted the urge to slap it. It was a warm night, but I shivered involuntarily.

And I needed to take a leak.

A branch snapped somewhere behind me and I forced myself to keep looking forward, scanning my sector. I had to trust my teammates had my back. The tree frogs went silent, and I heard a wheezing rasp of breath ahead of me.

I adjusted my sweaty grip on the knife. Six inches of steel felt *seriously* puny at a time like this, no matter how sharp, and I crouched lower in the ferns, willing myself to be invisible.

The smell came ahead of the visuals, and when the zombie materialized in front of me, she was only two paces away. I had no idea how she'd gotten so close. She loomed in my vision, washed out by the IR illumination. She was frighteningly hideous, dressed in a tattered cloth wrap skirt and naked from the waist up. Her distended belly and pendulous, sagging breasts were covered in tattoos. Half her face was corrupted with decay, but her good eye glowed malevolently in the green-on-green of my nods. She wore a battered feathered headdress and sugar skull war paint and opened her mouth in a tortured, silent scream that exposed rotted teeth filed into points as she leapt at me, swinging her macuahuitl.

I threw myself backwards, landing on my butt as the obsidian blades whistled inches from my throat. With shocking speed, she reversed the arc of her strike into a diagonal slash meant to cleave me from shoulder to hip. I rolled clear and got my feet under me, springing up and to the side as another slash aimed to spill my guts. She was shorter than me, but not by much—unusually tall for her tribe, and powerfully built. A corner of my mind wondered who she'd been and if Xochi had known her. It was a fleeting thought as she brought her war club up in a sweep that nearly caught me in the groin. Then she lunged and thrust, hitting my chest plate in a powerful blow that left me breathless as my back slammed against a tree.

Holy crap, she was *strong*.

She pressed the attack, jabbing my chest plate again, hard, and then held a fist in my face and blew into it. A fine, choking dust that smelled of sulfur and death filled my mouth and nose.

Swiftly withdrawing a pace, she swept her war club backhanded at me. Gagging and sneezing, I stepped into the attack, circling and grabbing at her wrist with my free hand, only to have the putrid flesh slough away in my grip.

I managed a couple quick kidney strikes with my knife before she pirouetted and slammed my face with the hilt of her macuahuitl. Blood erupted from my nose, and I felt several stitches in my cheek tear. The blow knocked my nods painfully off their mount, and I could feel my left eye swelling closed.

I blindly surged forward, tackling her, and we fell in a tangle of limbs, rolling along the ground. I hooked my legs around her hips and struck repeatedly with my knife. A skeletal hand with ragged nails closed around my throat, and she slammed her hilt against my side, hitting my unprotected ribs. I felt a searing pain and jammed my knife into her neck up to the hilt as I gasped for breath.

"Just… die!" I choked, twisting the blade.

I heard her jaws snapping and reared my head back, then gave her a head butt that ignited fireworks in the backs of my eyes. Ripping my knife free of the sucking flesh, I stabbed again, aiming for the dark, blurry shape that was her head. Steel scraped bone as I drove my blade as hard as I could into her ear. She bucked under me, and finally, rancid breath escaped her lips in a death rattle.

I rolled weakly off the twitching corpse and lay on my back, sucking in air and staring up into the blackness. Breathing was painful; I was pretty sure she'd cracked at least one rib. A strange coldness radiated out from my core and flowed into my limbs and face.

A beefy shape bent over me, and I felt a large hand on my shoulder.

"You alive, bro?" I heard Wilson's voice ask.

"I think so," I croaked. "Bitch wouldn't die."

Wilson laughed. "Swearing doesn't suit you, man. Don't start. Shit, your face is a mess. Here, lemme fix your nose."

I felt fingers feeling gently alongside my crushed nose, and then Wilson flexed his hands and a sudden searing, eye-watering pain hit me like a freight train.

"What the hell! You didn't warn me."

"No point," Wilson said, taking my hand and helping me to my feet. I wavered, and he steadied me.

"Can you stand?" he asked.

"Think so. I got a couple bruised ribs. Maybe cracked even. She blew something in my face. Some kinda dust. Tastes like rotten eggs and roadkill. I feel sick." I tried to wipe the blood off my tender face with my sleeve.

I could sense Wilson staring at me. His breathing grew heavy.

"Fuuuuck," he said slowly.

Wilson flashed his red light at my face.

"What's wrong?"

"Dude, your face…"

"You're starting to freak me out, Sergeant."

"Bennett, bro, you got all these black, spidery veins growing around your eyes and up and down your face and neck. Hate to say it, but it's just like Dee. Lemme see your arm." He grabbed a hand and pushed up my sleeve. "Dammit, there too."

I felt my heart stop. Was I *infected*?

Then I heard a knife slipping out of a sheath, and I stepped back, holding my hands up. "Whoa, whoa! I'm not going to eat your face."

"You're *turning*, man," Wilson said softly. "Just like Dee. I'll make it quick."

"What's going on?" Whitlock asked from somewhere in the darkness.

"Bennett's changing into one of those things that just attacked us," Wilson answered, closing on me.

I retreated another pace. Wilson took a matching step.

"I'm sorry, Nephi, I don't want to do this—you're my bro—but I have to, man." His voice wavered. "You know I do. I'm sorry, man. I'd want you to do the same if it happened to me. That's what bros do. You… you won't feel a thing. Promise."

"Sergeant Wilson," Whitlock snapped. "Put the knife away."

"Sergeant, please." It was Pierce's voice, moving between me and Wilson. "We don't know he'll turn. We've seen it before. *You've* seen it. Remember? You said Sergeant St. James was like this too."

"If he needs to be dealt with, that's my job, David, not yours," Whitlock said, more gently this time.

"*Dealt with*, sir?" I protested. "All due respect, I don't need to be *dealt* with. I'm fine." I leaned past Pierce to where I sensed Wilson was standing. "It's *me*, Wilson. I'm still *me*. I'm okay. Swear to God. Look at my eyes."

I heard metal clearing Kydex and a hammer being cocked. I had a feeling it was being aimed at me, not Wilson.

"Okay," Wilson said after a long moment, retreating, his voice a mixture of relief that Whitlock had taken the responsibility and suspicion that I was just trying to find a way to bite them all to death. "All right."

"Bennett, you understand that we can't take any chances," Whitlock said. "Secure him, Specialist."

"Sir?" Pierce said.

"Disarm him and tie him up. At least for the night. The captain can decide what to do with him when we get back."

"*Tie* me—sir, I'm *fine!*" I protested, putting my rifle down to show that I had full functionality, comprehension, and more importantly, no desire to harm my friends.

"Whatever you are, you're not 'fine,' Corporal Bennett. You're infected, and we can't take the risk. Let the specialist secure you."

I set down my sidearm and the claw knife I'd taken from the Chaneque who'd tried to knife me next to the rifle to create a pile of weapons on the ground. My primary was still in the zombie's skull.

Pierce moved behind me and flexi-cuffed my wrists. "Sorry, man," he mumbled.

"I'm *fine*," I snapped.

The truth was, I understood that the lieutenant was taking a sensible precaution. But it made me furious all the same. Like I wanted to scratch out his eyes and tear his throat out with my teeth.

The thought made me pause. *I* didn't want to do that. I really didn't. But something *inside* me… did.

I swallowed hard and let Pierce sit me down against a tree.

So maybe I wasn't fine.

And I still had to take a leak.

CHAPTER 44

"Will he turn?" Captain Brown asked.

Friar Bastía was among the survivors who had assembled at the ruins of Kuauchanko. It was he who the natives looked to when it came to my condition. The friar carefully examined my face, sorrow fully evident in his eyes, and then… relief.

"Not if his will is strong. No, I don't expect he'll turn. It's all in the willpower of the individual to resist. Willpower, and faith."

Xochi knelt by my side and put a hand on my shoulder. Whitlock had released my wrists for the ride back to Kuauchanko, but I had been zip-tied again as soon as we got within walking distance of the village. And now Captain Brown had set a guard on me: Lawrence. I don't think he liked it any more than I did.

"I've been studying the Children of Mictlāntēcuhtli for many years, daughter," the friar said, gently patting Xochi's arm to comfort the princess. Her distress was evident. I doubted this was how her vision had gone. "To be infected and not turn—it has happened before among your own people, more times than you might think. The last time… oh, you must have been only a child." He paused, considering his words, and seemed hesitant to continue. Eventually he shrugged. "Those who have become infected and do not turn choose to live apart, in their own community. But they are still part of my flock, and I watch over them."

"You keep a secret settlement of infected?" Xochi asked, narrowing her eyes.

"A very small community, yes, far from here." He waved his hand dismissively. "But not secret. Your mother knew. The practice predates my time with you."

"Like lepers," Brown said.

"I suppose so, yes." Bastía chuckled. "Something like that. They are harmless."

"Nothing harmless about murderous psychopaths," Sanchez said flatly. "And at best that's what Bennett will become."

I tried not to glare at Sanchez. Sitting, bound like a criminal, with everyone hovering over me and talking like I wasn't *right there* was annoying me. Probably more than it should have. Even Xochi's hand on my shoulder was annoying me. I swallowed my rancor like bile and forced myself to look at her, trying hard to think of what she meant to me.

"Well, now, that's a question of his character." Bastía held out both hands, like he was weighing something in the balance. "Does he incline to evil, or to good? Take away the veneer of civilization and a man will show his true nature, no? The infection strips away inhibitions. It isn't like rabies, my son. It's... think of it as a test of the soul. Even some of those who are initially violent learn to live in peace through a life dedicated to meditation and prayer."

"And those who *don't* learn to 'live in peace'?" Sanchez asked.

The friar frowned. "Unless they are stopped... they wander off to join the Children."

"Can it be cured?" Brown asked. "I don't mean just learning to live with it—I mean a full-on cure."

"No, *señor*. There is no cure that I know of. Your mention of leprosy is apt. This condition is similar in many ways. Its victims suffer physical deterioration, and I'm afraid it's fatal—eventually."

This was just getting better and better.

Xochi gave me a sad smile and shook her head as if she knew something the friar didn't. Something inside me wanted to slap that smile right off her face, but I killed the impulse. Smothered it. Ground it down. I leaned my head against her shoulder instead and willed myself to allow her to comfort me.

"We know they don't always turn right away," Brown said. "How long before we'll know if he's a danger?"

"I cannot say." Bastía shook his head. "But if one is going to become a Child, it tends to happen rather quickly in my experience. Before sundown anyway. Those who survive longer will sometimes wander to me in their condition to find solace."

"You're sure of this?" Brown asked. "I can't have a ticking time bomb walking around. The first man we lost to this… curse, acquired strength sufficient to break the bonds we have on Nephi."

"As sure as I can be, given the circumstances," Bastía insisted.

The captain frowned deeply and folded his arms. "We'll wait until morning, just to be safe. If he looks all right, I'd like to ask you to take him to your community."

"No!" Xochi cried, standing quickly. "Sir, no! You *cannot* send him away."

"You forget yourself, Chief." Brown leaned over her. "I know you have feelings for him, but—"

"That is *not* why I protest." She folded her arms and glared up at him. "What I desire does not matter. You cannot send him away. I forbid it. We *need* him."

"You forbid it?" Brown arched an eyebrow. "You'd better explain yourself, Princess, and quickly."

Whatever it was she wanted to say, it was clear she was unwilling to say it in front of all of us. Brown considered the small woman standing defiantly in front of him for a long moment. Sanchez looked like he had indigestion. Bastía's eyes twinkled with amusement.

"Walk with me," Brown said curtly.

Sanchez snorted after they left. "She has balls, I'll give her that much."

"Takes after her mother." The friar chuckled as he knelt down in front of me. "And you, my son, how are you faring?"

I sighed deeply, pushing down the incoherent rage that clawed at my belly. "I feel—like I'm fighting a battle with myself."

"Not with yourself," he replied gently. "But yes, you are fighting a battle. A war, even. A war of wills. A war you cannot win on your own. Who do you think will prevail?"

"I—I don't know," I whispered, my voice suddenly trembling. "I'm… afraid."

"Who is the source of fear, my son? And who told us to 'fear not'?"

I took that as a rhetorical question and nodded slowly that I understood him.

"Are you a praying man?" he asked.

"Yes, sometimes. I mean, I was," I admitted. "But not now as often as I should."

"May I pray with you?"

"I don't know your prayers."

"There are many forms of prayer, my son. Teach me yours." He motioned to Sanchez. "Will you join us, Sergeant?"

To my utter and complete surprise, the hardened old killer nodded gravely and knelt beside us, crossing himself.

"It's been a long time, Father," Sanchez grunted. "I'm rusty."

"A rusty prayer is the most beautiful to God's ears," the friar said.

***

Friar Bastía remained with me throughout the day. As sunset approached, a small crowd formed a vigil of sorts. It was deeply moving to be surrounded by so many strangers and friends. Throughout the day men like García and Pierce had taken time out from their preparations to pray with the friar and me, or if they weren't of a praying sort, like Wilson and Takahashi, to at least speak with me quietly and give encouragement. The outpouring of support strengthened my soul and helped to drive the malignant force that possessed me into the shadows. It wasn't vanquished—Bastía said it would be like a thorn in my side for as long as I lived, however short that might be—but I felt that it was in retreat, and I thought I was learning to master it.

Captain Brown had come to kneel by my side shortly before the vigil formed. He removed the old cavalry Stetson he always wore and held it in his lap. I knew he was a praying man if anyone was.

Although he kept his religion close to his chest, I had seen him alone in the wolf gray of dawn often enough, his great bald head bowed reverently. He never made a spectacle of it; he simply quietly withdrew a distance while most of us were still sleeping, and knelt in the dew silently.

The prayer he prayed for me that evening broke my heart with its passion and eloquence as his rich basso profondo voice poured over me. I knew he cared about his men, but I never knew he cared so much about *me*, as an individual. The revelation that he must feel equally deeply about *each* of us was sobering—as was the realization of how heavy each of our brothers' deaths must weigh on his soul. He carried a heavier burden than I ever suspected, and my respect for the man grew a hundredfold.

Greene was my guard at the time, and after the prayers, the captain sent him away so we could be alone.

"I will give you two some space as well," Bastía said. "I am old, and my knees aren't what they once were. I think I'll take a walk."

"Thank you… Father," I sniffed. "For staying with me."

"But of course, my son. It is not only my duty, but my pleasure. And… in your case… my great honor." I gave him a puzzled look, but he only smiled cherubically in reply before turning to Brown. "Your faith is humbling, Captain. As is your eloquence. You are a poet-warrior in the best of the tradition."

"I am a simple man, doing the best he can."

"All men should so aspire," the friar said, creakily rising to his feet. "God be with you both."

"And with you," the captain said. He watched Bastía shuffle off for a long moment and then turned to me. "I had a long discussion with Xochi. I understand she's told you some of what she's seen in her vision."

I wasn't sure where the captain was going with this. "Yes, sir. But very little."

"It's hers to share with you, and what she told me she shared in confidence. Suffice it to say she's seen things that have convinced me to not send you away."

"Assuming I don't turn," I pointed out quietly.

"There's no risk of that. You've a part to play in what will happen that precludes it. She convinced me of this."

I felt a weight fall away from my heart. "You... believe her vision, sir?"

"I believe she has seen the future, yes. Shadows of what will be. I believe in predestination—fate, destiny, call it what you will. I questioned why we came here for a long time. Questioned how it fit into God's plan for each of us, but I question no longer." He paused and cracked a brief smile, then tapped the side of his head. "It's not all *X-Men* comics up here. I can tell you that she saw that this would happen." He motioned to my face. "Or at least suspected it. That you'd be cursed and that you'd overcome it. She saw many other things, things that convinced me not only that her vision was true, but that it was a divine message, and a warning."

I felt a great relief, but I had so many questions, none of which the captain was likely to know the answer to... or would be willing to share even if he did. He was obviously choosing his words carefully. Those questions remained, though, and they churned in my mind like a boiling ocean.

Brown saw my distress and grasped my shoulder firmly.

"Be at peace, trooper," he said, gazing into my eyes. "'Sufficient unto the day is the evil thereof.' And you've experienced enough evil for one day. Rest your mind. The curse is strong, but you're stronger. You're a good man, a *righteous* man. I've known you long enough and seen enough to know that without a doubt. This is only a test, a purifying fire, and you'll emerge stronger for it."

I thanked him as he left, wondering what terrible task fate had in store for me that required this crucible. The demon inside me stirred, fighting against the chains I'd been forging all day.

***

Friar Bastía was with me as the black sun sank low in the sky and the vigil gathered. Most were there to hope and pray, but some, I didn't doubt, were hoping for a spectacle. Particularly some of them named Joe Stanley. He leered at me from the background, no doubt anticipating a transformation that would result in a bullet to my brain. I wasn't planning on giving him the satisfaction. I didn't understand why he hated me, but the expression on his face offered little doubt.

As the sun fell behind the trees and the shadows deepened, I began to feel feverish. The zip ties chafed at my wrists. My ribs ached with each labored breath I took, and my vision tunneled. Sweat poured down my face, stinging my wounds. My eyes were burning. It felt like in Basic, in the gas chamber, but if you were running a hundred-and-four-degree fever and suffering the worst flu imaginable at the same time. My bowels churned and turned to liquid, and I shifted to my knees, afraid I'd lose control and make an embarrassment of myself. As if that even mattered right now. Soiling myself was the least of my concerns.

The demon writhed in my guts and screamed in my mind. It raged against me and begged to be set free, promising relief from the pain one moment, threatening tortures I'd never contemplated the next. The sky grew red as blood, and I saw shades of the dead before my eyes. All the people we'd lost. All the people we'd killed. They drifted through the crowd, watching me intently. Captain had said I wouldn't succumb, I wouldn't turn, that Xochi had foreseen it... but I doubted. I was afraid. I felt my will battered like a sea wall in a hurricane, and I felt the cracks forming in my resolve.

It would be so, *so* easy to give in. It would be such sweet solace. All I had to do was say yes. Give my soul over to the dark.

One word and it would be over.

"Look!" someone cried. The voice was indistinct and far off, as if coming from another world. "His eyes are changing!"

I had entirely forgotten that there were others around me, watching.

A figure stood over me. Loomed. It might have been Friar Bastía. I didn't know. I didn't care. Someone was chanting in Latin. Droplets of water struck me, searing my flesh like acid.

And then my entire world coalesced into a single face. A graceful face, bearing a terrible scar, but like Kintsugi pottery, all the more beautiful for it. Eyes glowing like burnished gold, boring into my soul.

Delicate, strong hands caressed my face. The scent of her breath filled me. The warmth of her touch seeped through me. I stopped shivering and was suddenly still. Transfixed.

The demon howled in rage.

Her lips moved, forming words, and I strained to hear them as the chasm that separated us began to shrink. She was begging me to stop fighting and let go—not to surrender to the darkness, but to give myself up to the light.

And then I understood. I understood what Friar Bastía had been trying to teach me all day. I understood with clarity that while a sufficiently powerful will could prevent the demon from consuming one entirely, from enacting its transformation of the one possessed into a ravenous, deathless slave, it would corrupt the soul all the same. Only by allowing a greater will to intervene could the demon be permanently subdued.

And so... I had to let go. I wasn't strong enough. I could never be. No one could. The fight must be surrendered to a true champion.

After all, I was only human.

And so, I prayed.

And I let go.

And the three simple words that had the power to calm the storm ravaging the Sea of Galilee flowed through my soul.

And there was a great calm.

That's all. No climactic battle. No thunderous victory. No tortured screams as the demon was fettered and subdued.

Simply... calm.

Xochi pressed her face to mine, and I tasted her tears. Someone cut my restraints, and I enfolded her into my embrace. We knelt together for several minutes in silence. Others may have been speaking. I don't know. She was my entire world.

And then she held me at arm's length.

"I love you," she said.

"I love you too," I replied.

"But I cannot be so close to you any longer." She wrinkled her nose. "You smell terrible."

CHAPTER 45

"I don't need a babysitter. I'm just taking a bath," I complained. A *real* bath. The Kuauchanejkej bathhouse ritual wasn't going to cut it this time.

"Buddy system," Epasotl said. "Little Kahuna's orders."

"Okay, but why are *you* my buddy? Why can't it be—I don't know—a *male*?"

"Because I promised Little Kahuna I would kill you without hesitation if you get jumpy."

"Of course you did." I started stripping my gear and laying it beside the wide stream. "I'm not going to get 'jumpy.'"

She shrugged. "Little Kahuna said to keep an eye on you. Real close."

"What did *Big* Kahuna say?"

"Little Kahuna didn't ask."

I sighed and pulled off my blouse and shirt. Xochi was right: I stank. My clothes and gear were crusty with blood and dirt, and I think I still had pieces of zombie chick in my hair. It was going to take forever to clean everything.

I touched the black spiderweb of veins on my chest and grimaced. The entire left side of my torso was one massive purple and green bruise. Taking off my pants revealed more thick black veins running down my legs—and more bruises. Epasotl stared at me dispassionately as I stood there in my boxers.

"A little privacy, at least until I get into the water?" I asked.

"No can do." She pointed to her eyes and then to me. "Orders are orders. Besides, there may be ahuizotls in the water. Not safe. Buddy system."

I looked at the water warily. "You're not serious, right? Do they really have ahuizotls in this stream?"

"Could be more than one. Only one way to find out. Take off your big boy pants and see."

"That's not how the expression goes. And I'm keeping my boxers on, thanks."

I put a toe in the water and then took a deep breath before wading all the way in. The water was a little on the cool side, which felt good in the heat and humidity. But mostly, it felt good to *wash*. Someone from the village had supplied me with some kind of soap, and I sang a catchy tune that'd been all over the radio as I lathered up.

"Who is this woman in your song that drives you crazy such that you cannot help yourself?" Epasotl asked. "Are you singing of Xochi?"

"No. I'm singing the song of my people."

"Is it an ancient mating song?"

"Oh, sure. Very traditional. Billboard Top 100 in fact." I rinsed off and splashed back out of the stream. "Come on, help me wash my kit. I'll teach you the words."

We got to work doing the laundry, side by side, and Epasotl sniffed at me.

"You still stink," she said, wrinkling her flat, feline nose.

"Really?" I sniffed at myself. "Smells okay to me. That soap even has a nice scent to it, like flowers. I almost feel pretty."

"I doubt a human would notice, but to me you smell of death and corruption."

"Fantastic. Well, at least I don't feel like it anymore. I'm tired and achy, and of course my nose feels like pulp, and my ribs hurt every time I inhale, but let me tell you... compared to yesterday, I feel *great*. Near the end there it got brutal."

"It is good the old fat man cast a spell on you. Your eyes were changing quickly. I was about to kill you."

"It wasn't a spell."

"It looked like a spell. He was moving his hands and chanting and flicking magic water on you to summon your god. It burned your skin."

I touched the blisters on my face gingerly. I'd forgotten to include that in my catalog of aches and pains, but they hurt too.

"Perhaps he will teach me his magic," she continued cheerfully. "Do you think he would? I would like to be able to summon a god. That would be rad."

"That's… not how it works. You can't *summon* God, and the friar wasn't casting a spell. He doesn't use magic. And *anyway*, that's not what saved me. It might have helped. I don't know."

"Then what saved you?" she asked.

I thought about my answer for a long moment before speaking. "Humility, I guess. And faith… but mostly humility, I think. I had to admit I couldn't fight it on my own. I wasn't strong enough."

Epasotl made a face. "My gods do not favor the weak."

"Your gods don't seem very nice, either."

"No, they are not 'nice.' We do what we can to appease them, but otherwise we hope they take no notice of us. We are no more than ants to them. It is unwise to attract their attention."

"Which we're about to do in a very big way soon." I puffed out my cheeks. Tomorrow we would hit Outpost Kilo-Charlie.

"Yes, we will all die very soon," Epasotl said proudly. "Probably in the most horrible ways imaginable. To assault the Underworld and give battle to Broken Face is totally psycho. Brave, yes, but psycho." She looked around the ruined village and scowled. "It would go better for us if we made a few sacrifices first. Preferably a warrior or two, but even an old man or some children would work. Young ones. You would not even have to eat their hearts. I would do that for you, since you are squeamish about such things."

"We're not sacrificing anyone," I said firmly.

"I know." She sighed in wistful resignation. "I already asked Little Kahuna. I even offered myself as a sacrifice, but he is stubborn."

"Of course you did." I ruffled her hair playfully. "I forgot I was talking to Miss Walking Death Wish."

"I am prepared to give my account to the Hummingbird of the South," she said. She patted her haversack and gave me her unsettling version of a smile. "Though I have arranged some surprises."

"Oh yeah? What've you got cooked up?"

"Look and see."

I bent forward to peer into her haversack, and she pounced forward to vigorously tousle my hair in return.

"Psych!" she exclaimed with a hissing staccato laugh. "Finally got you."

I laughed. "Got me good."

"But seriously, I have made elixirs and potions. Many for me. Some for you."

"Oh, awesome, I think. Er… what's in them?"

"Ask me questions, I tell you lies," she said.

I corrected her misquote, and she rolled her eyes.

"Whatever," she said. "Is same. You do not want to know the ingredients because you are, 'Ooh, yuck, menstrual blood.' Bah!" She jabbed my chest with a finger. "But you *will* drink when I tell you."

"Yes, ma'am."

"Do not *ma'am* me. I work for a living." She twitched her ears. "Ah, Wilson comes," she said. "Good. I have things to do. He can watch you."

"How's it hanging?" Wilson asked us as he approached.

"Low and to the left," Epasotl replied, throwing him a lazy shaka as she walked off. "You watch Ben-Ette. If he gets jumpy, kill him."

"I'm not going to get *jumpy*," I said irritably. "And I don't need a babysitter, Wilson."

"Sanchez says you do," Wilson said. "Man, you look like absolute shit. You smell pretty, though."

"I do, don't I?" I went back to wringing out my stuff and then confessed something that had been on my mind. "You know, it's gonna be kinda hard to run an op with everyone watching me out of the corner of their eye."

"I'm sure if you can go a day not eating anyone's face, people will relax a little. For now, 'Toon Daddy figures better safe than sorry." He scratched at his beard uncomfortably. "Listen… about what happened out there…"

"It's fine," I said. It wasn't, though. Wilson was supposed to be my friend.

"No. It's not. Bros don't kill bros. I didn't know it was possible to survive… that." He gestured to my spider-veined body. "I thought I was doing you a solid. After watching what happened to Dee… I thought it was a mercy, you know? But I was wrong, and I'm sorry."

I could see that he meant it. And when I told him I forgave him, I meant that too.

"So, what did I miss?" I asked.

"We stage at zero dark thirty. Captain wants us in position and ready to attack at the ass crack of dawn. We've collected all the AT4s together and will hit the towers first, then blast the wire with grenades and barrel in guns blazing with the FAVs to make a breach. Then the SSGs and the male auxiliaries will flood the outpost and we'll secure the portal while they deal with the prisoners and mop up guards."

"Dead simple and incredibly violent," I said. The captain had named us dragoons, but he was about to use us like Rangers. "About what Pierce and I expected. Captain say where he wants us?"

"Part of why I came by, because you have the best job of all. You'll go in with Daddy and Little Miss Kitty before the attack and secure a tower so you can provide overwatch."

"You mean the towers you'll be hitting with eighty-four-millimeter HEAT rounds," I said dryly.

"Chill. They won't target *your* tower, obviously."

"Obviously."

"Don't sweat it, man. We've been over this at least a dozen times while you were busy not turning into a face-eater and everything. Anyway, Sanchez will get you in position and then pull back to join the main assault, so it'll just be you and Pierce up there. Think you can handle it?"

"If we can get in, we'll be fine," I said. "Captain wouldn't put us up there if he didn't think we could handle it."

"Point taken. I guess you're all grown up now. Balls finally dropped and everything. Seems like yesterday you were a PFC hunting around the motor pool for blinker fluid and asking the supply sergeant for chem light batteries."

"Hey, I never fell for that chem light battery crap. That was Arizona."

"Heh, yeah. Good kid. He drove me crazy, but I miss him."

"Me too. I miss a lot of people."

"Too many." Wilson frowned. "And maybe more tomorrow. Listen, bro. If my ticket gets punched, I just want you to know… you know."

"Same for me," I said solemnly.

"Good." He squared his massive shoulders and sniffed. "Dusty out today, ain't it? Come on. We got a shit ton of work to do."

CHAPTER 46

If the gear we'd received courtesy of Dietrich and the artifact had felt off to me before, it had become repellent after my... ordeal. Fortunately, Friar Bastía agreed to bless everyone's kit, which actually seemed to make a difference. It did for me anyway. Back home I'd have probably told you it was all mental, but here... well, my clothes didn't itch anymore, and my rifle felt lighter somehow.

"Dude, this is crazy," Wilson had said, looking at the lineup of weapons and gear waiting to receive the friar's blessing and sprinkling of holy water. "Like, everything here represents someone who had his heart cut out or whatever. Seriously bad vibrations, man."

I could tell Wilson was happy he had his original US Army-issued rig, and not potentially cursed soul-forged goods. He wasn't religious, but the man had a superstitious streak a mile wide.

We assembled deep in the jungle near Outpost Kilo-Charlie in the dead of night. Each of us scouts had led a string of warriors and auxiliaries to the rally point, since we were the only ones with night vision. Everyone had turned up as scheduled, and there hadn't been any encounters with hostiles. Not yet anyway.

So far, so good.

Captain Brown played his red light over the hasty sand table Sanchez had made on the forest floor while Greene went over the plan again. It wasn't uncommon for the captain to make a PFC give an ops briefing; he liked to make sure everyone knew the nuts and bolts, from the senior-most NCO down to the lowliest private.

"…after we take out two of the eastern towers, the northeast and southeast ones, *not* the central one"—Greene grinned at me —"Sergeant Sanchez and Specialist Woodward will hit the southeast corner with grenades to blast a passage through the wire. Sergeant García's team will advance in their FAV, with the FAV commanded by Captain Brown in support. Sergeants Sanchez and Yazzie will follow on the dirt bikes." He began pointing out locations in the sand table. "Once inside, Sergeant García's objective is to secure this avenue, while the HQ element holds the breach for the warriors, who will be staged here in advance, two hundred meters from the entrance we'll be creating. Once inside, our indigenous allies will mop up the resistance and handle the prisoners while Crazy Horse regroups and secures the portal, here at the eastern face of the temple pyramid." He paused. "Oh, and Corporal Bennett and Specialist Pierce will provide overwatch from the central eastern tower."

"And?" Brown prompted.

"Um, oh, right. Sorry, sir." Greene flushed. "Sergeant Wilson and his team will take out the towers on the western side and will regroup with us at the portal."

Wilson's team were a dozen hand-picked warriors he called "The Blackhearts." They were led by Dressed-in-Stars's older sister, a seasoned veteran named Flaming Feather who wore a great number of tattoos and bone piercings in painful-looking places and not much else.

"Things will move fast once we go kinetic," Brown told Wilson. "So don't dally."

"Roger that, sir. Me and the girls don't intend on missing the party."

The captain swept his eyes over us and cleared his throat. "It'll be frenetic once we're inside. Don't forget fire discipline and to communicate your movements. This is a situation ripe for friendly fire. Additionally, there's a sizable number of non-combatants at the objective. We'll do our best to avoid collateral damage, but not at the risk of our own people." His gaze fell on Xochi. "I'm relying on your people to contain the prisoners. If they get loose, there could be a riot, and a lot of innocent people will die."

"Understood, sir," she said. "It will not be a problem."

"Now, for the portal." Brown pursed his lips and exhaled slowly. "We have effectively no intel on what's on the other side, and I like that about as much as any of you. We need to be prepared to adapt to the situation as it evolves. Improvisation and extreme violence of action will be the watchwords of the operation from the moment we enter the portal. If you see a threat, even a suspected one, eliminate it without hesitation. The key to success will be establishing kinetic initiative and maintaining it."

He let that sink in for a minute and then took questions. I glanced at Xochi as the conversation flowed around the circle, and she smiled back at me. The face under her helmet was painted in the traditional grinning skull of her people, decorated with elaborate whorls and intricate flowers, and she wore her plate carrier over her quilted armor with its decorative fringe of feathers. A lot of the guys had taken a cue from her warriors and applied their own camo face paint in skull motifs. I was sure Army regulations frowned on that, but the captain knew it was good for morale and let it pass without comment. Besides, we were a long way from the Army, and we were about to storm the gates of Hell. Literally.

I wished I could have a last moment alone with her, but I knew there wouldn't be time. We'd said what needed to be said earlier in the day. All I could do now was embrace the confidence she felt. She *knew* we'd succeed. She'd seen it. I didn't need to offer any parting last words, because this wouldn't be the last of us.

Sanchez rose and walked past, tapping me lightly on the shoulder. I got off my knee and followed with Pierce to where Curly and Epasotl were waiting.

"You and Pierce stick to the rear," Sanchez told us. "The PFC will take point. This has to be quiet, so don't try and get in on any action. One of us will deal with anything that comes up."

I didn't object. Compared to Sanchez, Pierce and I were rank amateurs when it came to life-taking. I knew how to kill a man silently in theory, but I'd never actually done it. Sanchez had. As had

Epasotl—probably with her bare claws. And Curly had the look of a man who knew his business only too well.

"No talking and no IR," Sanchez added. "We don't know if they have night vision or not. The stars should be bright enough for nods once we get out from under the canopy. And clear your chambers. I don't want an ND screwing things up."

I flipped down my nods to do a function check. Well, Anderson's nods, actually. Sanchez had commandeered them from Gold Team, who would be staying behind with Dressed-in-Stars and her band of merry killers to pull security while the rest of us went to hell. *My* nods had been ruined when the zombie chick pulverized my face. Curly had a pair of his own as well—I don't know whose.

Epasotl didn't need image intensifiers. Her eyes did the job just fine.

"Bennett, you have the rear. We go single file. Epasotl will steer us clear of any traps. Stick to the man in front of you. Follow his footsteps. If any of you lands in a punji trap or sets off a mine, I'll have your ass. Hooah?"

"Hooah," Pierce and I echoed.

***

Pierce held up a fist and I took a knee, pivoting slightly to watch our six. We remained motionless for several minutes under the canopy of stars. I recognized several of the constellations from what Epasotl and Xochi had taught me—I even knew a few of the stories behind them—but the night sky still felt alien to me. I often wondered where we were in relation to Earth, assuming we were in the same universe. Maybe we weren't.

The night was warm and still. Insects trilled in the darkness, and the smell of decay hung heavy in the humid air. Not the unpleasant scent of death, but the heady aroma of rich soil. I enjoyed it while I could, knowing it'd soon be overpowered by the sickening smell of the outpost as we drew closer.

Pierce waved me forward, and we advanced. The outpost rose above the overgrown clearing of the killing ground ahead, its perimeter lit by torches and lanterns. The firelight meant they probably didn't have nods, but we couldn't be certain. We moved cautiously, crouching low, and my lower back was killing me from walking half bent for so long.

When Pierce motioned to the ground, I got down, following him in a high crawl. We were getting close to the wire. After several minutes he flattened out on knees and elbows, and I dropped lower. We snaked forward, stopping frequently and turning occasionally to skirt past traps. It was excruciatingly slow going.

I heard wire being clipped and dragged aside, and then I followed Pierce into a ditch between two concentric rows of concertina. Sanchez and Curly were posted up against the far side, and Pierce and I joined them. I was soaked through with sweat. After several moments, Epasotl slipped down into our midst and flashed the sign for seven before making the signs for a giant and an automatic weapon. She pointed to the north and held a hand up to listen.

So, a patrol of giants armed with machine guns. That was… less than awesome. It felt as though the power dynamic we'd grown accustomed to had changed in an instant. I wondered if these alliances had always been in place and we had been shown only what Dietrich wanted us to see, or whether some other big event—like whatever was set to happen on the Binding of the Years—had forged a new balance of power.

The ditch was in the shadow of the torchlight, but it was bright enough that we'd flipped up our nods. From somewhere above I heard a baby cry. Deep, hushed voices approached. I couldn't make out what they were saying, and I hugged myself tighter to the wall of the ditch. The stench had been growing worse as we neared the outpost, and now, this close to the prisoners, it was downright noxious.

The patrol passed overhead, and eventually the sound of their voices faded to the south.

Epasotl shot Sanchez another rapid set of signs. A few of them I recognized, but it appeared she and Sanchez had worked out a complex silent language all their own. He gave an approving nod as she finished her report and then motioned for Pierce and me to hold fast before subvocalizing into Curly's ear. The man acknowledged with a curt nod and drew his massive Bowie knife. He'd blackened the blade to prevent it from reflecting any light.

Epasotl slipped up and over the lip of the ditch silently, followed by the two men. Pierce caught my eye, and I shrugged. There was nothing to do but wait.

I heard some more wire being clipped and dragged aside. Then several minutes passed before Epasotl reached down and tapped both of us. Pierce went first. I followed, keeping low. We were near the central tower, in an area of semi-darkness formed by a gap in the torches and lanterns that lined the perimeter. I caught sight of fresh red-brown stains in the dirt and scuff marks as we followed Epasotl to where Sanchez waited at the base of the tower. They'd been busy. I wondered where they'd hidden the bodies.

Curly came flowing down the tower's ladder. His forearms and chest were covered in blood, but his face was calm and easy, like he was out on a Sunday stroll. Sanchez motioned me to the ladder, and I started climbing. Epasotl flashed me a shaka sign, but otherwise there were no parting words. We knew our mission.

I wasn't sure what I expected to find in the machine gun nest atop the tower. Bodies, maybe, but I certainly didn't expect to see so much blood. The two corpses had been neatly lined up, side by side, staring upward lifelessly. One of them had a twisted, tortured expression, but the other seemed to be smiling slightly. It was hella creepy.

Pierce joined me and leaned close to my ear. "What now?" he subvocalized.

"Now we pretend to be bored guards and hope they don't have replacements."

And that was where everything about this plan could go to hell in a handbasket. If the dead guards had a relief come before the attack was launched, things for Pierce and me could go pear-shaped real fast.

Instead of worrying, I scanned the outpost from our new vantage point. The central pyramid was broad and squat, shorter than the one at Hotel-Romeo, and I had a good view of the arch standing at its eastern side. There were barracks for about forty men, segregated pens for groups of prisoners, and equipment yards filled with crates and various goods. I spotted a couple of squad-sized patrols of men wandering inside the compound, and there was a corral with horses and another pen filled with turkeys. I tried to get an estimate of the prisoner population, but it was too dark, and everyone was sleeping in great huddled masses.

After a while, I spotted the squad of giants that Epasotl had seen earlier. They were pacing the perimeter and passed practically right below us. Each was armed with an M240 machine gun. The weapons looked like carbines in their hands.

Pierce had drawn his poncho over the dead guards and leaned on the machine gun in a slouch, feigning boredom. In the east I could see the sky beginning to lighten over the trees. Astronomical dawn meant we had maybe half an hour before the attack began.

The minutes dragged by like hours.

Sanchez's voice sounded in my earpiece, asking for a sitrep. I responded, giving an abbreviated report in code on what I'd observed. We didn't know if our short-range radios were being monitored, so we'd developed our own sort of shorthand, like police ten-codes, for communication.

"Roger. QM-dash-null," Sanchez said.

Fifteen minutes to go.

I keyed my radio twice to acknowledge. I didn't need to notify Pierce; he was on the same frequency. He gave me a look that expressed what I felt. We were both amped up as we waited for the axe to fall. That feeling only intensified as the sky further lightened and things became more visible—including the guards in the adjoining towers. Meaning we were also visible to them. Lucky for us, they looked about as bored as we were pretending to be and didn't pay us any particular attention.

Two soldiers on the ground caught my eye; they were approaching our tower. One of them stretched and yawned, saw me, and gave a lazy wave. I waved back in reply, hoping I appeared sufficiently sanguine, before turning my face. With the light behind us we probably were only silhouettes to them. I hoped. All the guards we'd seen so far appeared to be indigenous, and I, on the other hand, most certainly did not. Nor did Pierce. When the duo continued approaching, my heart began to race.

"I think we got company," I muttered.

"Friends of yours?" Pierce asked.

"Looks that way."

"Well, shit. How do you want to handle this?"

"We'll have to deal with them," I said, drawing my knife. "Quietly."

Pierce eyed my blade skeptically. "You're going to have to do the first one real quick and *real* quiet, or his buddy'll raise the alarm. Think you can? I don't know if I could."

We both glanced at the corpses on the floor with their boots sticking out from under Pierce's poncho, and then at the bloodstains everywhere. Curly had been efficient, and silent, but it had been messy.

"I'll deal with the first one," I said. "You take his buddy. Drag him up here by his helmet straps if you have to. The attack will launch soon. We only need to buy a few minutes."

"Roger that," he replied.

I moved to stand behind the trapdoor and Pierce turned slightly, leaning against the machine gun and hiding his face with a hand propped up like he was about to fall asleep. The dead guards were incredibly conspicuous, but you wouldn't see them first thing, not until you got to the top of the ladder and turned around.

I heard voices below us and then the ladder shook as someone ascended. They were both bantering as the first man drew nearer.

"Tlaloc, have I got a treat for you," he called up through the trapdoor. "Real nice flower, a young ripe one. I promise you Ehecatl and me didn't wear her out *too* much last night." He laughed as his head and shoulders appeared through the floor. "You'll have to get to her before the sergeant does, though. You know how he—"

He was stepping up off the ladder and I surged at him from behind, clapping a gloved hand over his mouth and frog-marching him forward as I drove my knife into his back, slipping it between his ribs and hoping I'd hit his lung. I kicked him to his knees, still holding my hand fast over his mouth as he jerked and fought against me. I think I'd expected him just to drop dead, and when he didn't, I wasn't sure what to do. I struck his kidney with two quick, deep jabs, and he arched powerfully before toppling forward with me on top of him, where he lay either unconscious or dead. There was a shout behind me and then a grunt of pain, followed by a low, crooning wail. I struggled to my feet, slipping on blood, and turned to see Pierce standing over the other man, just a kid really, who was sitting on the floor staring in shock at the steaming coil of guts spilling into his lap. He started whimpering for his mother.

Pierce made a strange, choked sound.

"We can't leave him like that," I said flatly.

Pierce gestured helplessly before turning and violently emptying his stomach in a corner of the guard tower.

I strode forward without thinking about it, grabbed the back of the kid's helmet, lifting it and forcing his head forward, and drove my knife into the back of his skull, twisting the blade swiftly. He twitched once and then fell over like a sack of grain.

Pierce continued retching for a minute before turning to me. His eyes were rimmed with red. "Sorry," he said softly, wiping his mouth with the back of a hand. "I really screwed that up, didn't I?"

I shrugged. I felt empty. Drained. Numb. I'd killed before, many times, and I'd always felt *something*. A mix of exhilaration and regret. Relief. Sadness. Maybe something stronger, but if I couldn't handle whatever it was, it went into the box. But this was up close and personal, and I was covered in their blood. And I felt *nothing*. Maybe I'd just seen too much death by now. Maybe it was the curse, gnawing at my humanity. Maybe I was overthinking it. Maybe it hadn't hit me yet. The four corpses at our feet reeked of blood, urine, and excrement, and I was numb to that too.

Sanchez's voice came in my ear. "All Crazy Horse elements. Dubs T-60."

Dubs meaning two, T-60 meaning minutes.

I blinked and looked at Pierce, meaning to check on him. Instead, he asked me if I was okay.

"No," I said after a moment. "But that doesn't matter. You'd better get Sybil ready."

"Yeah, guess it's showtime."

"Yeah," I echoed, wiping my knife and then sheathing it. "Showtime."

CHAPTER 47

The assault went exactly as planned. From our overwatch point, Pierce and I helped to coordinate fire, call out targets, and put down more than a few hostiles of our own. We each claimed at least one giant that night. But… throughout the battle I became increasingly aware of two things.

First was just how casual it all felt to me. I mentioned how devoid of emotion I'd been when it came to ending the life of a teenager, not much older than my youngest brother. Then, as the battle progressed, each shot and kill was just a little tick mark. It wasn't good or bad, it was nothing. I dropped an indig who was trying to flank one of our assault teams, sending a bullet through the guy's head before he had the chance to raise his weapon, but there was no sense of relief that I'd stopped him. It was all just so… empty. At the same time, I saw some seriously grisly carnage unfold among the prisoners. Women, children… and it just didn't register at all. I knew what I was seeing, knew that it was horrible, but it didn't even matter to me. I could not have cared less.

Life and death had lost all meaning.

While all this was unfolding, I got the overwhelming sense that my hands were dripping and slick with blood. My grip was fine. My finger didn't slip on the trigger at all. But they felt *so* covered in gore. I wanted to scream.

Pierce would talk to me and I couldn't muster the mental clarity to answer. The radio chirped in my ear more than once—same thing. Then, when we were out of targets and our guys were securing what was left of the outpost, I put my rifle down, dropped my gloves at my feet, and rummaged wordlessly through my pack until I found my canteen.

I hurriedly unscrewed the cap, splashed the water on my palms, and scrubbed at all the blood from the men I'd killed, all the blood that had seeped through my gloves. When it was gone I kept scrubbing, using my nails to scrape the skin clean.

Pierce was talking, but I couldn't hear him. The radio squawked, but no one said anything. At least nothing that reached my consciousness.

I sensed Sanchez climbing up through the trapdoor behind me. I didn't need to turn and look to know it was him. I could just tell. He has a presence. My ears felt hot, like they'd recovered their ability to hear.

Pierce was giving Sanchez a report. "Can't get a word out of him, Sergeant. He was totally cool during the assault. Like ice. All business. Then, after it all, he started doing... this. He cracked, man. I tried to pull him aside but he shrugged me off like I was nothing. He won't stop and he won't talk."

Had Pierce tried to stop me? I didn't remember.

Was this... was this part of the ravenous undead thing? Part of the curse?

I began to scrub harder.

Sanchez's voice was quiet as he asked me what had happened.

There was a lengthy pause. Flies buzzed thickly around the slaughterhouse of our thatch-roofed watchtower and took off from their perches of spent brass trapped in congealed blood as Sanchez's boots crunched through the carnage.

The sergeant stopped, looked at the vomit in the corner, and let out a sigh through his nostrils.

"That's... mine," Pierce said softly. "I made a real mess of that kid over there. He was my kill, my responsibility. I could've gotten us both killed. Or worse, I could've compromised the assault. I screwed up, royally. Bennett had to put the kid out of his misery for me. I—I couldn't do it."

"It is what it is. Don't beat yourself up over it," Sanchez grunted. "The captain will want to debrief you." He paused for a long moment and then spoke more gently. "That means now, son."

I heard Pierce move across to the ladder and then descend. Minutes passed. The only sound was the flies. I kept pouring out more water. Kept scrubbing.

Sanchez squatted and took my canteen away from me.

"Imagine that box is getting pretty full," he said in almost a whisper. "We've been downrange a long time. Takes a toll on the best of men."

I nodded slowly.

"You did what had to be done," he continued. "No shame in that. No shame in feeling whatever it is you're feeling either."

"But I don't feel *anything*," I said slowly, forcing the words out one at a time. "That's the problem."

I didn't have an answer for why I was scrubbing my hands, though.

"Don't bullshit me, son. You look guilty as sin."

"I feel guilty *because* I don't feel anything." The words came faster. "They were just kids."

"Kids who raped and tortured prisoners destined to be slaughtered like animals. Don't forget that. End of the day… a man's responsible for his own actions."

I gave another slow nod. But… that wasn't it. That was surface level. Convenient. It wasn't what I was afraid of and it wasn't what had driven me to obsessively cleanse my hands.

The truth was different, and right up until the point I spoke it, I wondered if I had the courage to admit it.

"What if I'm becoming a murderous psychopath, Sergeant? Like Alpha. What if this infection, this curse is taking over?"

Sanchez laughed bitterly. "God, you're a piece of work, kid. The fact you're having this little crisis is proof enough to me you've got whatever this thing is inside you beat. You're the furthest thing from a stone-cold killer on God's green earth. So you knifed a couple boys who needed knifing anyway and don't feel a damn thing. So what? There's no *right* way to feel, son. You feel what you feel. Sometimes, you don't feel nothin'. You had a job to do, and you did it. And it ain't over yet, not by a long shot, so stop the self-flagellation already. You hear me?"

"I hear you, Sergeant," I said, but not with conviction.

"Look, punishing you is my job, not yours. If you don't stop this bullshit, I'll smoke you into an early grave. That's a promise, Bennett."

That made me crack a smile. Sanchez stood and held out a hand. I took it and rose to my feet. He looked up at me sternly, but his hard, brown eyes weren't without compassion.

"You're a good soldier, Bennett, and a good kid. An odd kid, but a good one. I'm proud of you, son."

That meant far more to me than just about anything anyone could say. He didn't give praise or show warmth often, and his words felt like the sun coming out after a long, cold rain. Everything that had happened over the last few months started crashing down on me. All the horror. All the fear. Everyone we'd lost. The people I'd killed. The massacre at the village. The box that I'd thought was securely on the shelf teetered and crashed, spilling its contents across my soul. I clenched my trembling jaw and the tears came without warning, accompanied by sobs that wracked my body. I watched myself in shame, waiting for Sanchez to bring the hammer of God down on me for being so weak.

Instead, he embraced me firmly and pulled my head down to his shoulder, promising me it would be okay. He held me like a brother. Like a father.

And I wept.

***

"We good?" Captain Brown asked when the two of us came back down.

"We're good," Sanchez replied.

Everyone was looking at me side-eyed, looking but trying to look like they weren't looking, wondering what had gone on up in the tower. I wondered how much Pierce had shared. Everyone was sure to have questions.

Xochi stepped over and rubbed my back. "Are you okay?" she whispered.

I nodded.

We stood in front of the gleaming basalt arch, nearly all of us plus Curly and Wilson's Blackhearts. Xochi had her own royal contingent of warriors. It might take an army to defeat whatever waited for us inside; this was as close as we could get to assembling one. The Blackhearts had traded their hand weapons for rifles picked up on the battlefield, and Flaming Feather, now wielding an M240 liberated from a giant, looked like something from a *Heavy Metal* magazine cover. The rest of the Kuauchanejkej warriors were patrolling the outpost's perimeter on warbirds or helping the male auxiliaries tend to the freed prisoners.

I expected to have to give a debrief or an accounting, but instead all eyes were on Epasotl. Taking the outpost was just phase one. Now the real unknowns were before us.

Our Chaneque PFC studied the monument thoughtfully, hands on her hips.

"You sure you can do this?" Brown asked her.

"I am sure," she replied.

He gestured for her to proceed.

Epasotl bent down and lit incense in a small clay bowl beside her with Woodward's Zippo. Although it wasn't Woodward's anymore. When Sanchez had realized that the platoon had burned through every last lighter but one, he'd confiscated it for command use. Though I don't imagine this was the kind of use he'd had in mind.

Epasotl held out her hand, and Xochi handed over her ancient bronze dagger. Epasotl held it lightly with her eyes closed for a minute as the smoke curled around her, and then stood erect and started tracing it through the air.

At first, nothing happened. Then lines of energy began to spark off the dagger's tip, hanging in space as she drew a series of complex pictographs, just like we'd seen the priest do back at Outpost Hotel-Romeo. The incense smoke thickened and bloomed, filling the open space of the arch. Small spears of lightning flashed as the cloud darkened and began to spin. We stood with our weapons ready for anything. The vortex solidified momentarily and then flashed out of existence.

In its place, beneath the arch, now stood a long, wide hall. The walls were made of tightly fitted basalt blocks, the floor, obsidian shards. The entire passage glowed with a strange red-orange light that had no discernible source. Flecks of ash floated out from the portal and swirled around us, carried by a light, hot breeze smelling of sulfur and cadavers.

Epasotl frowned.

"This isn't what we saw before," Sanchez grumbled.

"One road, but many gates," Xochi said. "That's what Captain Yolotli said."

"*That* isn't the road," Sanchez insisted, pointing toward the open portal. "We saw a wide black road leading into a dark, open space, not a glowing passageway."

"What happened?" Brown asked Epasotl. "Are you sure you copied the pictographs exactly?"

"I do not know. I drew them as I remember them." She traced a finger in the air and then shrugged. "Perhaps I missed something."

"Where's the local priest?" Sanchez asked Xochi. "Bring him here."

"I doubt we could trust *him*," Epasotl said. "Even if we make him work the portal magic, he may create a trap."

"Oh, I'll convince him to be honest," Sanchez growled. "Believe you me."

"It does not matter," Xochi said. "He did not survive the assault."

"What?" Brown asked sharply. "He was an HVT. You had explicit orders to capture him alive."

"My warriors discovered unimaginable atrocities in his chambers. He and his guards were shown no mercy." Xochi shuddered, but her eyes were like steel. "What I saw will haunt me until I die. I cannot blame them."

"You had your orders," Sanchez said in a cold, hard voice.

"Which I repeated to my warriors," she insisted. "But I arrived too late for it to matter. The monster was dead and there was nothing to be done. Those women will forever bear the scars of what they witnessed. Do not be so sure that you would not do the same if those desecrated were *your* sisters and mothers."

"I would've followed my orders," Sanchez snapped. He turned to Brown.

"Well, sir, what now?"

"We proceed," the captain replied. "This hall leads *somewhere*." His boots crunched on the obsidian shards as he unceremoniously stepped through the portal and began walking.

We crossed the threshold after him, without questioning it. Captain Brown went, and so we would follow. The platoon. Curly. The Blackhearts. Xochi and her honor guard.

But not all of us went. Gold Team and Whitlock would stay in the outpost, as would the Sugar Skull Gal support teams led by Dressed-in-Stars. Together they were tasked with pulling security on the other side of the portal—not only to protect our rear from any enemy forces who might arrive unexpectedly, but also to ensure that nothing from the Underworld wandered out.

We found ourselves looking down a long hall that seemed to stretch away forever. Sanchez ordered a standard patrol formation with García on point. That meant Blue Team would lead, augmented by a handful of Blackhearts, followed by the captain, Xochi and her retinue, and Cohen, who'd come along as Brown's radio man, only to find that the SINCGARS didn't work in here. Sanchez and Doc would then trail me and Pierce, with Wilson's Blackhearts and Curly covering the rear. If anything needed scouting out, Pierce and I would likely be the ones dispatched forward to do the sneaking and peeking.

The passage was wide enough for each team to spread out in a tight wedge. Epasotl, our tour guide in Hell, made her way to the front to stand with García. She drank from a tiny gourd and then pulled a round, ivory-colored object out of her haversack and held it to her lips, mumbling to it. I craned my neck to get a better view of what she was holding, then drew back when I realized it was a skull. A very small, alien-looking skull. A newborn's skull. As she mumbled, a blue light began to glow in the eye sockets, and it gave a twittering laugh that made the hairs on the back of my neck stand up.

García stepped away and crossed himself. I saw Anderson visibly shiver.

A blue flame enveloped the skull as it slowly levitated out of her hand and came to rest floating above her right shoulder. Sound emanated from it, but I couldn't make out the words. It was a very singsong, high-pitched voice.

Epasotl turned to Captain Brown. "Atzi says we must go forward."

"As if there was anywhere else to go," Pierce muttered under his breath.

Brown was about to give the order to move out when a thunderclap boomed from behind us, ushering in a strong wind that buffeted us, tugging at our clothes and sending shards of obsidian scattering down the passage.

I spun around.

The portal was gone. The hall stretched behind us as far as the eye could see, just as it did in front of us.

"Whoa," Wilson said.

"That was our way out!" Greene cried in alarm. "How do we get out now? Are we stuck here? Oh my God, we're stuck in Hell, aren't we!"

I thought the kid was going to start hyperventilating. To be fair I wasn't exactly feeling zen myself at the moment.

"We'll find an alternate exfil," Brown said calmly. "Move out."

"All gonna end up here sooner or later," Doc announced, and then took the first step forward.

CHAPTER 48

"Why did the portal close?" I asked Epasotl. We'd been walking the hall for hours and had stopped to rest and eat. So far there hadn't been any change of scenery to suggest we were making any progress.

She rolled her eyes. "As I told Big Kahuna, I do not know. I am not a 'Portal Guru.' I am doing the best I can. Perhaps it only remains open for a short time. Perhaps the arch was destroyed. There could be many reasons. It does not matter."

"You think being stuck here doesn't matter?" I leaned against the wall and ran my hand through my hair.

She dug out her favorite MRE, ripped it open, and breathed in the Chicken a la King. "Big Kahuna is not concerned. Why should Ben-Ette be?"

"He's not?"

"Lieutenant Saitō and his porters went inside and did not leave their portal open. So there must be a way to open one from here. Duh."

"Oh. I didn't think of that."

"*That* is why you are not a kahuna."

The skull floating above her shoulder gave a twittering laugh, and the blue flame surrounding it danced. I'd almost blocked out its presence, *almost*, but its laugh set my nerves back on edge. It sounded far too much like a baby giggling. A demonic little goblin baby, but still.

"Should I ask where you found that skull?" I asked.

"Probably not," she said around a mouthful of food. She waved her spoon in the air. "I did not sacrifice a baby, if that is what you are thinking."

"The thought never occurred to me," I said dryly. "So... what is it, exactly?"

"*She* is a spirit, and her name is Atzi."

"Atzi, Atzi, Atzi!" the skull echoed in singsong.

"A spirit? Like the soul of a dead person?"

"No, a spirit, like a *spirit*. A creature of another world that intersects ours. They are mischievous and impulsive, but harmless. They can be excellent guides—"

"Slap me some skin, Bro-ski!" the skull twittered to me. I pulled back; it hadn't even occurred to me the thing could speak English, much less Wilson-English.

"—but they are flighty, and they have a perverse sense of humor," Epasotl continued. "They can be difficult to work with. No, Atzi, he is not the Bro-ski. He is Ben-Ette. The Bro-ski is cool. Ben-Ette is not cool."

"Hey, I can be cool," I said in an injured voice.

"No, you cannot," Epasotl said firmly. "I have learned this much in my bondage."

I frowned, having enough sense to know that it's never cool to try and convince someone of your own coolness. "And you learned how to summon spirits where?"

"I was an apprentice in *naualotl* for many seasons, remember? I learned much, but I sucked. I already told you this. I could not make magic and I flunked out. But I remembered the lessons. Now I do not suck. Now I rock. Now I am hardcore metal and bad to the bone." She made a "rock on" gesture and the skull bobbed up and down in the air, giggling.

"That you are," I said. "I wonder what changed?"

She shrugged. "I do not know."

"Break's over," Sanchez said as he passed by. "On your feet."

Grumbles came from Blue Team up ahead, and I stowed what was left of my meal in a cargo pocket. Epasotl bent to retie one of her boots. She'd been issued the diminutive footwear in Amoloyan, and although she often preferred to operate barefoot, it was a heck of a good thing she had them now; the obsidian shards paving the passage were sharp. It'd be like walking on glass.

Captain gave the order to move out, and we trudged forward, our boots crunching down the seemingly endless hall. It was monotonous. After another two hours of brain-numbing marching Brown threw up a fist, and I stopped and held up my own fist to signal those behind me. García walked back to Brown and handed him a red chem light. Epasotl joined them. They kept their voices low, but I was close enough to overhear.

"Interesting," the captain said. "I placed this when we first entered."

"How's that possible?" García asked. "We've been walking dead straight ahead all day."

"It would appear we've been going in a circle," Brown said.

García swore.

"Circles and circles!" Atzi giggled. "The damned stumble with bleeding feet on the path forever and ever!"

"Not acceptable." Brown threw Epasotl a knife hand. "How do we get out?"

Atzi, suddenly talkative, answered in Epasotl's stead. "Find the door. The door will break the circle."

Brown gave the skull a stern look. "You could've said that hours ago."

"Big Kahuna said walk, and we walked," Epasotl said apologetically. "This one is… difficult."

"Never ask!" Atzi said.

Brown looked like he'd swallowed a lemon. "Find me a way out, PFC."

"Only the death-touched can find the way," Atzi said with a bob. "Only those whom Death has marked."

"I'm not in the mood for riddles," Brown growled.

I stepped forward before Epasotl had even begun to tap her lips. It seemed obvious to me, but then, being a sort of living dead had been heavy on my mind as of late. "Think she means me," I said.

Brown's eyes lit up, and he nodded. "Yes, I believe so."

"Ben-Ette! Ben-Ette! Ben-Ette!" Atzi spun and fixed me with her glowing eye sockets. "Death walks with you."

A chill ran down my spine, and I shuddered involuntarily. I turned to Epasotl. "So… what do I do?"

"I can aid your sight." Epasotl dug into her haversack and produced another tiny gourd. She removed the stopper and waved a hand over it, chanting something I couldn't make out. Blue vapor began to issue out of the gourd.

"Inhale, quickly!" she commanded.

When I hesitated, she snapped her fingers irritably. With a sigh of resignation, I leaned forward and took a small whiff of the vapor. It had a sharp, acrid scent that made my eyes water. I sneezed.

"More! Breathe deeply!" Epasotl ordered. "Draw it into your core." She took a deep breath and held it low in her diaphragm to demonstrate. It didn't escape my notice that she was careful not to inhale the vapor herself. "Do not be a wuss."

I glanced at the captain, and he made a *go ahead* motion with his head. Both he and García were leaning back to avoid breathing whatever it was.

Closing my eyes, I inhaled deeply, letting the vapor fill my lungs until I started coughing in fits.

"That is good enough," Epasotl said, placing the stopper in the gourd and returning it to her bag.

"What now?" I asked with a final cough. I didn't feel any different. Maybe somewhat lightheaded for a moment, but that passed. My mouth felt a little dry and I sipped from my canteen.

"Now we search for the way out." Epasotl extended her hand to the front of the column. "Come. We walk."

I followed her past Blue Team and took point. She asked me what I saw, and I said that I saw the same thing we'd seen for hours and hours: a strangely glowing hall stretching away forever.

"Then we walk until you see something different," she said.

I waved the column forward and we advanced. The rhythmic crunching of boots on obsidian shards echoed lightly behind me. I wasn't sure what I was looking for. The walls were the same forever. Just huge blocks of basalt joined so tightly together you couldn't slip a knife between them. The ceiling was much the same, interspersed with lintels set atop engaged columns every fifty feet or so. Over time our footfalls became somewhat musical, more of a tinkling of glass than crunching.

I turned to Epasotl and saw that Atzi was no longer a floating, disembodied skull, but was fully fleshed now, though just as alien-looking, and possessed a body that looked like a naked squirrel married to a dragonfly. She sat on Epasotl's shoulder, her pearlescent skin shimmering.

Epasotl met my eye and smiled with a broad Cheshire grin I'd never seen before. Her face looked entirely too wide, her eyes big as saucers.

"You are beginning to see, aren't you?" she asked.

"He sees! He sees!" Atzi echoed in singsong.

I blinked, shook my head, and forced my eyes forward. The walls seemed to writhe, and complex shapes resolved to dance across the surface of the polished basalt. I held up a fist to halt the column. Stepping over to the wall, I traced my finger over the shifting pattern, mesmerized. Many of the shapes were simple geometric motifs, but others took the form of complicated pictographs depicting people, animals, and strange beasts. Some were benign, while others were the stuff of nightmares. They didn't frighten me, though.

The patterns seemed to pulse with a rhythm that matched my heartbeat, as if they were living extensions of myself. I could read the story of my life in them. As I studied the dancing shapes, I felt myself merging with them until I didn't know where I ended and they began. I was large enough to embrace the universe, while simultaneously no bigger than a grain of sand.

Atzi flew in front of me on her shimmering wings and took hold of my hand, leading me forward through the swirling patterns, giggling. "You can see now," she lilted. "So… what do you see?"

"I see… everything," I said in wonder.

"Yes," Atzi said. "The past, the present, and the future. All is contained in the moment. Death has touched you, an undying death of eternal hunger, but you conquered deathlessness and so now see past your mortality and walk transformed."

And I saw. My past, my present, and my future—all in one moment. I can't describe what I saw, because I can't remember; it was too much for a mind limited by flesh and blood to later comprehend. I only know I saw everything then, and I was unafraid.

"Who are you?" I asked.

"I am Atzi. I am the rains that fall from the heavens. I am the spirit of life and sustenance, of springtime and rebirth." Her aspect became frightening. "I am the storm that sunders the same heavens, the hail that pulverizes, the lightning that splits the great tree, the flood that drowns, but this too is rebirth." She smiled and was suddenly winsome again. "Life and death, death and life, circles in circles, and always the rain that falls to bring life from death. I am Atzi."

Her laughter was like the tinkling of bells, like raindrops on petals. "Come, step out of the circle. Walk with me, Nephi, and see."

And so we walked, though I could not afterward say where, or for how long, or what I saw or did there. The memories were like half-glimpsed shadows that teased at the corners of my mind, only to wriggle out of my grasp when I tried to pin them down.

The vision ended, eventually, if it was a vision, and I found myself standing in a cavernous subterranean chamber lit by braziers of glowing coals. The ceiling disappeared high overhead in smoky darkness. Passages led out in four directions.

Epasotl reached up and patted my shoulder. "Well done, Ben-Ette."

She looked normal again, and on her shoulder Atzi was once again a floating infant's skull shrouded in blue flame.

I turned and saw everyone behind me gazing around in wonder and confusion. Half of them were in the middle of eating. My mouth felt dry, and I was sweating, but that could've been the hot breeze sweeping through the chamber.

Captain Brown strode up to us. "Good work, you two."

Epasotl shrugged. "I did nothing. It was all Ben-Ette."

Brown examined me. "And the effects of the—"

"Are very temporary," Epasotl confirmed. "It has passed."

"Good. I don't need him stoned, at least not anymore." Captain Brown nodded to me. "You good, son?"

"Yes, sir."

Brown clapped my shoulder and then moved back into the formation. "García, back on point. Which way, PFC?"

Epasotl consulted with Atzi and then pointed to the passage leading off to our right. Brown ordered us to move out.

I fell back to walk beside Pierce.

"Dude," he muttered.

"What happened?" I asked.

"Nothing for a long time. You were wandering around touching the walls and talking to Epasotl's floating skull friend like you were best buds. Took a *damn* long time. Sanchez called another meal break. I had a nap. Then all of a sudden everything *melted*, and we were standing here. What happened to you, man? It looked like you were frying balls."

"I guess I was, basically."

"First trip is always the best."

"Better be the last," I grunted.

"Against your religion?"

I gave a slight nod.

Pierce elbowed me and winked. "But...?"

I cracked a smile. "Won't lie. Don't know if I'd want to take the Magical Mystery Tour again, but it was pretty bad."

"You mean good bad, right?"

"I mean radical."

"My man." He gave me a fist bump. "Now we just have to get you laid."

CHAPTER 49

"Contact!" Wilson cried from our rear.

Rifles barked, followed by the thunderous chitter of the M240. Brass tinkled as it struck the floor, and the sharp smell of cordite filled the passage. I heard human screams of rage and bloodlust—definitely not us.

"Eyes front, Blue Team!" Captain Brown barked.

The passage behind me was dark, and all I could make out was the strobing of muzzle flashes silhouetting my teammates.

"We're getting overrun!" one of the Blackhearts shouted from behind me as Flaming Feather's M240 erupted in a long belch of lead.

"Better get moving!" Sanchez called back to us.

"Blue Team, forward," Brown ordered. "Move with a purpose!"

"Contact front! Thirty meters!" García shouted from ahead. His team's rifles cracked as Cameron and Greene got on the M240 and started laying down the hate in short, controlled bursts. The tunnel was echoing with thunderous fire from both directions. Pierce and I couldn't do much but crouch and blink at the strobing light. What the hell was happening?

"There's too many of them!" Cameron cried.

The sound of gunfire intensified. Blue Team and their Blackhearts called out mag swaps and targets.

"Fall back!" García ordered.

"Nowhere to fall back to, Sergeant," Brown barked. "Push 'em forward!"

That's when I finally caught sight of the hostiles. It was the Children, pressing in on Blue Team, grabbing at barrels and snatching at plate carriers.

I heard a horrified scream, and then Woodward gave the tormented a name. "They got Greene!"

I caught a glimpse of García pulling Woodward back by his drag handle. A horrific, bloodcurdling howl of pain and terror that lasted far too long echoed down the passage.

"Fire in the hole!" Epasotl shrieked.

Blue flame erupted from the front of our column like dragon's breath, and I was hit by a sudden blast of hot air that smelled of burnt meat and hair. My lungs felt singed, and I gasped, holding my aching ribs.

"Clear!" García shouted after a stunned moment.

There was another burst from the machine gun behind me, and then Wilson echoed all clear from his end too.

"Greene?" Brown asked García flatly.

But the question was a formality. That scream, that final, last scream… it had left no doubt. Greene was dead.

"They got him, sir," García replied without emotion. "Them or that fire blast. There's nothing left but ash. Greene's gone, sir."

Someone up ahead was sobbing quietly. I think it was Woodward.

There had just been a sudden, major shitstorm, and I could barely say what had happened, only that it was as bad as it was fast. Brown kept his cool though, determined not to let us be rattled after our first encounter with the denizens of Hell.

"Cohen, you're Cameron's new AG," the captain ordered. "We can't lose inertia. Let's move, gentlemen!"

And so, on we pushed.

"That was brutal," Pierce panted. "How much further do we have to go?"

"However far it is, it's too far," I gasped. We had been following Atzi's directions—the flighty spirit was finally being cooperative, or at least we hoped it was—as we moved through a maze of passages and corridors that I'd long since given up on trying to keep track of. Most of that time we'd been moving at Ranger speed—not quite double time, but faster than a brisk walk—and my ribs were killing me.

After several minutes García called a halt. I rested my hands on my knees and winced as I drew air.

"You okay, Bennett?" Brown asked quietly.

"Ribs are still a bit sore, sir. I'll live."

He grunted and turned away. A minute later he motioned to me with a hand, and I signed to Pierce to move up with me. We joined Blue Team at a wide entrance opening into another chamber, this one massive. I nodded to García, and Pierce and I peeled off to the left while he and Woodward took the right. We flowed around the perimeter of the cavernous space, clearing shadowy nooks and exits to other passages, and met up with García at the far side.

"Clear," he spoke into his radio.

"Roger, moving," Sanchez's voice sounded in my ear.

We watched the exits as the rest of the team advanced into the chamber. I looked up and tapped García's shoulder.

"That's different," I said, pointing to a billowing white fluff high above us.

He frowned. "What the hell is that?"

"Looks like… giant cobwebs."

García squinted for a better look. "Can hardly see anything in the dark up there. Shit, if those are webs, there's a lot of them. What kinda spider could make a web like that?"

"Not the kind you can kill with the sole of your boot," I said.

"Yeah." He keyed his radio. "Possible contact. I repeat, possible contact."

The rest of our guys—and gals—were about halfway across the chamber and halted immediately to take a knee in a loose circle.

"Talk to me," Captain Brown said over the net.

"Look up," García replied. "I got a bad feeling about those webs."

"Roger that," Brown said. I could see him consulting with Epasotl. "Nightcrawler, secure the passage second to your right."

García squeezed Woodward's shoulder and the two of them moved across the floor to the indicated egress. Pierce and I followed at a distance, watching their six. I kept glancing above us too, thinking about spiders. So when something snapped and skittered across the ground in front of me, I freaked for a moment, thinking a giant spider had jumped down to eat me. It took me a moment to realize it was an arrow.

Spiders don't shoot arrows. Probably.

"Incoming!" I shouted, pivoting up and around, swinging my muzzle overhead. More missiles rained down, snapping against the stone floor at my feet.

Try as I might, I couldn't spot a target anywhere. I was considering just opening up when a large shape dropped out of the darkness. There was the spider I'd expected… only I hadn't expected it to look like *this*. Hanging upside down before me was a woman's torso affixed to the *body* of a giant spider.

She was hideous. Glowing red eyes. A mouth full of articulated, dripping fangs. Lank black hair that curtained below her as she hung inverted in the air. In her hand she held a bow, and she let three arrows loose simultaneously—all of them aimed at me. I staggered back as they impacted against my chest plate. They didn't break through, but my ribs were screaming.

My rifle was already up, and I squeezed off five rounds as fast as I could reset the trigger. Blooms of black ichor blossomed on her torso, her massive abdomen ruptured, and she hung limp from her silken thread.

Then more arrows rained down and a swarm of dark shapes descended, all of them looking just like the first. Gruesome spider-women.

I felt a jerk as Pierce grabbed my drag handle and pulled me back to the wall, taking cover in an alcove. By then the rest of the team had opened fire, sending rounds into the cavernous ceiling. There was a shrieking chorus of pain and hatred as bullets tore into flesh and chitin. Pierce was beside me, working his bolt and firing, and I joined him. Horrific bodies flailed to the floor in a sickening, splattering crunch of shattered limbs and ruptured organs.

But there were too many of them, and some reached the ground, long legs skittering over the stone as they drew whips that cracked the air with tongues of red flame. Now we had to be careful not to hit one another as the monsters darted between us.

Two of them rushed me and Pierce, red eyes flashing. He squeezed off a round, exploding one spider-woman head in a black mist. The other snapped her whip, and he screamed painfully in reply. I fired, reset the trigger, and fired again, putting two rounds into her heart. A third shot carried into her brain, and she rag-dolled to the ground.

Pierce was laid out, holding his right thigh and moaning. The wound was a long, cauterized laceration that reeked of burnt meat. His slashed pant leg was charred, and the skin around the injury was waxy and blistered. I fumbled for a morphine injector, but he waved me away.

"No good," he gasped. "Gotta… stay sharp."

"Doc, this is Longshot. I have wounded!" I called into my radio.

"So do I," the medic replied. "Do what you can for now. I'll send Miss Kitty."

"Not much to do anyway," I muttered to myself. And there wasn't. Aside from irrigating the wound with whatever water we had left, which wasn't much between us, all I could do was apply a loose dressing. Pierce needed proper medical attention. Probably skin grafts.

"Think you can stand?" I asked, holding out a hand.

"Don't know," he grunted.

I motioned for him to stay down. "Don't, then."

He pulled his sidearm and I brought up my rifle as another spider-woman skittered towards us. Pierce shot her in the throat before I could line up my holographic sight, and she veered off to the side, crashing into the wall, her nightmarish jaw spraying black blood.

I helped him into a sitting position in the alcove and took a knee beside him. Epasotl was racing toward us when a spider-woman dropped down out of nowhere and pounced on her. Epasotl rolled and slid across the floor, stitching the underside of the creature open with her MP5. The creature fell behind her as Epasotl lithely somersaulted to her feet.

She sprinted and bounded across the remaining distance to join us, her body steaming with splashes of black ichor. It smelled like… I have no words. Definitely a new contender for worst smell in this godforsaken realm.

Epasotl looked exhausted. Atzi came drifting up behind her, giggling.

"He will live," Epasotl said perfunctorily after examining the wound. She dressed it gently and kept the bandage loose, then handed Pierce something wrapped in leaves. "Eat. It will stop the pain."

"I wanna stay sharp," he said.

"You will. Clear mind. Much energy. No pain."

Pierce shrugged and ate it. "Not bad, Eps," he said around a mouthful. "Surprisingly. Not great, but not bad. Leg's feeling better already."

"All elements, make for the egress," Brown said over the net. "Move and fire."

"Watch your sectors, boys and girls," Sanchez warned.

The platoon moved in formation across the vast floor. Wilson had a body over his shoulder in a fireman's carry and was shooting his M16 one-handed.

"Come on," I said to Pierce and Epasotl. "Don't want the train to leave without us. Cover them."

Pierce and I were the last out and laid down steady fire as Sanchez and Woodward came up beside us and flooded the chamber with forty-millimeter grenades.

Sanchez paused firing to dig into his assault pack and pull out a demolition block. He grinned, baring his teeth as he affixed a remote detonator and pitched the brick of C-4 underhand, sending it sliding and spinning across the floor.

"Haul ass!" he shouted.

He didn't have to tell me twice. Or even once. I moved as fast as the man in front of me, firing behind as spider-women crawled into the passage, skittering along the floor and walls and ceiling. We'd moved maybe a hundred yards when Sanchez ordered us to hit the deck.

"Fire in the hole!"

The detonation thundered off the walls, echoing down the passage and shaking the floor. Dust fell from the ceiling, coating me with a fine white film as I fired at the last creature pursuing us. She fell, screaming, her multiple chitinous legs flailing, and Sanchez put a final bullet in her brain.

"Ugly bitches," he grunted before turning around. "What do we got, people? Team leaders, talk to me."

"Blue Team amber," García shouted back.

"X Team…" I hesitated and Pierce nodded. "Green."

"Blackhearts amber," Wilson called out. "One KIA."

Xochi gasped from somewhere up ahead. We tried not to crowd around in the confines of the tunnel as Xochi ran down to Wilson. "Who is it?"

"Golden Harvest," I heard Flaming Feather say in a husky voice.

"Can you carry her?" Captain Brown asked.

"She doesn't weigh a thing," Wilson replied. There wasn't really a question of leaving her behind, even dead. That's not how things were done in Brown's platoon.

"We good to proceed, Doc?" Brown asked.

"Multiple wounded, but all ambulatory. We're good, all things considered."

The captain ordered us forward once again. At this point we were all struggling. Multiple adrenaline dumps, miles upon miles of moving at a fast pace, hours upon hours of stress as we anticipated an attack. I had no idea how long we'd been pushing through these tunnels, but it felt like days. Sanchez held the rear with me and Pierce to give the Blackhearts a break, and I went to drink the last of my water, only to remember it was gone.

The grade of the floor gradually inclined and I could feel us moving upwards. Eventually we hit a steep staircase and began climbing. Up and up. Forever. My quads burned and my knees ached.

After, I don't know, *weeks* of climbing, I felt a hot wind coming from ahead and flakes of ash fell on me like snow. We halted, and everyone immediately plopped down to take a seat on the steps.

Word came down the column for me and Pierce, and suppressing groans, we struggled back to our feet and pushed forward to the captain.

We were relieved, at least, to see that we'd found the top of the stairs. There was an opening onto a larger space at the very top, and Pierce and I crouched down and then crawled when we saw Brown, García, and Epasotl lying on their stomachs just below the lip of the top stair, peering over cautiously. García waved us forward, and we ended up on our stomachs next to them.

The sight through the opening was almost incomprehensible in scale. It wasn't just cavernous. It was *immense*. An underground world. Above, red embers rained down constantly from a vast void filled with black clouds that flashed with lightning. Below, harsh red stone and jagged black obsidian shards formed an expanse that stretched almost farther than I could see. And in the center of it all sat a tall, wide pyramid topped by a temple. It was a colossal structure, easily bigger than the hill fort by half, with wide, steep staircases leading up each side. One face had scaffolding erected along the stairs, with ropes and pulleys that dragged platforms up and down the side. Some of the platforms held the forms of huddled prisoners.

We were at least a klick away, and the ground between us looked almost untraversable. Tripping and falling in that field of boulder-sized razors would leave you cut to ribbons. Heck, even just walking across it was life-threatening; brush up against one of them and you'd probably slice your leg wide open.

"That is the place," Epasotl said, pointing with her chin toward the pyramid.

I held my tongue. As if that wasn't obvious.

"Bennett, you and Pierce have first watch," Brown said. "We rest here."

"Yes, sir," I replied, settling my rifle on its bipod and trying to get comfortable on the stairs.

"Not long now," Epasotl said, patting my helmet. "Soon we die with much honor."

"Better get some sleep first," I said.

Pierce set up Sybil. I pulled my spotting scope out of my assault pack, got behind the glass, and watched men work the pulleys to bring captives up the lifts on one side of the pyramid, while bodies crashed and tumbled down another in broken heaps that teams of horses dragged away.

I felt nauseated. This was human sacrifice on an industrial scale.

Other, only vaguely humanoid shapes moved across the faces of the temple complex. No, *moved* isn't the right word. They *slithered*. I increased my magnification. Sure enough, they were snakes. Giant snakes. Or, like the spider-women, *half*-snakes. Their upper bodies, torsos and arms, were men. Most carried shields and were armed with spears and macuahuitls, but some had rifles. Looked like SCAR-Hs, same as us, but I couldn't be sure.

"Check it out, Pierce," I said. "You're gonna love this."

I moved over so he could get behind the glass. After a long moment, he groaned. "Batman, then Spider-Woman, and now snake-men with battle rifles. What the hell, man."

"Could be worse. They could be *flying* snake-men with battle rifles."

"*Don't*, Bennett. Don't jinx us."

CHAPTER 50

I felt a tap on my shoulder, and my eyes snapped open. For a moment I didn't know where I was. Then I panicked, thinking I'd fallen asleep on watch. But no, we'd been relieved and I was further down the staircase, curled up facing the wall, and everything ached. Sleeping on stone steps will do that. I sat up, stretched, and focused my vision on a gourd that was being held in front of my face. I quirked an eyebrow.

"It is for stamina," Epasotl said. "For the coming battle. Drink."

I steeled myself for the worst and swallowed a mouthful. It… wasn't revolting.

"Mmm. Tastes like a warm chocolate milkshake." I licked my top lip.

"I gave it a flavor humans would like," Epasotl said proudly. "Since you are so fussy."

"What else is in it? Let me guess: more menstrual blood."

"As if," she said. "It is seed."

"What kind of seeds?"

"Not seeds. *Seed*. The seed of stags."

I choked, and several of the guys around made gagging sounds. My guess was they'd already downed their own drinks and had been wise enough not to ask questions.

"It was very difficult to obtain," Epasotl said seriously.

"Stop right there. Don't want to know," Pierce said.

But Wilson eagerly snatched the gourd from me to take a chug. "I feel pumped already," he said. "This is some Egg Shen, *Big Trouble in Little China*, brew for sure, man."

I wouldn't say I felt *pumped*, but the crippling fatigue was definitely melting away. My senses felt sharper, and my aches and pains faded into the background. Even my ribs felt better.

Sanchez came up and down the stairs, checking ammo loads and redistributing magazines. What water was left was divvied up and shared. Someone amazingly still had a can of dip, and that too was passed around. Naturally, I declined the offer. Flaming Feather was about to hand out the leaves she and the other women were chewing, but Doc intercepted her.

"We'll politely decline," the medic said.

"Wilson enjoys the leaves," Flaming Feather said, ratting out the guy.

Wilson looked a little guilty, but only a little. He gave an innocent shrug when Doc shot him the evil eye.

We stripped our weapons and performed a fast round of field maintenance, double-checked our kit, and prepared ourselves for battle. This was it. This was for all the marbles.

When the order to advance was given, we did so swiftly and silently, flowing up the stairs and onto the field as one body. We moved cautiously, wary of the sharp rocks. The formation spread out into two wedges formed by García's and Wilson's teams, with me and Pierce trailing.

Eventually the razor-edged volcanic shards gave way to burnt stubble, and our rate of advance increased. But our respite was brief; the first of the serpent-men spotted us and raised the alarm when we were still three hundred meters out. Muzzle flashes lit up the face of the pyramid, and we engaged in kind, moving and firing in bounding overwatch as serpentine bodies slithered down the steps to meet us.

As we closed the distance, using soot-black boulders as cover, the ground began to shake, and Wilson called out a warning. A gigantic abomination was rounding the temple, towering twenty feet in the air and moving on two powerful humanoid legs thick as tree trunks. But like all the other nightmares down here, it was only half-human—in this case, from the waist down. Its upper half was a horrific fusion of a dozen human heads and scores of flailing arms, many of them wielding weapons.

"It is the Watcher!" Atzi giggled. "The Watcher of the Damned!"

Pierce groaned.

Flaming Feather set down a blistering hail of suppressive fire, and Sanchez began lobbing grenades. Heads exploded and arms went flying, but it only seemed to enrage the monster. We needed to kill it.

"Cohen!" Sanchez shouted. "Give me the AT4!"

The specialist scurried over, unslinging the tube behind his back and handing it over. Sanchez flipped it onto his shoulder, pulled the safety pins, and then uncovered the pop-up sights.

"Back-blast area clear!" he bellowed.

"Clear!" several of us echoed.

The recoilless gun belched flame from both ends as the warhead arced toward the Watcher. It impacted with a wet slap a moment before the monstrosity exploded.

I've heard they dispose of beached whales by blowing them up with TNT. But I'd never really thought about what that must look like until this moment.

A great red mist clouded the battlefield, and chunks of bloody flesh rained down on us as we pressed forward. We were past even the smallest boulders now, and there was no longer any cover or concealment; we were moving and firing in the open across the burnt ground.

As the crimson fog dissipated, I noticed one of the serpent-men on the temple stairs held a long staff affixed with skulls. He thrust a hand toward us, and a mortar barrage of meteors rocketed from his fingertips. Someone yelled "Incoming!" and we hit the deck.

The streaking bolides exploded around us, sending up big gouts of rock to pummel whatever wasn't already bleeding or bruised from making the dive to the deck. There was a lot of swearing, but no screams or cries for a medic indicating that anyone took a direct hit. Still, that kind of firepower wasn't the sort of thing we could endure for long.

"Pierce!" I yelled, grabbing his shoulder and pointing to the serpent-man with the skull-staff. The wizard or whatever he was. Pierce rolled into a sitting position and braced his elbows behind his knees to support Sybil, then calmly took a breath before squeezing the trigger.

The wizard was preparing another meteor shower when the 250-grain bullet plowed straight through his chest with something close to four thousand foot-pounds of energy. The kinetic force twisted his body around, and he collapsed instantly. It didn't look like much, but I knew from experience his internal organs were jelly.

We held back, Pierce and I, picking off targets of opportunity to clear the temple stairs as the platoon advanced. Once they hit the steps, we sprinted forward to join them. It was a good thing, too, because more serpent-men had appeared from somewhere behind us across the wide volcanic plain and were slithering to close the distance to our rear. Serpent-men and packs of the ravenous undead. A friendship made in hell, I suppose.

I called targets and Pierce took them down as we climbed backwards up the steep slope of the temple. Our pursuers were still a good half a klick away, a seething mass in the shadows, but there were a lot of them, and they were moving fast.

I heard a fierce firefight erupt at the summit. We pushed up all the same and arrived at a scene of carnage. Blood was everywhere. It was thick and sticky on the floor, some of it from the dead serpent-priests and their protective detail, but most from the untold number of human sacrifices that had taken place on the low altar before us.

Blue Team had interrupted the high priest as he was in the process of cutting out a woman's heart. She was lying supine on the altar, which was rounded so that her back arched painfully over it. Assistant priests had been holding her hands and feet. She was alive, barely, but the high priest had already sawed through her diaphragm and cracked apart the ribs. Doc didn't even bother attempting to treat her. He simply lifted her like a child, cradling her as her life drained away.

The way medics can keep tabs on their humanity and compassion in scenes like this instead of being given over to rage, fear, or any other more powerful emotions is something special. They're a rare breed.

The summit of the temple was wide and flat, with the bench-shaped altar for the victims at the center. Deep channels radiating from the altar allowed blood to flow over and down the sides of the pyramid. Behind the sacrificial altar, a pallet of MREs rested on a large bronze tray suspended on chains from a wide beam of dark, richly carved wood that loomed above us, the beam supported by a huge central post. My stomach churned at the sight, and not just because it was the vegetarian option. At the beam's opposite end hung a brazier filled with blazing coals and… human hearts.

It was a smell I'd never forget.

Dawning on me was the fact that we were looking at a giant scale —to weigh the balance between the object to be replicated and the cost in souls the artifact demanded.

My brain struggled to process—or even believe—what I was seeing, even as more serpent-men slithered onto the summit. Pierce had slung Sybil and was firing with his pistol.

Defenders called out mag swaps and the sergeants directed fire. I heard more of my teammates shouting that they were red on ammo. The sustained barks of the M240s grew tighter as the gunners fired shorter bursts at closer ranges. Doc had set down the dead woman and had drawn his claw knife. He was slashing at snake-men in a blur of deadly motion that sent great arcs of blood flying in all directions.

"Get me the C-4!" Sanchez shouted to García.

"How much?" the sergeant cried back.

"*All* of it! Every damned brick!"

Behind the altar and its diabolical soul-scale was a row of thick, towering stelae hewn from the blackest stone, their carvings inlaid with gold. Epasotl wandered around them, tracing pictographs, oblivious to the frenzy of killing around her. I was about to shout at her to get in the fight—we could have used her—when someone grabbed my plate carrier roughly and I whipped my head around to see Sanchez beside me.

"You're on heart detail," he yelled into my face.

"Sergeant?" I asked in confusion.

"I need *hearts*!" He pointed to the suspended brazier and then to the tray on the opposite end of the scale, now cleared of grenades and stacked with a few demolition blocks. "Hearts, Corporal! Understand? We don't have enough C-4."

Doc was cutting into a dead serpent-man behind Sanchez. The medic drove his arm up into its chest cavity and removed the creature's human-like heart, then ran to deposit it on the scale, dripping with gore up to his elbows.

Hearts… to power the artifact.

To generate more explosives.

I nodded briskly and moved to get what was needed. My mind was full of questions, though. Did the hearts have to be extracted from a living body? Would a fresh kill be good enough? Would serpent-men hearts even work?

And…

How am I any better than what we're seeking to destroy if I'm participating in this? This was exactly what Whitlock had proposed days ago—that somehow everything is okay if we only feed the artifact *evil* souls. Did the serpent-men even *have* souls? If they didn't… this wouldn't work. And if they did…

In the end, I fell back on that excuse that too many men have uttered when facing the specter of their own conscience. I was just following orders. Either this worked, or we were all dead. Heck, we might all be dead even if it *did* work. There was already enough C-4 stacked up to end everyone at the summit.

Sanchez must have intended to bring the whole pyramid down.

Only way to be sure.

I grabbed Pierce and told him to cover me as I slashed through the band-like scales just under the ribs of a fallen enemy. I thrust my hand up, groping in the hot, squelching innards for its heart. Blood spurted, blinding me. I wiped my eyes with a sleeve and got my other hand with my knife up in there. The open cavity steamed in my face. After several clumsy, blind cuts and a lot of tugging I held a slimy, dripping heart in my hand. Doc had made it look easy.

I called out to Sanchez and tossed him the prize, then moved on to the next donor.

"Do we even know how to work this thing?" Doc shouted somewhere behind me.

"Epasotl!" Sanchez barked.

And then I understood why Epasotl was studying the stelae. "I am looking," she snapped back. "I see no requirement for ritual. Hearts go there, samples go there, and with enough burned hearts, another of the samples appears with the first," she said, pointing to the ends of the scale. "It is goofproof."

People were going black on ammo, switching to backup hand weapons or battlefield pickups. Curly fought with his tomahawk and Bowie, delivering savage skull-cleaving hacks and great disemboweling slashes. The Blackhearts were in their element, dancing between swaying serpent-men, cleaving limbs and sundering bodies with their macuahuitls. Woodward had secured a spear. Even Captain Brown had gone to his knife, dodging and parrying and striking with a speed that seemed unnatural for a man so large.

A brick of C-4 can do a lot of damage, but it didn't compare to the power of whatever demon ran this hellhole. I spared a glance back at the artifact and saw the hearts being consumed in spiraling gouts of flame that rose heavenward. With each heart, a new det-brick appeared magically on the appointed platform, just as Epasotl had said.

I was getting better at the heart-extraction business and was well onto my sixth when Pierce called black on ammo. Not fifteen feet from me, he holstered his empty sidearm and was switching to Sybil when a serpent-man appeared before him and drove his spear through my friend's gut, just under the chest plate. The serpentine abomination twisted the obsidian point and withdrew it in a spray of blood and fluid.

Pierce gave a low grunt and fell to his knees.

I dropped my knife and brought up my rifle, surging to my feet and contact-firing into the monster's chest until my bolt locked back as I drove him to the edge, where he tumbled and fell, rolling down the steep stairs.

Stairs that were now swarming with Children, climbing and howling for our flesh.

To say that things looked bad was an understatement.

Sanchez was bellowing for us to regroup. I got under Pierce, hoisted him in a fireman's carry, and then stumbled into the defensive formation the platoon was establishing. García had Woodward over his shoulders and Wilson carried Golden Harvest's body. Flaming Feather bore one of her warriors on her back, Curly supported another, and Cohen was helping a limping Cameron. Everyone was wounded, including me. I'd been shot in the arm, though I didn't realize it at the time.

"We got everyone?" Brown asked. Another of the lithe warrior women was draped over his wide shoulders. It looked like Xochi. I felt my stomach drop for a moment before I realized she was standing right beside me. Her face was a mask of blood, and she gave me a weary smile. Even now, she harbored no doubt that we would come through this alive.

I used that to steel myself the best I could.

"Fall back to the lift!" the captain ordered, directing us to the scaffolding where the treasures to be replicated were hoisted to the top.

I looked to Sanchez, the remote detonator in his hand. The obvious question of whether we had stockpiled enough C-4 must have been evident on my face, because he gave the slightest of shrugs. There was all that there ever would be. We couldn't stick around to add any more.

Ropes were slashed once we were aboard the pulley-driven platform, and we careened down the side of the temple in a barely controlled crash that seemed to last forever, surging past serpent-men and Children who had been crowding up the stairs after us and now found us suddenly at their rear. We hit the ground limping and stumbling and made directly for an arch that stood empty and alone down a long black road. If there was a way out of here, that looked like it; the arch was identical to the one we'd entered this realm through.

We ran. Pierce was like a lead weight on my shoulders, and I could feel his blood, hot and sticky, as it soaked my back. My legs and lungs screamed at me that they couldn't keep going, but they could, and they did. We all did. I didn't look back but we knew the pursuit was there.

Then suddenly the arch was right in front of us. I blinked and skidded to a halt, wheezing for breath and clutching a hand to my ribs.

"Move with a purpose, PFC!" Sanchez barked.

"I am moving!" Epasotl said. "The dagger! I need the dagger!"

"Here!" Xochi cried, tossing the bronze relic. Epasotl caught it and flicked at the platoon's sole remaining Zippo, trying to ignite her small bowl of incense. "It will not light! I need smoke."

"They're coming," Brown warned.

"But I need smoke!" Epasotl caterwauled.

"So magic some up!" Sanchez said.

"It does not work that way! I need *natural* fire to light the incense."

"Willie Pete," Pierce groaned in my ear.

Despite our circumstances, I felt a wave of relief. Until that moment I hadn't been sure he was still alive.

"Seems like overkill," I muttered back.

He didn't reply.

"Will this work?" I asked, producing an M14 incendiary grenade. It wasn't white phosphorous, but at four thousand degrees it would ignite anything it came into contact with. A bowl of incense should light up just fine. And unlike the WP grenade, it didn't have a blast radius, which was a plus.

"Give me that," Sanchez huffed. "You shouldn't have one of these anyway."

"Never know, Sergeant," I said. Actually, we were lucky. Had Sanchez not ordered me to engage in heart extraction duty, I'm sure I would have used the weapon already.

He pulled the pin and grunted, then told Epasotl to stand back before setting it in the bowl. Holding it at arm's length and turning his head, he released the spoon and scuttled away as a blinding jet of flame erupted a second later.

It certainly ignited the incense. Heck, it ignited the bowl. Smoke curled and billowed. I looked back toward the temple and saw the shapes of hundreds of figures, some human, some serpentine, racing down the long black road. They'd overrun us in moments.

"Hurry up, PFC," Sanchez growled.

"If I screw the pooch, we could end up anywhere," Epasotl protested.

"So don't screw the damned thing," he replied through gritted teeth.

I tore my eyes away from the approaching horde and saw the vortex of smoke coalescing. It shimmered for a moment and then vanished, revealing a forest I'd never seen before. But it was better than being here.

"Detonating," Sanchez said simply as we surged past him through the portal. He still held the remote detonator in his hand.

Behind the horde, the temple erupted like a volcano, spewing stone blocks high into the air.

CHAPTER 51

I laid Pierce out on the forest ground carefully, trying not to jar him too much. His face was surprisingly serene for how much pain I imagined he must be in. I had no idea where we were, and several of the Sugar Skull Gals were inspecting the foliage, trying to get a sense as well. Whatever happened, it was clear that the exit was a different door than the entrance.

But for now, my attention was fixed on Pierce.

One of the Blackhearts, a warrior named Falling Leaves, knelt down beside us, took Pierce's head in her lap, and bent to kiss his forehead. Her eyes were wet.

"You and him?" I asked.

"Yes," she replied.

"When did *that* happen?"

"Here and there," Pierce groaned, trying to smile. "Hey, baby. Said we'd make it. Didn't I say we'd make it?"

"You did," she said.

"You fought like hell, baby." He grimaced. "My own Amazon queen."

I was pressing a bandage to his horrible gut wound and searched frantically for Epasotl. There wasn't anything Doc could do for him, but her magic might be able to save him.

"Epasotl!" I called out when I finally caught sight of her. "Pierce needs you!"

She stumbled hurriedly over. Great black circles sagged under her eyes, and she looked like the grave. She was beyond the point of exhaustion.

"I cannot help him," she said sadly.

I noticed then that one of her ears had several large notches cut out of it. Blood trickled down to her shoulder; she'd used her flesh to save others already. I hated asking more of her, but Pierce was my friend.

"Please, Eps," I begged.

"I cannot help him," she repeated, "because he is already gone."

My gaze flicked back to Pierce. His eyes were open, but dull and vacant. Falling Leaves's tears splashed on his face, and she crooned softly.

I closed his eyes. It wasn't easy, like in the movies.

I felt a light hand caress my shoulder, and sensed Xochi beside me. I took hold of her hand firmly, and she squeezed back.

"So sorry," she whispered. "Noah did not survive either."

"Woodward's gone too?" I choked. "Who else?"

"Break of Dawn was already dead when the captain carried her through the portal. Walks in Shadows will survive, thanks to Epasotl, but she will never ride into battle again. Cameron was grievously wounded, but will live to fight another day, also thanks to our savage friend. She saved many. She saved me. She saved us all."

Xochi had started speaking to me, but by the end she was talking directly to Epasotl, who knelt with her hands placed firmly on her knees. Our Chaneque medicine woman wavered slightly and closed her eyes. I was feeling a little faint myself. Blood dripped down my hand. I was covered in so much crimson mess that it hadn't occurred to me some of it might be my own until the light-headedness came.

"I think I might've been hit," I mumbled before passing out.

***

My wound was a deep graze that only needed to be closed up and bandaged. While I'd lost some blood, Doc declared that what had caused me to lose consciousness was, and I quote, "The sum total of all the shit you've gone through, Bennett. If it weren't for Xochi, I'd say the only luck you've got is bad luck."

I couldn't have agreed more.

Our forest location was on the edge of the woods patrolled by the Sugar Skull Gals. Epasotl had apparently found a portal arch that had been overgrown by vines and ivies. The natives had no idea it existed. We holed up while runners went to link up with those still at the outpost, and then all of us returned to the ruins of Kuauchanko.

Curly's very pregnant wife, Wind Dancer, had been serving as my nurse. Her husband had come to retrieve her at what amounted to the end of her shift, but they ended up staying with me far into the night as we exchanged stories.

"It grows late, and Mountain Dew is restless in my belly," Wind Dancer said.

I furrowed my brow in confusion. "Mountain Dew?"

"Our child," Curly explained. He stood to help his wife up. "Sergeant Wilson suggested the name."

Of course he did, I thought, but held my tongue. I must not have been able to hide my expression, though.

"You do not like it?" Wind Dancer asked. "We thought it was very beautiful."

"Oh, no, it's a fine name," I lied. "She will be a fierce warrior."

"*He* will be a fierce warrior," Curly corrected.

"Men do not fight, my love," Wind Dancer chided. "Besides, I know she is a girl."

Curly shrugged and nodded to me. He couldn't keep from smiling as he sarcastically said, "Sure *felt* like we just came through a fight, didn't it, Corporal? I certainly feel as though I fought at the gates of hell itself, in fact."

Wind Dancer shook her head and pulled him along by his shirt sleeve. "Come to bed, husband."

"Yes, ma'am," he said in mock surrender while giving me a long-suffering look over his shoulder.

I watched them stroll away before returning my gaze to the fire. It had been three days since the Battle of Mictlān, and I hadn't slept for more than an hour here or there. I couldn't. The nightmares were too intense.

There was worry about retaliatory strikes from Amoloyan, but none came. It was Brown's belief that with the destruction of the artifact, Dietrich now had far bigger concerns to focus on. Whatever modern resources he now possessed—and that included fuel and ammo—it was now all he would *ever* possess, and he couldn't afford to spend it on a mere act of retaliation. He was, for now at least, reduced to cautious defense and consolidation of power.

I recalled the statues of Dietrich all throughout Amoloyan, replacements of statues of the previous ruler, and I wondered how the people of that city would respond to this sudden change in their fortunes. There was always a next warlord waiting in the wings.

I wasn't sure what this meant for the war with Acalán, either. Without an all-powerful artifact for the two nations to struggle for control of, would that war have reason to continue? If both sides ran out of guns and ammo, would their mutual animosity find a way to rage on anyway, only with arrows and knives and spears?

It didn't really matter. We'd ended the ghastly human sacrifices, as we had set out to do. Now we just needed to recover. There would be plenty of time to ponder the political intricacies of the Land of the Black Sun later.

By the time Xochi came for a visit that night, I was staring at the burning embers. She tossed more fuel into the fire and then sat beside me, resting her head on my shoulder. "You must sleep, my love."

"I'm afraid to." It amazed me how vulnerable—how honest—I could be with her. No macho Cav posturing. It all came so naturally. "How's Falling Leaves doing?"

"She mourns Pierce greatly."

"They couldn't have known each other very long."

"Time means nothing where the heart is concerned."

We watched the fire for a bit, then Xochi nuzzled even closer against me. "Nephi, do your friends still mock you for your chastity?"

The question and the nearness of her body rattled me, and I was sure my blushing competed with the campfire for brightness. "Not, uh… not lately. I think, uh… I think all, um… what was the question?"

"It is not a question. It is a thought." She somehow pressed still closer until she was practically sitting in my lap. "I have a good imagination. I have given it much thought." She nibbled my ear. "In much detail." She paused to move a hand indiscreetly. "We almost died, and I am tired of imagining."

Now she *was* sitting in my lap. We were secluded and alone. Everyone else was sleeping. I wrapped my good arm around her, feeling the heat of her body, filled my lungs with the scent of her skin, and pulled her closer.

"Are you sure?" I whispered.

"What are words spoken by a priest? We are already of one heart in God's eyes."

"I don't think that's how it wo—"

She shut me up with a kiss.

Resistance was futile.

Captain Brown cleared his throat above us. I couldn't believe it. *Come on!* The man was built like an ox. How on earth had he crept up on us? I mean, we might have been a *little* distracted, but still…

Xochi jumped out of my lap, and I winced as she hit my injured arm. Her hair fell over her face, shielding her eyes, and she became suddenly extremely interested in a twig on the ground. I coughed. Brown just circled the fire to sit down. He gazed at us across it for a long, awkward minute.

"Caught you," he said.

"Yes, sir," I mumbled.

"What was that, Nephi?"

"You caught us, sir. Won't happen again."

"I doubt that." He chuckled. "I very *seriously* doubt that."

I didn't know what to say. What felt like several minutes of silence followed. Brown stirred the embers with a stick.

"I suppose you two are eager to jump the broom," he finally said. He gave a toothy grin. "Although it looked like you were about to forgo *that* business altogether." He held up his hands. "Not that I'm judging. But I know you both, and you'd be better off doing things in their proper order."

"You mean...?"

"Friar Bastía is more than willing. With my blessing."

"But, sir, an enlisted can't fraternize with—"

He waved a big hand dismissively. "God put you two together; who am I to keep you apart?"

The swelling excitement I felt soon gave way to a more pressing concern. "Xochi... listen. I want this. Desperately. But you heard what Friar Bastía said about my... condition. Physical deterioration. Eventually fatal. I may not have long to live."

"He is wrong," Xochi said softly from behind her hair.

"You don't know that," I said gently. "I'm death-touched, Xochi."

She swept her hair out of her eyes and gazed at me sternly. "I do *know* that. You will live to have many gray hairs."

"I already have gray hairs," I pointed out.

"Many more, then. I have seen it. And..." Her voice fell to the thinnest whisper. "... children. Many children. *Our* children. I have seen them. And I also saw—"

"You've already said too much," Brown interrupted. "Remember what we decided upon."

"Let her finish," I said. Ordered, really. Brown quirked an eyebrow and I retreated with a weak, "Sir."

"No, the captain is right." Xochi sighed. "I have said too much."

I felt a surge of annoyance at them for keeping secrets from me, but then I recalled my own vision, or whatever it was I'd seen. My trip. The hallucinations. There were things I'd seen, things I'd forgotten until this moment, and I wondered how I could have possibly forgotten them, even as I continued to struggle to hold on to them. I'd seen the future, even if the details were now shrouded in mist, and I'd been unafraid.

"You must have faith, Nephi," Xochi said after a long pause. "The Madonna will guide you."

I pressed my lips together. "I'm trying."

"Trust her," Brown said. "That's actually the reason I came looking for you. We need to talk, just the three of us."

"What about, sir?" I asked.

"About your vision. About the future. The future where you stay here and the two of you grow old together and make lots of little Bennetts. And more immediately, the future where I get everyone else back home. Epasotl found a map. On the stelae at the temple. A map to"—he spread his arms wide, as if encompassing the universe—"everything. I think we can use it to get ourselves back home."

"I said *perhaps* it could take you home," Epasotl said from beyond the campfire. Her voice was weak and tired.

Captain Brown turned to face the darkness. "May as well join us, Epasotl."

The Chaneque moved slowly toward the fire and sat down in a heap, devoid of her usual grace, cloaked in a blanket. She rolled the infant's skull in her hands. I didn't know if Atzi was gone, or just somewhere else at the moment, doing whatever spirits do.

"I understand the way the portals work now," she volunteered, then dropped the skull in her lap to pluck at two different pieces of her blanket and draw them together. "It is like so. See?"

I gave her a puzzled look. "It's like crumpling a blanket?"

"Folding space," Brown explained. "Bringing two places together so they touch. Folding space... *and even time.* I suspected as much, but we needed to know the specific mechanics. Now we do. Thanks to the map we found—more of a Rosetta stone than a map, I suppose—and with Atzi's help, Epasotl has a grasp on the language of intra-dimensional travel. The syntax of those pictographs."

"So... how does that work? She can just write in the coordinates for home?" I asked. "Draw a few doodles in the air and, poof, home free?"

"No, we... not yet," Brown admitted. "Travel between points in this world is—"

"Piece of cake," Epasotl said confidently.

"If it's that easy..." I said.

"I know what you're thinking," Brown said. "If it's so easy, why hasn't Dietrich, who seems to know a lot more about portals and how this all works than we do, used it as a means of travel beyond just accessing the artifact?"

"Exactly, sir. If you can just pop open space and even *time* in this world, 'piece of cake,' no enemy could stand against you. Not for long, anyway."

"Okay, maybe not *piece of cake*," Epasotl said. "And you need a guide." She held up the infant's skull. "Our enemies have no guide."

Brown nodded. "Without a navigator like Atzi, fixed points like the arches are required. They serve as lodestones, if you will. For example, the Lord of Mictlan's worshippers built the arches to access the Underworld." He tilted his head from side to side. "Theoretically, with Atzi's help, *we* can create portals to anywhere in this world... but travel between *other* worlds is a much more difficult feat, and traveling between *times*..."

"Hurts my head," Epasotl finished.

"It'll require something more than just a navigator," Brown said.

"But it's possible," I said, encouraged by what I was hearing.

Brown nodded. "It must be possible, or we wouldn't have traveled here in the first place. It's essentially a matter of defining coordinates—crafting the right description of the destination. If we can get Epasotl the intel she needs to 'describe' Panama, on Earth in 1989, with this portal language... then we can get everyone home."

"And how does my vision relate to this, sir?" Xochi asked.

Brown pinched his nose. "Think of it like this. Epasotl is the hand that turns the key. But the key itself is something we still need to find, the 'something more' I was referring to. And that's where you come in, Bennett."

"Uh... I don't understand. I have the key to Panama?"

"Not yet. But the real value of Xochi's vision, the critical intel she's provided, is that you will. And based on our review of that vision, I have a good idea of *where* that will occur."

I don't think I'd ever felt so confused in my life. Puberty was more straightforward than this. I looked to Epasotl, who was nodding as if it all made perfect sense.

I took a deep breath. "You're saying... Xochi's vision tells us what we have to do..." I paused thoughtfully. "But also it tells us where we need to go for me to get Epasotl the intel she needs to figure out the magic set of doodles that'll get everyone home."

"He is smarter than he looks," Epasotl said to Brown. The sarcasm was thick enough to bend an e-tool.

I spread my hands and grinned. "Hey, what do you expect? I'm only an E4."

"No excuse," Brown said. "Everyone's a leader in my outfit."

I forced an uneasy laugh. "So do I get a promotion since I'm the key to this and all?"

"Don't get delusions of grandeur, son. Quetzalcoatl and the 'something more' are the true key. We can't achieve mission success without either. You're the..." He fished around for the right word. "'Catalyst' is as good a word as any."

That sounded a lot less critical than what I'd been told a moment before. I guess they were breaking the news to me softly, or just didn't want me to get a big head about it.

"Better word than 'bait,'" Epasotl said, and then began a hissing laugh that turned into a coughing fit. After it passed, she rubbed her eyes with her palms. "I am, like, so totally beat."

"Get some rest," Brown said. "You deserve it more than anyone."

She yawned and lay down right there by the fire, closing her eyes and seeming to drift into an immediate, deep sleep before one eye struggled to open and looked at me. "Ben-Ette..."

"Yes?"

She made a lazy shaka sign. I smiled and returned the gesture.

EPILOGUE

The dream jolts me awake. I've had it before, but it always vanishes, forgotten when I open my eyes. Tonight, I can recall it clearly, and my heart races. Xochi—my wife—has her head on my chest, and she mumbles something as I slide out from under her and stand to dress. She sits up in bed, watching me through half-lidded eyes.

"What are you doing, Nephi?"

"I remembered something, something from my vision, or whatever it was. I need to tell the captain."

"It *was* a vision. Stop doubting that, my love. But why do you have to tell him now? It will be morning soon enough. Come back to bed."

"If I wait until morning, I'll forget again. I can't do that. It's important."

She runs a hand through her short, sleep-tousled hair. "Do you want me to come with you?"

"Probably. Yes. You should hear this too."

She nods and fishes around on the floor for something to wear, settling at last on a long, embroidered tunic of thin homespun cotton. We exit our little home, our nest, and our bare feet pad against the smooth bark of a wide bough. We climb down a rope ladder and the earth is warm under my feet; even at night it doesn't get cold in this forest.

Sanchez is sitting alone by a small fire, sipping from a gourd and staring at the flames.

"Didn't expect to find you awake, Sergeant."

"When did you ever see me sleep, boy?"

As a point of fact, I haven't. I've never really thought about it before. He's just always around, doing platoon sergeant stuff like barking at people. Softly. Because he's quiet and sinister like that.

"Surprised to see you two newlyweds out of the nest so soon," he says. "Bored of married life already?"

"I need to speak with Captain. You'll want to hear this too, Sergeant."

Sanchez arches an eyebrow. "At *this* hour?"

"It's important."

As if not fully believing me, or maybe just because he wants someone higher up the chain to pin the blame on if Captain Brown gets angry at being awoken early, Sanchez shoots Xochi a pointed look. She nods. He shakes his head as he stands. "Better be, son. I'll roust him and bring him over. Waking that man takes a light touch. He's liable to slip a knife into your kidney before he knows it's you."

I doubt he means that literally. I've never seen Captain Brown operate with less than a hundred and ten percent awareness of his surroundings.

Xochi sits by the fire, but I remain standing. I roll the remembered part of the vision around in my head, making sure I don't forget any details. I can feel it trying to slip away, and I latch on to it firmly, wrestling to keep it clear in my mind.

I'm about to just start telling it to Xochi, just so I have someone else to help me remember it, when Sanchez returns with the captain. Brown's uniform is impeccable, as always, and I wonder, not for the first time, if he sleeps dressed and standing. He's even wearing that old cavalry Stetson. The brass crossed sabers of the Ninth Cavalry Regiment flash in the firelight as he folds his massive arms and quirks an eyebrow at me.

"Something on your mind, Bennett?"

"Sorry to wake you, sir, but I didn't want to forget the details. I remembered something just now, from the vision I had in Mictlān. I was afraid if I waited, I'd forget. I remember things, little things, from it sometimes, but they always slip and—"

Sanchez clears his throat.

"Sorry, sir. What I mean to say is, part of my vision, the part I just remembered, it's about Sergeant St. James and the rest of Alpha."

The captain looks intrigued and motions for me to go on. We've talked about the few fragments I can recall of my vision, or trip, or hallucination, whatever you want to call it, Xochi and the captain and me. She believes it was a true vision, and the captain's inclined to trust her insight into what he's started calling METINT, or Metaphysical Intelligence. This is the first time Alpha has come into the picture, though.

I take a deep breath and start from the beginning.

I'm staring at a huge mirror, clouded by smoke, but the face I see is not my own. I'm looking through someone else's eyes. St. James's eyes. His face is hard, as if carved from stone, his olive skin deeply tanned and laced with black veins. He steps through the mirror and enters a vast hall made entirely of obsidian that glows with a ghostly, pulsating internal silver flame. Rows of warriors stand at attention, hundreds of them, dressed in quilted armor draped with cloaks of jaguar skins, the snarling maws of the great cats enveloping the men's heads. A spiderweb of black veins mark their grim faces. The warriors are all large, powerfully built men, armed with spears and obsidian-edged war clubs. They chant in unison and slam their weapons rhythmically against richly decorated hide-bound shields.

St. James strides down the length of the hall, passing rank after rank of Jaguar Knights.

At the far end of the hall is a high, stepped dais flanked by more knights; these men are even more imposing than the ranks lining the hall. At the summit is a great obsidian throne polished to a mirror sheen and wreathed in smoke.

A man sits on the throne, his features obscured. Four women stand with him, two on either side, each a vision of heart-wrenching beauty. One holds a bowl of salt, another is pregnant; one carries a bushel of corn, another a serpent.

St. James halts and genuflects at the base of the dais, and the man cloaked in smoke rises, holding up a hand that quiets the assembled warriors.

The silence is deafening.

The man descends the steps without a sound, his gait like flowing water. A cloak of swirling, inky smoke shrouds his body, but now his face materializes, revealing skin painted in yellow-and-black-striped war paint. His face is regal, with an aquiline nose and almond eyes the color of midnight. Atop his head rests a crown of flint knives adorned with raven feathers. Heavy strands of gold and jade hang from his neck.

He reaches the foot of the dais and bids St. James rise. The three other surviving members of Alpha Squad—Clark, Wright, and Bond —step forward into view.

"My lord and master, Broken Face, sends his everlasting fidelity and wishes the Dread Lord Smoking Mirror eternal life and glory," St. James announces formally.

"I am most displeased with my vassal, your lord," replies the painted man—no, the god Smoking Mirror—with a voice as sharp as flint and as terrible as a hurricane. "I placed the Soul Forge under his protection, and it has been destroyed."

"My lord most humbly begs your forgiveness and would appease you with the sacrifice of we, his warriors, who have served him faithfully and well. May the sight of our still-beating hearts placed at the foot of your throne bring you pleasure and ease your wrath toward your most unworthy servant."

The look on the face of Smoking Mirror is one of cold indifference flecked with fiery malice. "Your deaths would indeed please me, but only for a short time. No, it is the deaths of the other members of your war party that I desire. They entertained me greatly, for a time, but they amuse me no longer. I grow tired of the creatures and wish to be rid of them. I would destroy them myself, but there would be no pleasure in that. Instead, I would that *you* hunt them down and bring me their hearts. Yes… I should like to observe such sport. This would amuse me.

"I would you swear fealty to me and only me, above all other gods, to serve eternally at my pleasure. If you then succeed at this task, I shall heap upon you thrones and dominions, wives, concubines, slaves, and treasures beyond imagining.

"What say you? Shall you so swear?"

St. James looks to his men. Clark's face is inscrutable and his eyes crinkle as he regards Smoking Mirror for a long moment.

"Sergeant?" St. James says.

"I will so swear," Clark replies flatly.

Wright stands easy, a Barrett rifle across his shoulders and a necklace of human and Chaneque ears draping his neck. He gives a rictus smile, exposing teeth filed down to sharp points. "I'll swear to that."

A flicker of unease crosses Bond's face for an instant, but he suppresses it with a savage grin and lights a cigarette. "I'm in. All the way."

ABOUT THE AUTHORS

JASON ANSPACH (1979-) is the award-winning, Associated Press Best-selling author of Galaxy's Edge, Wayward Galaxy, and Forgotten Ruin. He is an American author raised in a military family (Go Army!) known for pulse-pounding military science fiction and adventurous space operas that deftly blend action, suspense, and comedy.

Together with his wife, their seven (not a typo) children, and a border collie named Charlotte, Jason resides in Puyallup, Washington. He remains undefeated at arm wrestling against his entire family.

Galaxy's Edge: www.InTheLegion.com

Author website: www.JasonAnspach.com

twitter.com/TheJasonAnspach

Ryan Williamson draws inspiration for his writing from his love of history and mythology as well as his past experience as a Cavalry Scout in the U.S. Army. His debut novel, "The Widow's Son" has been praised by readers and critics alike for its thrilling action, complex characters, and immersive worldbuilding. He is also the co-author of "Doomsday Recon," an epic new military fantasy series from WarGate Books. Ryan lives in the Pacific Northwest with his wife and children. When he is not writing, he enjoys exploring the back roads on his motorcycles. You can find him on Twitter as @rywilwrite or visit his website at **ryanwilliamson.com**.

WARGATE BOOKS

Discover more titles like DOOMSDAY SCOUTS, including several free options, at **www.WarGateBooks.com**.